Deep in an oak grove...

I ran into the circle. In the dark, I couldn't find anything.

"Go...go...go...go," croaked the frogs.

Perspiration pricked at my forehead. My stomach, empty from a day of fasting and a little ritual wine, heaved and I fought down the bile. I clutched my pentacle to my throat.

"Goddess, please...please."

"Go...go...go...go."

Nothing moved in the darkness except Nature.

"Go...go...go...go."

I clenched my fists to the sky. Death was close. Not just homage paid to the Wheel of Life, but Death itself. I knew it, felt it on the back of my neck. I smelled it hot in my nostrils. Heavy and blood-like. Sickly sweet.

"Go...go...go...go."

"Show me!" I cried. "I can't leave without knowing."

The starlight seemed to shift, a little to the left. Something white shimmered at my feet. White with dark blotches.

I bent and picked it up. My robe. My ritual robe.

Also by the Author

Witch Moon Waning
(a Prequel to *Access*)

Access

Dark Revelations
(Book #3 of the Madonna Key series)

Waiting on the Thunder

A Man Called Regret

A Fortune in Thorns

Thunderstorms and Convertibles

Until

Top Secret Affair

The Cure for Shyness

Flying By Night

A Coven of the Jeweled Dragon Mystery

Lorna Tedder

Spilled Candy Books
Niceville, Florida

Flying By Night
Copyright 2002

By Lorna Tedder

Published by: Spilled Candy Books,
          Spilled Candy Publications
          Post Office Box 5202
          Niceville, FL 32578-5202
          http://www.spilledcandy.com

ISBN-13: 978-1-892718-44-0 (trade paperback)

Cover art and design: Big Zen Dragon
First Release, October 2002
Re-Release, September 2006

Flying By Night

Author's Note

Spiritual circles grow and change over time, especially long-lasting ones. Members leave and return, and new initiates are welcomed in. Others go forth to start new circles, but in their hearts, they remember from whence they came.

The Coven of the Jeweled Dragon series of novels features members of the coven in different locations and different decades, from the early 1980's to modern day. Each story stands entirely on its own, with a reunion of the surviving members planned in the final book of the series, one in which they must all stand together.

Part One

Traveler, there is no path.
Paths are made by walking.
— *Old Spanish Proverb*

Chapter One

~Kestrel~

The last time I saw my two husbands alive, they were standing naked before the altar of the Goddess.

Darkfall came quickly that night, thanks to looming black clouds that overtook the sun before it set. The morning paper had predicted clear skies for May Eve, and the unexpected thunder made me edgier than I already was.

For weeks, I had been nervous about the Beltane festival. Halloween, or Samhain as we pagans sometimes call it, celebrates the memory of the dead, of those gone before us, and honors all that has passed. Beltane, six months later and the opposite spoke of the Wheel of Life, celebrates life and all things living. It is a night of couples and coupling, and being the only woman in the threesome, I feared that one of my lovers would be hurt when I had to choose for the night.

Grant? Or Cedric? Which would it be?

Hands shaking, I closed the heavy oak door behind me and stepped barefoot onto the front porch. The boards were slippery in the darkness. Curtains of rain, white against the distant streetlights, swished across the pavement, occasionally vanishing amid the bright flicker of sheet lightning. I took a step forward. Rain splattered my feet and dampened the hem of my white robe. The thin silk clung to my ankles. In the dark, I couldn't see the mist of raindrops on my sleeves, but I felt their damp weight. I was naked under my robe. Every touch came alive on my skin. Time was drawing near.

Grant? Or Cedric?

A pair of headlights cut through the night. My pulse quickened. Was it him? The car slowed for a deep, street-wide puddle, then plowed through with a spray of water rising from either side of the car like low wings. The car sputtered and choked, then sped out of the puddle with a lurch and passed the house.

My heart sank. Grant had never been so late. In the three years we'd been married, he had often worked twelve-hour days at the law firm where he'd just been named a partner, but he'd always been home early on a feast night. Snakes of dread twisted in my stomach. It wasn't like him to work this late, not on a night like tonight. Not on Beltane when I would choose the father of my child—*our* child.

Grant? Or Cedric? Who would lie with me in the circle tonight?

I took another step forward, my toes curling over the edge of the slippery porch floor, and thrust out my arms to the hard-pelting rain. I reached just beyond the protection of the roof. Cool water drenched my hands, splashed against my face.

"In Your hands," I whispered to the thundering night sky. "I leave my choices in Your hands, Goddess."

The oak door opened behind me. Light from the green candles inside filtered out over my feet in a soft glow and then thinned to blackness as the door closed. Heavy footsteps lingered at the door. Cedric.

"You're not starting without me, are you?" he asked in his lilting British brogue. I couldn't tell if he was hurt or teasing. I would need light for that.

Then I realized my stance: me in a ceremonial robe, barefoot, arms raised to the skies in a posture of gratitude, damp silk clinging to my body and outlining every curve in the brief air of candlelight. I must have flushed with embarrassment. Thankfully, the porch was too dark and the flickers of lightning too dim to betray me. I lowered my arms, crossed them, and turned to face Cedric, my second husband.

"I would never start without you," I told him. I meant it with all my heart.

Amid a distant roll of thunder, I heard him sigh. Was he wondering, too, if I would choose him to be my Beltane partner?

Grant? Or Cedric? Fire? Or water?

"So what are you doing out here in the storm?" he asked.

And yet, since my girlhood, I had always been caught in the storm. I had tasted its fury too often to run willingly into its midst.

In the dimness, I could see Cedric's smile and the huge, dark pupils of his eyes, his dark hair hanging loose on his shoulders. At twenty-three, two years my junior, he was a fine cut of man in the black silk robe I'd made for him. Grant and I had met him at an Ostara festival the year before, though his mother—to her chagrin—was firmly convinced she was responsible for our blasphemous union.

Cedric had been a chain smoker then and had hated every minute of it, largely because the habit interfered with his metal working. It was too hard for him to smoke a cigarette and hammer the chainmail helmets he sold by mail order. He and Grant had become fast friends—almost brothers—during the overnight camping trip. At Grant's urging I offered Cedric my hypnotherapy services.

I knew I had to do it. Cedric was all water and stillness, and fire was not his element. The habit would kill him, I'd thought. On the second day of the Ostara festival, I led Cedric into a deep trance that rid him of his desire to smoke. He awoke with memories of loving me in an ancient time. The same as Grant had done at the end of a stress management session some four years earlier.

They were water and fire, fire and water, the two of them. Existing so separately, yet together. I was the common bond. Me. Kestrel. Lover of the element of air and all things that flourish in sky and wind. Water could not exist without me. Nor could fire. Me, I could exist alone, but the three of us together were more powerful than any coven or circle I'd encountered.

In many ways—shallow ways—Grant was Cedric's opposite in looks and temperament. Grant, at thirty-five, kept his curly blond hair sharply trimmed and spent most of his days in dark business suits and reading glasses. Cedric's hair was longer than mine, and instead of bending over a desk or computer all day, he spent his time in shirtless overalls, barefoot, hair tied into a thick band at the base of his neck, a hammer in his hand, standing in the workshop behind the house. Grant was ambitious and high-strung, full of fire. Cedric was laid-back and gentle, having spent his college days in England and picked up a seductive accent. He was smooth-flowing as a mountain stream with a quiet depth no one truly knew.

Even though Grant spent more than half his breath in the office, it was Grant who more often shared my bed. Cedric, on the other hand, spent most of his time with me just talking, cuddling in the hammock while we watched a pair of mourning doves drinking from a saucer of water left in the grass.

Not that Cedric was a slacker. His handmade crafts outearned both my hypnotherapy income and Grant's attorney fees.

"You didn't answer me," Cedric said, interrupting my silent comparisons. "What are you doing alone out here in the storm?"

Again, I said nothing. Instead, I let him enclose me in his arms and pull me to his chest. I angled my head to watch for passing cars.

"It's Grant, isn't it?"

The back of my head against his hard chest, I nodded. The raindrops eased to a steady drizzle instead of torrents. An ambulance siren wailed in the distance, and I stiffened.

"I know." Cedric hugged me hard, then kissed my neck. "I was worried about him, too."

"Was?" I half-turned to look at Cedric's shadow-hidden face. *Oh, Goddess, no!*

"He'll be home soon."

I smiled to myself and relaxed against him. Cedric had a gift for sight, though it was usually barely into the future. Anything he said was likely to be misinterpreted as prophecy.

Cedric ran one long finger over the neckline of my ceremonial garment. He bent and kissed my throat. "Do you like the robe?"

"Very much." He and Grant had made the ritual robe for me, just as I had made a robe for each of them. The two of them had handsewn dozens of stones of Baltic amber and English jet into my bodice, sleeves, and hem.

"The rain's letting up," he whispered in my ear. I started to protest, but at that instant, the drizzle of spring rain pelted to nothing. Only the fresh scent of water hung in the air.

"Grant's home."

I traced the length of the street with my gaze. Except for a streetlight, darkness. Then fiery twin headlights pierced the night, and I knew the sound of Grant's car engine the moment I heard it.

Seconds later, Grant parked in the driveway. I met him on the steps with a hug. Woman's perfume assaulted my nose and stung my eyes. Someone—some *thing*—had been rubbing against my man, and I didn't like it one little bit. I didn't have to have Cedric's psychic abilities to know who it was.

"Whoa!" Grant gave me a nervous grin and hugged me back. "What's this for?"

"She was worried about you," Cedric said from behind me. As if he hadn't worried at all.

Grant pocketed his car keys and started up the steps with one arm around me. "I didn't think I'd ever get home. I had an absolutely awful day."

Great. And I had the power to make his night even worse.

Grant? Or Cedric?

"What happened?" I asked when we were safely inside with the oak door locked behind us. "More trouble with your senior partner?" Or trouble with a woman?

"The worst yet." He paused to sniff the air. "Something smells good. Roasted chicken? Honey cakes?" A frown plowed across his forehead. "Baby, I'm sorry I'm so late. I know how important tonight is to you." He glanced at Cedric. "To both of you."

"To all of us," Cedric corrected. "Is it that Gloria chick again?"

Ah, but sometimes Cedric could be so sweetly blunt.

Grant plopped down on the living room sofa and tugged at his shoes. One fell with a thud. "I can't believe it. She's filed a grievance against me." He rolled his eyes. The other shoe fell near the first. "For sexual harassment."

"What?" Cedric squatted in front of the sofa, and I lamely dropped down onto the cushions.

Not again! When was the little flirt going to give up? Gloria Stokes had been the proverbial thorn in Grant's side since March when Grant had been made a full partner in the law firm. She hadn't had any interest whatsoever in her daddy's law firm until the cocktail party where her father had announced the news with as much fanfare as lawyers in conservative pinstripes can muster.

Grant had been asked to bring along his girlfriend—or whoever it was he spent his spare time with—to the affair. I had to make a special trip to one of the fancier dress shops in the city just to make sure I had the right little black dress that didn't show too much leg or too much back. It certainly didn't look like the usual witchy wear I was so fond of. We didn't want Cedric to be left out, so at the last minute, Grant asked if his "younger brother" might join the celebration.

That was the day I first met Gloria and her husband, Floyd. From some of the pop culture references Floyd made, I knew he couldn't have been much older than Grant. He seemed bored with life and spent most of his conversations immersed in petty complaints about the banking industry and how banks had no moral right to exist. Not only that, but he believed none of us had any legal, moral, or biblical obligation to pay our income taxes, and he had plenty of monotonous references to prove it. If the listener seemed the slightest bit interested, however politely, he turned to his next complaint: white women who married black men and produced a dozen welfare children to sap his personal tax roles. Leaving her husband to bore every female guest, Gloria flirted with most of the men in the room, especially Grant.

"How do you ever keep your hair so blond?" she'd say in the wispy, little girl voice, all the while running her fingers through her Suicide Blonde #18 ringlets. Maybe she normally sounded that much like a damsel in distress, but she was my age, and the phony frailties ran thin with me. But she wasn't done by any means. No, sir-ee. The twit then ran her fingers through

Grant's hair. I'm not sure who was more appalled—me, Cedric, or Grant.

Grant's trouble at work started within a week after that. Gloria caught the firm's long-time receptionist stealing money from the petty cash box—or so Gloria said—and by some imaginary power vested in her by the power of her father, the senior partner, Gloria fired the poor woman on the spot and took her place as receptionist and personnel aide.

That night, the phone calls began. Not on Grant's pager but on our personal, unlisted home phone. In her new position at the law firm, Gloria had access to Grant's personnel files, including the most private information he'd ever disclosed. Thank the Goddess he'd had the foresight not to answer the questions on the application regarding religious and political preferences.

Soon after that, we started screening our calls at night, and if it was Gloria's number that showed up on our Caller ID, then it was I who answered the phone—only to hear her hang up.

Her next tactic was to make sure that Grant didn't leave the office to come home and refuse her calls. She arranged his schedule, keeping him in endless, useless meetings so that his paperwork didn't start until after three in the afternoon. She would hang around the office late into the evening in case he "needed anything." Once or twice, she even had the gall to order in dinner—with wine!—so he wouldn't have to leave his desk.

Still, Grant didn't say anything to Gloria's father. Not out of fear but out of respect for an old man who idolized his only child. If the old man had only known his daughter's intentions, it would have given his beleaguered heart a fatal jolt. Besides, Grant insisted, Gloria had the makings of a seeker. The only problem was, she was too immature spiritually to realize she eventually might become a seeker of anything beyond the physical realm, so she immersed herself in the trappings of baser glories.

When things really got out of hand was the night of the Spring Moon. Grant had had to work until eleven o'clock that night, the night of our last full moon feast which we'd intended after our midnight magick, as was our tradition. Gloria had tried to stop him, and from the way Grant told it, she'd literally thrown herself into his arms, demanding he stay and make love to her and free her from a life of passionless, mechanical sex with dull, boring Floyd. He'd let her down gently, figuratively speaking.

Gloria must have gone through his personnel records after he left because she showed up unexpectedly at our house. The three of us—Cedric, Grant, and me—were already in a sacred circle in the forest behind our house. For our magickal workings for that particular full moon, we'd chosen a spell of harmony and protection to fall over our household, largely because of the trouble Gloria had caused Grant.

Unfortunately, when Gloria rang our doorbell at midnight, no one answered. She must have heard our singing because half-way through our magick, something pulled my attention out of the hands of the Goddess, and there was Gloria, standing at the edge of the clearing with her mouth hanging open as if she'd never seen three naked people before in her life. She'd left running.

Cedric had fretted for days that our disrupted magick hadn't worked to bring us harmony and protection. In hindsight, he was right.

"So what did the boss' daughter do this time?" I asked Grant. I slid down onto the carpet. Cedric settled down beside me and rubbed my feet, though he remained attentive to Grant. I couldn't stand the thought of Gloria's hands on Grant, especially on a night when I might choose him as my partner. "And when is she going to leave us alone?"

"She lured me into the snack room this morning."

"Lured?" Cedric looked up. "Isn't that a bit kind for her?"

"Probably. Everything from 'please come get a donut' to 'help, there's a mouse!' Every twenty minutes it was something new. Then I heard a squeal and a thud, and I knew she'd fallen, and I...I was the first one there. She was lying on the floor, all sprawled out." Grant raked his fingers through his hair and held his head. "She had her skirt up just enough to show her, um, panties. And when I reached down to help her, that's when she wrapped one of those short, skinny legs around my ankle and threw me down. I damn near fell on top of her. Then her dad came in and a couple of clients, and oh, Kes, it was awful."

I reached out and rubbed his knee as a show of support, but my natural instinct was to wrap a vise grip around the bitch's throat and tell her to get the hell out of my husband's life. "What happened?" I asked in a hoarse but supportive voice. I wasn't sure I really wanted to know.

"I tried to explain that it wasn't what it looked like, and then Gloria started crying." He rested his face in his hands. "Gloria finally insisted it was an accident and that we'd both tripped over a couple of stray kernels of popcorn on the floor of the snack room and had just happened to fall like that. But I could tell nobody believed her and she wasn't trying real hard either to sound convincing. Just the opposite, in fact. The more she tried to explain it, the worse it got."

"What about her father?" Cedric asked. "Can't he tell when she's lying? Mine always could."

"In his eyes, Gloria can do no wrong. I thought he was going to fire me on the spot, but instead he just told me to get back to work. He said he never acts on temper." Grant slipped his hands down to his jaws and rested his chin. "Gloria left on time and went home—surprise, surprise—and I stayed late to finish up what I should have been doing instead of trying to help someone who had fallen on purpose."

"It took you this long to finish?" I glanced at the clock on the wall. Staying late and staying until after eleven o'clock were two different things.

"I finished a long time ago. I was getting ready to leave when Gloria came back to the office with all kinds of allegations. She claimed she wanted to make everything right between her dad and me."

"And you were willing to listen." I knew my Grant.

"For her dad's sake, yes. She said she was planning on leaving her husband because she'd married someone too old for her. She said he was boring and hated to party, and she thought we'd make a better couple. And that—" Grant swallowed hard— "that what she'd seen in our circle suggested I was available."

17

He blew out a long breath. Just because there were three people in a marriage didn't make one of them available. It wasn't against our vows for any one of us to sleep with someone else, but none of us had ever wanted to, and I could tell from the tension in Grant's neck that he didn't want to now.

"She left," Grant continued. "Angry. Rejected. Swearing she'd make me pay for turning her away. When I got to the car, I found all four tires slashed. That's why I was running so late tonight." Deep creases wracked his forehead. "Damn her! She knew I had to leave work on time. She knew I had a special function I had to be at tonight."

Cedric scurried to his feet and ran to the window. He pushed the curtain aside and peered into the night. "She didn't follow you home again, did she?"

I brought my hand to my mouth in horror. Cedric had that gift, that curse, of seeing quick visions of the future. But I never could guess if the flickers in his eyes were normal intuition and curiosity or something more.

Grant stiffened on the sofa and turned in silent apprehension to watch Cedric at the window. "I don't think so. Why?"

Cedric let the curtain fall closed and shook his head. "Just...just wondered." He crossed the room to us and stopped with both hands on his hips. His long hair had fallen into his eyes again. He gave his head a little jerk, and the hair fell back into place. "You know what you need, Grant? A hot, cleansing shower. Wash that wench's touch off your skin or our magick will be tainted. Again. And I've got a roasting chicken to check. We've got less than an hour before the ritual."

The ritual. An uneasy ribbon tightened in my throat. Caught up in Grant's latest tales of Gloria, I had for a moment forgotten my dilemma. Grant? Or Cedric? Which would it be? Tonight, a magickal night thousands of years old, I would ask the Goddess to give me a Child of the Green Wood.

"Yeah," Grant agreed, giving Cedric a thoughtful nod. "Maybe with a drop of cinnamon and cedar oil for purification." He curled his upper lip as he picked off a curly, white-blonde hair from his shirtsleeve. "Goddess knows, I need to rid myself of Gloria Stokes' smell." He bent and kissed my forehead. "Sorry, I'm in such a rotten mood. I promise to be much happier after my shower."

I kept my head bowed. I couldn't bear the look of guilt on his face. Not the kind of guilt that comes from a secret, sexual affair but the kind that comes from being the bringer of destruction to the home. Gloria Stokes meant unnecessary grief and pain for our little family, and Grant, our first line of defense, had been unable to shield us from the results of her actions. And for that, he bore more guilt than if he had slept with her.

"It's okay," I told him.

"It's not okay! This is *your* night." He paused, reaching out to brush my cheek. "Have you...have you made your choice yet?"

Grant? Or Cedric? Which would it be?

"I...no."

I saw Grant and Cedric exchange a sheepish glance. A secret. My guys had a secret that didn't include me. What a rarity!

"All right, boys. What's going on?"

Cedric cleared his throat. "This morning over breakfast, while you were in the shower, Grant and I had a talk about tonight."

"What kind of talk?" The guys were always doing little things to surprise me. I had a right to be suspicious.

Cedric looked to Grant, and Grant took a deep breath. "We want this child to be our child. A child to all three of us."

"Um, guys?" I stifled a giggle. "I hate to tell you, but there's going to be only one mother and only one father. At least, biologically. That's Mother Nature's way, you know? Only one of you can father this baby."

Grant's eyes glowed. "But we don't have to know which one of us is the biological father."

Grant's words sunk in. I was to have them both as my Beltane partner. Regardless of the consequences, both men would father my child. *Our* child. I smiled at both of them through tears. I had left my choice in the hands of the Goddess, and She had delivered to me the two most beautiful lovers on the face of Her soil.

"I should take my shower now," Grant said, "and you two should prepare and meditate."

I nodded, still too overcome with emotion to speak. Then I rose and walked out into the night.

Chapter Two

~Kestrel~

The rain had stopped as if the Goddess Herself had brushed away the clouds. Stars dotted the bowl of heaven.

Barefoot, I tiptoed through the wet herb garden where I spent so many of my afternoons. Rosemary, sage, hyssop, thyme, chamomile, mint, and more, all ingredients in the homemade soaps and shampoos I sold at Renaissance Faires and over the Internet. I paused and inhaled the strong scent of my labors. Out of habit, I picked a sprig of rosemary—for protection—and rubbed its soft spikes between my fingers and dabbed the oil on my neck, anointing myself as Grant and Cedric had anointed me just before Gloria had interrupted our last full moon ritual. I let the healing, protecting, warm light of the Goddess envelope me as I stood there, head cast back and eyes shut.

Tonight's ritual would be as special to the three of us as it had been to pagans throughout time. A night when I would take my lover into my arms and invoke the God in him, and when he would invoke the Goddess in me. Rain frogs chorused in the distance and up close as I made my way down the sole, winding path through the overgrown grasses and into the woods.

Try as I might, I couldn't help but tremble. There's nothing like a star-filled night in the Cathedral of Nature to draw me close to Deity. Especially on Beltane when we pagans celebrate all things living—plants, animals, and people. It is a time when Mother Earth is fertile and new green covers her with a mantle of renewal and hope for an abundant future. And nothing on that night was more fertile than I.

A spark of light leapt up beyond the first ridge of ancient oaks. The spark flamed out and up, into a brilliant bonfire. A tall silhouette stood dark against the glow. Had I lost all track of time? Cedric had somehow beat me to the ritual clearing, probably while I stood deep in meditation amid the herbs. Then again, his gift of sight gave him a distinct advantage.

The midnight hour was near. The smell of rain-touched dirt and dry kindling wafted toward me. Damp grass gave way to soft dirt and the occasional autumn-old acorn under my heel. Not even the wind disturbed the reverence of the moment, and the bonfire's smoke curled upward toward the circular opening in the canopy of trees.

I could almost feel someone watching me. Someone other than Cedric. I shook it off. Probably just the wood nymphs or my spirit guides. Perhaps the Goddess Herself. For once, I didn't listen to my intuition. I told myself that all of Nature was watching and this night would be one I'd never forget.

And on the last count, I was right.

I stepped into the clearing and met Cedric's merry eyes with a solemn smile. This night's doings were not about lust, but about life. Cedric was a playful lover, but tonight he would take the role of the Horned One, the God of all things wild and natural. For now, I said nothing but instead watched as he walked deosil around the fire. His clockwise circles, a symbol of increase, were no accident. We'd each written a part of the ritual. He carried a homemade besom and made sweeping motions widdershins, or counterclockwise, with the little broom to clear away all negatives and to create a sacred space for us.

The circle and the stone altar had been set with all the tools of the night's ritual. The altar held a chalice of sweet wine, two ceremonial swords, my own amethyst-encrusted athame, a scattering of honeysuckle flowers, stones of fiery carnelian and moonstone and amethyst, a small iron cauldron of fresh water, and candles of green and white to honor God and Goddess on this sacred night. On a small table near the altar rested my flute, a lyre, a tiny bell, and a drum. Flower petals had been strewn across the table and throughout the circle, the center of which roared with flame.

Grant appeared out of the dark beyond the clearing. He looked more relaxed than earlier and smelled of cinnamon and cedar. He'd wasted no time in purifying himself for the Great Rite. His blond hair was still wet from his shower, a fact betrayed by the gold ringlets on his forehead. He wore the black silk robe I'd made him. It clung to his damp chest and ready groin. Yes, not yet naked, already he looked like the young God.

On every Beltane, the young God, the young Year King, comes to His manhood. He falls in love with the Goddess and the Two of Them unite, male and female, the balance and the whole, in the Great Rite. The Goddess finds Herself with Child by Midsummer. At Samhain, the end and the beginning of the Celtic New Year, the Year King dies, an ultimate sacrifice. The earth grows cold and dark. And yet, at Yule, the Winter Solstice, the God is reborn as a Child of the Goddess, to live and love again in Light and joy. No matter what the religion, the young God is the bringer of Light, just as Grant and Cedric brought Light to the darkness I had embraced since my own parents' gruesome deaths. But the joy of my loving days was as short-lived as the Goddess' time with Her Year King.

Grant raised both hands to the bright constellations above. He carried dried herbs in each hand. After a silent prayer, he followed Cedric, deosil around the fire. With every bare footfall, he paused to toss a few sprigs of last summer's herbs into the flames. Sweet-smelling smoke from fertility herbs filled my lungs and then the woods.

For a moment, I thought I heard a cough. Then a frog croaked nearby and, for the second time since I'd come to the Beltane fire, I ignored whatever spirit guides were shouting in my inner ear to pay attention.

I joined the circle then, pausing only to retrieve the flute from its resting place. My heart thundered in my ears. It wasn't nervousness that pounded in my body, but rather, the anticipation and energy rising inside me. I joined my lovers—my *guys*—in their circle, walking slowly deosil, choosing some ancient tune from lifetimes ago to honor the God and Goddess.

Grant tossed the last of the herbs onto the fire and picked up the drum from the table. He beat in time with my flute as we circled round and round. Then Cedric exchanged the broom for the lyre and bell, and completed our musical trio as we danced round and round, our tempo rising with our energies. My heart pounded in rhythm with the drum. I felt my blood, my life force, rushing through my body. And then...

Stillness. Silence.

We each put down our instruments. I glanced from Grant to Cedric. Their chests heaved, the both of them, as did mine. We all felt it, felt the energies and the magick.

I turned then to the altar and raised my athame toward the East. I drew a pentacle in the air, then pressed the point of my nine-inch athame to its center in the air, thus sealing the circle. I walked slowly deosil, in an outer circle around my lovers, the altar, and the balefire.

In my mind's eye, I saw myself on the outer edge of a circle between this world and the unseen planes. A globe the color of indigo fire blazed over us, protecting us from all harm. I made one full circle, round again to the East, drew a second pentacle in the air there, and sealed it with the point of my amethyst-handled blade.

I pivoted to look at my husbands in the firelight. "The circle is cast," I said. It was all I needed to say.

I swished my blade over the fire. Orange flames licked at the metal but touched not my hand. I walked deosil around the circle until I stood toe to bare toe with Grant. I raised the blade to his heart, beating wildly under his heaving chest, and held the point gently against the spot of cloth that covered the triskele tattoo over his heart.

"I greet thee in perfect love and perfect trust," I said softly. "Thou art God." I stood on my tiptoes to kiss his cheek.

He took my athame from me, held it to the place above my heart and matching triskele tattoo, and whispered, "I greet thee in perfect love and perfect trust. Thou art Goddess." He bent to kiss my cheek.

In a grand gesture, he delivered the athame back to my own hand. I doused my blade again in the flame. I moved past Grant, clockwise, to Cedric and repeated the same words and actions. When I was done, I laid my athame on the altar and turned toward the East, arms raised high and open.

"I call upon the Guardians of the Watchtowers of the East," I said with as much voice as I could muster, "to witness and to protect. Powers of Air, lift me up, give me new breath, wings to soar, and wind to carry me. Come, and blessed be!"

The echo of my voice had scarcely died when Grant spoke, his voice fierce and booming. He raised his arms to the South. "I call upon the Guardians of the Watchtowers of the South to witness and to protect. Powers of Fire, burn through me with the flame of inspiration, let new blessings smoulder and spark, let passion glow. Come, and blessed be!"

Cedric lifted his arms to heavens. "I call upon the Guardians of the Watchtowers of the West, to witness and to protect. Powers of Water, cool me, flow through me and wash away the troubles that hinder, soothe me with the rain of tranquility. Come, and blessed be!"

Without a fourth to call the Northern quarter, the three of us faced North and raised our hands in invocation. "I call upon the Guardians of the Watchtowers of the North," we all said at once, "to witness and to protect. Powers of Earth, ground me, give me balance and solidity, nurture me as you do your fondest flowers, and give me grass to touch my feet and soul. Come, and blessed be!"

We were nearly shouting then. Not intentionally. Our excitement and gratitude would not stay quiet.

I lifted the chalice from the altar. Grant and Cedric exalted the two swords high above their heads. I knelt before my husbands, chalice raised to them and filled with a sweet wine, sweeter still with rare herbs that would undo any worries.

"As the blade is to the male, as the chalice is to the female," we chanted. "As the blade is to the male, as the chalice is to the female. As the blade is to the male, as the chalice is to the female."

We continued the chant, their blades ever nearing the life-giving wine in the shadows of the chalice as our voices grew louder, more frantic. My body went hot with fever of want. They plunged their blades into the chalice at the same instant.

After what seemed an eternity, they withdrew their swords and laid them crossed on the altar. I offered them both the chalice. Grant took it first and drank, then Cedric, then me.

"Blade and chalice," Grant said, taking another drink.

"Male and female," Cedric said. He drank long and deep.

"Balance and wholeness," I said. The wine tasted sweet on my lips and burned quickly through my blood with a fierce desire. I thought my entire body would take flight.

"Light and darkness," Grant said.

"Earth and sky."

"Water and fire."

"As above."

"So below."

"As within."

"So without."

"As turns the Wheel of Life."

"Merry Meet."

"And Merry Part."

"And Merry Meet Again."

"Lord and Lady, bless us," I ended. I rose and set the chalice atop the altar.

Grant and Cedric faced me then. Only the fire kept us apart. They tilted their faces to the night sky. "We consecrate our bodies to Thy use, Lord." Then silently, they shrugged off their black robes and laid them on the ground beside the fire to form a covering for the earth. Their bodies glowed magnificently in the firelight, both nervous with energy but erect and ready.

I held my breath, almost forgetting myself. Grant was the more experienced lover; Cedric the better endowed. I was by no means a virgin, but I had never coupled myself to one man with another watching. Nor would I this night, for both my husbands would take on the mantel of the God. Neither would be Grant nor Cedric, but the Lord, just as I would no longer be Kestrel, but the Lady. Lord and Lady, God and Goddess. Eternity and balance.

I tilted my face to the stars above. "I consecrate my body to Thy use, Lady."

Closing my eyes, I pulled my white gem-sewn robe from my skin. Then, eyes open, I laid the gown atop the two black robes. I watched with anxious amusement as my lovers' eyes widened with adoration. I didn't look down at my body, but I could see the reflection in their faces and I knew I was beautiful, naked, wearing nothing but my pentacle choker. I was still Maiden, soon to be Mother if this night fared well, and I was the very image of the Maiden Goddess herself with flowing, flower-laden hair, full breasts, and fertile hips.

"Blessed be," Cedric murmured.

"My Lord," I called, imitating with my body the five points of a star with raised arms and parted legs. "I invite Thee to this circle to join the Lady in sacred union. In this, bless us this night with Thy most sacred gift—a child! As I will it, so mote it be!"

"So mote it be!" echoed Grant and Cedric.

"My Lady," my lovers said together to the sky above me. They, too, stood in star position. "I invite Thee to this circle to join the Lord in sacred union. In this, bless us this night with Thy most sacred gift-a child! As I will it, so mote it be!"

"So mote it be," I whispered. "I invoke Thee, my Lord, into the bodies of these two men."

"I invoke thee, my Lady, into the body of this woman."

I don't remember exactly what happened next. I do remember Grant arranging me on the silky robes, the fire burning beside me and warmth burning inside me, too. I still recall my palms under my head as I offered up my body to him, legs parting slowly at first and then open wide to the heavens long before he knelt.

I remember feeling that I was outside my body somewhere, watching, worshipping as God and Goddess united and created life. She, beautiful and earthy in the fire's glow. He, wild and alive with green leaves and fur and the antlers of a stag.

I remember Cedric taking up the drum and beating a slow, steady rhythm that matched my Lord's strokes and then pounding wildly. I remember hearing my own breath ragged in my throat and thought perhaps I screamed.

I remember later that Grant was the drummer. I remember crying out as my body bent to a Stronger Will. I remember the total submission to something much greater than myself and the oneness with Grant and Cedric and Nature and the Universe. With God and Goddess. I felt my womb on fire and awash, my heart aching with love, my soul soaring.

It was done.

At some point, we thanked the God and Goddess, dismissed the corners, and closed the circle. Exhausted, content, I sank to the ground and bent my head against Mother Earth, not caring if the sweet, soft dirt tainted my skin or disheveled my hair. Cedric and Grant reclined beside me, one on either side, and the three of us gazed up at the dark sky.

I breathed in a long, lingering wish that this night would be with me always, and said, "Shall we feast now?"

With a gasp, Cedric bolted upright. Flower petals hung in his dark tangles. If he hadn't worn a scowl on his face, he would have looked sweet, sitting naked on the ground beside me. He started to say something, then seemed to think better of it and shook his head instead. Whatever had caught his attention, he was a million miles away from me. Either that or a few minutes into the future.

"Cedric?" I touched his shoulder. "What's wrong?"

The distance in his eyes startled me. "Nothing. Everything is as it's meant to be." He blinked, his eyes watering. His Adam's apple jumped with his swallow. "Everything is as it's meant to be," he said again, this time in a whisper.

I should have known. I should have known.

Even when I was a little girl, I had those feelings. Intuition, as some people call it. Devilment, Daddy had said. As young as kindergarten, I had learned to listen to those feelings, to the howls of the coming storm, and yet I chose to ignore my psychic antennae in favor of my heart.

The night had been so perfect. The magick left me tingling and happy, full of love, not wanting the night to end. Doubts niggled at the back of my mind, but I ignored them, refusing to give them the power of my thoughts. If I acknowledge my worries, I told myself, then I might bring them to fruition. I knew well that dwelling on a fear will give it physical form and breathe life into it. Precisely why most pagans don't believe in the Devil of the Christian Bible: give an evil a name and you give it power.

"Why don't we get a quick shower then," I heard myself say, "and then we can enjoy the feast and each other's fellowship." And, while we ate and drink, we would talk as we often did about the ritual and what we had felt of the worlds seen and unseen. It was always like that at sabbats and esbats and other feast nights. We'd stay up half the night and get our fill of fine food and talk.

My stomach growled then, a reminder that I'd fasted all day and the thought of the meal ahead of me was tempting. Already I could taste the chicken roasted in its own juices, the fresh fruits, the flat bread made from an ancient Mediterranean recipe, the wine—

"We're out of wine," Cedric interrupted my thoughts.

Grant shook his head. "No, we're not. I left several bottles of light spring wine on the table. My contribution to the feast you two spent all day cooking."

"We're out of wine," Cedric repeated. He gripped my hand. "You'll have to go to the store."

Grant stood up and brushed an oak leaf from his bare shoulder. His penis dangled wearily. "It's after midnight. There's no way we're sending her to the liquor store. If we need more wine, I'll go."

"No!" Cedric stood up, too, dragging me up with him. "We're out of wine. She'll go."

The two of them exchanged uneasy glances. Finally, Grant nodded and turned to me. "Yeah, baby. Go get some wine. Red wine. We don't have red wine."

"Guys!" I wailed. "We have plenty of wine. We don't need any more."

Cedric gripped my hand even harder. For a second I thought he would break my fingers. "Go," he said, that distant, watery look in his eyes.

Ah, I thought, ignoring those psychic antennae again, the guys are planning a surprise for me. Something special. Like they did at Valentine's Day. Although why they wanted to send me out alone on a stormy night after midnight, I couldn't understand. Sometimes when the guys were into romantic surprises, I could be a bit dense. At least, that's how I convinced myself to go along with their ploy.

"All right, all right," I said. "I'll go. But I'll be back in fifteen minutes. I'm just going to run up to the corner to the—"

"No." Cedric held up his hand as if to silence the wind in the trees. He seemed to listen for a second. "Not the liquor store. It's dangerous this late at night. Try the twenty-four hour grocery store."

"But that's an extra twenty minutes away from—"

"Try it!"

I'd never seen him so intense. Cedric was laid-back and easy. Never intense. "Okay. Okay, the grocery store it is." Then I tried to lighten his dark mood. "Just don't start the feast without me, okay?"

Cedric nodded once. I saw the tiniest hint of a smile in the corner of his mouth and tears in his eyes.

I left my robe on the root of an oak and, wearing nothing but my pentacle, sashayed skyclad back through the woods, through the herb garden, and through the unlocked back door of the house.

I never looked back. Not once.

I didn't have to. I felt both Cedric and Grant, as surely as if I had seen them with my own eyes. I knew they were standing behind me, still in the clearing, by the dwindling bonfire. Staring after me with the longing of a hundred men. Refusing to say good-bye.

And then, in that moment before I left their presence, I knew that they had reached for each other, brother to brother, and clasped hands.

Chapter Three

~Kestrel~

Inside the house, I took just enough time to grab a quick shower and wash the flower petals from my hair. I couldn't very well visit the local, all-night grocery store, looking as if I'd just rolled in the grass—even if I had. I compromised, though, and didn't bother to comb my wet tangles. I pulled on a pair of old jeans and my green T-shirt with the image of people dancing around Stonehenge over the words, "Give Me That Old-Time Religion." On the way out the front door, I slipped on a pair of old sandals, grabbed Grant's Mercedes keys from the rack on the wall, and stuffed my wallet into my jeans pocket.

Water puddled along the street in front of my house. It had started to rain again, almost as if the Goddess Herself had stopped the rain for our ceremony. I tapped the brakes and they sluggishly responded. The windows fogged up as I reached a quiet intersection. I swiped at the windshield with the butt of my palm and then fiddled with the knobs on the control panel before finding the de-fog button. I started across the intersection just as the windows cleared.

A swirl of motion passed me. I slammed on brakes. A large, light-colored car—headlights off—skidded through the intersection in front of me. Alone on the road, I sat there for several minutes, my heart pounding. Perhaps that near-miss was the source of my earlier unease. Too often, people complain about small delays that ultimately save their lives because they're not on railroad tracks when the train's coming or they're not on the plane that took off on time and crashed. Since Mama and Daddy died, I'd often enough endured premonitions that kept me off airplanes and out of dark alleys. I told myself the unsettling feeling now was because I needed to be late enough that my car didn't connect with that madman's car.

Except when the car had passed, the bad feeling remained.

I took a few deep, cleansing breaths to calm myself. Rain splattered against my windshield faster than the wipers could brush it aside. Why was I bothering to drive all the way into the nearest grocery store? The rains were getting heavier by the minute and already torrents of water gushed through the ditches and pooled on the roads. Much more water, I thought, and I'd get myself killed on these slick roads. Screw it. I'd buy the wine at the liquor store on the corner. Besides, I figured the guys just wanted me out of the house so they could surprise me with who-knew-what.

I pulled into a corner liquor store and killed the engine. It was an older building, but the exterior had been modernized with plenty of bright, safe lights. I'd been there once or twice before with Grant and a few times more to the small bar adjacent to the liquor store. None of us was a big fanatic of liquor or cocktails, but we usually incorporated some type of wine into our sabbat and esbat feasts. We always celebrated the pagan holidays and full moons with feasts of abundance. For that reason alone, it was handy to have a wine and liquor store a few miles from home.

By now, the rain had turned into a full-fledged downpour, and I, without my umbrella, decided to leave the car unlocked. The last thing I wanted to do was stand with bottles of wine under my arm while I fumbled with my keys at the driver's door. With my first step, I sank into muck and water and cursed. Grant and Cedric had better have a damned good reason for sending me out in the middle of a deluge, I told myself. The rain was colder than I had expected, like a thousand daggers of ice.

Inside the store wasn't much better. The thermostat must have been set at arctic. I was soaked to the bone, and the air conditioned breeze gave me even more chills. Hugging myself to hold in a little bit of heat, I selected three bottles of red wine from the finer section of the store. I dug my wallet out of my jeans pocket and laid a couple of twenties on the counter in front of a boy who looked half my age. I figured he was over twenty-one or he wouldn't have been working in the liquor store, but all the same, he still had the pimples of an awkward youth.

Rather than ring up the sale, he hesitated. "I'll, er, need to see some ID, miss."

I choked. "Excuse me?"

"ID, miss." He looked embarrassed, and I half-felt embarrassed for him. Then he added in a heavy drawl, "It's the law."

It was then that I felt someone standing behind me, the way those of us who are extra intuitive often do. Two presences, both warm and loving.

"Miss? An ID, please?" The boy held out his hand.

I fished in my wallet and handed him my driver's license. "Is this really necessary?"

He stared too long at my license. "You're twenty-five?" He glanced up at me and studied my face, which was framed by wet, blonde tangles and probably still flushed from passion. "You don't look twenty-five," he said.

"Well, um, thanks, I guess."

"And this name on here.... That's not your real name, is it? I mean, what kind of name is Kestrel Firehawk?"

"My legal name," I replied. He didn't need to know I'd had it changed twice, or the terrible reasons I no longer used the name I'd been born with.

He made a funny sound in the back of his throat. "I'm gonna, um, have to, um, keep this."

"Keep what?"

He brandished my driver's license. "This phony ID."

What? I didn't have time for this shit. I stopped just short of questioning both his intelligence and paternity but realized it wouldn't do me any good.

"That's my driver's license. I assure you it's real. See the state seal?"

"Uh, yeah. But you don't look no twenty-five and that's a fake name if I ever saw one." He eyed me carefully. "Unless you're a singer or actress or something."

"Or something. Look, are you going to sell me the wine or not?"

I felt a presence close in behind me. Large, warm hands rested on my shoulders, almost as if they were intent on keeping me there. I could feel the work calluses against my skin and knew instantly that it was Cedric. Good. Maybe he could get this idiot to give me back my ID, and then Cedric could explain why precisely he'd sent me on this wild goose chase to get me out of the house.

"Cedric—" I whirled to find no one there.

Between the door and me, near the pylons of cheap beer, stood Grant, arms crossed in front of his black-robed chest. I frowned and took a stride toward him. Then I stopped. He looked both sad and angry, as if he had no intentions of letting me out the door. Why had the guys sent me after wine, only to follow me? And why in the world would Grant show up in public in his ritual gear?

"Grant?" I ventured toward him, but he looked past me.

"Lady? Hey, Lady?"

I glared at the clerk with a contempt I no longer bothered to hide. He'd insisted I looked too young, and then called me by the same name my young priests had used in the ritual. "My husband will take care of this." I gestured at Grant.

He was gone.

"Grant?"

I ran to the door. He wasn't outside on the sidewalk. Sheets of rain beat against the plate glass store window.

"Grant?"

I poked my head out the door, closing my eyes against the mists that hug in the air. Not a car in sight other than the one I'd driven. Maybe Grant and Cedric had parked around the corner in the bar's parking lot.

"Where'd he go?" I asked the clerk.

"Where'd who go? Lady, you're talking to air."

Annoyed, I stood on my tiptoes and peeked over the aisles of wine and beer. Two aisles over, Cedric, dark hair flowing instead of clasped in his usual ponytail, made his way toward the rear of the store.

"Cedric!"

I ran to the open corridor, but he'd just rounded the rear of the aisle.

"Cedric, wait!"

I ducked into the next aisle, expecting to see Cedric waiting for me, but no one was there. I ran the length of the aisles and circled the store.

"Where did he go?" I asked the boy at the cash register.

He stared back at me. Furiously, he shook his head, then shoved my two twenties across the counter at me. "Take your money and get out of here before I call the cops! We don't need no druggies here."

I reclaimed my cash but watched in horror as he dropped my driver's license into a metal slot in the counter's surface. "What is wrong with you?" I demanded.

"Me? What's wrong with me?" His cheeks reddened. His hands shook as he stabbed a finger at his own scrawny chest. "Nothing's wrong with me, but Lady, you're a fucking loony!"

Argh! I'd deal with him later. I'd already let him ruin a perfect night. Well, him and Gloria. And too much rain. Without my driver's license, I could still drive the short distance home, but I probably couldn't buy wine elsewhere. The guys would just have to do without red wine. Right after they explained their game of hide and seek in the liquor store. And then we'd feast and talk until dawn and everything would be all right.

It would, I told myself.

I trudged back out into the rain. My nerves were on edge. Something was going on that I couldn't explain. The need for this midnight shopping excursion. The sudden appearance and disappearance of both Cedric and Grant. Had I imagined it? Perhaps if I'd taken some sort of hallucinogen, but those were strictly prohibited for our spiritual path. The only thing I'd consumed all day was a few swallows of herbed wine on an empty stomach. Hmmm. Maybe it was an aftereffect of the magick.

"Goddess, give me answers," I murmured into the rain. "Give me direction."

Standing in the downpour, I tugged hard at the door handle. The metal didn't give. My fingers slipped. I nearly lost my balance and fell flat of my back in the ankle-deep water pooling in the parking lot. I plied the handle again, and again it didn't give. So much for hurrying home, damn it!

An old man, drenched from the knees down, thrust a huge, green and white golf umbrella over me. "Lock yourself out, missy?" I could barely hear him over the thudding of raindrops on the plastic above us.

"It's locked," I told him, sounding helpless to my own ears. I know good and well that I'd left the door unlocked. Or thought I had. Sometimes I do things out of force of habit. Had I been so caught up in memories of the ritual or in getting the wine and heading back home that I'd forgotten? I didn't have an umbrella and I'd wanted to avoid standing in the rain, fumbling for my keys. Just run in quickly, buy the wine, and run out. Instead, I'd had my driver's license confiscated by the boy wonder, been soaked to the bone, nearly been sideswiped, and chased both of my disappearing lovers around a liquor store well after midnight. At last, a little bit of sanity on an otherwise crazy trip to the corner store.

"You all right, Missy?" the old man asked. He was dressed in a black, three-piece suit with a gold watch hanging from his vest, probably for practical use as much as for decoration. There wasn't another car in sight, and I couldn't tell where he'd come from. Why would a well-dressed elderly man be walking in a storm like this? If he hadn't been wet from the knees down, I would have thought I'd encountered a spirit.

"I-I'm fine," I told him. I extracted my keys from my jeans pocket. Without looking away from his pale, wrinkled face, I felt my way to the right key. "Thanks for keeping me dry." I offered him a little bit of an obligatory smile. The only one I'd had since I left home.

"That's my goal. Keeping you dry. Dry of rain—" he gestured toward the store— "and dry of liquor. No sense in frequenting a place like this. Especially a girl like you, pretty and too young to drink."

"I'm not—" I broke off quickly. He'd seen me come out of the store empty-handed and had assumed by my wet and waif-like appearance that I was too young to make the purchase. "Well, um, thank you," I said finally. I managed to get the key into the lock.

"Do you have a church?" he asked, almost cheerfully.

I paused and looked up at him. He meant well. But how could I tell him I worshipped in the Church Not Made of Hands? In the God and Goddess' Cathedral of Nature?

Then his gaze dropped from my face to my throat where my pentacle choker hung loosely. Of the dozens of pents I owned, the one I was wearing was the most prominent, the one used exclusively for rituals, the one I'd completely forgotten I was wearing. Made of intricately braided brass wires by my own Cedric, the pendant could not be missed.

"You're a witch," he hissed. Sheer sorrow coated his voice. "You're damned."

I started to sputter something about his allegation being nonsense, but he had it half right. "You don't understand" was all I could manage.

"I'd love to save you, but I can't. The Bible clearly says, 'Thou shalt not suffer a witch to live.' No matter how much I might like you, Missy, there's nothing I can do."

I started to explain how King James VI in the early 1600's had rewritten that verse to suit his political needs and rid himself of enemies, but it was no use. People believe what they want to believe, especially about those who are different.

"You're one of that coven over on Wide Oak Lane, aren't you? The Coven of the Jeweled Dragon. I've been by to witness to them many times. There's nothing I can do for them either. Poor things. You're all lost. All damned."

I started to tell him I wasn't part of a coven and I didn't know anything about Wide Oak Lane or any Coven of the Jeweled Dragon. For a moment, time stopped, the two of us standing there in the downpour, under his huge umbrella. The old man doing his best to keep me safe and dry but failing. He himself, from the knees up, remained untouched by the weather. Impossible not to get wet in this storm. Imposs—

Grant had stood in the doorway of the liquor store as if to bar my exit...and he'd been perfectly dry.

"Call the police!" I screeched at the old man. My body wouldn't move but my mind was already racing back to the circle in the clearing of oaks. "Call the police!" My voice rose an octave on the last word. "Tell them it's 37 Forest Way. Tell them—" Oh, I could almost see it! "Tell them it's an emergency."

I dove into the car and didn't think twice a few seconds later as I squealed out of the parking lot and splashed the poor man up to his waist. Something was wrong, dreadfully wrong, and I knew it. And worse yet, I had known it all along. Neither Grant nor Cedric had ever made it to the liquor store. But which one was in trouble? Grant? Or Cedric?

I'd felt them both there. Trying to tell me something. Trying to *keep me there*. That was it. They'd both known something bad was going to happen—something dark—and they'd sent me off into the light. To safety. That's why they'd insisted on wine we hadn't needed. They'd wanted to get me away from home. But why?

Was it Cedric's sight again? He always got these strange "flashes" of things not long before they happened. I couldn't forget the look on his face when he'd suggested I go for wine. Desperate, and maybe a little afraid.

I was already on the highway home before I jerked the headlights on. All I could concentrate on was my foot slammed down on the accelerator and my knuckles white on the steering wheel. I didn't even slow down at the four-way stop. I crashed through puddles on my street. I didn't brake at all to turn into my driveway. Just let off on accelerator a little. I hit a sheet of water and skidded, turning half-way around in the driveway and plowing into the front yard, leaving deep scars in the grass. The car came to rest headfirst in the thick border of azaleas I'd planted to keep all things negative away from my home. The azalea branches squawked their way across the hood and up against the windshield.

I tore at the car door and practically fell out into the muddy grass. I could go to the front door but it was just as quick to go the back way, given that I was standing in the middle of the side yard, equidistant between the two. In the deep shadows and in the poor light of some distant streetlight, I fumbled through the dark. My sandals squished in the rain-sodden grass.

Ahead of me, in deeper shadows still, the side gate through the twelve-foot-high fence that surrounded the back yard and the oak grove gaped open at me. The gate was wrought-iron and taller than our fence, but it didn't lock. Only a latch held it. I slid through the opening.

I sensed a stranger had been there. Someone filled with hatred like I'd never felt before in this lifetime. But whether that person had left the gate open by entering the back yard or leaving it, I didn't know.

A deadly fragrance caught on the night breeze. The rain had stopped as quickly as it had started. The smell was so strong, it stung my eyes and nostrils. Of all the incenses I'd ever made, I'd never smelled anything like this one. It was as if all the herbs of my garden had given up their essences at once.

I crept through the tall grass, following a path not my own. My feet slipped into craters of footprints larger than mine.

I held my breath.

Rain frogs chorused all around. Deafening. I squinted as I made my way through the herb garden. All the lights were out in the house and only a few of the candles still burned. The glow from the windows was too faint to light my way. The stars above me looked faded in the light pollution from the surrounding towns and the city. As many times as I'd complained of its infringement on Mother Nature, tonight I was thankful it afforded me sight in otherwise darkness.

As I made my way through the grass, something soft caught on my foot. A stalk? A flower? I picked it up, and though I could not see it well in the dimness, I knew the smell: rosemary. A huge branch. Rosemary—for protection.

I took another step and recognized the leaves under my feet. Mint. Even if a thunderstorm had flattened my many rosemary and mint bushes, the stalks would not have landed so far outside my garden.

I turned and stared back at the house. It seemed farther away than usual. I fought the sense of disorientation. I should have been standing in the middle of my vast herb garden instead of the grass. I felt lost.

Peering at my feet, I concentrated. Hard to see, as if scrying into a crystal ball. My heart skipped a beat. I wasn't standing in grass—I was standing in the midst of my garden. No wonder the smell of herbs had been so pungent! Every green thing in my garden had been demolished, chopped off knee-high or lower as if the Reaper with Her scythe had cut down everything young and green.

Grant. Cedric.

Should I flee now when I can still feel the presence of strangers around me? I wondered. Or find my guys? A spark of light glinted off something on the path near the grove. Grant's ceremonial sword! Driven deep into the ground like a Christian cross over a grave. Cedric's sword stood similarly beside it. I debated only a split second before I ran for the grove.

Sidestepping the swords, I ran panting into the woods. The thick canopy of trees blocked out not only light pollution but light. I felt myself fade into the majesty and mystery of the dark Cathedral of Nature all around me. Everything seemed to come alive. The rain frogs bleated as if to say, "Run...run...run...run." In the back of my mind, I was terrified, but my heart would not let me turn and leave. Not without knowing what had happened to my guys.

I stumbled forward, following the smell of burning, wet wood. On the path, up ahead, a glimmer of light broke through the trees and formed a perfect circle. The clearing. The bonfire no longer blazed and roared. Smokey, wet embers were strewn across the circle as if someone had kicked them this way and that. Black fabric curled and smoked across a charred log. The altar stretched in disarray over the ground, an overturned chalice and my flute beside it. The lower leaves of the northernmost oak smoked. I blinked in disbelief. Someone had destroyed our ritual site and set fire to our sacred oaks, but the Goddess had put out the fire Herself with the rain.

Grant. Cedric. Had the Goddess saved them, too?

I ran into the circle. In the dark, I couldn't find anything.

"Go...go...go...go," croaked the frogs.

Perspiration pricked at my forehead. My stomach, empty from a day of fasting and a little ritual wine, heaved and I fought down the bile. I clutched my pentacle to my throat.

"Goddess, please...please."

39

"Go...go...go...go."

Nothing moved in the darkness except Nature.

"Go...go...go...go."

I clenched my fists to the sky. Death was close. Not just homage paid to the Wheel of Life, but Death itself. I knew it, felt it on the back of my neck. I smelled it hot in my nostrils. Heavy and blood-like. Sickly sweet.

"Go...go...go...go."

"Show me!" I cried. "I can't leave without knowing."

The starlight seemed to shift, a little to the left. Something white shimmered at my feet. White with dark blotches.

I bent and picked it up. My robe. My ritual robe. The one the guys had made for me. I'd left it behind. I held it out, let the folds fall open. But the cloth was shredded in long, slashing cuts. The amber and jet torn from their threading. I knew without touching the bright, dark flowers of color that my ritual gown had been dipped in blood.

Clenching the robe, I crouched on the ground. It seemed safer there for some reason. Closer to Mother Earth. Closer to Holy Ground. I scooped up loose stones of amber and jet from the ground and held them to my chest.

Then I saw. Ah, sweet Goddess, I saw it!

What I had known was there all along. What I had refused to let myself see. Just like Mama and Daddy.

On either side of where my robe had been spread out were my guys, my sweet guys. The starlight caught the white of their eyes, open wide and staring at nothing. I knew without a second glance that they were dead, Grant and Cedric both. Nothing could bring them back, not to the bodies they'd lived in and loved me in.

I tried to look away from the awkward postures their bodies had been left in. Who could have done this to them? Toying with them, playing with them, designing them like an artist. Smearing their faces and chests with bloody, upside-down pentagrams in a twisted, obscene version of ritual.

I retched and fell flat to the ground beside them. Memories of another bloody scene flashed like dangerous lightning through my brain, and like then, I knew it was too late. Like that last time when I'd lost the two most important people in my life, my knees turned to jelly and my heart squeezed itself shut. I was eight years old again and all alone.

I stared longingly at my guys. I wanted to hug them, draw them both into my arms. But I couldn't bear to touch them. Their distorted positions, the perversion of the scene. I couldn't touch them. I couldn't taint the purity I had known with them by becoming a part of that ghastly scene. I looked from one to the other and retched again, swallowed bile.

My athame, I realized. Only my athame could have left those wounds. But where was it now? I closed my eyes and concentrated hard. I could feel it. Feel it in my fist. No. No, not my fist. Someone else's. Someone nearby. I could feel the presence all around me. Like some evil thing conjured by a novice.

I let out a little whimper, afraid to turn around for fear I'd find my own athame buried above my breast, deep into my heart and twisted. I drew in a deep breath and remembered that I was a Daughter of the Goddess. That to Her all things are as they must be. That She, too, has known grief and love and hope.

I dropped my bloody robe and pocketed the stones. I raised my hands in a V to the sky. "Lady, what of me now?" I cried out. "What of me now?"

I summoned all my strength and rose to my knees. Death would come soon. I knew it. I felt it coming. And then...and then...a veil of electric bluish-purple light surrounded me. It wrapped me up like harmony. Like a oneness with all things living—past, present, and future. Grant and Cedric were with me, too, and a part of me deep inside and as protected as She was of me.

I felt the pain of the young Maiden Goddess who'd lost Her Year King, Who'd seen Him slaughtered. I felt the joy of Him reborn inside of me, a testament to the immortality of the soul. I felt the clutch of sadness and great comfort all at the same time and being One with the Goddess.

I heard—no, felt—my athame rise behind me. High and damning and intent. Then I heard the sirens call. The air around me wavered and light hugged me. The air seemed to withdraw from me and take shape in the starlight. My emotions were raw, but I felt awed.

41

It looked at first to be an angel, but there were no wings. But I knew what it was. She stood before me, a perfect double, with long blonde hair both flowing and braided and flying out behind Her as if they'd encountered some phantom wind. Her skin seemed to glow almost as if it were light underneath instead of bone. She wore a long red tunic with intricate needlework of gold and silver threads and a solid, cream-colored sheath underneath. She wore bracelets on both arms and at Her brow, a circlet of gold with the sign of the moon in the center.

I reached out to my mirror image. So did She. Our fingertips touched and I felt the power surge through me. Strength. What I needed.

"Oh, Goddess, why?" My hands shook. It is never wise to question Deity and truly foolish to fault the Higher Power.

Out of grief, I lost myself in Her eyes, in Their deep pools of color. I saw the tears roll down Her cheeks. She was crying. The Goddess was crying! And then I realized that She was just a reflection of me. I pulled away and wiped a tear. She took my hand and opened it, touched where the tear had been.

"Out of your greatest grief," She said, "will come your greatest joys." She lowered Her hand and touched my belly. "But for tonight—" Her hand lifted my chin— "you must fly, My child."

I was aware then of the footsteps running away from me. The evil behind me had receded and taken its hatred with it.

"You must hide," She said. "Hide or you will die."

"Hide? I don't know where to hide. I don't know where to go."

"Find my children," She said with a smile. "You asked me for direction. I've already told you of them this night. The Coven of the Jeweled Dragon. They will take care of you. Until Grant and Cedric can rejoin you."

"Grant...Cedric...rejoin?"

"Hurry, My Kestrel, My little Firehawk." The police sirens grew louder. "Fly. Fly by night."

Then the light that had been the form of the Goddess seeped into my belly and vanished.

Part Two

It is asked first what is to be done when, as often happens, the accused denies everything. We answer that the Judge has three points to consider, namely, her bad reputation, the evidence of the fact, and the words of the witnesses ... then, according to the Canon Law, he must subject her to punishment, whether she has confessed her crime or not.

—*Malleus Maleficarum,*
the medieval Church's legal guide
to witch detection and "justice"

Chapter One

~*Dylan*~

The steady strobe of red and blue lights announced the location of the crime scene. Detective Dylan MacCool steered into their midst and, vaguely aware that his partner had craned her neck to get a good look through the rain-splattered windshield, he did the same. The house was nothing less than a stately mansion. Yeah, Death was a great equalizer, all right. A homeless man on the other side of town had been kicked to death, and he was just as dead as whatever rich snobs lived here.

Dylan blew out a long breath. "Jeez, I hate working nights."

"Almost as much as I do." Across the seat, Robyn Porter nodded, her dark red hair gleaming in the glow of police lights. She'd done her damnedest to get out of work tonight, citing personal plans, but the sergeant had nixed her attempts to discard her beeper for even a few hours and guaranteed instead that they would have fewer cases after the first of May.

Not that it mattered. He and Robyn and half the other detectives at his precinct spent most of their holidays, weekends, and time-off trying to solve murder cases that didn't want to be solved. Even when they did spend time at home, they couldn't let go of the job. There was always an unknown gunshot victim or a beautiful teenager pushed from a balcony or a drunk with his throat cut from ear to ear with a broken beer bottle. There was always the matter of figuring out how it happened and why it happened and who did it or any combination thereof. He spent every waking moment and most of his dreams preoccupied with the dead as if finding the answers to his questions would somehow validate their value among the living.

Which was why Dylan spent most of his time alone and why his wife of ten months had walked out and never looked back. Not that divorce among cops was unusual. Most wives simply got tired of waiting for the phone to ring to let them know their husbands were dead and managed to escape the marriage before the call ever came. Not Sherry. She could live with him if it meant being a widow, she'd said. Even if he'd taken out his frustrations on her with his fists, which he hadn't.

What she couldn't live with was an absentee husband, the solitude she felt in his presence. Moreso than the beeper that went off in the middle of birthday parties, anniversary dinners, and lovemaking, she resented the way he nodded and pretended to listen when they both knew he wanted—no, needed—to be elsewhere. Couldn't she understand? Most homicides were solved within the first seventy-two hours. After that, the trail was too cold and resolution rarely came. Thank God for Robyn, her sleeper sofa, and an understanding ear.

Robyn drew in a deep breath and grimaced. "You know, Finn? We should get out of this business." She caught his gaze and held it. "While we're still alive."

He reached for the door handle. "I'm not dead inside completely, you know. Although Sherry might argue that point."

"I don't mean alive as in enjoying life. I mean alive as in surviving. The odds aren't very good for us, you know."

He jerked his head in the direction of the house. "Better than whoever's in there. At least we go into this business knowing every minute that we could take a bullet. For most people, death just kind of sneaks up on them."

Dylan swung his legs out of the car and stood up, anchoring himself firmly in six inches of mud puddle. "Christ!" he cursed. Bad enough that he had to take a look at bodies in their rawest form, but couldn't God cut him a little slack?

"Hey, watch your mouth." Robyn glared at him.

"Oh. Sorry."

Robyn never talked about God. At least, not in front of him. He knew for a fact that she was devoutly religious though because he'd heard her praying late at night when she thought he was asleep. As for the way she lived, she was probably the most Christian of any woman he'd ever known.

She met him at the front fender of the car. No one seemed to pay any attention to either of them. Already a good thirty or so uniforms were milling around, not to mention another dozen bystanders, some still in pajamas. The cop closest to them clung to the trunk of a small oak tree and retched his guts out. Poor kid leaned far enough away to avoid the splatter on his shoes.

"Hey, Harrison?" Dylan called. "That you?"

The kid looked up sheepishly. He couldn't have been any more than twenty-one or twenty-two. Fresh out of the criminal justice department of the local college. Green as they come. The kid wiped vomit from his chin. Yeah, green in more ways than one.

Harrison Weaver backhanded a thin trail of saliva from his bottom lip and sniffled a few times. He blushed a little at the sight of Robyn. He had a massive crush on her, a type of puppy love that would never be returned. "Hey, Detective MacCool," he said. "Might've known you and Detective Porter would get the call."

"Just unlucky, I guess."

"Not as unlucky as—" He turned and retched again.

Poor kid. It took a while to get used to seeing dead bodies and stop puking your guts outs every time.

Harrison gulped in fresh air in an attempt to settle his stomach. "I'm going to stay right here, Detectives, if you don't mind. I think if I prayed a little bit, my nerves might calm down."

"Praying and puking," Dylan said with a sneer. He kept his voice low enough that only Robyn could hear.

"Leave the boy alone," she whispered. The glare she shot back warned him he was on dangerous ground. She'd said more than once that Harrison Weaver was a fine Christian man who led by example. Clearly, she respected his gentleness and sincerity. Admired him for it. Dylan knew better than to get on Robyn's bad list.

"Whatcha got in there, Harrison?" Dylan inclined his head toward the mansion.

The kid straightened up again. "It's not in there. It's out back in the middle of the woods, in a clearing. I've never seen anything like it before. Some kind of devil-worshipping."

Oh, shit. He didn't usually get those until Halloween. Somebody would find a grave in the local cemetery splattered with cat's blood and the headstone overturned. Maybe a little digging around the tombstone itself. Always, it turned out to be local high school boys. In most cases, they'd tortured a cat to death and then had to find an equally obnoxious way of getting rid of the evidence so they decided to make people think it was some kind of Satanic ritual. Once he determined that the case didn't involve any foul play—other than the stench—the case was deemed vandalism and he was called to take care of bigger and better crimes.

"What makes you think it was...devil worshippers?" Robyn asked, carefully choosing her words.

"The way their bodies are marked up. All those, er, you know. *Symbols.*"

Robyn raised an eyebrow. "I'd better take a look. For myself."

She took off in the direction of the house, walking briskly and side-stepping puddles. As usual, Dylan took the longer route. He had to see the scene from the point of action. That meant following in the footsteps of whomever had crashed their Mercedes into a bank of shrubbery in the side yard. He walked along the deep tire ruts left in the grass. Water squirted up around his shoes, occasionally seeping in around his ankles.

The driver's door was still open, the keys still dangling from the ignition. Normally, a soaked ground would have left imprints of footfalls but if the rain had lasted much longer—and it had—the technicians would never get a decent impression of footprints. Someone, probably young Harrison Weaver, had turned on the flood lights at the corners of the house. The light crept across the soggy lawn, barely reaching the shadows beyond the azaleas and the sky-blue hydrangea blossoms inter-twined with rain-beaten blossoms of yesterday's morning glo-ries.

Stupid, he thought. Shadowy bushes and recessed door-ways got more homes burglarized and people killed than any-thing else he could think of. If he had his way, he'd bulldoze everything green and turn the lawn into a bed of rocks. It might not be aesthetically pleasing, but it was better than having mon-sters hiding behind the elephant ear leaves that were as big as Medieval shields.

He took his time looking over the car. Had the driver been drunk? Scared? Made mistakes? The occupant had fled in a hurry. If he followed the most likely trail, maybe he'd find answers.

At the outer edge of lamp light and just within the reach of another flood light from the other side of a twelve or fifteen-foot fence, a huge, wrought-iron gate gaped and beckoned. Clearly, the gate was meant to intimidate, but for him there was something strangely fascinating about it. Something gothic. Enticing, as if from an ancient dream. In a way, it reminded him of himself—its strength, protection, and just a little differ-ent.

He shouldered his way through the gate, careful not to touch anything. The back of the house was even more impres-sive than the front. Lights gleamed from every window. Mur-der investigations could be bright and busy, especially in an af-fluent neighborhood like this one. The residents must have made a pretty penny doctoring or lawyering or hostile taking over or whatever they did. Not only had they settled their man-sion on a prime piece of real estate in one of the hottest new neighborhoods in Greenburg, but they'd bought the building lots adjacent to their home as well as ten or twelve lots behind their house. From what he could tell, their other building lots had been left untouched, affording them an illusion of privacy, almost as if this were some kind of refuge in the midst of a hos-tile civilization.

The lawn at his feet had been cut short, trimmed and manicured either, he mused, by servants or the best-paid land-scaping service in town. The extensive patio behind the house looked as if it were made out of marble with its huge urns of hibiscus and bougainvillea—and other flowers he didn't know— at intervals along the wall. A regular showplace, it was.

But beyond the patio, everything was chaos. A flower garden that looked more like a small farm had been destroyed. He picked his way gingerly through it and toward the woods beyond. Bright pink flowers with huge middles littered the ground. Tiny lavender thistles stuck to his pants leg. The smell of sweet and spice burned his eyes.

He stepped on something hard. He kicked at it in the leaves. Damn. A scythe with a blade three feet long. Whoever had wrecked the garden had done it by hand.

Dylan stood for a long time and peered ahead at the dark woods. Lanterns had been set up to light a path that might once have been overgrown but was now overrun with investigators. He'd never seen so many of the city's finest. They certainly had- n't turned out for the murder of the homeless man earlier. Great. If it was somebody famous, he'd have reporters from the national news crawling all over the scene in a few hours. The piddling few local news hounds would be bad enough.

Robyn emerged from the wooded path and stood waiting, visibly shaken. He hoped it wasn't a dead child. God, he hated it when it was a child. Back when he'd been a teenager and his parents had forced him to go to church every Sunday, the Bap- tist preacher often spent the morning service weaving tales of babies skinned alive and sacrificed to the devil. His stomach churned.

"Finn, it's bad." Robyn met him on the path and for a moment seemed to block his way. "Real bad."

He swallowed hard. "What have we got?"

"No, it's not a child," she said in that annoying way that she always seemed to read his mind. She turned and stepped around a pair of swords driven into the ground next to plastic markers with the numbers *6* and *7* on them. She gestured for him to follow her and he did. "Two white males," she said. "One thirties, one twenties. Buck naked. Bodies are still warm. Estimated time of death is one a.m."

Dylan glanced at his watch. A quarter of two. Sheesh! Someone must have heard the murder. How else could a crime hidden in those woods have been discovered so quickly?

"Naked, huh?" He turned the words over in his mind. "Homosexual murder-suicide?" He'd had one of those last year on Christmas Eve. *Merry Christmas, MacCool.*

"No," Robyn said slowly. "I don't think so. These wounds were definitely not self-inflicted."

"What makes you say that?"

A chorus of rainfrogs and wood life grew louder as the woods around them deepened.

"The older one, he was taken by surprise. There are defensive wounds on his hands. He put up quite a fight before he was stabbed through the heart."

"Maybe the younger one did it."

"No. Though I can't imagine what was going through his head." She stopped for a second and looked around, then continued on. "He didn't put up a fight at all. Just took it. Looks like he just stood there and let someone slash his throat." Her shoulders stiffened involuntarily. "Damned near cut his head off."

"Maybe he slashed his own throat. Strange, yes. Unheard of, no. It does happen."

"Possibly," Robyn conceded with a shaky sigh, "but you don't nearly behead yourself committing suicide and then, just to make sure you got it right, stab yourself in the heart. Besides, both men had symbols carved into their bodies, and that didn't happen until after their hearts had stopped pumping."

"What kind of symbols?"

Robyn shook her head. "You'll see." She let out an accidental whimper.

"You've seen worse," he said. He meant it to comfort her. Instead, he felt more uncomfortable than before. Robyn was a strong woman with nerves of steel. She'd grown up in the aftermath of two drugged-out, hippie parents. By the time she was twenty, she'd already seen more horrors than most cops saw in their whole careers.

He decided to put it bluntly. "What's getting to you, Robyn?"

She paused and nodded toward the lantern-lit clearing a hundred feet away. "Something isn't what it appears to be."

"Seldom is."

"No. I mean, this murder is all wrong."

"Most murders are."

"No, no. There's a woman involved."

"Often is. You're thinking a woman did that?"

Robyn shrugged. "I-I don't know."

"You're thinking a woman killed two men in their prime with one of them just standing by, waiting?"

"I-I don't know. A superhuman one perhaps. Doesn't seem likely. You know the force it takes to pierce a man's rib-cage with a knife, even if he's not defending himself. I don't think I have the strength to do what I saw up ahead, and I'm not exactly a petite little thing."

Petite? Not Robyn. She stood six feet tall if she stood an inch and could have played the part of Red Sonya or a warrior princess at any Halloween party.

"You think a petite woman was involved?"

"Involved somehow." Robyn began walking again. "There was a white silk robe on the ground between the two men. Bloody, cut up. Looked like it had been slashed with the same knife that...slashed both men. At first the guys on the scene thought the robe belong to a girl. Maybe a young teen."

Dylan groaned. He hated it when children were victims. When it came to kids getting hurt, he couldn't act rationally.

"It wasn't a girl's though. The robe was...definitely a woman's."

"How do you know?"

"I-I just know. The cut of the gown. The length of it. *The ornamentation.*" And something else she wasn't telling him.

"Maybe it belonged to the men."

"No."

"Damn it, Robyn. How do you know? Did a techni-cian—"

"No, I just know."

"You said there was blood on the robe. Was it the woman's?"

"Can't tell yet. The lab may be done by noon if we press hard. We'll know then."

"We may have a third victim or we may have a killer."

Robyn nodded. "I told Harrison to start searching the woods though I doubt we'll get very far before daylight. Woods are too thick. Dangerous, too."

Dylan winced. "Snakes."

"Snakes don't bother me. People do. Serpents don't slither out of the dark with the sole purpose of slaughtering anyone who doesn't believe like they do."

"Robyn, what the hell are you talking about?" He'd never seen her like this, shaken, nearly incoherent, mumbling on and on about snakes and serpents.

"There it is," she said as they walked into the clearing. "What's left of it, anyway. Whoever killed them tried to burn down their woods. Might've succeeded if it hadn't been for the thunderstorm."

But Dylan wasn't hearing her any more. He stared at the circle in the clearing, taking in every inch of it, committing it to memory as he did with every murder scene. A technician moved out of his way and readjusted one of the lanterns so he could see. The charred remnants of the bonfire, now damp and cold, had been scattered across the circle.

Robyn was right: someone had tried to set fire to the woods, but the rain had put it out. The ground in the clearing was no more than dirt and leaves and soft green grass, yet it seemed littered, fouled. Small rocks that looked like hardened liquid light gleamed in the lantern's beam. Amber? A brass goblet had fallen to the ground, red and rain still in its overturned bowl. Flower petals, unwilted, mingled with the debris. Under the nearest tree rested a flute and drum. A harp-like instrument had been broken beneath a footfall. A clump of white cloth, red in places and jagged in others, twisted at the photographer's feet as he crouched and swayed this way and that until he found the best angles. Several amber and black stones were sewn into the fabric.

As soon as Dylan cleared his throat, the photographer rose to his full height, excused himself, and moved to take pictures of two sticks on the ground. Dylan glanced from the cloth to the orange plastic *3* beside it, following a triangular line to the plastic *1* and *2* beside the bodies.

With a sign of finality, Dylan moved closer. He hated this part of the job. Hated arriving too late for a rescue. Looking at dead bodies always made him feel helpless, and he always wondered if he'd been there, could he have saved anyone? Almost as if he'd lived a lack of rescues many times before. But the out-side world would never know his doubts. He kept his aloofness. After all, he was cool Detective MacCool with all his emotions hidden.

He frowned down at the two men. He didn't notice na-ked bodies anymore with their usual scars and flab and excre-ment. They were anonymous enough when dead. He didn't notice faces either. He noticed wounds and clues. That was all. That had to be all. He'd go insane if he let it get any closer.

These two men were muscular and fit. Men in their prime. Men about *his* age and build. One had gashes across his hands and wrists where he'd tried to defend himself. He'd fended off at least six or seven strikes before his hands had been ripped apart. Whoever had stabbed him hadn't used a butter knife. The blade had made its way through finally and straight to the heart. Judging by the shape of the wound, the killer must have twisted the knife in a full circle before pulling it out.

The other man had a deep gash below his jaw line that left his windpipe exposed. He had a wound over his heart and it perfectly matched the other man's. They had been arranged side by side, arms outstretched as if crucified, and their ankles crossed. In death, they almost touched. The sign of the devil, the five-pointed star upside down, had been carved across their chests, in their right palms, and on their foreheads and smeared with their blood. He remembered enough of his childhood's Sunday School classes to understand the references to the *Book of Revelation.*

He tried not to notice the sightless eyes that stared back at him but they pulled him in, called to him, drew him. Bile rose in this throat. He swallowed, but it kept coming. He covered his mouth and raced for the edge of the circle so he wouldn't defile the crime scene.

"Finn?" Robyn laid a curious hand on his shoulder, but he shrugged it off. "Are you okay?"

He shook his head. He would never again be okay. How could he explain it to her? He'd never met either of the men, yet he was sure he knew them.

Chapter Two

~*Saadia*~

Saadia raised her withered hands to the full moon and prayed for a child as she had at every full moon for the past sixty-five years. She chuckled at the thought of it and knew she must be dreaming. Why now, after all these years, would the Goddess give her a young one? Saadia was no longer maiden or mother, but crone. A feeble wise woman. An old witch destined for a long-awaited rest in the Summerlands. Either she was dreaming or she was—

Saadia opened her eyes and stared up at the dark ceiling. No, the Goddess hadn't taken her. Edgar snored beside her, though the noise no longer bothered her. She'd long since lost the sharpness of hearing even before the gleaming in her eyes had begun to fade.

The air around her vibrated in three steady strums. Her sense of touch had strengthened as her other senses had faded. It wasn't his footsteps she heard when Edgar shuffled to their bed but rather his footfalls she felt. And now, even without her high-powered hearing aid, she knew someone was at the front door pounding away.

She fumbled and found her eyeglasses on the nightstand and then shoved them on with all her strength. With her hearing aids in and turned up all the way, she squinted at the digital alarm clock with its six-inch tall red numbers: *3:33 AM.*

Who could be at their door at this hour? Certainly not good news. Callers in the middle of the night were sure signs of death or impending death. Celebrations waited for sunlight. Tragedy came when it pleased.

Saadia swung her legs over the bed's edge and slowly lowered her feet to the carpet. Her nightdress fell loosely from her hunched shoulders as she reached for her four-footed cane. She didn't bother to turn on the lights. She could sense the distance of the walls and knew exactly where she was.

It seemed to take forever to reach the front door. The knocking had ceased. Whoever had awakened her was likely gone by now.

In the dark living room, Saadia leaned her forehead against the door and peered through the peephole at night. No one. She twisted the door knob, wincing at the touch of arthritis that lingered, and tugged open the door. Nothing. She stepped out onto the porch—and nearly stumbled over the poor little bird.

The girl sat with her back against the wall, her arms wrapped around her knees. Even though the night was warm, the child shivered, shivered, shivered. A tiny little thing. Young and lost. A child from the Goddess.

"Please?" the girl said, lifting her head. "I need help. I was told the children of the Goddess would help me."

Saadia leaned into the house and flicked on the living room light behind her. The girl's face fell.

"I-I'm sorry, ma'am. I must've gotten the directions wrong. I saw the sign for Wide Oak Lane. I saw the rosemary at your gate. Smelled sandalwood incense from your windows...." She clutched the pendant at her throat and rubbed its outer circle. A pentacle.

Saadia drew in a deep breath and let the oxygen feed her blood. Yes, yes! A child of the Goddess.

"You were sent to me." Not a question. Reassurance for the girl.

"Well, sent *here*. But there was some mix-up. I-I'm sorry I disturbed you, ma'am. I-I'll go now."

Ma'am. Did the girl think a woman of eighty-five too old to be a daughter of the Goddess, too?

The girl's cheeks were wet but not from rain. Only tears ran those trails.

Saadia drew herself up to her full height, what was left of it. The bones of her upper back crackled. "Go? You'll do no such thing. You'll come inside and let me make you some tea."

The girl sniffed. "I can't. Really. I have to find someone. Tonight." She started out into the darkness, away from the reach of the light.

"In the old times," Saadia said, "in lands where girl children meant more mouths to feed and less food for their brothers, newborn daughters were taken to the forests and left to the wolves or the cold. Except in lands that valued their daughters, lands that followed the Goddess."

The child stopped suddenly, then turned, a look of relief and wonder on her face. "You're a...?"

"Like you." Saadia nodded and smiled as much as she could without her dentures. "Now come inside, my child. The Goddess brought you to me for a reason."

The girl stepped into the light. Her yellow hair hung in tangles and thin braids. She couldn't stop shivering. She was older than Saadia had thought. Maybe nineteen or twenty. Everyone looked so young these days.

"You're soaked to the bone," Saadia realized as she locked the door. "Stay right here." She shuffled to the closet and came back with a long, white flannel gown. Then she told the girl to put it on while Saadia made tea, peppermint for herself and chamomile with a little something extra for the girl.

When the girl came out of the bathroom, the white gown dragged the ground and puddled at her feet. She'd combed her hair and untangled her braids, but the wetness on her cheeks seemed fresh. She held a dozen or so stones of amber and jet— high priestess symbols—in her hand. She laid them lovingly on top of the coffee table and, staring but not seeing, arranged the stones in a small circle.

"Sit down, child." Saadia motioned to a sofa she'd bought new in the 1950's and handed the girl a saucer and cup of tea. Then Saadia eased her own creaking bones onto the cushions. The girl's hands shook so badly the cup rattled on its saucer. Saadia reached her feeble hand to steady the girl's young one. "Drink up and tell me what brought you here."

The girl lifted the cup to her lips and gulped, her gaze on some imaginary spot across the room. "They're dead," she said in a whimper too soft to be heard, but Saadia could read lips well enough.

"Who's dead?" Saadia leaned closer. She couldn't afford to miss a word.

The girl gulped down the tea too fast. Her eyes misted over, lost in memories. Whatever she had witnessed had left her nigh shock, and the pain of it was just now beginning to seep in. With one last swallow, she finished the tea and then left the cup and saucer empty in her lap. She closed her eyes, either to re-member or to shut out the memories.

If a crime had been committed, then Saadia would need to call someone, report it. But so far, the girl hadn't made sense. You could never tell with kids these days, whether they were on dope or not. Even bedraggled young ones. The girl's aura flick-ered and wavered, and in Saadia's experience, only one of two things could weaken an aura so: drugs or pain—either of the physical or emotional type.

"Tell me, child." She took the girl's hand and rubbed it. The fierceness of life inside such a limp little thing stunned her. "Has a crime been committed?"

"Yes."

Saadia drew in a slow breath and continued to rub the young hand. "Child, what kind of crime?" She held her breath and waited for an answer.

"A crime against the Goddess."

"Listen carefully," Saadia said, squeezing the young hand until her arthritis stung, "don't go to sleep on me yet." But too late. The soothing herbs were already at work. "Stay with me, child. You said someone was dead. Who's dead?"

The slightest frown passed the girl's brow. She opened her mouth to say something and finally murmured words Saadia couldn't understand. It sounded like she'd said, "My year kings."

Saadia rose and shuffled to the closet in the hallway. She found the quilt with stars and crescent moons on it, then took it back and covered the girl with it, carefully removing the empty dishes from her lap and tucking her in around the arms and legs.

The poor thing was exhausted. The girl must not have eaten in a long time because the herbs had worked very quickly. Much more quickly than Saadia had expected. Perhaps she was homeless. Perhaps she'd witnessed a murder. Or perhaps she was drunk off ritual wine. It was, after all, Beltane. Perhaps—ah, no use in wondering. There was another way to find out.

She went to the altar on the other side of the room and cleared away the laurels of oak leaves and rose petals she'd left there to celebrate her own May Eve. She let the small black cauldron remain. She'd filled it with fresh rainwater—a gift from the Goddess—and floated in it blossoms from the garden—a gift from the Green Man. She arranged a tall white candle to stand above it and, with a flick of a match, set the wick ablaze. Then, finally, she tossed the girl's amber and jet into the water.

Saadia stared at the flame's reflection inside the cauldron. Better to use the moon's reflection, especially when full, but there was no moon at this hour, so a weaker light would have to do. She placed her palms firmly on the oak altar to brace herself and stared hard into the pot. The water seemed to shimmer and swirl. Her old eyes burned, as they often did more and more, but scrying had never failed to give her answers.

The water swirled again. She looked past the water to the flame, past the flame, and into a glade where three people danced and sang and loved. Saadia smiled to herself, remembering Beltane fires of long ago in England. The girl had been happy. A priestess to the two men who worshipped the Goddess through her. No.... No. Saadia looked more closely. They not only worshipped the Goddess through her—they worshipped *her*. An enviable position for any woman. The three of them with their matching tattoos over the heart and, on their faces, expressions of utter joy.

Then the waters wavered. The scene changed. The ground was wet. The girl, soaked to the bone, tripped and stumbled through the woods and into the glade. Something dark stood at the edge of the clearing, just in the shadows where she couldn't see it. Neither Saadia nor the girl. But she felt it. They both did.

The girl looked around, confused, lost. Then she stopped, stared at the ground. At her feet were positioned the two men who had sung and danced and loved with her. Abominations of their sacred pentagrams had been carved upside down into their bare skin. Knife wounds, the kind made by a nine-inch athame, obliterated the tattoos on their chests. The little triple spiral tattoos, symbols of their unity, had been mutilated until they were no longer there. Saadia squeezed her eyes shut. One of the three had escaped and found her way to Saadia's door.

Saadia lifted her face to the nearest window. How little she could do at this hour of darkness! Both she and the girl needed their sleep. Come sunrise, Saadia would call the rest of her coven—the Coven of the Jeweled Dragon--and invite them to her little house on Wide Oak with its tell-tale witch signs of rosemary at the gate and sandalwood incense wafting into the street.

Chapter Three

~Dylan~

Fighting the need for either a good night's sleep or a barrel of coffee, Dylan stood in the dewy grass behind the mansion and wished he were alone so he could take his shoes off and feel the ground beneath his feet. It seemed he never had a chance to connect with nature any more. He never took his shoes off except to sleep. And what if he did? He'd just find himself walking on concrete. Which was probably for the best. He felt hardened, disconnected. Such was the life of a homicide detective.

"Coming through," someone called from behind him.

He stepped aside and, with a sadness he couldn't conquer, watched as the two heavy body bags were carried away. The photographer was gone. The scene had been cleaned up, much of it carted away for analysis. Now, just as the sun was coming up, Harrison had begun to assemble a team to scour the woods for signs of the missing woman.

Dylan shook his head and averted his eyes from the body bags. Even in death with their cold eyes staring upward, he'd felt he'd known them. Not recently. Maybe...maybe in elementary school. But it went deeper than that. As if they'd been brothers or playmates or best friends some long, long time ago. It didn't make sense. Everyone knew Detective MacCool was a pro.

Time, he decided. He blew the hair out of his eyes and stalked toward the house. Time to talk to the dead. Let the coroner examine the bodies and the technicians dust for finger-prints, but Dylan had found that the answers to most murders came when he got to know the victims. He wanted to know everything there was to know about them. Who they were, what they did, what they had for lunch. He would spend the next day or two finding out all those things. From neighbors, childhood friends, old sweethearts, and most importantly from their own homes and workspaces. Talking to the dead, he called it. He let the life they had lived tell him how they had died.

He paused inside the back door. The furnishings inside weren't quite as he'd expected. As a matter of fact, he wasn't sure what he had expected. When he'd taken his first look at the house through his rainy windshield, he'd been positive that every room boasted at least $25,000 in fine furniture and that the lady of the house kept an interior decorator on retainer. The home inside was not the showplace he'd expected.

He'd been wrong, too, after he'd seen the carnage in the grove, to think the interior would be decorated with red shag carpet and black walls and goats' heads painted on the ceiling. The interior was more like a garden with large leafy shrubs in ceramic pots and wooden baskets. Some of the rooms had ta-bletop fountains. Others had saltwater aquariums of blue and yellow fish. Most rooms had banners hanging from the ceiling or windchimes or feathered dreamcatchers. Every corner was filled with something: plants, crystals, candles, an arrangement of brass bowls, a dish of potpourri. Not so much cluttered as natural, relaxing.

Dylan tiptoed across the hardwood floor and tried not to track grit—as if anyone alive still cared. There was a richness to the textures and colors in this house. A good feeling about it. Nothing but harmony and none of the chaos of the garden out-side. He had a feeling the murderer had never stepped foot in-side this house.

Beyond all the rooms designed for entertaining, he dis-covered an office, typical of any home office except that it sported five very nice computer systems. In the back of the house, with a door opening directly into the garden, was a huge workshop with separate areas for metalworking and what appeared to be some kind of garden crafts. For a moment, he thought he'd stumbled onto a private drug manufacturing shop, but the green leaves in the baskets smelled more of peppermint than pot and the small white squares resembled cakes of home-made soap with fleck of herbs shining through. On the adjacent tables stood bins of metal ringlets and heavy blankets of something that looked like chainmail.

Strange people, he concluded as moved toward the four bedrooms.

The first bedroom was empty. Not even carpeting on the floor or pictures on the cedar-paneled wall. Not a stick of furniture. As if it were waiting for someone to move in.

The second bedroom was decidedly masculine with its fireplace, massive brass bed, heavy oak dressers, accents of red, brass fixtures, lanterns hanging from the wall, and tiers of candles. The picture on the mantel was of the blond man from the grove and a young woman in bridal gear and brownish-blonde hair. The two of them were smiling and happy, lost in an embrace, the garden behind them bearing witness. From the looks of the bathroom and the adjoining closet, this room belonged to the blond man. If the woman in picture was his wife, Dylan found no sign that she shared his room.

The third bedroom was also decidedly male, yet different. The colors were a cool blue and the furniture, cypress. No tabletop fountain for this room! The one in the corner was nearly six feet tall, bubbling and gurgling louder than the two aquariums on the opposite wall. A mobile of fish dangled from the ceiling. On the dresser, next to a goldfish bowl teeming with tadpoles, stood an elegantly framed photograph of a dark-haired man with hair loose on his shoulders and the bride from the other man's photograph. He was dressed in a green robe and she in white with flower blossoms tucked behind her ears and braided into her long hair, which was blonder than in the first photograph. He wore a laurel of oak leaves and grinned at the camera as he caught the woman's hand in his. It was almost a wedding picture but not quite. The thing that intrigued him most was the satin ribbon wrapped around their wrists and hands, uniting them as much as any exchange of wedding bands. Like the other man's bathroom and closet, this room also bore no sign of a woman's touch.

The fourth bedroom was at the far end of the hall. It was nearly twice the size of the other rooms and where they were heavy and dark, this room was light and airy with birch furniture and sheers for window coverings. In the center of the ceiling, a large white fan turned slowly, stirring enough of a breeze to disturb the long windchimes in the corner of the room and a wreath of feathers on the opposite wall. With every circle of the fan, the chimes resonated a single low tone as if from a church pipe organ. Ornamental bird cages decorated the top of the armoire and dressers.

The bath area sported a Jacuzzi encased in glass bricks. He could just make out the garden through the wall. These rooms were obviously the woman's.

On the left side of her bed, on the nightstand, stood a picture of the blond man. On the right, stood a picture of the dark-haired man. What kind of relationship did these three people have? He waited for the dead to talk to him, but they didn't. Not in the usual way. Here were three people living together under one roof, each with their separate rooms. Yet they were more than roommates. His gut told him the men weren't brothers allowing themselves to be photographed with a sisterly bride. Each one seemed to have some claim to her. Maybe what Reverend Jones had said was true....

"Strange," he said aloud, shaking his head.

"Not really," Robyn said from behind him. "It's pretty obvious, isn't it?"

He turned and blinked at her. To him, nothing seemed obvious.

"She's air," Robyn said. "Don't you see it? Bird cages, feathers, wind chimes, the kite." She pointed at the ceiling. He'd missed the hand-painted kite with its interlocking Celtic designs. "They all have to do with air and wind. Whoever she is—or was—she aligns herself with the powers of air."

He shrugged. "What are you talking about?"

"The other rooms. The bedrooms. One is fire and one is water. She's air. Independent of either and necessary to both."

"Fire, water, air—Robyn, you lost me."

She sighed heavily. "Each of the three of them felt very close to one of the four elements. Air, fire, water, and earth."

Ah. He understood. "But what about the empty bedroom. That would be earth. Whose bedroom is that?"

"I don't know, but maybe it has something to do with who killed them and why. Or maybe they're waiting for a forth person to join them."

Dylan shook his head. "I don't get it. What's the big deal about the four elements? And why would anyone want to, um, align themselves with an element? I just don't get it."

Robyn rolled her eyes. "I'm not surprised."

Dylan grunted and wondered why he felt insulted. "What were they doing? Trying to re-enact that Captain Planet cartoon where each one calls out the name of an element and they put their hands together and suddenly a superhero appears?"

"Finn? Sarcasm does not become you."

Where had he heard that before? At least Robyn said it in a nice way. Not like Sherry had. But then, Robyn understood him and Sherry never had.

"What we are," Robyn explained, "is a delicate balance of the four elements, plus spirit. Our...personalities, for lack of a better word, share something of each of the elements, but when we find ourselves more greatly attuned to one of the elements over all the others, we tend to align ourselves with that particular element, depending on where our souls are in their evolution."

"Souls? Evolution?" Dylan blinked at her. "What the hell are you talking about? These people are devil worshippers."

Robyn shot him a wounded look, almost as if he'd struck her across the face. "Where did you get that idea?"

"From Reverend Jones. I interviewed him an hour ago while you were talking to the neighbors."

"Reverend Jones? You mean the man who initiated the 911 call that Harrison answered?"

"That's the one. He showed up a little while ago. Offered counseling to any of us who needed it after what we'd seen here tonight. He said the woman was a witch."

"Oh? And what is Reverend Jones? Her *pastor*?"

"Now you're the one who's being sarcastic." He picked up a purple rock from the top of the dresser and ran his thumb across the crystalline edges. Amethyst. "He said she looked unkempt and nervous, like she'd just rolled out of bed."

"And that makes her a devil worshipper. You should see yourself on Sunday mornings! You don't look so hot yourself until you've had six cups of coffee."

Dylan let go of an exasperated sigh. He was tired, damn it. The last thing he wanted to do was to argue with Robyn. "Look, he said she was wearing a pentagram. Okay? One of those five-pointed stars? You know, like the ones carved into our friends in the woods?"

"No. Not like that."

His fingers tingled and burned, almost as if the rock had come alive in his hand. He set it down quickly on the dresser and drew his hand against his chest. He needed rest, sleep. All this talk of devil worship was getting to him. "You saw them, Robyn. They were clearly involved in some kind of devil-worshipping ritual."

"No, they were not clearly involved in some kind of devil-worshipping ritual. A ritual, yes. But they didn't carve those marks on their own foreheads and palms."

"Then maybe the woman did. Maybe they were her sacrifice or something."

Robyn shook her head, her jaw tighter than a vice. "You watch too many stupid movies, you know? Witchcraft is not about devil worship. It's not about slaughtering newborns or stirring up storms to kill your enemies or carving up the people you love. Whatever those three people were doing tonight, it wasn't about death. It was about life."

"Yeah, well, we need to find the witch and find out how her two warlocks felt about life."

Robyn sank her hands into her pockets. "Like I said, you watch too many stupid movies. A man who practices witchcraft is a witch, not a warlock. Get your terminology straight."

"Just where do you get your terminology?" He'd never heard her talk this way. As far as he knew, she was a very religious person, and yet she was taking the side of witches?

"I..." She swallowed. "I read a lot."

"Hmmm. Obviously not from the same library I read from."

"Did Reverend Jones tell you anything useful?"

Dylan thought for a moment. "Yeah. Yeah, he did. One thing did seem a bit odd. Odder than witches and devil worship, that is. The witch was the one who told him to call 911 and told them exactly where to go. Then she took off like a bat out of hell."

"She knew something," Robyn murmured.

"Yeah, like maybe she killed them. Did you get any good dirt from the neighbors?"

"Not really. Grant Firehawk was a corporate lawyer."

"Any enemies?

"None known. He was well-liked in the neighborhood, though. Before he made partner and got too busy, he spent Sunday afternoons at the community center, tutoring high school kids in math. Couple of neighbors described him as a nice, young Christian man, though they didn't know what church he attended. Some people thought the other man, Cedric Firehawk was his brother. Or maybe half-brother because they looked nothing alike."

"Did this Cedric Firehawk have any enemies?"

"None known. He built treehouses for half kids in the neighborhood. Built goldfish ponds for their moms. Played handyman for every old woman on the street. The blue-haired lady on the cul-de-sac was crying harder than anybody because, quote, 'that nice young Cedric' unquote, took her to the grocery store once a week and helped her with her bags."

"Jeez. That clean?"

"There was some discrepancy over which brother was married to the woman. Nobody really knew the men quite that well, and as usual, everybody was plenty willing to take whatever these people were willing to give."

"So what about the woman?" Dylan asked. He found himself staring at the chunk of amethyst. His fingers itched to pick it up again.

Robyn caught a glimpse of herself in the mirror over the dresser. Her fingertips moved to the circles under eyes. Flustered, she turned and instead leaned against the wall. "Nobody knew much about her, though most agreed she had something of a bad reputation. They couldn't really say why they thought so. She tended to keep to herself. One neighbor told me she left for work—or assumed she left for work—every morning around eight and returned home around noon."

"Sheesh." Dylan hated nosy neighbors, but on the other hand, many a nosy neighbor helped solve a crime. "Any friends?"

"None anyone could name. Like I said, she kept to herself. They thought her name was Kestrel, but none of the neighbors I talked to were really sure. A couple of the stay-at-home wives in the neighborhood had stopped by several times to ask her to have tea with them. One woman thought Kestrel was shy. The others all agreed that she was stuck-up."

"Did they think she was strange or different or anything?"

"Eccentric, maybe. But they couldn't tie it to the anything other than that she was unsociable to the other women in the neighborhood." Robyn narrowed her eyes at him. "That's not a crime, you know."

Dylan leaned against the wall beside Robyn and looked down at her. "We've got a lot of work to do. I suggest we talk to employers and parents next." They had less than seventy-two hours before the trail grew cold. The big question now was whether to grab some shut-eye or keep going.

"Detective MacCool! Detective Porter!" Harrison huffed into the room. "Come quick! We found something in the woods."

"The woman?" Dylan choked out.

"No. Not yet, anyway. But we found a woman's purse. Hasn't been exposed to the elements for very long. We figure it was dropped during the night."

Dylan brushed past the young officer. "You guys haven't opened it yet, have you?" Inexperienced officers were notorious for destroying evidence.

"Um, no, Detective MacCool. But it was open when it hit the ground because lipstick and tampons"—he reddened—"and other stuff spilled out on the ground all over the place. Including her credit cards. Good firm footprints nearby, too, like she was running hard."

Dylan turned back to Robyn and nodded. "Kestrel Firehawk. She can't be far away."

"Who?" Harrison asked. "No, this purse belonged to someone else. A Gloria Stokes."

Dylan and Robyn exchanged glances. "I guess that answers that question," he said. "No nap for us."

Chapter Four

~*Saadia*~

"Jeez," the woman at the door said under her breath. "Albion, you look terrible. What's happened?"

Saadia opened the door a little wider. She put one bony finger to her lips and motioned Tara inside. Tara was the Maiden of the Coven, Saadia's right arm. One day soon Tara would take over as the High Priestess of the Coven of the Jeweled Dragon. She would have already except everyone insisted Saadia——Albion was her Craft name——lead them spiritually for as long as she was able. Having a crone lead such a vibrant young group of Wiccans was unusual, but the Goddess obviously had need of her in such a position.

"You came," Saadia said.

"Of course, I came. We all did. All except Phoenix, and she'll be here soon."

Saadia smiled back. Her eyes stung. Of course, they'd come. They were more than friends and closer than family. They were her brothers and sisters in the Goddess, and for these past few years of her cronehood, they had been her life.

One by one they trudged through the door, following Tara's lead and not making a sound. Quiet as mice, they made their way through the door and into the hall. They'd come through the same door last night, laughing and joyous and celebrating the coming Beltane ritual and dressed in robes of purple, the sacred color of their coven.

This morning, they were somber, their eyes showing the weariness of a late night as well as fear for a dawn's summons. Some of them, she'd reached at work, and they'd come right away, still wearing their mundane clothes. Others had chosen to take the day off and spend it at Saadia's beckon.

They came in, every one of them, with expectant eyes. Tara in her green nurse's scrubs had come straight from the labor and delivery room. Starr Quietwater, a high school history teacher, had dressed for work in a tiny, floral print with a Peter Pan collar, but she'd found a substitute at the last minute. They were an eclectic mix for a coven of thirteen. A shy botany major at the local college, an obstetrics nurse, a bartender, a high school teacher, the best female mechanic in Greenburg, a restaurant manager, an assistant manager at a bookstore, a web designer, a bookkeeper, a stockbroker, a police officer, dear old Edgar, and Saadia. They came from all walks of life, but they followed the same path.

Saadia led them, one by one, to the chair where the girl slept. They looked her over, every one of them, as if examining the relic of a saint. Careful and worshipful. One by one, they nodded and followed Saadia out into her rose garden. Each of them were told all the details Saadia knew, plus those she had seen in the scrying pool. One by one, they found places to sit or stand in the garden, the garden they had all made together.

Three years ago, to celebrate Ostara, the vernal equinox or the mundane first day of spring, eleven of them had gathered to bring life again to the plot of land feeble fingers could no longer tend. Each had brought a rose bush, along with a small box of flowering herbs. As a service to her and to their Goddess, they had planted the most wonderful garden. Each year, they gathered seeds from their own back yards, farms, and neighborhoods, and brought them to Saadia's as an offering at Ostara, the pagan Easter, and planted the seeds. Now, on a bright May morning, the roses were in bloom and the other flowers grew madly around them.

"Who is she?" Tara was first to ask. She found a seat on an upturned clay pot.

Saadia blinked at her matter-of-factly. "A child of the Goddess."

Tara pushed her dark but prematurely graying hair out of her eyes. She was thirty, maybe thirty-five, and wise beyond her years. Only the silver threads among the black gave any evidence of her age. "Did she tell you her name?" Tara persisted.

"Not yet."

"Did she have any identification on her?"

"A wallet. Single fold. Tapestry weave." Saadia lifted one eyebrow.

"What about a driver's license?"

"There wasn't one. No license. No credit cards. Just a handful of money. Sixty-three dollars," Saadia added with a frown. "In twenties and ones."

"What about keys?" asked Morgana, the mechanic. "She couldn't have walked all this way."

"No keys. Wherever she came from, she did walk all this way. Her sandals are ruined."

"Was she...was she raped? Or hurt?" someone else asked from the far side of the garden. Renwen, the assistant manager at the local chain bookstore.

"No. Not physically. But I do know this: the two people she loved most in the world were killed last night, and whoever did it means to kill her, too. And will, if we don't do something about it."

Echo Dragonfly, a petite blonde stockbroker in her early forties, shifted on the mosaic tile bench and extracted a small package from her purse. She untied a satin string from the package, then on the bench beside her, she unraveled the silk cloth that had been folded in triangles.

She picked up a well-worn deck of Rider-Waite Tarot cards and shuffled them to release any energies remaining from previous readings. She paused for a moment, closing her eyes and frowning a thought, then nodding to herself and shuffled seven more times. Then, while everyone waited in silence, she carefully laid the deck in three small stacks on the bench with her right hand. With a deep, cleansing breath, she moved her left hand, her receptive hand, palm down over each stack. Her hand moved slightly up and down over the last stack as if something nearly repelled her skin. She checked the middle pile again, smiled to herself, then picked it up and shuffled the others underneath it.

She slid the top card off the deck. "This," she said, "is behind her." She turned the card over and laid it flat on the stone.

Lucretia, the college student, peeked over Echo's shoulder and gasped. "The Tower!" Her black and blue hair flopped forward, hiding her eyes and the heavy, Gothic eyeliner. She chewed at her black lipstick. "Tragedy. Change."

Echo nodded. *"Catastrophic* change."

Saadia could no longer see the drawing of the Tower with people leaping from its walls, shaken to their foundations. It was the most dreaded card in the deck but thankfully for the girl, the Tower was behind her now.

"This card," Echo said, slipping the next from the deck and pausing before turning it over, "represents where she is now."

A beautiful woman in a yellow dress sat on a throne and looked quite content in the artist's rendering.

"Guess you're wrong on that one," Lucretia commented. "That's definitely not the girl asleep in Albion's chair."

Shaking out her left hand as if it tingled, Echo frowned up at Lucretia. "Actually, I think it is her. I know this is going to sound strange, but...." She glanced around the other members of the coven.

"Go on," Grail prodded. The bartender's husky voice cracked. "Go on."

"The...the girl's pregnant."

Tara startled. An obstetrics nurse, she took a quick interest. "I'll check on the girl when she wakes. We'll see then what we can find out."

"But she didn't look pregnant." Lucretia crossed her arms and uncrossed them impatiently. "Maybe she got pregnant last night. I mean, it *was* Beltane."

"Yes," Saadia agreed, remembering the images in the water. "Yes, you're right."

"And this card," Echo said, slipping the third card from the deck, "represents her near future. This is what will happen if she stays on her present course." Echo turned over the card and gave a little cry.

A big red heart with three swords sticking through it shimmered in the morning light. They stared at the card, all of them, and without saying a word. Only Saadia broke the silence. She had to. She was their High Priestess.

"If that is the course before her, then we must change her course. We're not helpless. We may leave our choices in the hands of the Goddess, but She allows us to pick our own fate if we choose to do so. By using our magick to change our courses, together we can save this girl and the child she carries."

Children, Saadia heard in the back of her mind.

"How do we do it?" Lucretia asked, wide-eyed.

"Tonight. In the midnight hour. We'll make her disappear." Saadia glanced at the back door, toward where the girl slept inside. "But first, we must have her permission."

Chapter Five

~Dylan~

Dylan carried a pen and a small notepad with him, but he rarely used them during interviews. Too often, witnesses clammed up or worse—-misinterpreted his jottings and then ad libbed. That wasn't true of all detectives, but he knew what worked best for him.

It was 8:05 in the morning. Robyn had taken off for God knew where at a quarter 'til eight. It wasn't like her to leave the more interesting interviews to him alone, but then she hadn't had any sleep in the past twenty-four hours either. Plus, they'd argued.

He and Robyn rarely argued. They listened to each other rant about other people, but they rarely ranted about each other. This morning had been different. They had yet to find Kestrel Firehawk, and more and more the evidence—in Dylan's mind— pointed to the petite witch as the cold-blooded killer. Robyn, at least half a foot taller than their suspect and thirty to fifty pounds heavier, argued that she probably would not have had the physical strength to kill two men in the prime of their lives and in the prime of health. The angle of the wounds, the ferocity of the thrusts—they didn't match expectations for a petite woman in her twenties. Not unless she really was a witch and had supernatural powers or something like they always did on TV and in the movies. The only way a woman of her stature could possibly have inflicted those wounds was if the men had readily submitted to their sacrifice without flinching. One of them had, one hadn't. Dylan could only hope, as he rang Gloria Stokes' doorbell for the third time, that his interviewee was six feet, two hundred fifty pounds of muscle.

The door opened a crack, just until the chain caught it. A baby-faced blonde stared up at him. "Yes?" she asked in a whispery voice.

"Ms. Stokes?"

"Uh-huh?"

Damn. So much for that illusion. She wasn't any bigger than Kestrel.

"I need to talk to you about last night." He showed his badge. He didn't flash it. He let her take a long, slow look at it.

"I don't know anything about last night." She answered too quickly, barely gave him time to finish his sentence. She started to close the door in his face.

"Your purse is down at the station, being held as evidence for a murder trial. You want to talk here or there?"

"I—I.... My husband just left."

"Good. Then we can talk in private."

She closed the door to unchain it, then opened it wide. Unlike the Firehawk's mansion, this house was a real showplace but a little smaller. Everything had its place, but it was the kind of perfection that came in a model home. Not a speck of dust, as if no one really lived here at all but rather, only came out to take appointments to show it off.

"Could I offer you something?" she asked. "Tea? I've got an exotic blend brewing right now. It's some kind of health food stuff that's supposed to stimulate your mind and help you remember things."

"No, thank you." He noticed the bags under her eyes and the way her hands shook. "But help yourself to some."

She was a pretty woman, this Gloria Stokes. Early twenties. Certainly no older than Kestrel Firehawk. Her long, curly blonde hair had been combed but not thoroughly. She still had tangles at the ends and in the back. She wore make-up, but it didn't look fresh. No lipstick. Good grief! Had the woman been up all night?

She sat him down at the kitchen table, a contraption of glass and steel, and sat across from him with a cup of tea. Nervously, she tightened the belt on her lacy robe. From the way it hung at her breasts, he could tell she wore nothing underneath.

He laid his pad and pen—capped—on the table between them, then leaned forward on his elbows and folded his hands under his chin. "Don't you want to tell me about last night?"

She didn't look up. "What about it?"

"We found your purse at the scene of a murder." He watched carefully, but she didn't flinch. Most people who were unaware of a crime would jerk their heads up and demand to know who had been harmed and what had happened and when.

"Yeah, somebody stole my purse a few days ago."

She was lying. He could tell by the way she held her head. "Ms. Stokes? Are you certain?"

"Yes."

"We found a receipt in your purse. From a local convenience store. One pack of gum."

She sipped her tea. She was nervous and doing her damnedest to hide it. "So?"

"So the receipt was dated yesterday. At 10:07 last night to be precise."

"Oh, that's right. I picked up some gum on my way home from work."

Sheesh. If there were a stereotype for dumb blondes, this woman was the template. "If you bought gum on your way home from work and the receipt was in your purse, and your purse was stolen several days ago.... Ms. Stokes, are you even thinking about what you're saying?"

She took another sip and blinked at the table in front of her. "Huh? I'm sorry. I haven't had much sleep, and you're not making much sense. I'm usually perky in the mornings. Really, I am. Just today...."

"Just today is the day after you saw a murder. Isn't that right? Or were you part of it?"

"I-I didn't see anything. I don't know what you're talking about. You should leave. My husband will be angry."

"You just told me he left for work a little while ago."

"Oh. Yeah, that's right. I guess he did. But he'll be angry if he knows you're here."

"Why would he be angry? Is there something you're not telling me? Ms. Stokes?"

"No, no. That's not it at all." She still hadn't looked up at him. "He'd be angry if he knew...I'd lost my purse."

"Or where you'd lost it?"

Her eyes watered. Then tears spilled down her cheeks. "Floyd's a good man."

Dylan sat in silence and let her blubber all she needed to. When snot started hanging from her right nostril, he did the gentlemanly thing and handed her a coarse white napkin from the silver napkin holder on the table. She blew her nose on the paper, then buried the napkin in her lap.

"Floyd? Is that your husband?"

"Yes."

"I don't understand. What does your husband have to do with the murder that took place last night?"

"Everything."

Dylan's pulse quickened. "You're saying your husband killed two men last night, in cold blood, then carved them up with Satanic symbols?"

She raised her chin, her eyes still downcast. Slowly she raised her lids to look at him. "No. No! My husband didn't kill anybody in cold blood. He wouldn't do that. He's a good man."

"Then what does your husband have to do with last night?"

"He's...he's...." She sighed and looked at Dylan helplessly. "He's a fine Christian man. Really, he is. He goes to church several times a week. Twice on Sundays. Prayer meetings on Wednesday nights. He's a deacon in the church. He's a good man. A good man."

If he's so good, Dylan wanted to say, why are you looking at me like that?

Gloria slanted her head to one side, then reached across the table and ever so gently rubbed the back of Dylan's hand. "He's a good man. A good provider and all. I mean, I have everything I could ever ask for. But he's, well, boring." Her index finger wagged along the top of his hand. "I'm only twenty-three. He's almost forty but he looks a lot older. Thinks a lot older, too. I'm in the prime of my life and he's...boring."

Dylan retrieved his hand from her touch. "I think you've lost me. What do your marital problems have to do with a double murder?"

She slowly withdrew her hand, dragging it back across the table toward her. "Nothing. But that's why I was there last night."

"You were there? You actually saw the murders?"

"No. But I heard their screams. And I hid in the woods for a while because I knew he was there."

"He who?"

"I don't know. Maybe the Prince of Darkness. You know, the Devil?" Her eyes glittered with fear. "It was like he was waiting. He was waiting for the woman to come back. And...and...."

What a flake! He'd never had a witness so intent on contradicting every sentence that issued from her mouth. Nothing she said made sense. Trustworthy sense.

"Whoa. Wait a minute. Why don't you start at the very beginning? What is your connection with the two men who were killed?" He didn't mean to exclude Kestrel Firehawk. "And the woman?"

"I didn't really know the dark-haired man. Or the woman. I think I met them at a party once. You know, one of those boring get-togethers my dad has at his law firm. Grant was the only one I really knew."

"Grant Firehawk?"

She frowned. "Grant Sullivan. He was a lawyer in my dad's firm. Corporate law. Contract disputes, stuff like that. Bo-ring!"

Dylan wondered if criminal law held any more interest for her.

"I was his receptionist."

Ah. At last. A real connection. "So you worked for Grant."

"No. I was his receptionist. He worked for my father. Everybody works for my father. I was Grant's receptionist."

Ah ha. Why hadn't he seen it before? "And Grant was *not* boring?"

Gloria backhanded a tear. For a change, her eyes gleamed. "Oh, yeah. Grant was great. He was smart. He was funny. He was ambitious. He was...he was on fire with life!"

"But? He was taken?"

She grunted. "Well, he said he was, but he really wasn't. I mean, most guys you meet in singles bars claim they're not married, but they really are and they don't wear their wedding bands. But Grant, well, he claimed he was married, but he wouldn't wear a wedding band. He said gold bands were based on material tradition or—oh, I don't know—some gibberish like that. But that what he had with his wife went far deeper and he wore a different kind of symbol. I don't know. I thought it was a bunch of crap. You know? To put me off? I tried to get him to tell me what kind of symbol he meant, but all he would say was that he and his wife had this little tattoo over their hearts and that it meant something very special to them. I tried to get him to show me one time, but he kind of freaked out when I unbuttoned his shirt."

No wedding band. That made sense. The blond man murdered in the woods hadn't worn a wedding band. He hadn't had a tattoo either. The only thing he'd worn above his heart was a knife wound. A deep gash that destroyed much of the skin on impact.

"So you made a play for a married man and he rejected you?"

"No! It wasn't like that at all! He loved me." Her eyes clouded over. "Or he would have if he hadn't been under that woman's spell."

"Spell?" His ears perked up at that. "You mean the, um, witch he was living with?"

"Yeah," she breathed, leaning forward. "You know about that?"

"The question is, Ms. Stokes, how do you know about it?"

She leaned back in her seat and gnawed on her lip for a good minute and a half. "I kept hinting to Grant that he should invite me over sometime to see his house. I'd heard it was quite elegant. On the outside, anyway. I don't know anybody who's ever been inside it. He wouldn't tell me, so I...I..." She picked at her fingernail.

"You what?" Dylan prodded.

"I followed him home one night. It was kind of exciting and a little bit stupid, I guess. I felt like I was in high school or something."

Dylan didn't say anything. Except for the harsher lines on her face, it was hard to tell that she wasn't in high school any more.

"Anyway, I followed his car to see where he pulled into a driveway, and he stopped at this great, big house. So I drove a little ways down the street and parked in the driveway of this house that was for sale. I sat there for a long time. Several hours maybe."

Dylan picked up his pen and doodled on the pad. "Why was that?"

"I don't know. It seems a little silly now. I'd told my husband I was working late. He was at a late-night church meeting, so I knew he wouldn't miss me. Not for a while, anyway. I wanted—" She paused, swallowed, and gathered her nerve again. "I wanted, um—"

"Wanted what?"

"I wanted Grant to—to seduce me."

Gloria bowed her head and began crying again. Dylan couldn't see much difference between her and a teenager. She had all of the intensity of young love but none of the restraint that comes with growing up. She was little more than a budding schoolgirl who didn't comprehend her own consequences. She walked the borderline of aggressor, still wanting the man to be the one to take her, to seduce her, to relieve her of any responsibility for her own actions.

"So what happened after you sat in the car for a long time?" he prodded.

"Now or never, I told myself. If I was going to leave Floyd for Grant—"

"Whoa, wait. You were going to leave your husband for Grant Firehawk?"

"You mean Grant *Sullivan*. Yes."

"Had Grant, um, Sullivan given you any indication that he would be there for you if you left your, er, boring husband?"

81

"Not in so many words, but he would have. I know he would have. I knew it the minute I met him."

"Even though he was married."

She waved her hand. "I never believed that crap—not one word of it—about him being married. People who are married wear wedding bands. Okay?" Her voice took on a sing-songy, mocking tone. "They don't wear tattoos over their hearts or shit like that to show they have a commitment. They wear *wedding* bands. Gold wedding bands."

He glanced down at her hand on the table, at the gold wedding band on her finger and the two-carat diamond accompanying it. So much for commitment.

"Grant even had this picture of her, this woman he said he was 'committed' to. He had this picture of her on his desk, and if you look real close, you could see that she was wearing this...this witch's star necklace."

"Witch's star?"

"Yeah. You know. It has five points. You turn it upside down and it makes a goat's head with horns and ears and mouth?"

Yeah, he knew. The same symbol had been carved into the still warm flesh of two men.

"Did he talk about her much?" Dylan asked.

"No. Just when asked. He didn't talk much about his private life. After what I saw that night and last night, I can see why."

"So what did you see that night?"

"After a while, I got out of my car and I walked up to Grant's door, and I started to ring the doorbell. But then I heard singing."

"From inside?"

"No. At first I thought it was a radio or CD or something playing inside. Kinda soft, low music like you might play in your bedroom. Celtic-sounding, you know? But I listened for a minute and I realized it was coming from the back yard so I tip-toed around to the back fence and...."

"And what?"

"It wasn't that hard to climb."

Oh, shit.

"I mean, if you want to keep somebody out of your rose garden, you put razor-wire around the top of the fence, right?"

Dylan didn't say anything. He kept doodling on the pad, making absent-minded, interlocking spirals. "Go on."

"The singing wasn't coming from the backyard. It was coming from down in the woods. It was a full moon that night, and it was really bright, and I could see well enough, so I followed the sound of the singing. There were two men and a woman singing. It was real pretty. It sounded old, you know like that Celtic music that's so popular? They were standing around this bonfire in the middle of a clearing, and they were singing, and they were...naked." She closed her eyes. "I'll never forget the smell of that bonfire. It smelled like rosemary. I have a shampoo that has rosemary in it, so I knew what it was."

"And one of those three people was Grant?"

She opened her eyes. "Yes. And that woman. And—this was really weird—Grant's brother, Cedric. He was really cute, you know. And closer to my age. But he didn't look anything at all like Grant. Plus it kind of freaked me out the way he and that woman were so friendly to each other at that business cocktail party. A little too friendly to be with your brother-in-law, if you know what I mean."

Yet Gloria had been quite friendly with Grant. Sometimes witnesses to crimes were as despicable as the criminals.

"So, *Mrs.* Stokes, what did you do when you saw the three of them dancing naked around the bonfire?" Dylan could hardly believe he was asking the question. People were people, and there were certainly worse things people could do than dance naked in a secluded forest clearing on their own property and under a sky full of stars. "Did you...watch?"

"No! I mean, yes. For a little while. They were talking to the moon or the trees or the sky or something. Like they were talking to somebody. Guardians, they called them. And they asked for protection. And harmony. And...and the rosemary was really strong and I sneezed, just like I do whenever I use that rosemary shampoo." She took another sip of tea. Her hands shook as she replaced the cup in the saucer. "Then everything stopped and they started putting on their clothes real quick and coming after me and—and I ran."

"How did Grant react to you on the next work day?"

83

"H-he pulled me aside and told me that if I ever told any-body what I'd seen, he'd have me arrested for trespassing. And I told him I wasn't scared of him or anything he had to say be-cause if he did have me arrested for trespassing, then I'd have to tell everybody what I'd seen, and I thought that he'd like it a lot less if everybody knew what I'd seen than I would like it if I got arrested or something. I mean, worshipping the devil is not something you want your clients to know you do, right?"

"Are you sure they were worshipping the devil?" He sounded like Robyn now.

"Well, they sure weren't praying to Jesus, so what else could they be doing?"

These people weren't worshipping the devil, Robyn had told him just before she left for parts unknown. These people didn't even believe in a devil. The devil is a Christian concept based on the antlered Green Man of the Forest. Because he was crucial to many Earth-based religions, the Christian religion pre-sented this sacred god as evil even though the devil of the Bible is never described as having horns or cloven feet. According to Robyn, most pagans didn't believe anything was pure good or pure evil, but rather, as in Nature, a balance of both. To give evil a name—to call it "The Devil"—was to give it power. At least, that's what Robyn had said. Still, it was hard to believe there was anything good at all in the person who had carved up last night's victims. Dylan had seen enough murders to believe that there certainly was such a thing as pure evil, whether you gave it a name or not.

"It wasn't his fault, though," Gloria continued. "Grant wasn't acting of his own free will."

"What makes you so sure of that?"

"It was her. It was that woman. She's bewitched them both. I told Grant that, but he just got really, really mad. He told me to stay away from his house or else."

"Or else what?"

"He didn't say. I told him he should let his brother have her, that I was a better match for him."

"What did he do then?"

Gloria shrugged. "He just walked away. After that, it was like he wouldn't be alone in the room with me unless there was somebody else in the room, too."

"So you weren't alone with him at all after that."

"Oh, yeah. Several times. There were times when he had to work late."

Dylan smirked. "And you stayed to help?"

"Of course."

Dylan shook his head, then stopped himself. He wasn't there to pass judgment, just to collect the facts—or her version of them. "He did nothing to help you get away from your boring husband?"

"Well, not yet, but he's— I mean, he *was* going to. Once I got him away from that woman. That witch. He didn't know what he was doing or he wouldn't have been with her. Isn't that obvious?" Gloria peered deep into Dylan's eyes. "Isn't it?"

"So what were you doing at Grant's house last night?"

"He invited me."

"He did?"

"Yeah. Yeah, he asked my help. You know, to break the spell that woman had on him. He'd been talking all day about how he had to leave on time because he had this special event to go to so he wanted me to schedule his appointments a certain way but I couldn't, so he ended up having to work late even though he had something special he had to do, he said. A big dinner or something. I had to stay late and help him, of course."

"Help to do what?"

"You know, file things. Get books for him. He was working on this real important case about intellectual property and proprietary rights and crap like that. And somehow all his notes from the previous week got accidentally thrown into the shredder. So he had to start over, and I helped him all I could."

Dylan stopped doodling. That's why he kept his important notes in his head. Too many things that were meant to be shredded got faxed and too many things meant to be faxed got shredded by accident. At least, he had a good memory to back up his mental notes.

"He never did finish. I called home about nine and told Floyd that I was going to have to work even later, maybe even after midnight, and what had happened with Grant's papers. This big thunderstorm had come up, and it had been raining ever since dark. I sat in my car for a while. I didn't really want to drive in that weather. I waited in the parking lot across the street and watched the windows of Grant's office until the lights went off. I watched him run through the rain to the car. He took off way too fast for the rain." She lowered her gaze, a sure sign she'd omitted something important. "I waited a little while and then I followed him home. I parked in the driveway across the street."

"Someone else's driveway? Why would you do that? You said he invited you to his home."

"Because of her. The witch. It would have made life a lot harder on him if I'd forced him to confront her like that. Besides, I didn't know if she might come after me with that knife she carried."

"Knife?" They hadn't found a knife at the crime scene and one had most definitely been used. "What kind of knife?"

"Long. With a real fancy silver handle that looked like it had purple jewels in it. Like amethysts."

The murder weapon had been conspicuously missing from the crime scene. No jewel-handled knives had been found. Or anything matching the description just given him.

"I was terrified that she might fly out of her house and chase me around on a broom or something." She rubbed at both eyes. Mascara smeared, giving her the look of a thieving raccoon. "I even wore a cross." She held up a pendant that dangled from a gold chain around her neck. "Witches are afraid of crosses, you know."

"Um, I think that's vampires."

She shrugged. "Anyway, I knew I could break the spell. If anyone could, I could."

Dylan took a deep breath and tapped his pen against the pad. Of all the romantic notions! Who could resist the idea of a lover breaking through an unbreakable barrier? From the un-monied heroines of early romance novels breaking through barriers to win the hearts of wealthy heroes to the human hero in *The Terminator* coming back through time to save the woman he loved to a law firm receptionist breaking the unbreakable spell of a witch to rescue the man who would save her from a hellish life with a boring husband.

"Finally, a few minutes before midnight, the rain stopped, and I took it as a sign from God that I should do something right then and there. So I walked up to the front door, and instead of ringing the doorbell, I knocked very, very softly. Grant opened the door and when he saw me—oh, there was this awful look on his face. He was just out of the shower. Still had towel-hair. He started begging me to leave. I know it was for my own safety. He said the others were waiting for him and he had to go and I should leave and not ever come back. He begged me, Detective. *Begged.* He was wearing this long black robe and I could tell"—she blushed— "that he was naked underneath. He smelled really good though."

"Did you leave?"

"Not exactly. I went back to the car and I sat there for a long time. Then I thought, no, no, he needs me."

"So what did you do then?"

"I went back to the fence I'd climbed the time before, but it was too wet. I couldn't climb it. So I followed the fence perimeter all the way around the house to the other side, and I found this gate there. It was a huge gate. Like something you'd see at a haunted house."

Yeah, he knew the one.

"But it was open a little ways, and I figured that Grant had left it open for me to come through. I mean, why else would it be open? So I walked through, and I could hear music down in the woods where I'd heard the singing the last time, and it was very...I don't know...like flute music. I didn't take the path this time. I was afraid they'd see me if I did, so I went a different way into the woods."

The footprints they'd found in the woods. At least parts of her story Dylan could corroborate with other evidence.

"That's where I dropped my purse. I couldn't see in the woods. I was just walking blindly through the dark toward the music. My purse strap caught on a limb and it tore the strap off my shoulder and spilled everything, and I couldn't find anything in the dark."

Dylan nodded to himself. How much of the rest rang true, he didn't know, but this part sounded right. The woods were certainly dark enough at night, and the limbs were low and thick. If she'd been able to see the spilled contents of her purse or find it in the underbrush, then surely she would have removed all evidence of her presence. At least in this case she had a story to go with the facts and facts to match her story.

"What did you witness in the woods?" Dylan asked, urging her toward the heart of the matter.

Her eyes widened. "An orgy. It took me a while to get there, but it was in full bloom when I came on it. They didn't even notice me standing there. So I backed up into the shadows."

Likes to watch, Dylan made a mental note to himself.

"That woman didn't have a spell on just Grant. She had one on his brother, too. After it was over, things got real quiet, and I was afraid to leave then because there were leaves on the ground from last winter and if took a step, I'd go crunch into the leaves and that witch would hear me. Then the three of them started talking again, and the woman got up and walked away. But a few minutes later, I saw her come back. They rejected her."

"Rejected her how?"

"Well, I think that's what happened. She walked away because they rejected her. I think she was kind of mad."

"What makes you say that?"

"She kept insisting that she didn't need to leave. After she did, I waited to see what was going to happen next. Grant and his brother started arguing."

"About what?"

"About her. The woman. They argued a long time. A long time. Then she came back. She was wearing a yellow raincoat with big, tall, rubber boots and a big yellow rain hat. You know, like you see in those pictures of lobster men from Maine. She walked over and started stabbing them. First, Grant's brother. He didn't fight or anything. And then she stabbed Grant. He fought back, but she must have used her supernatural powers to subdue him."

Odd. The one that fought back waited his turn?

"And what did you do?"

"Me? I ran like hell. Through the woods and through the house. Out the front door and to the locked car."

"Your keys weren't in your purse," he reminded her. He remembered the contents of the small handbag as perfectly as remembered everything else about a crime scene. Strange that she'd managed to pick them out of the litter possessions she'd left in the underbrush.

"No, no. I kept the keys in my hand. Like a bear claw. It was a trick I learned when I was in high school. You know, if you're ever walking alone after dark, you just put each key between your knuckles and that way, if you're attacked, you can swipe and slash their face and maybe put an eye out."

"Oh. I see. So why didn't you call the police?"

"I guess I was too scared to."

"You went straight home?"

"It must have been—I don't know—maybe one in the morning by then."

"And your husband can corroborate the time?"

"Umm." She chewed at her bottom lip. "No."

"You witness a double homicide and run home to safety, and you don't tell your husband? How is it you crawled into bed without him knowing his wife had come home after midnight?" Any sane woman who'd witnessed what Gloria Stokes had seen would have been shaking so hard the man in her bed would have assumed an earthquake had hit his box springs.

"I, um, I moved out of his bed a month ago. Floyd snores, you know? I moved into the guest room. I got home last night and went straight to bed, then slept in. This morning, my husband got up and went in to work before I got out of bed. I only saw him to kiss him goodbye."

And she didn't mention a word of it to him? Better yet, she didn't wake his ass up when she got home? Why not? Was she hiding something? Protecting someone? Or was she afraid of what her husband might say or do?

Something else bothered Dylan. The more he thought about it, the more convinced he was that Kestrel Firehawk wasn't strong enough physically to pull off the double homicide. Perhaps she was strong enough to slaughter small animals, if that was really what her religion was about and according to Robyn, it wasn't. But two grown men? The last time he'd witnessed the aftermath of a woman her size trying to stab a full-grown man, the woman had left hesitation marks all over the hospitalized man's ribs where she hadn't had the strength to puncture the chest wall with her knife. The Firehawks had been strong, virile. Either one could have thrown Kestrel Firehawk aside like the proverbial rag doll. Unless, of course, they'd come willingly to the sacrifice. If Grant had been the second to die, why hadn't he run? Something was not right with Gloria's story.

"Tell me again about the murderer. Are you sure it was a woman?"

"Well, yeah. I saw her long blonde hair hanging down out from under her hat. It was all wet."

"But are you sure it was the woman who'd been with them earlier as part of their, um, ritual?"

"Positive." She studied her fingernails.

"How can you be so sure? It was dark."

Gloria finished the last of her tea and set the cup down on the saucer ever so gently. "Easy. When she picked up that dagger of hers off her stone altar or whatever it was, she looked right at me. And...and she winked."

Dylan expelled a slow breath. "Okay, thank you, Mrs. Stokes. We're going to need you to come down to the station and get all of this down on record."

"My husband doesn't have to know about this, does he?" She sat back suddenly, alarm in her black-smudged eyes. She looked like a raccoon caught in her own trap.

"Mrs. Stokes, you are the sole witness to a double homicide. You can identify a killer and put her away for good. There's a good possibility—no, probability—that you'll have to testify against Kestrel Firehawk."

"Testify? How can I keep this a secret from my husband if you expect me to testify? I told you who did it. Can't you just go arrest her? I'm sure she'll be convicted and executed, and we won't have to worry about her ever again."

"Ma'am, you're not going to be able to keep this a secret from your husband. I'm sorry, but you were planning on leaving him. Maybe it's time you had that little talk."

"If I have to tell my husband everything I saw last night—everything I told you—then I take it all back."

"You can't 'take it all back,' Mrs. Stokes."

"Watch me."

"Mrs. Stokes?"

Abruptly, she scooted her chair back from the table and stood up. "No, the truth is, I was on my way home last night and stopped by a convenience store to get some gum and a black teenager wearing gang colors grabbed my purse and ran."

Chapter Six

~*Dylan*~

Shortly before one o'clock in the afternoon, Dylan met up with Robyn outside their favorite sidewalk café. She'd changed clothes and her breath smelled fresh. He recognized the slacks and blouse right away. Robyn, prepared as she always was, kept a gallon-sized plastic baggie under the seat of her car at all times. In it, she kept an emergency change of clothes, including—he presumed—fresh underwear plus a trial-sized toothbrush and toothpaste and a couple of breath mints.

Peppermints. Sometimes their stake-outs didn't allow them to go home and change, but Robyn always said she felt like a new woman if she could simply get out of her old clothes, even if she couldn't get to a shower. He smiled to himself. Robyn was the most organized, together woman he knew. Ready for anything. Ready for everything.

"You look rested," he said. The bags under her eyes were gone. "You grabbed some shut-eye, didn't you?"

"Actually, no. But I'm scheming for a nap this after-noon."

"I don't believe you. You've rested. I can see it in your eyes."

"Rested, yes. Slept, no. I took a walk in the grass and now I feel much better. Much."

"Oh, yeah. Right." He'd slurped down eight cups of coffee since dawn and he was still stumbling around. Mainly to the john.

Robyn shrugged off his sarcasm. "I guess I'm just a nature girl. If I can wiggle my toes in the grass and reconnect with Mother Earth, then I'm okay."

"Careful," he warned, motioning to a waiter. "You're beginning to sound like some of these tree-hugging freaks we're investigating."

They ordered ham and cheese croissants, more coffee, and fresh orange juice. With the business of lunch out of the way, Dylan told her all about his conversation with Gloria.

"So which is it?" Robyn asked, popping a straw into her juice. "Did she witness the murders or not?"

"She knows too many details not to have been there, but I don't see how Kestrel Firehawk could have had the opportunity to kill both her lovers and escape before the police arrived."

"I've had a busy morning, too, Finn. I talked to Reverend Jones."

"Why? I already talked to him at the scene while you were inside the house."

"I know, but I had to talk to him myself." She shuddered. "I can't stand that man. I can't put my finger on it, but I just don't like him. And then I talked to the kid at the liquor store where Kestrel went. Turns out he'd confiscated her driver's license because he thought she was acting weird. He thought she might have been on drugs or something." She shrugged. "Which isn't totally incongruent with these rituals. Some sects practice their religion with ritualistic use of drugs. Most don't. Anyway, the clerk let me review his security tapes from the night before. Kestrel Firehawk walked into the store at one-oh-seven and walked out at one-twelve."

"So was she acting strange on the tapes?"

"No. I've seen worse after midnight. Well, maybe a little," Robyn conceded. "Anyway, then she talked to Reverend Jones in the parking lot and no later than one-fifteen, she asked him to call 911 and send the police immediately to her home.

She barely had enough time to get home, plow her car into her soggy yard, and run to the grove. Sorry, Finn, but I don't believe Gloria Stokes. Not for a moment."

"I agree that she's not the most mature witness but does that make her unreliable? Why would she lie about witnessing a murder?"

"Gloria stayed in the woods a long time. At least, that's what she says. We don't know for sure what time she witnessed the murders or what time she left. Or what time she got home."

"I think we need to pull out all the stops," he said, "and find out all we can about Kestrel Firehawk." He munched on his ham and cheese and washed it down with juice.

"I'm not seeing the motive," Robyn admitted.

"Then I guess it's time we break the news to the next of kin. And I don't mean Kestrel Firehawk."

"Been there, done that. It wasn't pretty. We're fortunate that both sets of parents live in the city, close by."

"Both sets? Parents and step-parents of the brothers?"

"They weren't brothers."

Dylan nearly choked. "So they weren't really related?"

She smirked. "Only by marriage. I was able to talk to both men's parents."

"How bad?" He reached across the table and stroked the back of her hand and retreated before she could think anything of it.

"Bad. I started with Mr. and Mrs. Grant Sullivan the Third."

"Sullivan?" He'd heard that twice now, once from Gloria and now from Robyn.

"Yeah. That was Grant's real name before he changed it to Firehawk. He still went by Sullivan professionally. The blond man we found last night was Grant Rupert Sullivan the Fourth. Age thirty-five. Corporate lawyer and the newest partner at Simmons, Waker, Stokes, and Holley."

Dylan frowned but continued to munch. "So. Gloria was the daughter of *that* Stokes."

"Mr. and Mrs. Sullivan had high hopes for their son. They're solidly middle-class. Neither went to college, but they both had good jobs. They scrimped and saved to put Grant through law school. They didn't want him to graduate in debt. They wanted him to leave with a law degree and a fresh start, so Mr. Sullivan worked three jobs for ten years."

"So what's the problem? Grant got his law degree, made partner by thirty-five, lived in a mansion. Sounds pretty good to me." Dylan shoved his chair to one side to get out of the hot, mid-day sunshine. Unlike Robyn, he hadn't stopped for a shower yet and his skin felt rank.

"The problem was, once Grant got his law degree, he quit his mommy and daddy's church."

"And that's a problem? I can't remember when the last time was that I was in a church, except maybe for a wedding or a cop's funeral."

"As long as Grant was in law school, he went to church faithfully every Sunday. I got the impression it was because the Sullivans let him know how much they'd sacrificed for him, so he attended services out of guilt. His parents kept pushing him to go to church. They wanted him to meet 'the right girl.' Instead, he spent more and more time alone. Fell in with some, well, healer types. Those are my words, not theirs. You could tell how disappointed his parents were. He'd been a 'good boy' all his life and didn't rebel—their words—until he was thirty or so. About the time he met Kestrel Hawkins."

"They blamed her for his rebellion?" Dylan smiled to himself. He wasn't quite thirty yet. Maybe he had some rebelling to do yet, too. Or maybe rebellion was just another word for transformation.

"I think they blamed Kestrel for everything. If not everything bad, then certainly everything they didn't agree with. The mother found out by accident that her son and Kestrel were planning to elope, and the woman had a conniption fit. She insisted on a big church wedding, and Kestrel insisted on no church. The couple wanted to marry in a garden. They compromised, though it was strained. Grant insisted one of the justices of the peace, a colleague of his, perform the ceremony instead of the Baptist pastor who'd been ministering to the groom's parents for the past thirty-plus years. Grant's mother kept saying *hurt* to me as if the word had three syllables. Then the shit hit the fan when the parents found out that the couple had changed their legal name to Firehawk, a name they'd chosen together."

"So Firehawk wasn't her name or his name before."

"No. They made it up. Said it meant something personal to them. Grant's father said *Sullivan* meant something personal to him, that Grant's mother and he were expecting to have a grandchild eventually to take over the Sullivan name. Little Grant Rupert Sullivan the Fifth. And that Grant owed his parents that for all their years of sacrifice. And...well, you can guess the rest of that story." She stopped talking long enough to finish her croissant and gulp down her juice.

"So they were estranged at the time of Grant's death?"

"Hmmm, yes and no. Both sides seemed to try to make amends, but the couple didn't take the Sullivan name. Grant's mother wasn't too exuberant about her concession. She decided to force the issue. She held Kestrel responsible for Grant's lack of church life, so dear ol' Mom arranged with the ladies of the church to give Kestrel a proper wedding shower. Nobody told Kestrel what it was. She just got a message to come to the church, that her mother-in-law needed her right away. Kestrel walked in, frantic and worried, and they all yelled 'Surprise!'"

"A bit tacky, isn't it?" Not that he knew a whole lot about weddings and showers except for the miserable one he'd been involved with when Sherry had solicited the services of a distant relative to throw her a bridal shower when no one else would. "Then again, how tacky can you get with pots and pans and the occasional toaster?"

"They gave her things like Bibles, good inspirational reading for Christian women, and the special present from her new mother-in-law. A necklace. To be exact, a huge gold pendant with Jesus hanging on a cross."

"I'll bet Kestrel loved that."

"She took one look at it, burst into tears, and ran out of the room. Grant's mother was, of course, embarrassed in front of all of her buddies and never forgave Kestrel for that. Grant's parents hadn't spoken to either of them in almost three years."

Dylan wiped his mouth, then shook his head. So sad that someone with living parents couldn't talk to them when so many like him would've given anything to feel that understanding hand on his shoulder just one more time. "I don't know, Robyn. It seems kind of silly to break up a family over a cross pendant."

She frowned across the table at him, sadness wearing heavily on her face. "I guess it depends on what a cross means to you. So many sacred symbols have been perverted over time. The ancient swastika that once stood for harmony was flipped over by Hitler to define chaos. I don't think there's any way of ever reclaiming the sacredness of that symbol. The ancient pagan crosses couldn't be stamped out by early Christians so they adopted them for their own symbols. The five-pointed star, a symbol of the four elements plus spirit, was adopted by the Church to represent the five wounds of Christ, and it's now been adopted by gangs for who-knows-what meanings. Negative meanings. Funny how people who don't know any better can look at a five-pointed star and see only evil and yet those same people wear crosses around their necks without actively thinking about how crucifixion was a terrible Roman torture that many people endured during the reign of the Roman Empire. It was a horrid way to die. You, Finn, as a Christian may find this hard to believe, but some people find *crosses* offensive because they was used as tool of torture. Do you ever wonder, if Jesus came back and saw all the instruments of His torture hanging around peoples' necks, would He be really mad?"

Dylan stared back at her. "Where are you getting all this stuff?"

"I keep my eyes and ears open. And I try not to pass judgment just because I don't know anything about it. You might know these things, too, if you bothered to read outside your religion."

Religion? He'd always called himself a Christian. He barely remembered those days as a child in his church. He mostly remembered envying the adults as they partook of communion, the grape juice they pretended was wine which they pretended was the blood of Jesus and the little wafers they pretended was bread which they pretended was the body of Jesus. He swallowed hard. All those years of pretending he was drinking blood and eating the flesh of God. Yet if a pagan ritual had included such things, he would have denounced it as devil worship.

"What's wrong?" Robyn asked. She pushed back her plate and paused long enough for the waiter to take the plate from her.

"Nothing's wrong." He stopped. "Everything's wrong. I guess I haven't had enough sleep, have I? This case has got me questioning what I believe." He shrugged. "Or if I believe. I went to church because my parents went to church. I became a Christian because that was the only religion I was ever exposed to. If I'd been born into a Hindu family, would I have followed the Hindu religion? If I'd been born into a Jewish family, would that mean I couldn't be a Catholic? Are religions pre-ordained?"

Why was he having these doubts so suddenly? Too bad he couldn't be like young Harrison, devoutly pausing at every office breakfast or after-work get-together to say grace. Dylan had been content for so long he wasn't sure what he believed any more. Or why.

He finished his coffee and motioned to the waiter for another cup. The conversation lapsed into silence while a boy of no more than seventeen poured the scalding coffee and then politely backed out of earshot.

He tested out the words in his mind before he finally spoke. "It's strange to me," he said. "This idea of witchcraft being a religion. It's the most bizarre thing I've ever heard."

"That's only because you were raised among Christians. You isolated yourself to their beliefs. Didn't you ever take comparative religion in college?"

"Started to. But my family's minister warned me not to. Said it would introduce beliefs that might be harmful to me."

"How can opening yourself to spiritual truths be harmful?" Robyn smiled at him from across the table, and he was in sunlight again. "Knowledge enlightens. Gives validation to beliefs."

"Maybe these witches are just misguided people," Dylan suggested. "Even if their intentions are good, they're fooled into thinking—"

"Stop! Just stop right there. Divinity comes to each of us in the form that's best for us. Maybe that's God to you.

Maybe that's the Goddess to some. Maybe it's Mother Earth to others." Robyn leaned forward across the table in an angry whisper. "But what gives you the right to have such arrogance as to think that *you* know what's going on between someone else and Divinity? When you imply that people are stupid for believing something other than what you believe, isn't that like playing God?"

"Okay, okay." He held up his hands in defense. "But you've got to admit that this case is a little weird. One woman and two husbands. That's what this looks like to me. All living happily ever after under one roof. That's completely unheard of in the civilized world."

"Have you told that to the Mormons?"

"Not that I've read as much about these things as you, Miss Fount of Knowledge, but that was just done back in the nineteenth century when women needed the protection of a man and there weren't enough men to go around."

"Oh, how convenient. But it's still being done today. Against the law or not, there are still Mormon men—and some unusual right-wing Baptists—who have five, six, seven wives. Some of those girls are married as young as fourteen or fifteen. By the time they're eighteen, they have a couple of toddlers and maybe another baby on the way, and they're trapped economically and emotionally with their sister wives."

"Maybe there are a couple of Mormon families like that, but I would think that they're the exception and not the rule."

"I think you're right," she said. "And there are also pagan families like the Firehawks who are also the exceptions and not the rule. It's true that Wiccans and some other pagans, too, live by a rule that says you can do what you will but don't harm others. It's hard to have two mates and not hurt somebody, so most pagans don't do it. Just practicality, you know? But then as usual with the double standard of patriarchal religions, it's a bit more okay for a man to have many wives than a woman to have more than one husband. In a religion that follows the Goddess, the opposite might be true."

Dylan scooted his chair sideways to avoid the brightness. He reached for his coffee, cup number—what? Ten?—of the day.

"Look, Finn, many pagans—probably most pagans—are happy, content people who live their lives with the one person of their choice. That is the life they are called to live, and they and their God or Goddess or both are satisfied with that life. Who are we to judge, right? If this woman has two men who love her and it is a choice made by all three of them to live as husband and wife and husband, and that's okay between them and their path, then what right do mere humans like you and me have to tell them otherwise? Am I not correct?"

He shook his head furiously. This was too foreign to him. Robyn obviously wanted to talk, to fight almost. But he wasn't ready to continue the discussion. He was in over his head. This was something he needed time to research, but first he needed sleep.

"So what did Cedric Firehawk's parents have to say?" He caught himself. "I guess his name wasn't Firehawk either, huh?"

"Wiley. And his parents weren't any happier with Kestrel than the Sullivans were. Their son had always been an artistic type but he smoked all the time. His mother suggested he see a hypnotist to quit. She'd had a few sessions herself with Kestrel Firehawk and had lost about twenty pounds, so she figured it would work for her son, too. She was tired of smelling smoke in her house and in her clothes. Cedric was living with his parents at the time, so for his birthday, she gave him a gift certificate for six thirty-minute sessions of hypnosis to help him see what a filthy habit it was. He'd studied in London but changed his mind about becoming an international consultant. His parents kept hoping he'd get a real job. You know, something other than art and selling his wares at Renaissance Festivals and through online auctions. They had no idea how much money he was stashing away. They'd hoped he'd meet a nice, normal girl and settle down and get married. Instead, Kestrel Firehawk started accompanying him to the Ren-Fests."

"Ooh. Not what Mommy was thinking, huh?"

"Actually Mommy was pretty pissed off when she found out Kestrel and Cedric already knew each other and had arranged for Mommy's hypnosis sessions first and that Cedric had already quit smoking by the time Mommy suggested it. But that was just extra fuel for the proverbial fire."

"She felt deceived. Either that or she hated being the last to know."

Robyn nodded. "Kestrel and Cedric became quite an item. Mrs. Wiley had an old-fashioned hissy fit. Not only was Kestrel Firehawk a few years older than her little boy, but she was also a married woman. Mrs. Wiley insisted her son straighten up and abide by her rules as long as he lived under her roof. So he moved out, bought a mansion with the money he'd made from his 'hobby,' and moved in with Kestrel and her husband. Then he had his last name legally changed to Firehawk."

"Yet more fuel for the fire."

"Definitely. In a way, the Wileys kinda felt sorry for Grant, the other man in their son's life. But they hated Kestrel. They said she had the audacity to call several times and invite them to dinner or to ask them if Cedric might go over and visit them. They hung up on her every time. She wanted them to spend time with their son, but to them, they were perfectly justified in turning their backs. The last time Cedric's parents talked to him, he'd called to invite them to a handfasting. But—my interpretation from what they said—the Wileys went nuts when they realized what a handfasting was."

"A what?"

Robyn leaned back and squinted into air as if to seek the answers. "A handfasting is like a, well, it's sorta like a wedding. It's a commitment of sorts. It's not legally binding unless of course the person performing it has the legal power to marry a couple in that state. But then, Cedric and Kestrel's marriage couldn't have been legally binding anyway. She was already married to Grant Sullivan."

Ah. That explained everything. The photograph in Cedric's room, the man and woman in ritual robes with flowers and leaves and their hair and a satin ribbon binding their wrists. Not quite bride and groom, but definitely, definitely something.

"So Kestrel Firehawk had two husbands, and she managed to alienate both men from their parents." Dylan nodded to himself. He'd seen enough feuds with in-laws during his years of investigations.

"Not intentionally. What both sets of parents told me, even though they didn't realize it, was that Kestrel did her damnedest to make sure the men stayed in touch with their parents, even if she was out of the picture. It was the parents who turned their backs. And both men were willing to lose their parents if their parents wouldn't accept Kestrel."

"What about Kestrel Firehawk's parents?" Dylan asked. "Have you spoken to them yet?"

"Not without a medium."

Robyn was cracking jokes again. He was pretty sure of that, even though she had such a dry sense of humor that he often couldn't tell.

"Care to elaborate, Robyn?"

"Kestrel Firehawk's parents are dead. Both of them. Both violently."

"She didn't...?"

"Oh, no," Robyn assured him. "Hardly. She was eight years old at the time. About all we know is that her mother killed her father."

"What?" He leaned forward. "Now this is news! Were they pagan, too?"

"No. Not at all. He was a deacon at the First Baptist Church. Her mother was a Sunday School teacher. And little Marilu Eddington, as she was known then, had a perfect attendance pin for Sunday School by the time she was six weeks old. According to the neighbors the police interviewed at the time, everything seemed to be perfect. The ideal little family."

Dylan snorted. Ideal little families always had the worst skeletons in the closet.

"Then one Sunday afternoon," Robyn continued, "little Marilu's mother killed little Marilu's father."

"Are we sure it wasn't an accident?"

"Only if the woman accidentally unloaded her gun into him six times. Then she reloaded, asked Marilu to leave the room, and shot herself once. Through the heart. Marilu spent the next ten years being shuffled from relative to relative. An aunt had the girl's name legally changed to Kestrel Hawkins to distance her from the tragedy."

"Christ! You mean the mother killed the father in front of the child? No wonder she's so screwed up."

"That's all I know for now, but I have a full agenda this afternoon, including a nice, long nap. I'll call you tomorrow morning, okay?"

Dylan barely heard her. All he could think was that Kestrel Firehawk was out there in the world somewhere, all alone. And whether she was a murderer or a victim, she had no one—no one!—to vouch for her.

Chapter Seven

~Saadia~

Saadia stared at her naked, wrinkled body in the mirror and fought back the sadness. It seemed like only yesterday that she'd worn the raiment of the Maiden Goddess, when her flesh had been smooth and pink, her hair long and ungrayed. It seemed as if it had been only yesterday and not a lifetime ago. But just as sowing and harvest moved in cycles, so too did life.

In time, not too long a time now, she would die, Saadia knew. But then be reborn in that endless circle of life, death, rebirth. Then she would come back into the world to learn some new lesson to further the evolution of her soul. Perhaps with strangers, perhaps with those she'd known in this lifetime, perhaps with those she'd known in other lifetimes and missed this time around. Perhaps even as a child of the girl who'd sought her out. Perhaps— No matter. The one thing she was sure of was that she would be back.

She stared the length of the mirror at the body she didn't recognize. The folds of flesh, once tight, had shifted like desert sands into an eerie landscape of loose skin that she wore like pale pajamas. Had it not been her own skin, she might have been fascinated by its texture. How long ago had she stood in front of a long mirror and gazed at her body before a man had ever touched her?

She gave out a long sigh. Then she pulled down her purple robe from where she had hooked it over the post of the mirror's frame. She struggled into the soft folds of cloth. She raised the hood over her gray tangles and stared into the mirror at her face, bathed in shadow. In the hooded, deep purple, she cut a most ominous figure, she realized suddenly, but she didn't mean to be ominous. The hood was not to hide her identity or to scare small children. It protected, as it might have in the old days, from the cold and the rain. A night such as last.

At least it wasn't a pointed black hat from children's cartoons. Somehow over the years, witches had become synonymous with disfigured crones, warts on their ugly, pointed noses, green and moldy hair. Broomstick-flying monsters. The greatest disrespect of all was shown toward witches like herself. Old women were once regaled for their wisdom but now were harangued for their lost beauty. The stereotypical ugly old witch was nothing more than an insult flung at old women like her.

"Albion?" Starr Quietwater whispered from the doorway. "Are you ready?"

Saadia nodded. "Yes, but weary."

"No wonder. You hardly slept at all this afternoon. And probably even less last night."

True. Every bone in her body ached. The arthritis in her joints burned. Still, she had to do what she had to do tonight. She had to make Kestrel Firehawk disappear.

Saadia turned to the young woman in the purple robe that matched her own. Starr looked nothing like a high school teacher. "Is everyone else ready?"

"Almost. Edgar wants to sit this one out, poor dear."

She'd suspected as much. Edgar had once been an active thirteenth member of the Coven of the Jeweled Dragon, but no more.

"And Phoenix is still making phone calls. She's going to have to leave her beeper inside. It keeps going off like crazy," Starr added with a little laugh.

Of course, beepers and cell phones and the like would stay inside during rituals. Inside and out of earshot. The rituals connected them back to Mother Earth, back to Nature. The last thing they needed was an intrusion back to mundane life.

"Very well," Saadia said. "Tell everyone I'll be there momentarily."

Starr didn't move. "Albion? May I ask you a question? Shouldn't we wait until the moon is waning before we try to make our charge disappear? We do rituals for decrease when the moon is waning, and we do rituals for increase when the moon is waxing. It would seem to make sense for us to wait until after the full moon. The astrological timing could be better, too."

"Yes, it could be. But if we wait for a decrease in the moon, then it might be too late for Kestrel. So, as the moon waxes, we'll ask for an increase in her cover, her invisibility. It's all a matter of perspective, my child. When the moon phase waxes, ask for an increase in wealth. When the moon phase wanes, ask for a decrease in debt and expense. Do you understand? We'll make her as transparent as moonlight and at the same time, we'll ask that as the moon waxes and shines brighter and fuller, so too will the moonlight reveal the true murderer of Kestrel's young Year Kings. And we'll ask the blanket of safety to cover her more fully. Now go and make sure everyone is ready."

~

The mood was somber when the Coven of the Jeweled Dragon walked back indoors. They all had felt the hand of the Goddess. Her power had glittered inside them. Energy that they had raised—the magick they had performed—had worked. Kestrel would be safe now. No one in the coven would breathe a word of her presence. Saadia would keep the girl here in her own home and protect the girl with her own life as she would the child she'd never had.

Renwen and Lucretia, both college freshmen, busied themselves in the kitchen while they prepared cakes and juice. The cakes were really just sugar cookies without the sugar and the juice was white grape juice. The sobriety of the evening gave way slowly to a quiet banter among the sons and daughters of the Goddess. Worry lapsed into relief.

Gryphon lowered his hood and shook free his wild mane of blond hair. He drew Morgana close to him in a quick hug and quicker kiss. The two had been married for over ten years and were bringing up three beautiful daughters in the Craft. Saadia smiled and remembered the days when she and Edgar had frolicked. No longer. With his health failing, he could barely join the circle on these occasions and more often than not, napped instead of raising energy.

Tara, the nurse, knelt near the sofa where Kestrel stared into nothingness, seeming to hear voices no one else could here, not even the most intuitive of the coven. Tara stroked the girl's hair and whispered something comforting to her. At last, the girl blinked, but nothing more. Saadia could only hope that before the girl disappeared, she didn't disappear into herself.

Saadia caught the eye of her own husband across the room. They were so hard of hearing these days that they rarely even spoke any more, yet they never needed to. The passion of youthful fire had cooled between them in the sixty-plus years they'd been married, particularly after his bypass surgery, but just looking at him still warmed her heart.

"Jesus H. Christ!" screeched a woman's voice from across the room. Saadia recognized it immediately: Phoenix Red Sword. The tall woman who stood near the telephone with her hood still on. The woman slammed the phone back into its cradle, then pressed both palms against her face.

Saadia shuffled across the room and laid a hand on the Amazon's shoulder. "Phoenix." The entire room had quieted again. It was unlike Phoenix to show disrespect for a great teacher and prophet like Jesus. "Are you all right?"

Phoenix swallowed a rush of ugly tones. "No," she said with a sigh. "I am not all right. I'm sorry, Albion. I lost control."

Saadia stood on her tiptoes and reached high to push back Phoenix's purple hood. Dark, red hair tumbled out. Phoenix blinked back tears of frustration.

"Child," Saadia said, "if you can do something about what's bothering you, then do it. But if you can't, then put it in the hands of the Goddess."

Phoenix Red Sword nodded. She was twenty-six years old in this lifetime but an old soul. She had to be pushed and pushed hard before she lost control.

"Now tell me, child. What's wrong?"

"Somewhere out there is someone who's going to get away with murder if I can't stop it. And not only is he going to get away with murder, but he—or she—is going to frame an innocent woman." She gave a slight inclination of her head toward Kestrel Firehawk's place on the sofa. Phoenix had seen her fair share of pain. Enough to know more pain existed in the world than she could ever take away.

"Why don't you take another barefoot walk in my garden?" Saadia suggested. "It'll give you a better handle on the questions you have. It always does."

Darling Phoenix. She couldn't see that she needed to change her line of work. She couldn't see how it was destroying her. Her soul's archetype was that of a warrior.

And a warrior involved in police work fought to the death.

"You're going back out to work on Kestrel's case, aren't you?"

Phoenix nodded. "I have to. I can't let justice go undone. There's another man who could be just as dangerous to her as whoever murdered her husbands. He's a bulldog at police work. He won't stop until he finds all the answers and then he'll expose her, whether he means to or not. No matter what happens, we have to keep him away from Kestrel."

"Who is he?" Saadia asked, rubbing the younger woman's shoulder. "Your boss?"

"No. He's my partner. Detective Dylan MacCool."

Chapter Eight

~Dylan~

Dylan slanted his wrist to catch the light of a distant street lamp on his watch face. A quarter 'til one. He brushed the fog from the windshield and peered out at the Firehawk mansion. A scant twenty-four hours ago, the people who had lived there had been carefree, happy, *alive*. The worst of their concerns had been what changes to make on the web sites where they sold soaps and chain mail and auctioned off costumes for Renaissance Festivals and reenactments.

They had no monetary woes, the three of them. He'd determined that later in the afternoon. Three incomes. A huge house completely paid for. Cars bought with cash. Investments of stocks, coins, bonds, mutual funds, property. Other than their activities under a night sky, their financial situation was possibly the most unusual thing about them, compared to most people he investigated. The Firehawks weren't just solvent; they were downright wealthy. Yet they had chosen to put their wealth primarily into earth.

The two men had been outgoing and friendly. The woman had kept to herself. She had no friends. No neighbors to share afternoon tea and gossip. Too often, the TV news showed neighborhood strangers passing judgment on some neighbor who had allegedly committed a crime. Invariably, the neighbor talked about how the person was quiet or reclusive. Dylan had put off reporters all day long and let the department handle it while he tended to real business, but sooner or later, the news hounds would interview the same people he and Robyn had and they, too, would discover that Kestrel Firehawk didn't conform to societal norms. Anyone not wanting bad press should go to church at least once or twice a month, play softball with the neighborhood kids, or participate in a school bake-sale. People who were comfortable alone weren't welcome in the world.

He glanced up at the night sky. It was clear and full of stars. Not a cloud in sight. The same night sky watched over Kestrel Firehawk somewhere out there. Assuming she was still alive. Whether she was murderer or victim or witness, he had to find her. He had too many questions unanswered and there was truth waiting to be unfolded. *If Robyn ever gets here.* He could do this without her, but he was always a better detective—a better man—when he had Robyn on his team. There was something special about her, and if she weren't his partner, Robyn might have been the partner Sherry never could.

The headlights of Robyn's car spanned the driveway where he had parked. The yellow police-line tape gleamed for a moment in the light, then faded back into obscurity. He hopped out of the car and ran to meet her. He opened her door before she could kill the engine.

She scowled up at him. "I came as fast as I could. Can't you give me another five seconds to take the keys out of the ignition?"

"As fast as you could? What took you so long? I called you twenty minutes ago. You weren't asleep."

She exhaled as loud as she possibly could, one of her subtler ways of letting him know she was pissed off at him. She unfolded herself from the car and then slammed the door behind her. "I do have a life outside police work, you know?" She shrugged. "Not much of one, maybe, but a life."

Dylan choked. She hadn't been asleep. The time had been well after midnight. She had a life outside of him? With whom? He swallowed the pang of jealousy. He had no right to envy another man her companionship. They weren't lovers. Hell, they were closer. Not that was he in love with her, but he did care for Robyn. He knew better than to admit that he loved anyone or anything.

"Sorry," he mumbled. "I'm tired."

Robyn's face softened. "Did you get any sleep at all today?"

"A few hours, maybe. But it wasn't good sleep if you know what I mean." He'd napped fitfully in a cocktail of coffee and exhaustion. Images of the day's police work played their way out over and over in his head, and he'd spent his restless dreams searching for Kestrel Firehawk.

"Finn? What was so important that it couldn't wait until morning?" Her voice was still ragged with anger.

"Finding Kestrel Firehawk. The techs scoured every inch of Firehawk property. Including all ten acres of woods. They found rabbits, squirrels, foxes, one snake, more birds than they could count, a small armadillo, and what they disputed to be a coyote."

Robyn's eyes widened. "You found all those animals dead? Impossible."

"No, no, no." He calmed her down. "Those animals were very much alive. To borrow a phrase, the woods were teeming with wildlife."

Robyn looked relieved. "Well, of course. This place was sanctuary. Not just for them but for all living things."

"But that's not what you thought I meant, was it?"

"What are you talking about?"

"When I mentioned the animals, you thought I meant we'd found them slaughtered. Sacrificed."

"I did not."

"Yes, you did. I saw the look in your eyes."

"Yeah? If I inferred anything wrong with your statement, then it was because of the way you stated it. Not because of any knowledge I had. I'm not sure exactly what sect of paganism those three people followed, whether it was Wicca or witchcraft or Druidry or some other Earth-based religion, but I do know by the signs and by the tools they used that they were life-loving, that they would speak to Nature, and Mother Earth, and all living things, and that last night's ritual was about life and not death. Finn, everything in the universe has a vibration to it. Everything is alive. Whether it's dirt under your feet or the air around you, it vibrates. And if you practice at becoming sensitive enough, you'll feel those vibrations the way most of Her followers do."

"Her?"

"I know witches who can tell the vibrations of a gem stone or crystal even if they're blindfolded. A tiger's eye or a rose quartz. Amethyst or lapis. All those stones vibrate to a different frequency. Celestite comes alive in your hand like a small bird with its heart thrashing in its chest against your palm. Aragonite is the same way. And moldavite. And meteorite. They vibrate with such intensity that you can get this terrible headache and—"

"Robyn."

She caught herself and looked up at him in surprise. He didn't understand this mumbo-jumbo about rocks and vibrations and frequencies, except for one thing. He'd touched the purple stone on Kestrel's dresser—the amethyst—and a burning tingle had spread through his hand. More importantly, he'd heard what Robyn had said just now.

"Robyn, what witches are you talking about?"

"Huh?"

"You said most witches you know. What witches do you know?"

"I meant...I meant most witches I know of. I told you, I read a lot."

"Yes, you've said that before. Robyn, it's not how much you know about witches that bothers me. It's how well you defend them. You've been so on edge since the Firehawk murders. Talking about witches and weirdoes. I don't remember the last time you fought so hard about something that didn't matter to you."

She'd always been devout about her religion, but quiet in it. Once or twice, she'd mentioned the teachings of Jesus and once, the teachings of Buddha. She talked about angels to children who'd lost their parents. She'd held the hands of weeping mothers while they prayed for their missing kids. She gave to charities on a regular basis. In fact, he'd been with her at the grocery store when she'd bought a few extra cans of soup for a needy family in the community. He'd laughed at her in Wal-Mart when she'd bought a package of men's tube socks which she later dropped off at the local homeless shelter. Robyn was a good Christian woman, and good Christian women didn't routinely defend witches.

"What makes you think it doesn't matter to me?" Robyn asked quietly.

Dylan turned his back and stalked to the car. He felt around the back seat until he found two flashlights. He needed light to get at the truth.

"Did you hear me?" Robyn asked, her voice shaking.

He ignored her. He had a bad feeling about what she was going to say. That he wasn't going to like it. That it was going to change his life in ways he couldn't imagine. He didn't want to hear it, didn't want to know it. He refused to listen even when on so many nights when he'd been the one who wanted to talk, Robyn had been the only one willing to listen. Sherry had failed him, but Robyn...Robyn was his partner in almost every way. To her, he could say anything. And now, when she was about to say something he didn't want to hear, he turned his back.

"Finn? I asked if you heard me." She let out a sigh that sounded more like a wail. "You don't know how bad I hate hiding this from you."

Without looking into her eyes, he handed her one of the lanterns and stomped away. "Come with me. I need to look at something."

"What? What do you have to look at that's more important that what I have to tell you?"

He couldn't stand the sound of her voice. She sounded as if she might cry at any moment—and Robyn never cried.

"There's something that's been bothering me all day," he told her. He tried to force his mind away from Robyn and concentrate on the case. He ducked under the yellow police tape. "Well? Aren't you coming?" he asked as if nothing had happened.

"Coming? T-to where?"

"The clearing in the woods. Something's been bothering me all day. Something Gloria Stokes said. Doesn't make sense." He heard Robyn shuffling along behind him and walked faster. The beam of her flashlight mixed with his, mating and growing brighter at his feet. He led her around the side yard to the tall gate with the broken lock. He slid through and trampled the wilted herbs and flowers. "I'm positive Gloria Stokes witnessed the murder. She gave me too many details that can be corroborated for her to have made it all up. Frankly, I don't think she's bright enough, but there's something fishy about the details."

"We're not going to talk about this, are we?" Robyn asked. "We're not going to talk about *me*."

He walked faster. "Gloria mentioned a nine-inch knife with a jeweled handle. Amethysts on the pommel."

"An athame," Robyn said from behind him. "A ritual knife."

"Gloria said that Kestrel used it to kill both men."

"That's insane. An athame should never be used to draw blood. At least, that's what most witches I know believe. I'm sure there are a few sects that practice small animal sacrifice...somewhere...out of reverence for some distant past, but it is not as commonplace as you're thinking. I told you, Finn. Witches honor life."

"Not according to Gloria Stokes. According to her, Kestrel Firehawk is a cold-blooded killer."

"I don't believe it."

"Robyn, no offense, but I really don't want to hear what you believe."

"Then if you don't want to hear what I *believe*, let me tell you what I *am*." Her strained words assaulted him from behind. "Finn, I'm a pagan. A follower of the Goddess." She paused for a split second. "A witch. A Wiccan, to be specific. I have a coven, and together, we perform magick."

Dylan clapped one hand over his ear and steadied the flashlight in his fist. "I don't want to hear this, Robyn. Not now. Not ever."

"You have to, Finn. You *have* to hear me. I do magick. Do you understand? That's magick with a 'k.' Without the 'k,' it's just silly tricks. This stuff is for real. Do you understand,

Finn? Do you? I defy physics. I change the laws of physics on a daily basis. You have to understand," she added, "whether you call it prayer or meditation or just sheer will, it's all the same thing. Personal power connecting with Divine power and changing that which could not be otherwise changed."

"I don't believe in hocus-pocus." He walked faster, harder.

"It isn't hocus-pocus. It's not special powers we inherit or some bullshit like that you see on TV. It's not special powers we're born with and don't know exist until our sixteenth birthdays. It's a conscious decision to be a witch. It is our connection with the Divine," she insisted. "Not a bunch of Hollywood special effects. It's the power that's inside you. The power we all have if we reach deep enough and connect with our souls and with our Creator."

Dylan brushed his beam of light over the path and into the woods. The well-trodden path had been narrow less than twenty-four hours ago but had now broadened as a result of the trampling of so many technicians, detectives, police, and reporters.

"I don't understand you," he said. And that's what really hurt. That for the first time in their partnership, he didn't understand her, didn't really know her at all. She'd kept a part of her life hidden from him all this time when he'd opened every vein to her. He felt deceived, betrayed.

"Ah, Finn, please. Please stop. Turn around and listen to me for a minute." She panted behind him. With her height, she rarely had trouble keeping up with him, but he was walking so hard, so fast. "Finn, I know you don't understand, and if you don't understand something, you fear it. That's human nature. Nobody really knew or understood who Kestrel Firehawk was. They say she was a little eccentric, a little weird maybe. But definitely different. People hate different. They loathe it. They kill it. A hundred years ago, people who were different were ostracized. Several hundred years ago, people who were different were burned at the stake as witches, whether they were or weren't. We like to think that we're such an evolved society, but we still tend to isolate people who are different because our society sees them as threats."

"Enough already!" He spun on one foot and caught her face full in the ray of his flashlight. Flustered and fragile, her face shone like a beacon. For the first time since he'd known her, she wasn't the strongest woman in history.

Her forehead furrowed in pain. "Finn, please don't let this come between us. Not any more. I've let it come between us for too long. I knew one day I'd have to tell you about my religious life before I could tell you how I really feel about you."

His throat tightened. His chest ached as if he'd been punched. How she felt about him? She had feelings about him? Was that why she was so angry? Angry with herself for feeling the way she did?

Robyn took a deep breath and exhaled slowly. "Finn?" She took another breath. "Finn, I love you."

She'd told him she was a witch and now she was telling him she loved him? It was too much. Too much. She blinked into the light, waiting for an answer he would never give her. Ever. She wasn't the person he'd thought. But he'd think about that later. Slowly he let the light fall from her face. Then, when it reached the ground, he spun back around and stalked down the path.

"Finn?" she wailed. "Aren't you going to say anything?"

"Yes. I'm asking to be taken off this case."

"But why?" She trudged along behind him.

"Because I think you'd better ask for another partner. One who can be a little more 'understanding' than I am. As for right now, the only thing I want to know and the only opinion of yours I want to hear—if you have one on it—is whether Gloria Stokes was telling the truth about the murders she witnessed."

His own voice shook, but it wasn't because of Kestrel or Gloria but because of Robyn. He'd had a theory about Gloria and he'd wanted to bounce it off Robyn, but now nothing seemed right. Everything in his world had been turned upside down by one little confession of a different kind of faith.

Gloria had specifically mentioned the way Kestrel entered the clearing and picked up the athame from stone altar and then spied Gloria hiding in the woods. But if his theory was correct, Gloria could never have seen Kestrel's face because Kestrel would have been silhouetted against the fire. If the killer had indeed spotted Gloria in the woods and turned to taunt her with a diabolical smile, Gloria would have seen only darkness. Not a smile. Not even a face! Without that, she couldn't be certain she'd seen Kestrel. Just as in the shadows, Gloria couldn't have been certain if the person had long, dark hair. Or even if the killer was female. But, to satisfy his suspicions, Dylan had to see the clearing again. Had to examine the logistics of who stood where and how the firelight had cast shadows.

The trees parted ahead and he stepped into the clearing. Robyn bumped into him from behind and gave a little cry of surprise. Both aimed their flashlights at the previous night's campfire and the scattered remnants of cold embers. After a few seconds of silence, he broke away and swept his light across the clearing floor to the stone altar—and to the sacrifice atop it.

Robyn gasped from behind him.

It took a few seconds before recognition set in. The woman sprawled naked across the stone altar. Her legs flopped this way and that off one end. Her head lolled backwards, exposing a long, slender neck and a slash to the throat that almost decapitated her. Blood from the throat wound drenched her hair and face, dripped onto the carpet of oak leaves. An upside down pentacle had been carved into her forehead and into her open, right palm. A single stab wound pierced her heart. A post-mortem wound.

He reached out one hand to touch the body. He didn't recognize her for all the red. Warm. She was still warm.

"Do you know her?" Robyn whispered from behind.

He glanced down at the blood-dyed hair and groaned. "Yes."

"Who is it?"

"Our eye witness. Gloria Stokes."

Part Three

In the middle of the journey of our life,
I came to my self in a dark wood
where the straight way was lost.
—*Dante*

Chapter One

~Kestrel~

The last time I spoke with the ghosts of my two husbands, I was nine months pregnant with twins. My time was near. I could feel it with every breath I tried to take, with every step I waddled. Yet they were there with me, every moment. Talking to me, soothing me, stroking me. Almost as if they weren't really gone. I could feel their presence, hear their whispers. Even though they'd been torn away from me, they couldn't leave me. Not yet. I think they knew I couldn't have made it back then without them. And because I was never really alone, their presence lessened the blow of losing them.

I heard Grant and Cedric so often in my dreams that I thought I was going crazy. Robyn wanted to call in a therapist to talk to me, but we were all anxious about the potential for exposure. Saadia simply nodded and agreed with me that the spirit world was highly active in her home, particularly since Edgar had passed to the Summerlands a scant two months after Saadia had taken me in, the result of a stroke. Outside the Coven of the Jeweled Dragon, talk like that would have made the average person really nervous.

As for Grant and Cedric, I never feared my guys, ever. Just because someone is dead doesn't turn him into a monster. The energy remains when the body is gone. He doesn't become evil or scary. He's just transformed, that's all.

There have been many, many documented cases of people who don't believe ghosts and yet they've seen and felt their loved ones a good six weeks after the funeral. That's because it usually takes the dead around forty days to cut their ties with their earthly lives and move on to the next life or to a place of rest. In some cases the dead don't realize they're dead and never follow the light into the arms of the Summerlands or heaven or whatever they choose to call it. In other cases, they turn their backs on the light because they can't bear to leave behind a child or a lover. They make themselves known in the whisper of the wind or a warmness on the cheek, but the easiest method of visitation is in dreams.

Both my husbands came to me in that dream-filled night. They rubbed my huge belly in warm circles, soothing me as I reclined miserably, too large to roll over to even sit up without help.

"Time to pick a name for your daughters," they said to me.

I smiled in my dream. One the Coven of the Jeweled Dragon, Tara—I never knew her mundane name—was a labor and delivery nurse, which meant, she said, she took care of 90% of the delivery and the obstetrician arrived just in time to catch the baby, if that early. Tara gave me monthly and then weekly checkups and promised to be on hand for the twins' delivery. To forsake obstetric care was dangerous but coming out of hiding when there was a murderer still on the loose was nothing short of suicide. Tara had warned me of the problems with twins so I was prepared for that.

But daughters? I hadn't been able to get tests I needed to know the babies' sex or if there were any deformities, not without making myself and my condition known outside my hiding place. The only time I'd left safe haven in all those months was to enjoy the Moroccan basilla I'd had a craving for, and even then, I'd been discreet. Robyn wouldn't have it any other way. She'd spirited me out into the night for a terrific meal and right back to my hiding place.

But daughters! I hadn't the slightest glimmer of hope for daughters. My heart soared for the first time since their conception for, to a witch, daughters are a gift from the Goddess.

"Do you know the story of Deirdre?" Cedric asked, and I shook my head. He kissed me then, in the middle of my forehead, where my third eye is, my sixth chakra, and I saw an olden time as clearly as if I'd been there in the flesh.

The floor of the castle of young King Conchobar had been strewn with fresh straw. The fires glowed brightly in the furnaces, and the tables were laden with the bounties of the harvest and tankards of mead. The bard regaled the festive crowds with stories of Conchobar's feats in battle, even tales not heard before. The people laughed and danced and cheered in celebration. All except for two.

The bard's wife, heavy with child, reclined miserably in one corner of the festival hall. Her time was near, and no amount of festivity could aid her weariness.

The other quiet one was Cathbad the Druid. He sat in the opposite corner, watching the ailing woman. He said nothing, only watched.

In the midst of the revelry, someone screamed. High-piercing, but muffled. The music-making and singing ceased and all turned to look at the bard's wife. She hunkered there on the ground, clutching her belly, terrified.

The scream came not from the woman, Cathbad explained, standing to calm the crowd, but had come from within the woman. It was her baby, protesting its own birth, weeping even before it came into this lifetime.

The crowd was horrified. What terrible tragedy could a child unborn foresee?

But Cathbad saw it. He had the Druid sight, for the bard's wife was his daughter and the talent for prophecy ran deep in his roots and in his seed.

There, before Conchobar, his brave warriors, and all his people, Cathbad explained that the child inside his daughter would fall in love with the greatest of Conchobar's heroes and would be the ruin of the Kingdom of Ulster. Men would fight over her, he said. Men would lose their kingdom for her. The ground would run red with the blood of noble men.

The crowd murmured angrily. Warriors talked of drawing their swords and cutting the child from its mother's womb.
They would do whatever was necessary to protect their king.

Cathbad held up his hand. He explained that the baby,
Deirdre, would grow to become the most beautiful woman in all
the known worlds, and many men would want her for wife. He
purposely did not tell them that she, too, would have his Druid
sight.

Conchobar was a vain and powerful man who could
bring any woman in the kingdom to his bed if he so chose. The
idea of a woman so beautiful intrigued him, and he rose. Rather
than have the child slaughtered at birth, he wanted to see this
great beauty foretold. He reminded Cathbad of what Cathbad
so often said of prophecy, that the events to come could be
changed if one knew before they came. Conchobar fancied
himself more powerful than Cathbad the Druid, and Cathbad
allowed this, as he always had.

Conchobar insisted he would deny the Druid his prophecy. The king would have the child taken from its parents upon
birth and sent to a secret place to live, and when she was six-
teen, he himself would marry her. In this way, no warrior could
want her for wife when she belonged to their King. No harm
would come to her, for to own the most beautiful woman in the
known worlds was a king's right and a king's right alone.

And so within three days' time, the bard's wife gave
birth to a daughter, and the babe was taken from her ere she
had the chance to hold the child against her swollen breasts.
Though the young mother pleaded, both parents knew that the
child's survival depended on Conchobar's cruel plan.

The girl-child was named Deirdre, as Cathbad had foretold. Conchobar sent the child away into the mountains, far
from the sight of his warriors and the people of his court, deep
into a hiding place that some might have thought a prison. She
lived first with her nurse, then came a foster mother and a
teacher to train her such that she would be worthy of her king.
And only these three servants and no other human face passed
in her presence.

My dream faded and returned, and fifteen years had
passed. I knew when I saw her in my dream that she was not
me. She was Cedric, lifetimes ago.

Deirdre had grown into a beautiful woman-child, having fulfilled her grandfather's prophecy in the isolation of her golden prison. She did not so mind the mountains, for she loved the land and loved all nature. But she was lonely for others like her. She knew more than she had been told, for she had the sight of the Druids and she lived close to Nature. She knew Conchobar meant to take her for wife within a year, and she knew why. Conchobar had taken her from the very womb of a loving mother and cruelly sentenced her to be his prisoner until she could be his bed-mate. She had heard the tales of the great king and his many wonderful deeds, but she could not trust these stories when she herself was a trophy of his vanity.

Deirdre knew these things because she had endured visions since childhood, though she never spoke of them. Then one day, not long before the day when she was to be bound over to the king, she had a vision of a man with black hair, healthy red cheeks, and pale skin. And she knew then that she would love him.

I gasped in my dream, for I recognized this man, this Naoise, as he was called. He was *me*. In that lifetime.

Deirdre followed her visions and slipped away from her prison one afternoon on the pretense of bringing home a lost sheep. When she and Naoise laid eyes on one another, they felt the jolt of memory from many lives past and knew instantly that they belonged together.

Naoise was a fierce warrior, the best of King Conchobar's men. He knew by her beauty that the woman he'd fallen in love with must be Deirdre, the future wife of his king. Naoise knew that to have his greatest joy meant he and Deirdre would have to fly by night and never return to the land of their birth.

And so Deirdre, Naoise, and his two brothers slipped quietly away in the night and headed for the rugged mountains of Scotland. His brothers were great warriors, too. Ardan I knew immediately as the soul of my beloved Grant. Ainle, I recognized as a soul I have spent many lifetimes loving, but at the time of my dream, I did not know his name. Both brothers loved Deirdre, too, though only Naoise touched her in the nights.

They spent ten years in the mountains of Scotland and settled finally near a deer-surrounded loch. The four of them lived and loved together there. And they were happy, though sometimes Ardan longed for the home fires of Ireland and sometimes Ainle missed long walks on the land of his youth.

Conchobar meanwhile seethed at his loss. His warriors and all the people of his kingdom knew that he'd lost not only his prized possession, but also his three finest warriors. And so he plotted revenge every night for those ten years. He would never let the Druid's prophecy better him.

The king told his men he had forgiven Deirdre of her foolishness. Though she was still rightfully his, he believed, he would give her up to have his three best warriors back in his fold. After all, for an aging king, he needed warriors to defend his kingdom more than he needed women to defend his bed.

He sent out a champion to plead for the quick return of the four and promised a celebration when they arrived. The three brothers readily agreed, all longing to see their homeland and happy that both they and Deirdre were welcome to return. But Deirdre did not wish to leave Scotland. Her visions nagged her with blood and worry. The men ignored her prophecies, accepting the yearning of the heart for home over the anxiety of a woman who had come from a childhood of isolation.

But Deirdre was right. The warm welcome home quickly became a trap, and the three brothers fought hard into the night to keep her safe. At the worst of the battle, they encircled her, protected her, holding up their shields to stave off injury and fighting their way out of a burning house. They escaped, but not for long.

Angry, the king called forth Cathbad the Druid, who was now old and very powerful in his magick. The king demanded the Druid use his magick to kill the four, but the life-loving Druid of course refused. The king then gave his word that no harm would come to the four if Cathbad would simply stop their escape.

The Druid used his magick to create an illusion of a tempest all around the four. In rising seas, the brothers dropped their weapons and swam, bearing Deirdre high in the water, on their shoulders. She begged them to let her drown, for she had seen the future. When the brothers grew too weary to swim, Cathbad dried up the water with his magick. Conchobar's warriors seized the exhausted brothers.

The king then withdrew his promises to Cathbad, and condemned the brothers to death, but his people saw his treachery and refused to do his bidding. He drew his axe and killed the weary brothers, one by one, and killed Naoise last so that Deirdre could only watch helplessly. She felt her heart torn out with each blow of Conchobar's axe and hoped she would be next. She didn't want to live without her husband and his brothers. But no axe came for her.

The people of the kingdom admired the brothers who had fought bravely, and they buried them where they had fallen, with three standing stones to mark them. Deirdre had seen her visions come to pass. She was numb and silent. But the king was not done with her.

He condemned her to serve him in bed for a year, and then he would have her sent to each of his treacherous allies, for one year each, to serve each one in bed. Deirdre no longer cared. She wished for death, to be reunited with the men of her heart and begin their next journey together, a happier lifetime perhaps. But Conchobar refused even death for her. He would make her suffer dearly for the ten years she had denied him her company.

Cathbad and Deirdre looked at one another and both knew. Cathbad offered to deliver her from the killing field to the king's chambers. She was bound at the hands and at the feet, and a cloth over her mouth and eyes so she could not escape again. Several of the warriors—for there were not many left to do the king's bidding—lifted her into a horse-drawn cart with Cathbad.

They rode fast—the old Druid, Deirdre, and several warriors. Deirdre could not see through the cloth over her face, but she could see through Cathbad's eyes. They rode hard through the woods, and at the exact moment, she stood.

The tree branch struck her hard across the forehead, crushed her skull and broke her neck, and Cathbad knew she had died instantly. He and the remaining warriors took her broken body and buried it next to the three men she had loved most. They erected a fourth standing stone, all in a circle now, for together in a circle they were most powerful. Cathbad cursed the kingdom to fall to ruin, just as he had prophesied so long ago.

Conchobar ruled still, but before the turn of the year, his kingdom had turned from green to brown, the warriors had left him to ally with his enemies, and Cathbad the Druid had taken his magick far away.

Then in my dream, I sobbed. I understood too well Deirdre's loss, and the vision given me by Cedric made me re-live the grief of my own loss, a loss that had never been com-plete because Cedric and Grant had never completely left me. My wounds had never healed—they had merely been numbed. Now, Cedric's vision peeled back layers of mourning and pain. I had refused to feel. I didn't think I'd ever heard a story as wrenching as that of Deirdre.

Then Grant bent forward and whispered in my ear, "Do you know the story of Branwen, daughter of Lyr?" He kissed my third eye and a vision jolted through me like lightning.

In another time, not too far away from the days of Deirdre, an Irish king sailed to Dyfed, the Isle of the Mighty. Matholwch, the High King of the Irish, made a proposal to the people of Dyfed: join the two warring nations in peace with a marriage between the High King of Ireland and Branwen, the beautiful daughter of King Lyr.

In my dream, I knew Branwen immediately as the incarna-tion of my beloved Grant.

No one asked Branwen if she wished to marry, though she was a woman who upheld the great honor of her people and, without question, would have surrendered her happiness for their good. So her father and her brothers agreed readily to give Branwen in marriage to a foreigner she had never met. Both of the brothers were familiar to me in my dream. Ma-nawyddan, who had the same soul as my beloved Cedric, and Bran, another soul I recognized but did not know and the same as the soul of Ainle in Deirdre's tale. But where was I in that lifetime?

After much feasting and celebration, Branwen was sent with the Irish king to a special dwelling where he could consum-mate their marriage on Welsh ground before sailing back to Ire-land with his new bride. King Matholwch could not believe his good fortune: the people of the Isle of the Mighty had given him their beautiful Branwen and many gifts to secure a peace with his people. He could not have been happier.

But during the wedding night, Branwen's half-brother, Efnisien, who was a troublemaker, was returning home from his travels and came upon the dwelling and dozens of horses. He asked a man standing watch at the dwelling's door to tell him the name of these fine horses' owner.

The man explained that the horses were a wedding gift from King Lyr to the Irish king, who was now the husband of Efnisien's sister. Efnisien was incensed at the news. No one had consulted him in the marriage of Branwen. Stung by the slight, Efnisien quietly sent the watchman home, volunteering to stand guard himself. All alone, he took his dagger and cut the eyes and ears and nostrils of the fine horses, mutilating them, destroying their value.

News spread quickly the next morning that the Irish King had been disgraced, his fine horses mutilated while he slept with his new bride. Insulted, he gathered his men and prepared to sail straight away with Branwen and have nothing more to do with Dyfed and peace.

News then reached Bran of the horses' maiming, and he rushed to stop the hasty departure. To smooth the peace with Ireland, Bran presented Matholwch with a sacred cauldron that held magick powerful enough to give life back to the newly dead. And all was well for a while.

In Ireland, Branwen was welcomed with celebration and given many gifts by the Irish people. She conceived and in time, bore a child, a boy named Gwern.

I gasped in my dream, for I was that little boy. In Ireland, the son of the king would inherit the throne. In Dyfed where mother-right was the law of the land, the king's sister would bear the next king. Since Lyr had no sister, Bran was heir to his throne and Branwen's child would be heir to Bran. Gwern was a child who might one day rule both kingdoms and seal the peace between the countries.

And all was well for another year until the people tired of celebration and began to murmur against Branwen. The celebrations over, they began to remember the maiming of the horses and nothing more. They began to feel insults where none had been felt before. The people turned against her. Matholwch, tiring of Branwen's beauty, took her royal position from her and sent her down to the cooking pits to feed the men.

She toiled over the ovens for three years, each day beaten and insulted by the overseers and the men she fed. She was not allowed to see her son. She lived in the cooking pit, dirty and bedraggled, no longer beautiful under the soot and dirt. Her husband's people cursed and spit at her.

One night she rescued an injured bird that was native to her land. She nursed it, for though she was untrained, she had the gift for healing. When the bird could fly, she tied a letter to its claw and sent it on its way, back to Dyfed. Go, little one, she said to the bird. Go and fly by night. And the bird did fly by night and was found and taken to Bran who was now king. Bran read the news and mourned both his sister and the insults done to her.

Bran raised the greatest army in the history of the land. All the men of Wales left their homes and children to fight for Branwen, for in dishonoring her, the Irish had dishonored all of the Isle of the Mighty. Only seven men remained in all of the land.

In Ireland, the Druids saw a strange sight, even before the swine-herds on the coasts. It seemed to be a forest of trees marching toward them. When the Irish demanded Branwen tell what she knew of this, she told them her brother Bran was a terrible giant and that this was his retribution. Her embellishments brought great fear to the Irish and could not have been better planned.

The Irish stood at the sea's edge and watched the trees coming closer across the waters. Manawyddan, who was a skilled sea master, crafted the flat-bottomed boats of Wales with masts made of tall trees, some still leafy and green, to strike fear in the hearts of his enemies. Bran, who was indeed a tall man, leaned forward in his boat as they neared the Irish shore, and he almost turned the boat on its side. To calm the men on his boat, he slipped down into the watery marsh and waded ashore. The Irish saw this and thought surely he must be a giant to have walked across the sea's floor.

Terrified, the Irish set Branwen free from the cooking pits and reunited her with her little boy, Gwern. The moment Bran faced Matholwch, they named the little boy, Bran's nephew, their new king. The Irish prepared feasts for their hostile guests to smooth the peace, though the Irish were crafty and hid warriors in the pillars of the feasting halls so that the Irish could overtake the men of Wales when much wine had been drunk.

But Efnisien, Branwen's half-brother, was craftier. He discovered the hidden soldiers and quietly killed them one by one. Then, still angry that he had been excluded from decisions regarding Branwen's fate, he sat by the fires and played with little Gwern, the new king. When he had gained Gwern's trust, he picked up the child, playing a swinging game with him at first— and then threw the child into the flames.

The crackling of flesh shook me in my dreams, but then the lifetime was gone and could no longer hurt me. Still, I continued to look, for this vision was Grant's gift to me.

Branwen screamed and flung herself at the fire to save her child, but Bran caught and held her. He asked for the sacred cauldron, for if they gave the little boy to its magick, he might live again. But the Irish picked up their swords instead and the battle began until it was too late to resurrect the boy.

In the morning, Efnisien saw the bodies of more men than he could count and realized his terrible deed. He threw himself into the cauldron and pushed with all his might until the cauldron broke apart and the powerful magick inside covered the land and ended the war.

All the Irish men were killed that day. Only Branwen and seven men, including Bran and Manawyddan, survived. Bran, alas, had been struck in the back by a poisoned spear and could not move any of his body below his neck. The remaining men carried the head of Bran, his useless body with it, back to the shores of home, where he ordered his warriors to end his life. Branwen's healing touch could not heal her brother's paralysis. That knowledge dealt a final blow to her will.

When Branwen saw the destruction caused on her behalf, she fell to the ground heartbroken. At her fingers she found an herb, meant for making salve but deadly when tasted. She thought of her sweet little boy, of her paralyzed brother Bran, and of Manawyddan, suddenly older than his years. All this death because of her. And she plucked the berries of the herb and ate.

I curled up on the bed, then, sobbing, unsure of whether I was lost in a dream or wide awake. I felt Branwen's pain, her loss, the rawness of the carnage around her.

"Branwen and Deirdre," I croaked out. Both names evoked the exact emotions I'd felt the night I found Grant and Cedric's mutilated bodies and wanted to die myself. "That's what you're telling me to name our daughters?"

"Merry part," Cedric said, and kissed my left cheek.

"Merry part," Grant said, and kissed my right cheek.

"And merry meet again," they said in unison.

Then my belly pulled and bunched up and knotted hard and fierce. My eyes flew open wide, and I struggled to sit up but could not.

My labor had begun.

Chapter Two

~*Dylan*~

Dylan propped his feet on his desk and leaned back in his chair. He cradled the back of his head in his hands. One of these days, the department would have enough of a budget to paint over the stains on the ceiling. For now, given a choice, he'd pick ear plugs over paint.

Clive paced around their adjacent desks for the twelfth time, jabbering away about nothing. His son had an ear infection, his wife hated her part-time job in a dog-dipping clinic, his golf game sucked, and his gastrointestinal problems were festering. Who cared? Clive never shut up and never slowed down. He had more energy than the Energizer bunny, but that energy had to come from somewhere and Dylan suspected it was drained from all living creatures within earshot of the blabbermouth. Oh, Clive was a good detective and a nice enough guy, but he had one huge fault worse than his wagging tongue: he wasn't Robyn.

Dylan missed her dearly, both as a partner and as a friend. And he had no one to blame but himself. The night they'd found Gloria Stokes, their sole witness to the Firehawk murders, dead at the scene of the former crime, he'd been hurt and angry with Robyn.

Until that night, she'd kept a deep, dark secret from him. All those times when he'd spilled his guts to her, all those long stake-outs when they'd told each other everything—warts and all—she'd held back. He didn't even know it then but he'd longed so many times for her to love him back and when she finally did, her love came with the dark realization that he didn't really know her at all and he'd opened his insides to a stranger. Because if he had known her well enough to love her, he would have known she was a witch before she spelled it out in black and white. He'd felt like a fool and he'd lashed back at her by exposing her to the sergeant. Only days after that, she'd been pressured out of her job. The last he heard, she'd been forced to take a job as a night watchman for a mini-warehouse complex. He couldn't blame her for hating him.

"Hey, MacCool!"

A ball of wadded paper hit him squarely in the forehead. He glared at his new partner. "That's assault, buddy."

"You didn't hear a word I said. Off in la-la land again?"

"Naw. Still fighting the remnants of the flu." Which was true. He'd spent half a month at home with the knock-you-down-and-stomp-on-your-guts flu bug. If he and Robyn had been on speaking terms, she would have fed him chicken soup and mysterious herbs and had him back on his feet in a few days' time. As it was, he'd lost ten pounds and two weeks of work and still felt a bit weak in the knees.

"I was saying," Clive babbled on, "that it looks like a pretty clear-cut case of a liquor store robbery gone awry. I got a statement from the Reverend Jones yesterday while you were puking your guts out at home."

Dylan jerked his head up. Clive was right: he *hadn't* been listening. "Reverend Jones?"

"Yeah. He's gonna have one hellacious sermon next week. The evils of liquor and all that." Clive burped distract-edly into his hand. "Oops. Sorry, Mac. Blooming heartburn. Got anything for it?"

For a heart that burned? No. "Sorry," he told Clive. "Maybe Linda. She's a walking infirmary."

Clive wandered off to bother someone else with his latest ill-fought battle with a chili dog. Dylan waited until Clive was out of the room and slid the folder on Clive's desk to his own. He glanced at the doorway one last time to make sure Clive didn't catch him. Not that Clive would mind sharing his police work, but looking at the paperwork would only prove to Clive that Dylan had had his partner on "ignore" all day long. No use in alienating him completely. Dylan had to work with the guy.

The case wasn't a humdinger as murder cases went. A local liquor store adjacent to a popular bar had been held up near midnight two days ago. The clerk, Byron Steiner, age twenty-four, had decided to play hero and got himself shot once through the neck. A surveillance camera had caught the whole incident on tape and the suspect had already been apprehended. The college freshman in custody had been high and in need of money for more drugs when he'd made a split-second decision to use his daddy's revolver to earn a quick buck. Bad guy caught, case closed.

Dylan studied a couple of stills from the surveillance tape. They were fuzzy, but he recognized the clerk immediately. The man behind the counter—the guy taking a bullet to the throat— was the same liquor store clerk who had confiscated Kestrel Firehawk's driver's license as a phony ID not more than eight or nine months ago. His death might have been a coincidence, but the fact that Reverend Jones had witnessed this murder from the sidewalk outside the liquor store—*that* wasn't a coincidence.

Dylan had never gotten a straight answer out of Jones as to why the pastor had been lurking in the shadows outside the liquor store the night of the Firehawk murders. No one had reported him proselytizing or screeching Bible verses from street corners. If anything, the old man had a reputation as a solid Southern Baptist with a kind heart and a sincere wish to help those less fortunate. So why did he make a habit of hanging out at a local den of iniquity?

Robyn would know. She had that uncanny way of putting together puzzle pieces that didn't seem to fit. That would never happen with Clive. He looked for Band-Aid answers when tourniquets were needed.

As far as Dylan knew, Robyn had spoken only once with Reverend Jones and had returned with the heebie-jeebies. She'd sworn the pastor was lying, but she'd never found the proof. Since then, Robyn had lost her job, Dylan had lost his best friend, and the Firehawk and Stokes case had been shelved as unsolved. And Kestrel Firehawk—or her body—had never been found.

He had to tell Robyn. He knew it in his gut. Even if the case was no longer any of her business, she needed to know. But would she even talk to him?

Dylan took a deep breath, lifted the phone receiver, and then cradled it in his hand until the off-the-hook beep sounded furiously. He glanced around to make sure no one was watching or listening. Then, before the beeps started again, he punched those old, familiar numbers and waited for the ring.

The voice that answered was impersonal and devastating. "We're sorry. The number you dialed is no longer in service. This is a recording."

Can't be. He hung up and dialed again. Same voice, same condemning message. He slammed down the phone. Christ! What had happened to her?

Head throbbing, Dylan dragged the Greenburg directory from the corner of his desk and flipped through until he found the phone number of the warehouse where Robyn had taken a minimum wage job months ago.

He barely waited for the assistant manager to give the warehouse name, her name and title, and a sugary "How may I help you?" before bursting in. "This is Detective Dylan Mac-Cool. I need to locate Robyn Porter."

"I knew it."

"I beg your pardon?"

"I knew she was trouble. I can always tell."

Dylan snorted. "Can you give me the number for wherever she's working tonight?"

"She isn't. Not for us anyway."

Dylan felt the blood drain from his face. Whatever ill had happened to Robyn was all his fault because he couldn't take being in the dark about her when he'd spent too many evenings talking through the shockwaves Sherry had done his ego. He was a detective and a damned good one. Something major like your partner being a witch was not something you let slip by and still be any good at the job.

"What do you mean, she doesn't work for you any more?"

"We don't hire her kind."

"What kind is that?" He was confused. Robyn's kind was hard-working, loyal, ethical, and gentle-hearted.

"We got an anonymous complaint last month saying she was a Satanist. You know, that Wicca stuff."

"She's not—" Sheesh. Was this what Robyn put up with all the time? No point in telling the stupid bitch that Robyn did not worship Satan. He swallowed and started over. "Even if she is Wiccan, you can't fire her on the basis of her religion." Okay, so a little bit of Robyn had seeped into his veins.

"Wicca is not a religion we recognize," the assistant manager snapped back. "Christian, Jew, Hindu, Muslim—those are all legitimate religions."

"Legitimate? Who are you to decide whether a person's relationship with God is legitimate or not?"

"The guy who complained dropped some ugly hints that our warehouses might burn down if we didn't get rid of her."

"An anonymous tip suggested Robyn Porter is an arsonist and you fired her for that?"

"Not at all. Our impression was that he would burn us out himself if we didn't comply. So we confronted her and she admitted she was Wiccan and we fired her for being a security risk. Two birds with one stone."

"Why didn't you call the police?"

Laughter. "We did. You guys brushed us off. A detective Clive something. An anonymous threat, no harm done, call us if anything burns, he said. That's why we decided to get rid of Ms. Porter. We're just starting to turn a profit, Detective. You have to understand. We don't need trouble."

Spineless jerks.

Just like him. Abandon a loyal friend at the first test of character. He could keep kicking himself or he could call Robyn and try to make it up to her. More than anything, he wanted her forgiveness.

Yeah, and people in hell want ice water.

He dialed Information, but the results were disappointing. Not a single listing in Greenburg for a Robyn Porter or R. Porter or any derivative of her name. She couldn't have left town. Robyn had no family to move home to if her life turned disastrous. As far as he knew, Robyn had no one. No one but him. Now she had no one at all.

He threw Clive's folder back onto the other desk, grabbed his coat, then ran for the door.

Twenty minutes later, just as the sun was setting, he parked in front of the duplex Robyn had made her home for five years. It still looked the same. In the heart of a Southern winter, the azaleas didn't bloom and the hummingbirds didn't flutter at the tubes of red sugar water still hanging from the awning above the kitchen window, but the place still screamed of Robyn. An evergreen shrub at the door made his eyes water with memory. How often had Robyn plucked a few needles of rosemary from that very plant to season pots of spaghetti when he was low on Sherry and needed a willing ear?

He bounded up the empty driveway and then banged on the door. No answer. He punched the buzzer but nothing happened. Had the electricity been turned off? He waded through the wintering azaleas planted in front of the living room window. Pulling his coat against his face to shield him from the January wind, he wiped frost from the panes and peered inside. Not a stick of furniture remained.

"You looking for Robyn?"

Dylan glanced up at the lean, muscular man propped against the front porch column leading to the other half of the duplex. Close-trimmed beard, brooding eyes. Stuart, if Dylan remembered correctly. Robyn's gay neighbor who'd spent his share of time crying on Robyn's shoulder, too. Had Stuart ever been there for Robyn's tears? Had *he*?

Swallowing hard, Dylan allowed his gaze to lock with Stuart's. Dylan was confident enough in his sexuality, yet gay men always made him a little uneasy. He didn't know why. Nary a gay man had ever hit on him but his looks were fine enough that plenty of heterosexual women had hit on him—still did every week—but he rarely felt uncomfortable in their presence. On the other hand, plenty of heterosexual women had absolutely no interest in sleeping with him so the same might be possible of gay men, he reasoned.

Dylan cleared his throat. "Yeah, I'm looking for Robyn. Have you seen her?"

"Not in the past week." He paused and gawked at Dylan with hatred instead of raging sexuality. "I would have thought her so-called partner knew."

"Knew what?"

"That she's lost three jobs in the past month because some idiot keeps threatening her employers." He narrowed his eyes at Dylan. "Was it you?"

"No. No, it wasn't me! I'd never do something like that to Robyn." But he had. He himself had ratted her out to the sergeant. He refused to work with a practicing witch, he'd said. He'd ended up with Clive, and Robyn's new partner, a devout Catholic, had heard the rumors and followed suit. No one would work with an evil, Satan-worshipping witch who probably liked to cast spells over the men in the office to make them impotent.

Dylan swallowed hard again and asked the question he dreaded. "So she's left town?"

"No. She's still around...somewhere."

Dylan gestured at the empty apartment. "But her things are gone."

"Landlady liked Robyn a lot. Thought having a police detective living in this neighborhood made her properties on this street safer. That's why she held out so long."

"Held out?" Dread snaked its way down his spine.

"Somebody threatened her. Just like they threatened Robyn's employers. 'Get rid of the witch or you'll burn, too.' Landlady wasn't going to kick Robyn out, but Robyn was afraid for the rest of us. People who don't like witches usually don't like gays and interracial couples, you know. There's a lot of us alternative lifestyles on this street. So Robyn left." Stuart squinted at Dylan. *"Because she cared."*

"Any idea where she went?" The $64,000 question.

"Like I'd tell you?"

All right, he deserved that. "Look, I'm still a cop. Robyn is being stalked and she hasn't reported it."

"Like her cop ex-buddies are going to help? You're such a loyal bunch, aren't you? You'd feed her to the wolves and she knows that. Why would she ever call you for help? If she were on fire, you'd bring gasoline and kindling."

Dylan gripped the hand rail, vaguely aware that his knuckles had turned white. All he could think of was the upside down pentagrams carved into the bodies of the Firehawk men and Gloria Stokes. "I had no idea Robyn was in trouble. Look—Stuart—I need to know where she is. I may be wrong—again—but if her stalker has anything to do with a murder we investigated last spring, then Robyn's in bigger trouble than you think. I have to warn her."

"I could do that for you."

"No, you can't. It's official police work."

"I suspect you're the last person she wants to see."

"And I suspect you're right, Stuart. But I'm good at solving murder cases, and turning killers over to the justice system." Who just as often as not let them loose on technicalities that had nothing to do with him. Then he obsessed for days about the futility of it all—another minor talent that had driven his wife away from him.

"Last year, I let a killer get away from me. Maybe if I'd been less focused on Robyn's personal confessions and more attentive to catching a killer who liked to think his victims where devil-worshippers, I would have caught him. But I didn't. I fucked up. Robyn and I were a great team." His voice cracked. "And I broke up that team. How can I ever make up what I've done to Robyn if I don't find her in time?"

He held his breath and waited. Out of all the wonderful and terrible things that had happened to him in his life, Robyn was the best part of it all. He'd been the teenaged hellion his parents couldn't bring to the right side of the law...until after their deaths. Now it was too late and he had to live with that. He'd run off his crazy-in-love wife, too, never realizing how much she meant to him until it was too late. And now he'd destroyed his relationship with Robyn. Was it too late again? Would he ever get a second chance to prove he'd learned from his mistakes?

The months without Robyn had been hell, sheer hell. He had to find her, win back her job, and her heart. His apartment was tiny and not nearly enough for more than one lonely cop, but with her help he could make it a home for both of them. She had the gift to transform everything she touched, including him, from pale and bland to full of passion, life. He was withering without her.

"Please," he croaked at Stuart. He would have fallen to his knees if he'd thought begging would help. "This is one time when she needs me more than I need her. And I need her a hell of a lot more than I ever dreamed."

Stuart gazed at some imaginary spot in the distance, then blinked—a sure sign he was about to relent. "Wait here," he said at last. He disappeared through the doorway, and, a few minutes later, returned with a folded scrap of paper. He crushed it into Dylan's palm. "You do anything else to hurt Robyn and, cop or not, I swear I'll cut your heart out myself."

Dylan took one look at the scrawled phone number, mumbled his gratitude, and retreated to the relative warmth of his car. He dialed the numbers on his cell phone and waited, holding his breath. The last pink of the sky painted the western horizon through the silhouette of leafless trees. Woodsmoke drifted from a neighbor's chimney and settled like fog across the remnant of sunset. The phone rang a third time before it clicked.

"Hello?" a feeble voice answered. Maybe Robyn did have a grandmother after all.

"Who is this?" he demanded.

No answer. Then, a cautious "Who do you want?"

"I'm trying to find Robyn Porter. It's a matter of life and death."

No response.

"Okay, okay. Just tell her I called. Tell her...tell her...." If the old woman was screening calls, she wouldn't turn over the phone for just anybody. But "Finn" had been Robyn's special nickname for him, a play on the name of legendary Irish warrior, Finn MacCool. Dylan was neither Irish nor legendary, but he liked the warrior part. Warriors from olden times often went to war, never to see their family or homes again. That much he understood. His job was like that every day. "Tell her it's Finn."

The old woman must have covered the phone's mouthpiece with her hand. He heard bits and pieces of a muffled argument, then finally, finally, Robyn's voice. "Finn?"

He swallowed. He didn't know where to begin. Except with honesty. "I miss you."

Hesitation.

Then, at last, "I miss you, too, Finn."

Chapter Three

~Saadia~

Saadia set the match to the wick and watched the flame grow. With a whispered prayer, she placed the candle on the kitchen table.

"Lady, let her labors be brief and the pain without fury."

The Goddess had kept Kestrel safe and well-hidden for so long. Surely it would not be for naught.

Tara returned from the girl's bedroom, unease in her eyes. "It would probably do us all well to perform a little ritual for Kestrel. This is not going to be easy for her."

Saadia pushed the chair back with a squawk and eased her weary bones into it. "We can't take her to a hospital. You know that."

"I know."

"You have to do it, Tara. You're the one."

"I'm a nurse, not a doctor."

"You're a witch, a healer. You can do it. The Goddess is strong in you. Tonight may be the entire reason she came to our coven for help. For your talents."

Tara pulled up a chair beside Saadia and buried her hands in her face. "I'll do it because I have to." She looked up. "But I have to tell you, I'm afraid. She's eight and a half months pregnant, and she has not had the kind of medical care she should have had with an obstetrician once or twice a month."

"You've examined her daily for two months. You know her condition better than anyone."

"Yes, but if anything goes wrong with the babies...." Tears welled in her eyes. "Albion, I just couldn't live with that."

Saadia reached across the table and patted the younger woman's hand. "We'll do everything that is within our power, and for everything outside our power, we'll ask the Goddess' help. Throughout time, women have given birth without the assistance of fancy doctors." She paused, fully aware that she herself had never experienced childbirth. Easy to talk when your body wasn't being split open by a new life. "For weeks, I've given her raspberry tea and special herbs. When the time comes, she'll be ready."

"She's delirious." Tara wrung her hands. "I can't calm her down. Even if I could give her heavy drugs, that wouldn't be good for the babies."

"She's calm enough."

"No. She keeps insisting she can't feel Grant or Cedric with her any more. Albion, they've been dead for over eight months."

"And Edgar's been dead for two months, but I can still feel him around me. Kestrel's young men will move on to their next lives when the time is right. Perhaps when they're confident that Kestrel can make it on her own."

"They may be confident, but Kestrel isn't. All this tension is having an adverse effect on her health. Albion, we've got to get her to a hospital."

Saadia squeezed the unwrinkled hand. In the fourteen years she'd known Tara and tutored her in the ways of Wicca, Tara had been serious, reserved, but most of all, confident in her abilities. If Tara was worried, then there was reason to worry.

"All right, child," Saadia said softly. "Short of calling a doctor, what do you propose we do?"

The nurse quieted for what seemed a long time, then finally nodded to herself. "I've been contemplating this for months. You know, just in case. There's a clinic on the outskirts of town. It's open only on weekdays as an immediate care facility. But it does have proper equipment for labor and delivery."

"You're sure of this?"

"Yes. I sometimes substitute there on my days off. There's a combination lock on the side door." She met Saadia's eyes. "And I know the combination."

Saadia nearly smiled. Tara not only had been thinking about it, she'd put a back-up plan in motion months ago when she'd started this part-time job. "Won't someone call the police?" she asked.

"Not if we're careful. The building is situated away from the road with a forest of scrub pines on both sides and behind it. There are streetlamps in front and a couple in back, but you can park directly behind the building without being seen from the front. At least, I think you can. We'd have to meet here. Take as few cars there as possible so we won't be seen."

Saadia rubbed at spot on the table and gave a little shrug. "Then that's what we'll do."

Tara toyed with her collar, pulling it away from her skin as though it were a noose. "It's not that simple. I'll need help. I can't run the equipment alone and I'll need help in getting things cleaned up when we're done. A *lot* of help."

"As I said, we'll do it. All of us. We'll call the whole coven."

Tara glanced down at her watch, then held it to her ear just to make sure. "We have at least another hour until dark. We need to spend that time getting the coven together. Some labors last thirty hours. This one," she added with a sigh, "had better last less than twelve."

Saadia rose with her cane and hobbled to the cupboard where she kept her rarest herbs. "It will."

Chapter Four

~*Saadia*~

The clinic was far enough off the road and surrounded on three sides by trees. The security lights were ample, but still, if they parked very closely, none of the traffic from the road would spot them. The blinds in the windows blocked any view of the inside except for the dimness of a few token lights left on inside. What would a few more matter as long they weren't lit up like the proverbial Christmas tree? Perhaps they wouldn't invite too much attention after all, and if they did, they could easily be mistaken for a cleaning crew.

Saadia walked a waddling Kestrel through the door. Perspiration dotted the girl's brow and dampened the dark roots that had grown out beneath her blonde hair. Saadia watched helplessly as Tara tugged the girl out of her clothes and pulled a hospital gown over the girl's huge belly. Tara opened several packages of blue plastic-lined sheets, fumbling and nearly dropping one.

Phoenix, biting her lip, stood next to Saadia and cringed as Kestrel moaned, long and loud. "Can't you give her something?" Phoenix asked Tara. "Kes is really hurting."

"No, I can't." Tara turned on a machine with lots of flashing lights. She connected two thin, black wires to a couple of wide belts, then slipped them underneath Kestrel's back and buckled them in front. A loud heartbeat boomed through the room and then something just as loud—a chugga-chugga like a train. "Baby's heartbeat," Tara explained, glancing up for a second.

A strip of paper rolled slowly out of the machine. Some sort of graph, starting slowing like an earthquake tremor and then going off the scale at the same instant Kestrel nearly bent double and moaned again. Moaning was all Kestrel did. No screaming. No crying. Except for the occasional whimpered plea for Grant and Cedric to come back to her.

Saadia had faithfully fed her all the right herbal teas, especially the ones made from raspberry leaves. The labor should not have been so hard on her except for that last herb to speed to labor and beat the dawn.

Gryphon backed away from the bed just as Tara unlatched the stirrups from under the bed, raised them, and then gently slid Kestrel's ankles into place. "Can't you give her an epidural or anything?" he choked out. He'd watched Morgana bear him three children, but all within the comfort of a bustling hospital full of obstetricians. Gryphon was a big man but damned himself to see anything or anyone in pain.

Tara shook her head. "I told you, I can't. I'm not an anesthesiologist."

"Well, some kind of painkiller," Gryphon insisted. "I know women have been having babies without the benefit of drugs for thousands of years, but...but this—" he grimaced— "this is torture."

He was right. It hurt to watch Kestrel hurt. Yet, no one in the Coven of the Jeweled Dragon had ever known her when she wasn't hurting. She'd come to them in fresh pain, and somehow, one way or another, in pain she would leave.

Tara stopped and stood up straight, her age showing suddenly on her face. Tiny wrinkles scrunched up at the corners of her eyes and two prongs of concern creased her brow above her nose. "You don't understand. No matter how many painkillers there are in this building, they are all very carefully controlled. It takes two combinations to unlock the clinic pharmacy, and I have only one. Like it or not, Kes is going to have these babies Rambo-style."

Tara donned a smock and then latex gloves. "There'll be plenty of clean-up work to do later," she said, voice shaking, "but if you want to make yourselves useful now, I suggest everyone focus on a quick and safe birth. For both of these babies. And Kes. Because if anything goes wrong, and I get in over my head, we'll have to call for emergency back-up. And if that happens, everyone will know about Kestrel's babies, and the rest of us get to explain to the police what we're doing here."

"She's right," Saadia said, taking control. "We're all going to send a little energy Kestrel's way."

They took turns then, some of them pacing the floor deep in prayer and others stroking Kestrel's black and blonde hair or gripping her hand or rubbing her belly as the train sounds chugged away from the machine.

Saadia glanced at a clock: 8:15. The girl on the table was all she had left in the world. Saadia had come to love her as the daughter the Goddess had given her. She'd do anything for Kestrel, Kestrel and her babies. Give anything. Everything she owned.

The next time Saadia looked at the clock, it was almost ten-thirty. Kestrel panted on cue. Made hee-hee-hoo sounds. At times she had that wild look of an animal trapped in a cage. No escape from the pain, no escape from impending childbirth.

Tara, perspiration dripping from her brow, backed away from the table and shot a desperate look at Saadia. The old woman shuffled to her. Tara pulled her sideways and whispered in her ear. Saadia adjusted her hearing aid to catch every word.

"I'm nervous, Albion. Twin births usually get the worst of both worlds. The first baby comes out vaginally. By the time the second one is ready for delivery, the mother is worn out. She can't push enough. Or the birth is breach and we have to do a C-section. We may have to turn the second baby, and if we can't, we may lose one of these children. At this point, we could be in a world of trouble."

"Not at this point. No. It's in the hands of the Goddess."

Tara nodded and went back to her post. "Okay, sweetie," she said to Kestrel, "are you ready to push now?"

Kestrel nodded twice, firmly, one for each babe.

Someone began to sing. Nightsong, the coven member with the sweetest voice of all. "Isis, Astarte, Diana, Hecate, Demeter, Kali, Inanna."

The rest, even Tara, joined their voices very softly in the Goddess Chant, not too loudly so as not to draw mortal attention. "Isis, Astarte, Diana, Hecate, Demeter, Kali, Inanna...Isis, Astarte, Diana, Hecate, Demeter, Kali, Inanna...."

Everyone in the Coven of the Jeweled Dragon focused on Kestrel. Energy thrummed through the room.

"Isis, Astarte, Diana, Hecate, Demeter, Kali, Inanna...."

A pale, violet glow seemed to outline Kestrel's body as she grabbed two hands offered by her brothers and sisters and bore down hard.

"Isis, Astarte, Diana, Hecate, Demeter, Kali, Inanna...."

"Isis, Astarte, Diana, Hecate, Demeter, Kali, Inanna...."

"Isis, Astarte, Diana, Hecate, Demeter, Kali, Inanna!"

~

Saadia leaned over the babies, one each under Kestrel's arms, to give them a closer look. Echo and Starr had bathed and swaddled the baby girls while Tara tended to the afterbirth. The child under her right arm was wide awake and staring at nothing, yet seemed to take in everything. Her eyes weren't quite focused yet, but Saadia knew beyond a doubt that this child had a touch of the Sight. Saadia smiled down at the child with her wee, bright eyes and peach-fuzz for hair.

"This one was born of water."

Saadia twisted to get a better look at the twin on the other side. The tiny thing slept, her black hair drying into dark ringlets all over her head. Rather than wake her, Saadia pressed one old finger into the baby's hand and felt the tiny grip tighten around her feeble flesh. Her finger tingled and arthritis that had plagued her for decades seemed to fade. This child had a healing touch.

"Born of fire, this one was. Of heat and light. What are their names?" she whispered to Kestrel.

Exhausted from her labor, the new mother smiled. Her bonding with her children had been immediate, as if she knew them both the instant they were born. "They told me what to name their daughters." She shouldered away a stray tear on her cheek. "Oh, I wish they could be here with me now!"

Saadia patted her hand. "They are, hon."

"I mean, in the flesh. In the physical realm." She glanced around at the rest of the coven, half of them listening attentively while the other half scrubbed away at the blood, urine, and feces on the floor in an effort to leave the clinic as pristine as before their arrival. "You have all been so good to me," she sobbed, "but it's not the same as if their fathers were here. Still, bless you. Bless you all."

"You don't have to name to children right away," Tara said. "Give it a few days. I have a cousin in another state. He follows a Druid path, and I'm sure he'd help us. His wife is a healer and has been known to do some midwifery. We can figure out a way to make it look like these children were born elsewhere. That'll give you time to name them."

Kestrel let the tears stand on her cheeks, preferring to keep her arms around her babies to wiping away the grief. "But I already know their names. This one—the blonde—that's Grant's daughter. She has his eyes. Her name is Branwen. And this one, she has long, dark hair like Cedric's. Her name is Deirdre."

Saadia shook her head. "No, child. You have that backwards."

Kestrel shot her a weary but perplexed look in Saadia's direction, then closed her eyes. "I'm so tired, so sleepy."

Tara laughed. "Of course you are, sweetie. That's why they call it labor. If it were easy, they'd call it fun, and there's nothing fun about childbirth."

"Pssst. Robyn! Come here!" Lucretia stood at the interior door, one fingers still tight on the knob though her black Gothic sleeves hid most of her hand. Panic shone in her black-lidded eyes. She'd left the delivery room some time ago to take her turn as look-out in the front room of the clinic.

Phoenix pressed a discreet finger to her lips, a gesture for the teenager to stay calm, and then crossed the room to meet her. Saadia followed. Phoenix motioned for the three of them to step into the hallway, and then she closed the interior door so Kestrel and the others couldn't hear.

"Come with me," Lucretia whispered. "Quick! Somebody's out there."

The dread that had ridden Saadia's back all day pressed hard against her chest. She shuffled after Lucretia and Phoenix's quick steps and wished she'd brought her cane with her. Gasping for breath by the time she caught up with them in the front room, Saadia leaned against a straight chair. She would need her strength before this night was over. All of it and more.

Phoenix peered through the blinds. "I don't see anything," she said.

In the dim light, Lucretia wrung her hands. "Count the fifth lamp post from the road."

"I still don't see anything."

"In the moonshadows. He's parked between two pine trees. It's a white car. Big car. He's outside the car. He's leaning up against the driver's door. I don't think I would have noticed him at all except that I saw something glint in the moonlight. Something in his hand. It looked like a knife."

"Knife?" Saadia tripped over the word.

"Yeah, but not a kitchen knife. It had a long blade and a sparkly handle and it looked like some kind of dagger. An athame, maybe. Except that I don't know what an average Joe Blow off the street would be doing with an athame."

Saadia and Phoenix exchanged gazes and Saadia knew that Phoenix couldn't think of a reason either. Phoenix's lips moved. "The Firehawks," Saadia read. She turned up her hearing aid a little more. No need for her to look out the window. Her old eyes simply wouldn't see that far. So much of her life now depended on the sights and sounds of younger folks.

Phoenix squinted through a crack in the blinds as if her squinting somehow improved her night vision. "There he is. I see him." Saadia couldn't hear well, but she could distinguish Phoenix's breaths coming in ragged gasps. "Yes, yes, that's him! I can't quite make out what he's carrying. Oh, I wish I had a telescope or binoculars or something."

"Grail does." Lucretia brightened. "He keeps an old pair under his front seat for birdwatching in the park. You want me to go get them?" She winced, suddenly remembering. "Ooh, I mean, do you want me to get them and there being a guy out there with a knife?"

"Please," Phoenix said, staring into the night.

"But...but he's outside."

"He's outside *out front.* Grail's Jeep is parked out back. Any idea how long that clown's been out there?"

Lucretia shrugged. "I didn't notice him for nearly an hour. Everybody keeping watch ahead of me said nothing was going on outside, so I'm not sure when he got here. Maybe he was here before us."

"No." Phoenix was sure of herself. "I remember seeing a white car parked in a driveway across the street when we dropped my car back at my house." She'd said something then about having been followed lately and she was afraid someone would notice her car, so she'd taken Saadia's keys from her and driven like a bat out of hell to the clinic.

Saadia's old heart beat faster. There was nothing in the world she wouldn't do for Kestrel, and now for those two precious babies in bed with their mother.

Lucretia padded nervously out of the room, tiptoeing in her granny boots. Saadia reached out and touched Phoenix on the shoulder, and Phoenix startled.

"Don't worry," Phoenix said. "I'm not going to let anything happen to Kes and those babies."

"Do you really think whoever's waiting out there is the same person who killed Grant and Cedric Firehawk?"

She gulped and nodded. "I do. I talked to Finn today. First time in months. Funny how the Goddess works, huh?" Her voice sounded dreamy and far away. "He's uncovered a big clue in the murders. He thought I should know."

"He loves you, you know."

"He has to love himself first. He doesn't know how. Not yet. He's cursed himself with so many old hurts that—" She broke off and squinted even harder out through the blinds.

"What is it?" Saadia pressed.

"I saw the glint of the knife Cretia was talking about. He's pacing around the car now. I can see him in the moonlight. It's brighter than the lamplight, you know? He's getting impatient. Maybe he'll...maybe he'll come in here and attack us all."

"I don't think so." From what Saadia had seen that night when Kestrel had first come to her, this man was a coward. A sniper. A man who came out of darkness to attack and kill. He'd mutilated bodies in a way he never would have if they'd been alive to fight back. "This man will never confront us as a group. He'll never risk having us invoke the kind of power we have as a circle. He may prey on us one by one, if he knows who we are, but he will never face us all together. That's not his way. Now or ever." Saadia leaned against the wall. Her back hurt from standing for so long. "Phoenix," she said, then reached out and touched the younger woman. *"Robyn."*

The younger witch's eyes widened. Saadia never called her by her mundane name. Never. But the point had been made, and Saadia had her full attention.

"Robyn, have you done a ritual tonight to ask for the Goddess' protection?"

"For Kestrel? Of course."

"Not for Kestrel. For *you.* Have you asked for protection for yourself?"

Robyn the Phoenix moved away from the window and sank her hands into her jeans pockets. She stared down at the floor. "I don't ask the Goddess for much of anything lately. Nothing for myself. Except that...that I can find my purpose in this life."

Saadia rubbed the girl's arm. Yes, very much a girl at the moment, lost and alone in the big, ugly world. "You know your purpose."

"I thought I did. I know that in my lifetimes past, it's been my purpose to protect. I thought that's what it was in this lifetime, too, but I'm not a cop any more. I'm not much of anything."

"It's okay, honey. This time will pass. You have the soul of a protector. You know that. It's just a matter of finding how to use it again."

"Sometimes I think that...if I'm not able to be a protector in this life again, then I should just end this life and start all over again. The sooner I become a protector again—"

Lucretia burst back into the room and waved a small pair of black binoculars. "I found them! They're kind of dusty.

I wiped them off on my sleeve. I hope that's okay." She thrust them into Phoenix's hands. "Is he still out there?" she asked before Phoenix could bring the binoculars to her eyes and peel back the blinds once again.

"You're right," Phoenix said. "It does look like an athame in his hand. I can't make out his face, though. It is a man—I know that. Looks like he's wearing a...a...raincoat? I can't see his face. He's wearing some kind of...I think it's a rain hat of some kind."

"Why would anyone be wearing a raincoat and rain hat tonight?" Lucretia asked. "It's a clear night. Not a cloud in the sky."

"I've got a bad feeling about this," Phoenix continued. She glanced up. "Please understand that I wouldn't be telling you this if we weren't in danger now. Before our murder witness died, she told us it was Kestrel who killed her husbands."

"What?" Lucretia shrieked.

"Shhh. Keep your voice down. I didn't say I believed the woman, but that was her official story. When Finn tried to get her to agree to testify, that conniving little bitch recanted. She didn't live long enough for us to find out either way. But she said that Kestrel was wearing a rain hat and a raincoat when she committed the murders."

"That's fucking absurd," Lucretia seethed, giving voice to Saadia's thoughts.

"She was lying about Kes for some reason," Phoenix continued. "But now, I'm beginning to think she was right about the raincoat. Gloria Stokes wasn't imaginative enough to make up that kind of detail. Encasing yourself in plastic has a way of protecting one from blood spatter." She winced as she said it.

"You know, Robyn, if you could tell who it is out there, we could call the cops," Lucretia suggested. She wrung her hands as if she were chilled.

"No. We can't call the cops. Not until we get Kes and those babies out of here. There's no way we can explain what we're doing here, remember?"

"What about the car?" Saadia asked. "Can you tell anything about the car? Anything that identifies it? Bumper stickers?"

Phoenix squinted, leaning into the binocula٠ bumper stickers. Big car. Light-colored. Maybe whi. sized. Can't tell the make. It's too deep into t٠ Wait...wait a minute. There's something dangling fror. ror. Like a prism or something. It's on a cord. Turnin٠ catching the moonlight. It's...oh, Goddess, help us!"

"What is it?" Lucretia demanded, again taking th٠ right out of Saadia's slower moving mouth.

"It's a cross. No, not just a cross. A crucifix."

"You're certain?" Saadia asked.

"Positive." Phoenix handed the binoculars back tc cretia. "I know who it is. When I interviewed the guy, I k he was lying to me. It's Reverend Jones. It all makes sensc me now." She slapped her forehead. "Of course! Why didn see it before? He was following Kestrel the night of the mu ders. He called the police almost before the murders happenec We thought it odd that the bodies were still so warm. We go٠ there so soon after they'd been killed. Reverend Jones made the 911 call. Claimed later that Kestrel asked him to. Still, he made the call, and he showed up afterward when we were cleaning up the mess. He showed up at the scene of the crime and he knew way too much about what had happened."

"What'll we do?" Lucretia asked.

"You stand watch. I'm calling Finn." She snatched up the phone at the receptionist's desk and punched in the numbers. "Detective MacCool," she spat out. "It's an emergency. Yes, I'll...I'll...you tell him it's Robyn."

An eternity passed while Robyn the Phoenix waited. Saadia took over the hand-wringing from Lucretia who in turn took over as lookout. Saadia's arthritic hands throbbed. She willed Finn to answer soon and send help.

"Finn! I'm so glad to hear your voice! You were right. About what? About everything. I know who killed the Firehawks. And Gloria Stokes. I've been watching him from the window." Thankfully, she didn't say whose window she'd been watching from. "No. No, don't come yet."

Lucretia motioned frantically. "He's moving around out there."

"Look, Finn. There's something I have to do here for Saadia first." She cringed, obviously realizing she should never have divulged Saadia's name to someone outside the circle. "If you don't hear back from me in ten minutes, I want you to meet me at...um, the Emergency Day Clinic on County Line Road. No, no, I'm not hurt. Just make sure that you're there."

Saadia watched Robyn's Adam's apple bob up and down in her slender throat. "Finn? Don't say anything to anyone, okay? I've never asked you for much, but I'm asking you now."

Before she could hang up the phone, Lucretia began waving her arms wildly again. "He's coming up to the front door! I think he's trying to see in—see who's here!"

Robyn the Phoenix fished Saadia's car keys out of her pocket and slipped them into Saadia's hands. Robyn had driven while Saadia had comforted the mother-to-be. "My purse is under the seat of your car," Robyn reminded her. "There's a couple hundred dollars in it. It's about all I've got left, but it'll get you a hotel room for a night or two if you're careful with it. Are you up to driving?"

Saadia crunched the keys together in her hands. She understood. Tonight was what she'd been waiting for all her life. "Yes."

"Good. Cretia, I want you to make sure Tara and the others get Kes and the babies into the backseat of Saadia's car. They're going to make a run for it and never look back. I want the rest of you to get everything cleaned up as fast as you can and get out of here before Finn and the cops show up. Got that?" Robyn wiped her sweaty palms on her jeans and headed for the front door of the clinic.

"But...but," Lucretia squeaked, "where are *you* going?"

"Somebody has to distract Reverend Jones so he won't follow
Saadia's car."

Chapter Five

~*Dylan/Finn*~

Dylan slid the telephone receiver back into its cradle. With the exception of the night in the Firehawk grove when Robyn had begged him to understand what witchcraft was and had been desperate to make him accept her for what she was, he'd never heard Robyn sound as desperate as she did tonight. If she was standing there, looking at a killer from her window, there was no way he was going to wait ten minutes before meeting her at some clinic.

He'd never tell her this, but he'd bought a couple of books on witchcraft, Wicca, Earth Magick, and Druidry. Okay, not a couple. A dozen or so. Mostly Buckland, Cunningham, and Ravenwolf. He'd started reading a book on the Celtic tradition among Wiccans, although he hadn't quite grasped it yet. Some Wiccans called themselves witches. Some didn't. Some witches didn't consider their spirituality synonymous with Wicca and Goddess worship. It was all so confusing to him. Different paths meant different things to different people. Hodge-podge Earth religions, Buddhist beliefs, and odd traditions all thrown together, all tailored to each person for whatever an individual's soul needed, for whatever path God wanted that person to walk.

It wasn't so different, he supposed, from the First Baptist Church he'd grown up in. His church had believed dancing was okay, but the Church of Christ down the street considered dancing to be an offense punishable by hellfire. The fundamentalist church on the other side of town had insisted that wives stay home and have the babies, that they wear their hair in beehives with no makeup, and that the only instrument appropriate to making music for the glory of God was the human voice. Some Baptist churches insisted on dressing up every Sunday in suits and designer dresses while others didn't care if you came dressed for the beach as long as you showed up for worship. Yet other churches didn't allow women in pants to walk through their doors. Yes, different religions and the variants of each religion could be confusing, whether it was a pagan religion or a Christian one.

Maybe Robyn could sort it all out for him later, he decided. He pushed his chair backwards, letting it squawk across the floor. He paused. He'd almost forgotten he had a visitor.

"I'm sorry, Reverend Jones," he said. "Could we have this discussion some other time?" The older man rose to protest, but Dylan held up his palm to silence him. "We do appreciate all the help you've given us to help us find the man who robbed that liquor store and killed the kid behind the counter, but I'm afraid we can't arrest all the liquor store distributors and hold them accountable in that young man's death. Believe me, I appreciate the sentiment, but it just doesn't work that way."

With that, Dylan stalked out, leaving the preacher slack-jawed with all his demands. Dylan pushed through the outer doors and half-ran to the parking lot. He couldn't crank his car fast enough. He checked his watch. Ten-thirty. If he waited ten minutes for Robyn to call back, then it would take nearly twenty minutes for him to reach County Line Road. With his light flashing and his foot pressing the accelerator to the floor, he'd simply drop by Robyn's home on his way there. No matter what, he'd make it to the clinic on schedule, but if Robyn was in real trouble and there really was a murderer stalking her from outside her house, he wasn't about to waste ten precious minutes.

Moments later, he pulled into traffic and stomped the accelerator. Side roads flew by, almost too fast for him to read the street signs. Dylan hadn't realized quite how low Robyn had sunk until she had mentioned earlier in the day that her new home was at 48 Water Street. Housing was cheap on Water Street and perfectly within Robyn's new budget. But Water Street was also a home to drug dealers, drive-by shootings, and domestic violence. Certainly not the safest place for an ex-cop to live, particularly when said ex-cop had probably arrested half of her neighbors.

He slammed on brakes. He'd nearly missed the road. He angled through a shallow ditch and around a stop sign across the wrong side of the lane. He had to slow down enough to get a good look at the numbers on the mailboxes, but some of the boxes had been shot through several times and the numbers were unreadable.

There's 40...42...44...46...48!

Her car was in the driveway. He screeched to a halt in front of a small, dingy white house that had seen its glory days perhaps seventy years ago. It didn't look like a home at all for Robyn. Bars on the windows, barred gate across the door, the yard scorched of all vegetation. He would take her away from this place, from all its barrenness, and together he would learn what he needed to grow and be whole again.

He bounded up the steps to Robyn's door. Everything inside the house was dark. No light came from the windows. He banged on the door, then banged again. He jiggled the cast-iron grate over the door, but it was locked. It held fast. She'd just called him—what?—ten minutes ago? And where was the murderer outside her window?

"Robyn?" he screamed. Maybe she was hiding some-where inside. He tugged his oversized flashlight out of the belt at his back. He aimed the beam of light through the small pane in the front door. No sign of Robyn. A shabby sofa and rock-ing chair. Beyond that, a simple wooden table with some cold candles atop it. An altar? It reminded him of the one that sat below the pulpit, on level with the congregation, in the church he'd attended as a kid except that this altar was smaller and al-most meager by comparison. No finely-embroidered altar cloth. No layer of plate glass beneath an offering plate and a gargan-tuan bouquet placed in memory of some church member's dead relative. Just a simple table with candles, a silver goblet of sorts, a couple of pretty rocks, and a single flower. No, not meager. Simple. Respectful. He'd seen the same table in her previous home on so many occasions and had never realized what it was.

"Robyn!" He pounded on the door but nothing moved inside.

Damn. Maybe she'd already called his office back while he'd been rushing over to her house to save her. Okay, okay. Her car was there, but everything was dark. Maybe she'd caught a ride with a neighbor? Called a taxi? He aimed the flashlight at his watch and cursed. Fifteen minutes had passed. Either way, he had to get to Day Clinic and find Robyn.

He made it in six minutes.

Burning rubber singed the air as he steered into the parking lot. His headlights spanned four people—one man and three women—shining flashlights into the woods. Robyn wasn't among them. One looked like one of the dismal Goth chicks with unnaturally black hair and heavy make-up. They froze for a split second and, in another, dove for a Jeep idling under a streetlamp. He couldn't tell what the hell they were doing but by the looks on their faces as they passed his car, they were frightened by more than the prospect of being caught trespassing.

Barely braking to stare back at them, Dylan spun toward clinic building. No sign of Robyn. Or anyone else for that matter. He circled the low building. No cars. No one. Lights were on inside the clinic, but they were low and unobtrusive as if every fifth light had been left on for the sake of security and not for vision. Other than the foursome with the flashlights, he couldn't tell anyone had been on the property all evening, let alone Robyn.

He eased his car along the edge of the woods where the Jeep had parked. He swiped the beam of his own flashlight over the woods near the parking lot. Nothing. The foursome had been so intent, and his gut told him their anxiety had something to do with why Robyn had asked him to meet her here. But where was she?

Something moved beneath the trees. He held his breath. Robyn? He stopped the car, ran his palm over the hilt of his revolver, and then stepped cautiously out onto the black asphalt of the parking lot.

"Who's there?" he demanded, spraying the woods with light.

It moved again.

Whew. Only a shadow of waving pine needles in the light of the full moon. From what he'd read, covens and solitary witches often held rituals under a full moon because their power was at its height. Maybe that's what the foursome was doing?

Before turning back, he panned the light over the woods. Fresh ruts flattened the deep grasses and thick pine straw under the trees where someone, probably the Jeep, had parked. The straw between the ruts and the asphalt had been kicked up in places as if dogs had enjoyed an afternoon of playing in the shade. The foursome had probably spent the evening hiding out there, rolling a joint, and had ended up losing an earring or contact or something. If they still had drugs in their vehicle, then that would explain why they were so intent on scouring the area but quick to leave at the sign of another car. It didn't explain why Robyn wanted to meet him here.

Dylan climbed back into the car and waited. Five minutes. Ten minutes. Fifteen.

"Where are you, Robyn?" he asked himself through gritted teeth.

Everything around him was silent. The pines swayed in the night breeze, their shadows dancing eerily in the moonlight. The windshield fogged over. He rolled down his window for a better look out. His breath came out in clouds.

Robyn should have been there by now. If she was coming. Why this place? She'd seen the killer outside her window, she'd said. Yet her home seemed safe and sound, if unoccupied. She'd asked him to meet her here if he didn't hear from her in ten minutes. But Robyn wasn't anywhere to be found.

Damn it. He should have waited at the office another ten minutes, even if it meant humoring Reverend Jones. Instead, he'd rushed to the rescue like some kind of knight in shining armor to Robyn's damsel in distress. If he'd waited, she might have called and sent him elsewhere, some mysterious elsewhere where he should be now.

High beam headlights blinded him for a second as a familiar car zoomed up beside him from the highway. The horn honked a couple of times. The car stopped a few inches from his front fender, and a man hopped out enthusiastically.

"Clive?" Dylan couldn't believe it. "What are you doing here?" Then his heart skipped a beat. "Did Robyn call back?"

"Haven't heard from the Good Witch of the North since her untimely departure from the force." Clive looked over his shoulder a time or two and beyond Dylan's car. "What are you doing out here in the middle of nowhere?"

"Robyn asked me to meet her here."

"She put a spell on you or something?"

"What are you doing here, Clive?"

"Oh." He bunched his lips together and surveyed the expanse of parking lot. "You got a weird call after you left. Sorry, but I answered your phone for you. And by the way, don't you ever leave me again to entertain a Baptist preacher by myself."

"Who called me?" Perspiration pricked at Dylan's brow.

Clive shrugged. "I don't know. Some girl. Said her name was Lucretia but it wasn't really Lucretia, whatever that means. Said she was a friend of Robyn's. You'd been gone maybe five minutes when she called. She thought I was you 'cause I answered your phone. Couldn't get her to understand that I wasn't you and—"

"Get to the point, Clive."

"She wanted you to hurry up. Never would give me her name, but she said Robyn was in trouble and she'd gone to confront the man who killed the Firehawks. Well, I thought it was a prank. You know, somebody trying to give me a scare because of Robyn practicing witchcraft and tonight being a full moon and all. Kinda like that joke the guys pulled on Harrison last month. Anyways, I didn't buy it and I hung up on her. But I thought you should know. Besides, it gave me an excuse to get out of the office and away from Reverend Jones."

Dylan wanted to grab him by the throat and choke the living daylights out of him. "This girl told you Robyn needed help and you hung up on her?"

"Well, yeah. I don't have time for pranks. Even good ones meant for you." He laughed. "She even stopped a couple of times to yell at some other kids to get in the car and get out of there." Clive shook his head. "Dumb kids."

Oh, God. Robyn was in trouble and Clive had blown it off. Dylan took a deep breath and tried again. "Think carefully, Clive." A tough thing for the stupid son of a bitch to do. "Did Robyn's friend say where she was?"

"Nope. I got to thinking after the call and hit the recall button. Turns out the call was made from the Day Clinic." He squinted at the dimly lit building. "Hey, we may have a case of breaking and entering if she really did call from here."

A kid. The dreary-looking Goth girl in the Jeep. Why would a teenaged girl follow up Robyn's call from inside the clinic? If Robyn were home when she saw the Firehawks' killer....

"What's wrong?" Clive asked. "You look like you've seen a ghost."

Dylan pressed his hand against his mouth. Robyn couldn't have called him from her home. She didn't have a phone. Robyn had called from here, from the clinic. Robyn, for whatever reason she'd chosen to hide in the clinic, had watched the killer from inside the clinic. He'd been here. Right here.

But where was he now? Where was Robyn? The Goth girl and her cohorts?

What was it Robyn had said? She had to take care of something with Saadia first, and then she'd meet him at the clinic. But who was Saadia? A roommate? The Goth girl?

"Call for back-up," he instructed his partner. "Get some lights out here—quick—and get somebody who can open that clinic. And just pray you don't find any bodies in there."

He cranked the car, his hands jerking nervously. "I'll be back in a little while."

"Where are you going?"

"To get some answers."

It took five minutes to reach Robyn's house on Water Street. This time, the front porch light was on, and Dylan let out a long sigh of relief. In the five minute eternity it had taken to break every speed limit in town to get to Robyn's, he'd let a terrible image flash in his brain. He kept thinking of the night they'd found Gloria Stokes on the Firehawks' altar and how the killer had gone back to the scene of the crime. Robyn had said she knew who the killer was, and he couldn't wait to walk through her theory with her at the Firehawk's abandoned property.

He parked in the driveway behind Robyn's car and wondered who she'd shared a ride with to the Day Clinic. He pulled his coat tight around his throat and watched his breath turn to fog in the glow of the porch light. Robyn had a habit of turning on porch lights when she expected a guest, and the light wasn't on earlier. Clive must have gotten a message mixed up or something and Robyn had called to tell him to meet her back here. Par for the course for Clive.

Music wafted from the house. Something Celtic and bittersweet. An old Loreena McKennitt tape, he thought. A lyrical, sad-sounding song that repeated the words, "Please remember me." The last song on the tape. Oddly enough she used to play that one whenever she was happy and wanted to celebrate. He wondered what kind of evidence she'd uncovered against a murderer for her to be so pleased with herself. No doubt she'd found some humdinger of proof and wanted to turn it over to him in his official capacity of detective. It would be a boon to his career, and maybe, just maybe, it could help her reclaim hers.

"Robyn," he called out, bounding up the steps. "Where've you been? I waited for you at the clinic."

The iron gate over her door was unlocked and slightly cracked. He pulled it back and knocked hard on the door. He could see the small flowers of candle flame inside, but the music was too loud. She couldn't hear his pounding for the tunes.

He knocked again, glancing down at his shoes. Something red caught his eye. Fur? He'd seen foxes with fur that color. Pretty and red like Robyn's—

Sweet Jesus. It was too long to be animal fur. It was *hair.*

"Robyn!" he screamed. "Robyn!"

He kicked the heavy door but it wasn't latched. It flew against the wall with a bang and white sheetrock chunks fell in his wake. He drew his revolver and aimed it at the shadows.

Not a light was on in the house. Candles flickered everywhere. Tea lights had been set directly on the carpet, burning down and puddling wax on the floor. The candles hadn't burned down enough to start a house fire—they hadn't been burning that long—but it was just a matter of time before the whole place became an inferno.

He waded through clumps of red hair. Robyn's hair. Nothing jumped out at him from the shadows.

Side-stepping candles, he crept forward. One taller candle toppled under the pressure of his footfalls on the carpet. Fire sprouted at his foot, and he stamped it out before it could spread.

He stepped over a blouse, jeans, and short boots neatly arranged on the floor with the legs and sleeves spread-eagled. Red splotches bloomed across the white blouse and met in a bizarre artistry. At the center of each scarlet blossom was a slit no larger than his thumb.

"Robyn!" he screamed again. The loud, somber music drowned his pleas. He could barely see in the candlelight, let alone breathe. Incense, the kind that smoked and reeked, choked the air. Dylan had seen Robyn burn incense on several occasions, with wisps of scented smoke curling into the night, but the smoke was so thick that her whole stockpile must have burned. It was white and spicy and stung his eyes. It bounced the beam of his flashlight back at him. He swatted at the smoke in front of him and moved deeper into the house.

He slid past the shabby sofa and into the living room. He reached for the altar to steady himself, but it was no longer there. Dylan plugged his flashlight into his pants between his lower back and his belt. The light wasn't doing him any good in all the white smoke anyway.

The smoke seemed to billow from the center of the room. He crouched to get below the cloud of smoke and saw the base of the altar inside a circle of candles that burned faithfully toward the carpeted floor. A small black cauldron that had once graced the hearth at Robyn's old home sat directly in front of the altar. Instead of Halloween candy, it now held hundreds of sticks of incense, all of them glowing and smoldering.

"Robyn!" he shrieked.

A moan rent the air, just barely louder than the plaintive song.

Dylan dropped to his knees and crawled toward the circle of candles around the altar.

Now would be a good time to wake up, he told himself and kept crawling.

Holstering his revolver, he grabbed the edge of the altar and pulled himself up. Something wet and hot coated his hand. Then his eyes fixed on the sacrifice left on Robyn's altar. He shook himself, willing himself to wake.

It couldn't be.

It couldn't be.

Robyn.

He barely recognized her. Eyes staring, mouth torn but open, gasping. An upside down pentagram carved into her forehead and right hand. Her beautiful red hair clipped within a fraction of her scalp. And blood. So much blood he couldn't tell for certain if she was naked.

But she was alive. Oh, God, she was alive!

Alive. Whoever had done this to her had purposely left her alive. The gushing wounds to her shoulders and between her legs—safely away from heart and lungs—were meant to prolong her agony. He'd meant to burn her alive. Torture her, shear her hair, and burn her alive, just as the witchhunters of hundreds of years ago had done to their wise women and healers.

Her lips moved. A flicker of recognition pierced the suffering in her eyes. He couldn't see her well enough in the choking smoke, couldn't hear her over the volume of the music.

"Shhh, I'm going to get you out of here." His words vanished into the music. He lifted her carefully from the altar and held her gently against him. A candle at his feet oozed wax and a burning wick onto the carpet. The flame raced toward the sofa. He stepped through the fire and around another candle that had collapsed near the door.

A bracing wind met him at the door. Holding his breath, he laid Robyn on the half-frozen ground and fell to his knees beside her. As fast as he could, he yanked off his heavy coat and wrapped it around her nakedness. He was too numb to feel the cold himself. Robyn moaned softly at every touch.

"Who did this to you?" he begged, pulling her against his chest and rocking her like a mother would her broken baby. "Who did this?"

He caressed her bloody cheek, then threw his head back to the night sky. A full, winter moon gleamed directly above. He closed his eyes and squeezed out hot tears.

"Somebody!" he yelled at the top of his lungs. "Somebody help me!"

He could feel the strength draining out of her and into the ground, into her precious Mother Earth, her blood feeding the frozen soil.

"Somebody!" he screeched, voice breaking. Then, softly, he whispered in her ear, "It's all right, it's gonna be all right."

Her lips moved again, and he held her just far enough away from his face to focus his eyes on hers. Pain glazed her eyes. He would almost rather let her slip away than hurt for another second.

"Who did this to you?" he pleaded. He kissed a lone, soft patch of hair. Whoever had sheared her beautiful hair had recklessly sliced the scalp in places. No wonder accused witches of long ago gained little pity by the time they faced the stake or gallows. Days and sometimes weeks of torture left them scarred and broken and hideous. They must have looked like monsters by the time the first flames burned away their coarse shifts and licked at their ravaged bodies.

"Somebody!" he screamed again. Behind him, he heard people on the street. He'd gladly wake the whole neighborhood and all of hell if he had to. "Somebody call an ambulance!"

He rocked her, rocked her, warming her now by the growing fire from inside the house. Blood seeped through the coat he'd wrapped her in. She raised one mangled hand to his face and tried to speak.

"I'm here," he choked out. "Tell me who did this to you and I swear I'll spend the rest of my life making it right." Or paying for a cold-blooded murder.

She coughed, then wet her lips. She hauled in another breath and drew his face closer to hers. Her whole body shivered violently. Her lips moved against his ear. The words came out in a whisper of breath. "Never thirst."

Her head lolled against his chest. Her body shuddered and stilled in his arms. And she was gone.

"Robyn!" He blinked up at the cold moon, then dissolved into wracking sobs.

She'd had only enough strength to utter two words, and instead of naming her murderer, she'd used her dying breath to bless him.

Part Four

Behold,
I send you forth as sheep in the midst of wolves:
Be ye therefore wise as serpents,
And harmless as doves.
—*Matthew 10:16*

Chapter One

~ Finn ~

Nine years later....

In sketched dark green lines on light green paper, a hawk stretched its wings of flame and threatened to fly off the wrapper.

"You gonna buy that bar of soap or make love to it?" The woman's voice was worse than fingernails on chalkboard. She was a poor substitute for Trish, the woman who usually stood behind the counter at his favorite health food store and chatted with him. Trish's daughter was recovering from a tonsillectomy and Trish would be home for another week. That meant someone completely ignorant of essential oils and healing herbs watched the store in her absence.

"Hey, I asked you a question."

Finn glanced up at her from the bar of soap in his hands. No wonder the store was so sparse of customers today. The woman was doing a fantastic job of running them off.

"I'm just browsing," he muttered and put the bar of soap back on the shelf.

"You've been in here almost thirty minutes and ain't bought nothing yet."

How observant. He'd come in for a bottle of tea tree shampoo and natural toothpaste, but Trish's substitute hadn't restocked the shelves so he'd spent half an hour wandering up and down the tiny aisles and looking for a second choice.

He moved down the aisle to the big, glass-doored refrigerator where Trish kept goat cheese, flax seed, and unsalted sunflower seeds. He paused to pick up another bar of soap in the same shape as the one that had called to him earlier. Same ingredients, different scent, different magickal properties. Same burning bird on the wrapper. A hawk...on fire.

Saadia's Peppermint Soap.

He frowned. Something about *Saadia* tugged at his memory.

Trish's replacement sighed loudly. She could see him, he guessed, from the neck up but now that he had moved away from her, she couldn't tell what he was doing. She sighed again, stomped around the cash register, and then stood—arms crossed—at the end of the aisle. "You'd better not be stealing anything."

Him? Steal? He almost laughed.

"Whatever you send out," he tried to explain, "comes back to you times three, be it bane or good."

The woman blinked stupidly at him. Okay, so she'd never heard of the rule of three. Wasn't hard to figure out that the woman wasn't a witch. That he could tell by her demeanor. She also showed a complete lack of balance and understanding. Not to mention knowledge of The Craft.

"You need to leave," she said simply. "I don't like your kind here."

He stifled a smile. What would she say if she knew that, less than ten years ago, he'd been a cop? A homicide detective at that. "Trish doesn't mind my kind." In fact, Trish had commissioned him to sculpt an angel playing a harp and had paid him nicely.

"Then I'm doing Trish a favor by getting rid of all the freaks who hang out here."

A freak? Him? Because he'd changed his religion? Because he'd changed his priorities in life? Or because he'd changed his wardrobe? Maybe the poor woman had had too many past lives full of joy and enlightenment, and she'd come to this life preordained to be a stupid bitch.

He caught of glimpse of himself in the wall mirror and cringed. Ten years ago, he would have given a cautious eye to a man who looked like him, too. Black boots, black pants, black silk shirt. A single adornment in each ear. Flowing blond and silver hair that fell to the shoulders of his open, floor-length, leather coat. Yes, ten years ago, he too would have accused such a man of worshipping the devil. Ten years ago, he didn't know any better.

Finn tried to smile to offer the woman a little reassurance that he didn't plan to slash her throat and drink her blood as an offering to the gods. "This bar of soap," he said. "Is there anything you can tell me about it?"

The woman frowned. "You wash with it?" she tried.

"No. I mean, about the manufacturer. This—" he rubbed his fingertip across the script on the paper casing—"this Saadia Soap. That name sounds familiar."

"Could it be possible you washed with it...once?"

Okay, there was no call for that. Absolutely no call. Yes, he looked unusual to a conservative middle-aged woman in the Bible Belt, but he was perfectly groomed with perfect hygiene. The benefits of his morning shower certainly had not worn off this early in the morning.

"Look, I just want to know more about the people who make the soap."

Something niggled at the back of his memory. *There's something I have to do here for Saadia first,"* Robyn's voice echoed in the back of his head. He seldom heard her anymore. She'd stayed close to him for the first two years after her death, or at least, her spirit had. By the time he felt her fade and move on, he was decidedly entrenched in the religion that had given her happiness when he'd been so miserable. In honor of her, he'd taken her secret nickname for him as his Craft name. He was no longer a detective but an artist. He never thought of himself as Dylan MacCool any more. In his own mind, if not legally, he was simply Finn.

"There's something I have to do here for Saadia first," he heard Robyn say again as clearly as if she'd whispered it in his

ear instead of over the phone that night. *"I know who killed the Firehawks. And Gloria Stokes. I've been watching him from the window."*

Whoever Saadia was, he'd waited for nine years to find out. Was this Saadia the killer? The one who'd murdered her and carved up her body with upside down pentagrams? Artist or not, sometimes the detective inside him wanted to wriggle free, but he unleashed that part of himself only when he had to. Already his mind was spinning. There had to be a connection between Robyn and Saadia and between Robyn and whoever had killed the Firehawks. The minute he got home, he'd call Harrison, no longer the green-gilled kid who'd found the murder victims, but a detective in his own right. Maybe Harrison could tell him something about someone named Saadia who'd lived in Greenburg ten years ago. Then he'd find the phone numbers for Reverend Jones, Gloria Stokes' husband, and the Firehawks' parents and see if *Saadia* rang any bells with them.

"All I want to know," he persisted, "is where this soap came from. If I could get a telephone number or office address, I could work with that."

The woman's jaw dropped. She shook her head. "Weirdo," she muttered under her breath. Then louder, she asked, "How am I supposed to know that? I only work here."

His detective's mind started cranking away again. "If you could check the invoices.... You know, get me an address."

"Either buy that soap or get out, but if I have to look at you for another five minutes, I'm calling the cops."

He smiled to himself. The local police would show up and yell at him. Then they'd run his name through their computer and wonder what had happened to him, not knowing that what had happened to him was the best thing in the world for a cop on the edge of burnout.

Finn fished his wallet out of his pocket and handed the woman a twenty dollar bill. "Keep the change," he said and started out the door with the bar of soap in hand.

The windchimes on the door tinkled and sang as he stepped out into the August heat. He pressed the bar of soap to his nose and inhaled the sweet scent of peppermint. It reminded him of the peppermint candies Robyn used to carry with her. Whenever she worked on a case for too many hours and had to interview a new witness, she wanted fresh breath, but more importantly, the smell of peppermint always seemed to relax her witnesses, made her seem like less of an interrogator and more of a friend. Maybe, just maybe, Robyn was trying to tell him something now.

He studied the bar of soap in his hands with its bird on fire—the Firehawk. There had to be some connection. As many times as he'd shopped in Trish's store since he'd been in Atlanta, he'd never noticed the Saadia soaps before. But he, better than anyone else, knew that when the student is ready, the teacher appears.

He studied the fine script on the back of the wrapper with its short list of ingredients. Then he saw what he'd missed inside the door with the substitute haranguing him. He'd mistaken the script in its entirety for the usual long list of ingredients and preservatives in commercial soaps. This soap wrapper instead launched into a brief interpretation of the benefits of natural products and ended with *Saadia Soap, made with love in Lingering Shade, North Carolina.*

Chapter Two

~Kestrel~

I always celebrated the dark moon. *New* moon, as most people call it. New beginnings. But for me, it was always the time when the Crone aspect of the Goddess Trinity revealed to me her secrets. You might think that I would identify the Crone Goddess with Saadia, given that she was ninety-three years old when she passed on to the Goddess' embrace in the Summerlands. Instead of crone, Saadia was really more mother to me. More even than the woman who gave birth to me, because I knew her so few years and she herself was a wounded child driven to kill. But, just as the Goddess comes to me at full moon, fully ripe with child, She comes to me at dark moon, with silver hair tumbling to Her shoulders and framing Her wrinkled face and blue eyes that look too much like my own.

I stopped seeing the Maiden Goddess in myself the night the girls were born. That was the same night Saadia put the three of us in the back of her car and started the long, slow drive to Lingering Shade where Saadia's husband still owned land from his youth. I never even had a chance to thank the Robyn, red-haired witch who helped protect my babies, but after that night, it was the Mother Goddess I met in my prayers.

Saadia was wonderful to me. She gave to me everything she would have given to a child of her own—love, encouragement, her home, and finally her name. At eighty-six, she sold her house and lands in Greenburg, cashed out her savings, and we started over in a little mountain town where Edgar's relatives and friends were long since dead, and where no one knew us and where we could practice our magick and raise our babies alone. But most of all, we fled to a place where the person who'd killed Grant and Cedric would never find us. I could never thank Saadia enough for the sacrifices she made for me, including her request to be buried in a hidden spot in the mountains where no one would ever find her grave and reveal our secrets.

Life in the mountains with the four of us was sweet, and after a time, I put away my worries of being stalked and slaughtered. Or worse yet, of someone coming after the children. My life with Grant and Cedric had been sweet but that had been long ago and far away. By the time the girls were nine-and-a-half and going into the fourth grade at Lingering Shade Elementary, I was sure the Goddess had granted me sanctuary if not justice.

Until the dark moon in August.

Until *he* came.

Near midnight, while the girls were spending the night with their friend Becca, I drove up to the top of Saadia's mountain. Her mountain because she'd owned so much of the land there that we had plenty of privacy. The town itself was on a small plateau high in the mountains, so the drive wasn't that far. In my black ritual gown with my hair hanging loose at my shoulders, I carefully lit the candles and planted them in a circle, being especially careful not to catch my sleeves or hem on fire.

There in the darkness, with only the stars as witness, I invoked the Crone and asked Her to reveal Her secrets to me. For a moment, I remembered Grant and Cedric and how happy we were when we performed this ritual together. The chant choked in my throat.

"Goddess," I interrupted myself, "will I ever heal?" My fingertips tingled with the power. I touched my necklace, a simple choker made of amber and jet salvaged from a ritual robe one Beltane night.

The circle will be complete came back the answer surely as if the Goddess Herself had stood in front of me and spoke the words. *The circle will be complete* came the answer again, sweet and reassuring, in my head.

But what did that mean? That I would fall in love again? That I would rejoin my beloveds through reincarnation? Or that their murderer might find me yet?

Your fourth will return.

My fourth? There had been four of us before Saadia had died. Did She mean Saadia was coming back? Sometimes messages from the Goddess were cryptic but easily understood later. Perhaps if I had more insight. Perhaps if I'd meditated more, I might have understood earlier.

He will bring you danger, I heard the Goddess say, *and great joy.*

The revelation stunned me, and I foolishly broke the circle and ran without closing the circle and grounding the power. I didn't want to hear what the Goddess had to say. Not about joy. I'd known great joy, and I'd known the great pain that goes with it. I never wanted to be at that crossroads again. What I'd wanted was healing, not fresh wounds. And at the same time, I gave myself a quick mental kick. I'd turned my back on the Goddess and fled.

Ashamed, I glanced back at the circle of candles, but the wind had blown them out.

Chapter Three

~Branwen~

"Come on, will you?" Branwen tugged at her sister's bell-shaped sleeve, but Deirdre just shook her head.

"Mom will be mad. Really mad."

"Only if she catches us. Now come on."

School had started two days ago, and they were supposed to be doing homework. Or, worst case, playing by the little stream behind the house. Certainly not spying on their mother. They knew she made special soaps for health food stores and places on the computer where you could order stuff like that. They'd always known about the soap. Branwen and Deirdre had helped make a few batches, but mostly they helped to gather herbs in the back yard and woods in the summer months. Now that they could read and write pretty good, Mom usually let them fill orders.

That was the most fun, the funnest thing, about Mom's home business—filling the orders. The girls were real careful about how they packaged the soaps. Deirdre arranged the soaps in the boxes and put the packing around them. Branwen taped the box and stuck the label on top. They took turns at the old-timey manual typewriter, pecking out names and addresses, stores across the country. They were a team, the three of them. Branwen, Deirdre, and Mom. All of them working together, whether it was to clean the house, make soaps, or do their math homework. And all three of them playing together, too, whether it was Branwen chasing dragonflies or Deirdre capturing tadpoles, or the three of them dancing under a bright full moon and singing to the Goddess, they were the best team in the whole, wide world.

Sometimes Miss Tracey and her daughter, Becca, who lived in the cabin just down the mountain, would invite the girls to spend the night there or take a trip over the Smoky Mountains into Gatlinburg for the day to visit Becca's daddy. Miss Tracey had been a teacher once, before they fired her for being a witch, and she was trying to talk Mom into letting her homeschool the three kids because Deirdre kept getting into trouble at school.

They didn't like to leave Mom alone for long. She didn't have many friends. Grandma had died a while back and since then, Mom didn't leave the mountain very often except to go into town to pick up supplies. Most everything came and went by the mail or by packaging services, and even then, Miss Tracey often made deliveries herself after she drove the girls to school every day.

People did come up the mountain to see Mom, but not a lot. Sometimes trout fishermen got lost and didn't realize they were trespassing. Occasionally it was some man trying to tell Mom she ought to have her daughters in church every Sunday and how God was this awful old man who makes you burn in this awful place for forever and ever when you die. Mostly people who came up the mountain came to get hypnotized. She helped teach people not to smoke and not to be fat and not to have heart attacks and stuff like that. And sometimes she talked with them about times when they lived a long time ago, when they were other people, to help them figure out how to be better people now.

People had to really want to be hypnotized to come see Mom, she always said. The only decent road to their house went in unpaved looped-de-loops around the mountain and dead-ended on a steep road that went up to their cabin. Mom never advertised that she could hypnotize people, but word got around, especially between Asheville and Knoxville. The woman who'd come to their house half an hour ago must have been a millionaire. Her car was twice as big as Mom's Jeep and she dressed like a movie star, even though she cried a lot before she ever told them why she'd come.

"Well? Are you coming or not?" Branwen stalked toward the footbridge that led over the mountain stream separating their home from the even smaller cabin their mom called an office.

During the summer months, Mom took a lawn chair out into the middle of the shallowest part of the stream, far below the waterfall's thunder on the mountain, and hypnotized her customers right there. But a lot of the tourists, especially the rich ones, weren't comfortable taking off their high heels and sticking their feet in the cool water, so they rested their feet on the rocks above the gurgling stream.

Branwen glanced over her shoulder at her twin. Tiny green leaves rained down between them and swirled onto the the water. "I thought you wanted to do this."

"No. Not really. It was your idea."

"Well, you said it was a good idea."

"I know," Deirdre admitted, "but if we go over that bridge, Mom's gonna see us and we're gonna get caught. Trust me."

Uh-oh. The magic words. Deirdre had this thing for seeing into the future. Not real far into the future, like what they were gonna be when they grew up or how old they were gonna be when they died or anything like that. But she could see little things. Like when a teacher was gonna spring a pop quiz on them. Or when Joe Frank, the school bully in kindergarten, was gonna push somebody down and bloody their nose.

The only problem with something like that was that Deirdre saw things and ran to tell a teacher who arrived just in time to witness whatever was about to happen, so Deirdre got weird looks sometimes from other people. Joe Frank's teacher had called Mom to have a little talk with her about how Deirdre knew Joe Frank was gonna hurt somebody and Mom had totally freaked. Deirdre had seen that coming, too, and had a ready answer for Mom. Joe Frank was always pushing down people and bloodying their noses, so when he started picking on Donny for the third time in five minutes, she knew what was coming. Mom had calmed down about that, but Deirdre had learned an important lesson: don't tell Mom about the "flashes."

Branwen stopped and pretended to swat at a firefly. "You, um, had a flash?" she asked cautiously.

"Uh-huh. Mom saw us walking over the bridge, and she was waiting on us when we got to the other side. We lost all computer games and TV for two whole weeks."

"Two whole weeks? She wouldn't!"

"Well, she will if we go over that bridge."

Branwen planted her hands on her barely-there hips. "Yeah? Well, what do you think we should do then?"

Deirdre circled around her and headed off toward their favorite path, which was twisty and steep. Her long, blonde ponytail swished with every footfall. "We'll cross the stream and go the back way," Deirdre said.

Branwen grinned to herself and ran after her sister, careful to avoid the roots stabbing upward through the twigs and pine needles trodden to a smooth carpet. Huffing and puffing, she caught up with Deirdre at the edge of the stream where it was deepest. Some kind of water bug with long, spidery legs swam slowly across the stillest waters. Smooth, pretty rocks from the size of pebbles all the way up to boulders blocked the stream and jutted out of the deep water just above the waterfall that was maybe twice as tall as Mom. Maybe taller. Not far across the rushing stream was a rock twice the size of their dinner table. The girls had affectionately nicknamed it "the picnic rock" because they sometimes had lunch there against Mom's wishes. It hadn't rained in a few weeks and the stream was a little more than a trickle right now, so getting to the picnic rock or crossing the stream, if they wanted, was a little easier now. When it was really tough was after a couple of thunderstorms and most of the stepping stone rocks were under water except for the very tippy-tops.

Deirdre bounced from stone to stone before climbing up on picnic rock and staring back impatiently. She flicked a couple of daddy longlegs off the rock while she waited. "Watch that flat rock," she warned. "It gets slime on it and you don't realize how slippery it is. You have to step on the—"

"I know what I'm doing. Just be glad I hate you gently."

"Slow down," Deirdre yelled. "You're going to fall in!"

Branwen stopped abruptly on a steep, triangle-shaped rock and studied her precarious feet. Lush green moss grew on one side of the stone. Sometimes Deirdre could be awfully bossy, and she'd say things that really weren't going to happen. Sometimes Deirdre could tell the future for real, but you just never knew when. If she meant to tell the future, she was always right and it almost always got her into trouble. Like with Joe Frank.

She'd done it another time at school back in the first grade when she'd warned a teacher that the chalkboard was going to fall and bop the teacher on the head. The teacher hadn't listened though. She'd been mad at Deirdre for saying things that made their classmates laugh.

She'd been even madder when the chalkboard *did* fall—right on top of her head. The principal had called Mom for a big talk with him and the teacher and Deirdre. The teacher thought Deirdre had done something to the chalkbaord before class to make it fall but Branwen knew for a fact her blonde-haired twin was innocent. The teacher and principal finally gave up on forcing a confession and simply punished her instead with no recess for a month. The twins had both been disturbed by their first brush with injustice but Mom...Mom had cried for days. Something about not understanding how Deirdre had inherited a trait from Branwen's father. After that, Deirdre always phrased her warning in such a way that you couldn't tell whether she knew the future or simply offered good advice.

"I know this stream better than anyone," Deirdre reminded her. "Just follow my steps and you won't get wet."

The worst rock to fall off of was the one Branwen perched on. The part that stuck out of the water was like a long, thin, mountain peak. Branwen always needed both arms out to balance herself as she crossed the stream, but Deirdre always hopped across it like the fish that sometimes jumped out of the swift water.

Both arms out, Branwen patted a tentative right foot on the next stone before pressing down firmly and luring her left foot from safety to its new foothold. Good thing it hadn't rained in a week. If she fell after a big rainstorm, the thundering currents would drag her to the waterfall downstream and fling her over and onto the rocks.

Which was why Mom always insisted they take the hanging bridge downstream on the rare occasions when they were allowed to visit her small cabin of an office on the other side or the two graves over there. Mom wanted privacy for her customers? She got it. The ones afraid to cross could opt to sit in the lounge chair in the stream where it quieted and gurgled instead of roaring.

"Watch your step," Deirdre yelled almost angrily from the picnic rock.

Branwen wasn't worried about the next step. The rock, the one Deirdre had been concerned about, was high on the right side but broad and flat on the left with a wet, slick-looking dip near the center that let the stream trickle through. Deirdre had splashed through the center. Branwen hesitated. The center was wet, inviting disaster. Instead, Branwen touched the outer, dry edge with her left foot and then shifted her weight as she lunged for the rock.

A mistake. She knew it the second her balance eased from one stepping stone to the next. Her foot landed on the dry side of the rock, the side where mold had grown and flourished and dried up in the sun. All that was left of the mold now was a slippery film. Her foot touched it, skidded, skidded, skidded, and—sploosh!—down she went. She grabbed the high end of the rock and went down on one knee in the center of the hard stone, onto the wet place where Deirdre had stepped, where Branwen should have stepped. Only her left leg, up to her knee, got wet.

"You okay?" Deirdre called, her blond curls falling into her eyes as she leaned forward to stretch out a helping hand to her sister. "I told you to follow my footsteps and you wouldn't fall."

Branwen ignored the outstretched hand and climbed onto picnic rock without any help. She muttered something mean under her breath and rubbed her skinned knee. She should have been wearing jeans like Deirdre but a growth spurt had left her with a nothing but home-sewn shorts made from remnants of Mom's latest altar cloth. The sparkly silver pentacles shimmered in the sunlight but offered little protection against scrapes.

It wasn't fair that Deirdre got warnings and she didn't. Maybe this was a bad sign. Maybe spying on Mom and the rich lady was a bad idea after all.

"Hey, why don't we forget about this hypnosis thing," Deirdre suggested. "We can go to the caves instead." An equally forbidden landmark.

Branwen would have been perfectly willing, after dampening her enthusiasm, to forgo Mom's office for the caves, but Deirdre had suggested it and if Branwen agreed, then her sister had won. No matter that they weren't competing for anything, they were sisters and that was reason enough to keep tabs on who got whose way.

"No," Branwen said. "I want to see if Mom's gonna make that fancy lady bark like a dog."

"Aw, Mom won't make her do *that*."

"We'll never know if we don't go." Branwen pranced on ahead over the remaining stepping stones, knowing Deirdre would follow. She always did.

The two tiptoed in silence across the forest trail, careful not to slip on the protruding tree roots and stumble to the ground. Normally they ran and jumped and chased the occasional bunny or paused to watch a deer. Not today. Today they had to be quiet and quick. If they got caught and Mom punished them, she'd pick something really horrible, like not letting them play outside for a week.

The cabin—Mom's office—wasn't nearly as big as their house on the other side of the stream. The largest room was big enough for a straight chair and two recliners. Mom kept the blinds down when she had a customer because the office was darker that way and, according to Mom, helped the customer relax better. Behind that room was a small bathroom. All told, the office wasn't even as big as the twins' bedroom. If they were going to spy on Mom, they had to try it while the weather was still warm because the office wasn't air-conditioned and Mom raised the two windows in the cool summer. Come winter, they'd never be able to hear Mom's secret words.

A few feet from the eastern side of the cabin, Branwen stepped on a twig. It snapped beneath her foot and she froze, certain Mom would come flying out of the cabin, demanding to know what Branwen thought she was doing. Nothing happened though, and Deirdre punched her in the upper arm as a sisterly warning not to let it happen again.

Soft music poured out the open windows. Mom always played a CD of Celtic lullabies to relax her customers and give their—how did she say it?—their "conscious minds something else to do while they explored the subconscious." Branwen knew the songs well enough that she was tempted to hum along.

The girls found a clean, leaf-carpeted spot under the eastern window and crouched, eager to hear a rich lady bark. Mom's voice came through—smoothly, softly—just above the music.

"Okay, Mrs. Walsh. May I call you Helen?...Okay, Helen, now that I've given you my credentials and you've told me a little about yourself and your concerns, let's begin."

Branwen shifted in the sunlight. The August sunshine, warm and inviting, bathed her face. The creek below the waterfall gurgled and soothed. She stretched out her legs in front of her, leaned against the cabin wall, and waited to hear the woman do something foolish. Deirdre glanced at Branwen and mimicked her posture.

"Helen, have you ever been hypnotized before?...Okay, well, there's nothing for you to worry about. It's really not like you see on TV or on stage in comedy clubs. I won't make you stiff as a board so I can balance you between two chairs and stand on your stomach. I won't make you do anything silly, like crow like a rooster. Or bark like a dog."

The two women laughed softly inside the cabin, but Branwen exchanged a nervous glance with her twin. They held their breath and waited to see if they'd been busted.

"In fact," Mom continued, apparently unaware of the spies outside, "I can't *make* you do anything. That's not what hypnosis is about. I can't make you do anything silly. I can't even make someone stop biting their nails or quit smoking. Those are things they have to *want* to do. Now if you *want* to bark like a dog, I'll be happy to make that suggestion to you."

More soft laughter.

"Hypnosis is not about mind control but about freedom from physical constraints. It's about becoming so relaxed that you forget about your body and your mind is free to roam and create and focus on things you haven't thought about in years. Or, in your case, lifetimes."

"I understand," the rich lady replied. "I'm nervous though. I don't want to relive facing a headman's axe or dying in childbirth. I'm not ready for that. Not yet."

"Then this time," Mom said, "we'll look only at happy times in some of your past lives. Okay?"

With one finger, Deirdre poked Branwen in the ribs. "I'm bored," she whispered. "Let's go to the caves."

A tempting suggestion, particularly since Mom didn't plan to make the rich lady bark or anything fun. If Deirdre hadn't suggested it, it would have been a great idea.

"Later," Branwen whispered back and looked away.

"Okay, Helen. Feel free to lean that recliner all the way the back, if you'd like. Are you comfortable?"

Branwen glanced back at Deirdre, who had closed her eyes. Deirdre nodded.

"I want you to close your eyes," Mom said.

Branwen closed her eyes.

"Clear your mind of all your troubles and concentrate on the sound of my voice."

Mom's voice had never seemed so soft and sweet and soothing. Her voice moved up and down, like music, and it seemed more like singing than talking.

"I want you to take a deep, deep breath."

Branwen sucked in a mouthful of air. She heard Deirdre do the same.

"Now hold that breath. Feel the oxygen feeding the cells of your body. Now release the breath.

"Again...breathe...hold...release. And...again. Breathe...hold...release. Feel your body relax...starting with your toes and working up slowly, slowly into the arches of your feet...."

Branwen lost herself first in her mother's voice, then lost track of her toes, her feet, her kneecaps, her thighs, and all the way up until even her eyebrows seemed to fade away. She seemed to float in a place between sleep and waking, like the few twilight minutes in the mornings before her alarm clock clanged her into the ordinary world.

"And now you are at the top of a beautiful wooden staircase."

Yes. Yes, Branwen could see it. Or imagine it. She wasn't sure there was a difference. A spiral staircase in a sparkling castle. Extravagant paintings on the wall, paintings of long-dead ancestors. Shining treasures at the bottom of the staircase.

"Now, I'm going to count backward as you descend that staircase, one step at a time. Slowly, slowly, one step with each count. Twenty...nineteen...."

Branwen thought she stepped down, one foot at a time, pausing at each to feel the solidity of each stair under her feet. She ran her right hand over the smooth railing.

"Twelve...eleven...ten...."

Branwen moved deeper, deeper, further into this floaty dreamworld where everything looked more seen, sounded more heard, felt more touched. Her senses were alive and pulsating in this place.

"Two...one. Now look at the wall in front of you. You see a full-length mirror. Walk to the mirror and see what you are in this incarnation."

Branwen spied the gold-framed mirror on the far side of the room of treasures. She stepped over pirates' chests of coins and jewels and pearl necklaces, spilling out. The figure in the mirror walked closer to her. Branwen didn't understand. She narrowed her eyes at the glass. Where was her image? Where was the big fourth-grader with bright eyes and dark brown hair in a ponytail like a fountain on top of her head?

Then she remembered and smiled.

In the mirror, a blond man in a black robe grinned back at her.

Chapter Four

~ Finn ~

If he had to drive another half-mile, he'd throw up. Actually, he'd probably feel better if he did throw up. Finn wasn't used to winding, curving, slithering, twisting mountain roads. If he took a hairpin curve at any speed over 15 m.p.h., he had to crank the air conditioner up to full blast and direct it at his face. Nausea prickled around his hairline. His ears popped for the umpteenth time.

He had to do this. The detective in him would accept no less than the truth.

Thankfully, the road straightened ahead, though it was still woefully narrow. If two luxury cars met up here, one would have to seek the ditch. Still, North Carolina was prettier than he'd imagined. All the mountains, rocks, Mother Earth. Sun-rays trickled down through the trees where their branches met over the road. The leaves fluttered in the breeze, and the thick veils of sunlight swirled and danced. On one side of the highway a bank of brilliant yellow black-eyed susans, the only thing between the narrow road and an impossibly steep drop-off of trees and grass and something too far away to distinguish. On the opposite side, a stark sheet of rock rose straight up. No room for mistakes.

A small rectangular sign welcomed him to Lingering Shade, North Carolina. Yes, Lingering Shade, home of Saadia Soap. Home also to one Saadia Payne. He'd called in a couple of favors with Harrison back in Greenburg. Harrison had done a little checking in the past week and discovered that an old woman named Saadia Payne had lived in Greenburg up until nine and a half years ago. Then the woman had vanished, leaving her power of attorney with a local obstetrical nurse who promptly emptied the old woman's bank accounts and sold every inch of property Saadia owned. Even her car had been sold. Saadia Payne had left behind nothing but a cemetery plot, half of it already dedicated to her husband, Edgar, who'd died the year before.

And the most damning connection: Robyn's emergency phone number, the one Stuart had reluctantly given him, had belonged to Saadia Payne's residence.

There's something I have to do here for Saadia first.

Robyn's words still echoed in his head. Robyn's murderer had never been found. Neither had the girl, Lucretia-who-wasn't-really-named-Lucretia who'd followed up Robyn's distress call. Too many fingerprints in the clinic to single out Robyn, the girl, or any other intruder.

But Robyn had meant to contact this Saadia between the time Robyn talked to Finn and the time she died. Had she actually contacted the old woman? And why had the old woman deserted town so abruptly? Had she seen something? Or was she somehow involved in Robyn's murder? Robyn had stood an even six feet tall, young and strong. No old woman in her eighties could possibly have dragged Robyn back to her altar or inflicted those wounds on her body.

Finn flinched, remembering the mangled flesh between Robyn's thighs. No, no woman could have done that to another woman. He wasn't sure how a *human being* could have done that to another.

He had to find this Saadia. If he ever found the truth behind Robyn's death, it was Saadia who knew it. She must have fled out of fear. Otherwise, if she had cared for Robyn, she would have attended Robyn's graveside service.

Finn gritted his teeth as he drove through the town of Lingering Shade with its gas station, general store, and little more. With the exception of a dozen reporters and one funeral director, he'd been all alone at Robyn's funeral. He'd made the arrangements himself, purposely choosing not to ask a local chaplain to lead the ceremony but instead asking that attendees simply say a few words over her grave.

But no one came. No one. Not Harrison, still traumatized in his puppy love but too sick with the flu to crawl. Not Stuart, who feared the same fate as Robyn if anyone identified him as a friend of the witch. Not her landlady, who herself had been threatened with burning. Not the cops she'd stood with to protect and serve, the ones who'd later refused to work side by side with a practicing witch. Not the volunteers at the domestic abuse shelter where she'd spent her time and assets. They were too scandalized by the news that she wasn't a Christian. And most disappointingly, no one from her coven bothered to come. Maybe they had good reason.

Still, for the next few months, fresh flowers had graced Robyn's grave. He never knew who placed them there, though he did once catch sight of the Goth girl, with black hair and black fingernails, near the grave. He'd chased her through the cemetery, but the little gazelle had actually outrun him.

On Halloween of that year, the local papers had run a story of the unsolved murder of a local witch named Robyn Porter, and a couple of teenage boys supposedly interested in Satanism had desecrated her grave, getting only as far as unearthing the casket before the cops hauled them off. From what Finn heard on the street, a witch's skull held great magickal power for some sects and Robyn was the only known witch in Greenburg, dead or alive. Her grave was certain to be tampered with again. It was only a matter of time.

On his first visit to her grave in November that year, Finn found an empty hole where Robyn's body had lain. A distant relative had exhumed and moved the body, according to the cemetery manager. He'd checked the graves of Gloria Stokes and the Firehawks, but they remained untouched. Those three victims had a living spouse and parents. No distant, unknown relative could whisk them away.

Finn pulled over at the lone stop sign in Lingering Shade and checked his map. He was running two days late, damn it, thanks to a brief fender bender in Atlanta. The police had arrived on the scene and automatically assumed the guy with earrings and leather was at fault. It took one day to straighten that out and another full day to claim his car from an unscrupulous tow truck company. Thank God, Mercury wasn't in retrograde or no telling how long it would have taken him to reach the mountains.

According to a little detective work of his own, Saadia Payne owned most of the mountain, though little of the area above Lingering Shade was reachable by car. He closed the map and drove on, finding at last a wooden bridge over a creek and then a narrow dirt road that meandered along a mountain stream. He braked and blinked at a pair of mailboxes at the foot of the dirt road: S. P. on the larger one near the entrance and T. Z. on the smaller box next to it.

His car puffed and churned up the first quarter mile of road. When it came to endurance, the vehicle was definitely a lightweight and the mountain roads had taken their toll. Luckily for him, Saadia's residence wasn't far up the mountain. The house was tinier than the dung heap Robyn had rented before her death, except that this place was clean and the garden alive with butterflies and cascades of pink, old-fashioned roses. He steeled himself and climbed out of the car, ignoring the steam that streamed out from under the hood.

Before he could knock, a young woman with a curtain of wheat-colored hair dangling at her shoulders met him at the door. Twenty-something, he'd guess. Cute, too. But her youth reminded him painfully that he himself was pushing forty.

"Hi there!" the woman drawled. Probably Saadia's great granddaughter. She looked a little like Kestrel Firehawk had in those photographs at their mansion. Maybe it was her hair. Maybe it was the ethereal look in her eyes. Maybe she and Kestrel had been related.

"What can I do for you?" she teased, not seeming to mind that he was at least a decade her senior. His looks had held. If anything, his face looked younger since he'd given up the life of a cop on the edge of burn-out and taken up the peaceful life of an artist selling consistently well.

"I'm looking for Saadia Payne. This is her home, isn't it?"

"I'm afraid you're mistaken."

A girl of maybe ten or twelve joined her on the doorstep. Her daughter, no doubt. Same bright hair and green eyes. They would have made perfect models for mommy-daughter dresses.

"Saadia lives just up the mountain from us," she continued. She gestured at the dirt road that wound up the hill and reappeared a level higher than the woman's house and vanished high and away. "I'm Tracey Zachary."

T. Z.

"Oh. The, um, mailbox," he mumbled, feeling stupid.

"No problem. Saadia's mail box was there first and there wasn't room for a box between hers and the road when I moved here. Doesn't really matter to us, but it seems to confuse everyone else."

She smiled and Finn felt he'd found a kindred spirit. A good-hearted person whose charity beamed through her eyes.

"It's a long way by foot," she said, still smiling.

"I have a car." He gestured over his shoulder, then followed her dubious gaze. Smoke still boiled from underneath the hood. "I'll have to wait for it to cool, I suppose."

"I'll give you a lift, if you'd like." The woman stroked her daughter's long hair. "You can leave your car here for now."

"Y-you'd do that for me?" His look must have been incredulous because she merely laughed.

"Only two kinds of people come up here looking for Saadia. And you don't look like a Baptist preacher."

No, he guessed he didn't. Not in all-black, a dragon on his T-shirt, and a Celtic knot of pewter hanging from his neck. "What's the other kind?"

Her smile turned to a grin. "Your kind." She breezed toward a four-wheel drive truck, the quiet little girl in tow with an overnight bag nearly dragging the ground.

"You sure it's no trouble?" He trailed along after her and slid into the front seat, the child and bag between them. He kept his window down so he could breathe the cool summer air the mountains had to offer. The breezes smelled slightly of rotting leaves and fresh flowers.

"No, no trouble at all. I have a good feeling about you. I hope you don't think this unethical of me, but I can read your aura." She winked. "Besides, I was just on my way to take Becca to her grandmother's for the night." Then she lowered her voice. "Big plans tonight."

"Boyfriend?" It didn't hurt to ask. Or to make small talk. She wore a ring on every finger but none of them looked like wedding bands. Amber, pewter snakes, Celtic knots, braided rings, spirals, moonstone—all typical witchy wear. He met plenty of pagan women, but most tended to be either very young and totally enamored of movie magic and the power and sex the glamorized Craft could provide, or they were married and just finding their way home to a quiet and raging spirituality that would take time to explore. For the women in between, they usually were divorced with one or two kids and a low-paying job or home business that kept them close to both Mother Earth and their children but seldom near any real material gain. From what he'd seen so far, Tracey fit that category to a T.

"A boyfriend? Me?" She laughed. "No, full moon," she added as if she knew he'd understand.

Full moon. Of course. He'd been so caught up in finding Saadia that he'd forgotten the moon. Still, in spite of the subtle hints, Tracey wasn't overtly a witch. Pagans learned early not to be too obvious. A comment regarding the moon could easily be mistaken as an intention of romance or an astronomical hobby. Spirals and Celtic knots were not uncommon among college kids and people with an affinity for Ireland. It was now up to him to drop the hint that he'd be accepting if he knew she was pagan.

"Do you gaze at the moon alone? Or with others?"

She urged the truck uphill. "Definitely alone. That's my time to commune."

She didn't say what or whom she planned to commune with. God? The Goddess? Nature? Another hint. But he understood. She was a solitary, as if there ever is such a thing when Deity is involved. But she worshipped alone instead of with a coven.

He understood. He'd grown up in a Baptist church with five hundred people in the congregation every Sunday. Since converting to Wicca, he'd found religion to be an intensely personal matter. So personal, in fact, that he refused to answer any paperwork that asked his religious preference. He could easily write in Wicca or Pagan or Neo-pagan or Celtic or Earth Religion or something similar and all would be accurate for his spirituality, and yet, categorizing his relationship with Deity seemed...small and offensive.

Tracey steered around a curve, and the truck climbed higher. Out the window, Finn could see Tracey and Becca's home on the slope below.

"How can you see the moon through all the trees?" he asked. Sunshine rarely touched the forest floor.

"They're all covenants with Mother Earth. Just like church steeples are for Christians. Trees, moon, stars, birds, streams. She is all around me, not just in the sky."

He nodded. "I know, but I love the moon. Especially that tiniest crescent when she's new and the cycle of rebirth starts all over."

Tracey twirled the steering wheel again and the truck wove up the mountainside. They were safe now, both of them. *A little bit of confession is good for finding other souls.*

"If you need meditation time tonight, there's a clearing up near the top of the mountain. It's on top of some caves so you'll find the sound vibrates under you if you get too loud."

He grinned at her over her daughter's head. Loud, heart-felt rituals. How rare to find the space. No wonder she left the child with a grandparent.

"Anyone else use that sacred space?" he fished.

"Only Saadia. She's been a wonderful teacher and high priestess to me. And a great friend. I met her through her company when I was down and out, and she took me in and gave me a place to live. But we both tend to keep to ourselves when it gets down to brass tacks." Brass tacks being rituals and spell-work. "But it's a big mountain and there's room up there if you'd like to spend some time alone with the moon."

Finn nodded as the dirt road forked into two small paths from a circle just big enough to turn around in. Someone had parked a white Jeep under a carport in the edge of the forest. They were literally in the middle of nowhere, with uneven light falling on trees and everything green.

195

"Hmmm, I may do that," he told her. "But how will I know you're up there? I don't want to walk up on you and scare the living daylights out of you."

She stopped her truck and waited, he supposed, for him to get out. "I like drumming. Very soothing, hypnotic, you know?"

He nodded again. He knew quite well. Catholics use rosaries to count their prayers as they talk to God. Finn didn't do that much talking to the God or Goddess, but he spent a lot of time listening, especially when he was drumming.

"Yeah," Tracey continued, "sometimes when I have a hard day, I go sit up on the mountaintop and drum, and then, from about sunset until night when the first stars come out, I hear Saadia and her two daughters drumming. And it's like we're putting on this concert with the whole bowl of heaven above us as spectators and—"

Saadia's daughters? Somehow he'd managed to overlook that little tidbit of information when he'd researched Saadia Payne of Greenburg. He could well imagine three crones spending their evenings drumming on the mountain instead of sitting at bingo parlors or wasting away gossiping. He wasn't surprised to hear that Saadia was a witch, but a witch with two daughters? Maybe one of them could tell him about the night Robyn died. Or whatever had happened to Kestrel Firehawk.

"Saadia's already had two clients this morning. She's probably relaxing with her feet in the stream. Take the path to the left.. You'll find her easily enough. She'll bring you back to your vehicle at my house when she's done with you."

"What if she's not there?"

"If you don't see her at the stream, there's a gong at the base of the foot bridge."

"A gong?" He stared out into the forest and frowned.

"Long ago, when the priestesses of the Old Ways lived on the Isle of Avalon, if you wanted entry, you would have to sound the gong hanging from an apple tree on the banks of the water, and they would send a boatman across to get you."

"And how do you know that?"

Tracey blinked at him as though he were stupid. "Past life regression, of course. Anyway, it works quite well."

"What about the other path?" He pointed at the fork in the road. "Where does that lead?"

"That," she said with a smile, "leads to Saadia's house. But don't worry. You shouldn't have any need to go there."

They said their good-byes quickly. Finn slipped out of the truck and then watched as the vehicle drove slowly back in the direction it had come and then out of sight on the road into Lingering Shade.

He stood at the fork in the path and wondered what Tracey had meant about him not having a reason to go to Saadia's house. He felt a natural tug in that direction as if it were forbidden and therefore more desirable. He couldn't explain the terrible yearning pressing against his lungs. His life had been a series of crossroads and forked paths. Too often he'd made the wrong choice. Like the night he'd turned away from Robyn when she'd confessed her faith to him. Or that fatal night when she'd called for help and he'd gone to the wrong place, thinking he was helping her. If only he'd been wiser, smarter, faster, more patient, more anything than he was, he might have made it in time to save Robyn before that monster brutalized her and left her to die in agony and flames like her predecessors in the Craft. Today, however, he would take the road already chosen for him.

He crunched through the forest's stillness, in and out of swirls of sunlight descending through the leafy canopy. His footfalls seemed loud to his own ears as if he were all alone in the world and all of Nature listened and watched. A brown rabbit jumped a few feet in front of him, startling him, and it scurried away, quickly blending in with the ground cover and vanishing into plain sight. He stopped, as still as the unseen rabbit, and listened. The distant roar of a waterfall. The gurgling of a stream.

Like one of those Magic Eye puzzles, an image formed a few feet in front of him. A stag. A symbol of protection and new adventure. But was he the protected or the protector? Finn held his breath and waited, remembering to be patient and enjoy the beauty of the moment. After what seemed a long while, the deer looked him over and gracefully moved away. A second later, the stag was again invisible in the mountain foliage.

A visit from the God.

Finn exhaled and walked lightly down the path. The correct path. Maybe to another crossroads, yes, but still down the right path. He knew it now. He'd been asking for signs all morning and, as always, God and Goddess delivered.

A single beam of sunlight pierced the forest canopy and struck the metal disc suspended from a low-hanging oak limb by a wide, shallow stream. The light flashed and beckoned. The bridge was there as Tracey had described it, except more rustic with rope railings and plank flooring a good six feet above water that twisted and turned white when it touched the huge gray stones jutting out of the depths. The banks of the stream were still wet from a recent shower. His hands itched to lift the mallet dangling from the limb and sound the gong.

Except that, just upstream, someone relaxed on a lawn chair in the middle of the stream. A woman. A woman wearing a sun hat. A second lawn chair, empty, perched in the water beside her. A dozen or more butterflies—big yellow and small blue ones—fluttered in circles around her. Saadia?

No, too young. Her bare legs stretched out onto a footstool of a stone. Firm, pale legs not splotched by the purple of varicose veins. One foot tapped as if she listened to some imaginary music. She dipped the other foot into the stream and splashed water upward. Clearly, she was content amid her surroundings.

The crush against his chest ached. He'd never seen this woman before and yet there was something about her that pulled him forward, like the magnet of her soul drawing him in. He couldn't even see her face, but still the current of want and familiarity ran deep to the bone. The longing was more than he could bear. He trudged forward, pausing only to yawn and clear his ears from that god-awful popping.

Finn took a deep breath and cleared his throat. "Excuse me. Saadia Payne?"

"Join me," she said, her voice light, airy, young. She patted the seat of the chair beside her.

"I'm sorry." He'd made a mistake. He'd come looking for a woman in her nineties. He'd found...who? Her barefoot granddaughter in a red halter top and cut-offs? Was she really that sexy or was it his imagination? He was sure he felt the pull of this woman's soul. Maybe that's why Tracey had warned him that Saadia's house wasn't meant for him.

He cleared his throat again. "I'm here to see Saadia Payne," he said. He frowned at the string of amber and jet at her throat. It reminded him of the stones he'd found at the Firehawks' altar. "Could you tell me where to find Ms. Payne?"

The woman twisted in her chair to look up at him as she swept her straw hat back from her face. Long dark curls fell to her shoulders. A few strands of silver shimmered in the sunlight. She smiled reassuringly at him and extended her hand. "You've found her. I'm Saadia."

He stared at the woman. She was *not* Saadia Payne. Kestrel Firehawk? It had to be. Older, yes, but not so changed by the seasons that he didn't recognize her. A lifetime ago, he'd stood in the Firehawk mansion and admired the blonde-haired beauty—*dyed blonde*—in a wedding photo with her husband, Grant. He'd admired the same beauty in a picture with Cedric Firehawk.

Oh, the ache inside! There was something about Kestrel Firehawk that he hadn't seen in those long-ago photographs. Something that could only be felt in person. And only close enough to sense the soul. There was something about her that pulled him inward, and the sheer want to be in her presence was greater than any emotion he'd ever had. Ever.

How could this be? He'd been told by an eyewitness, now dead, that she'd murdered two men in cold blood. He'd fretted over whether she had survived the crime as a victim or as a killer. And now, as he stood over her, she sat calmly looking up at him as if nothing had ever happened.

Answers. Damn it, he wanted answers. To more questions than he knew how to ask.

"Are you okay?" She dropped her hand to her side. Genuine concern crossed her brow. "You look like you've seen a ghost."

He blinked, then remembered to close his mouth. "You're...." *Easy. Easy. She might run—again.* "You're not what I expected."

She laughed, soft and gilded. As if she'd never had a trouble in the world. Never lost anyone she loved. She was young and beautiful and eternal. Only the small crinkles at the corners of her eyes when she laughed reminded him that she was now in her mid thirties.

"I'm never what anyone expects. Half the time, people who come to me for hypnosis expect to find a gypsy with a bandana and huge gold earrings."

"And the other half?"

"An old woman with blue hair and gnarled hands." She patted the chair beside her yet again. "Please. Have a seat. This won't hurt, I promise."

He frowned down at his boots. They weren't meant for hiking or for hopping from one slippery stone to another. They certainly weren't meant for getting wet, but his balance was good. Instead of toeing them off and leaving them on the leafy bank, he picked his way carefully across the large stones and then sat gingerly on the lawn chair. It leaned to the side a little too much, so he shifted the chair over a few inches. Trying not to betray his unease, he leaned back and braced his feet on the nearest stone.

"Ah. I should have suspected."

He jerked his head up. Did she know he was the detective who'd combed through her home, looking for clues either of her whereabouts or her motive as a murderess? He'd held her fine silky underthings in his hands in hopes of finding the murder weapon hidden away. He'd perused what he'd thought then was a diary strange poetry and astrological phenomena but he'd since come to understand that it was her book of shadows, the journal of the magick she and her lovers performed.

She must have noticed the blush of his cheeks. "I just meant that I should have suspected you were an earth person."

"Earth person?"

"I can tell a lot about a person by the way they sit when they come to me." She scooped up a handful of water and let it trickle through her fingers. "Water people sit with their feet in the stream. That's what relaxes them most." She raised her hand to the light breeze at their backs. "Air people tend to let at least one foot swing." She pointed at the sunshine sifting down to the spot between them. "Fire people stay in the sun, don't move the chair. You, you're earth."

"Process of elimination?"

"That and the fact that earth people kick their feet up on that rock, first thing. Usually barefoot if they don't think they're taking liberties with social etiquette."

He nodded and stared down at his booted feet against the chunk of mica. He slid the boots off and laid them atop the rock. He wiggled his toes without thinking. Made sense. He'd always had a fascination for crystals and plants, sculpture and sand. Still, that wasn't why he was here. "You always analyze your, um, guests in the middle of a mountain stream?"

"Only when they don't have appointments. Who recommended me?" She squinted as if trying to figure him out. "Gwynhywfar at the candle shop in Asheville?"

He took a deep breath and concentrated on playing it cool—which he'd be better able to do if her presence didn't have such a strong effect on his second chakra. He was no longer a cop who could lead her on with silly games, convince her to spill her guts, and then arrest her on the spot. All he could hope for now was the truth about what had happened to the Firehawks, to Gloria Stokes, and most especially, to Robyn.

"I found out about you by accident," he admitted. "Health food store down in Savannah."

"You're kidding." She didn't sound thrilled. If anything, she sounded upset. "That far, huh?"

He shrugged it off. "Good marketing."

"I don't market my skills," she said with a sigh, settling back into her own chair. "People just show up. Like you. And I tell them what they need to know."

"What do you think I want to hear?"

"What you want to hear doesn't matter. Only what you need to hear. So why did you want to be hypnotized?" She eyed him from head to bare toes. "Hmmm, you're not here for weight loss. I don't smell smoke on your clothes or in your hair, so I'd guess you're not here to kick that habit. You do seem a little tense. Hmmm, you're looking for stress reduction? That I can help with."

"Actually, I'm looking for something else—"

"Your past?"

"In a manner of speaking." Sometimes his years in police work seemed a lifetime ago.

"Have you been hypnotized before?" she asked, reaching to take his hand.

She rubbed her palm over his hand. Her skin was warm, inviting, vibrating to his touch. He felt her energy calling to him. He shivered but blamed it on the mid-sixty temperatures so high in the mountains.

"No, I've never been under hypnosis. I've thought about it for years, but never had the opportunity." Which was true. He'd met the occasional hypnotist at pagan festivals but he'd never succumbed to the gentle urgings to give himself over to soft-spoken words of guidance.

She turned his hand over and studied the lines on his palm. With one fingertip she traced each line. He closed his eyes and took a deep breath, willing his body not to respond to her and failing. He'd studied this woman, interviewed her neighbors and in-laws, researched her beliefs—everything and anything in an attempt to find the Firehawks' killer. Robyn's killer.

And yet, she'd been so reclusive that no living soul back in Greenburg really knew who she was or what made her hurt or laugh. Yet, looking at her now, he knew she hadn't killed Robyn. Or her lovers. Husbands. Her body was a little larger now than ten years ago, but no matter. She was simply too petite to have had the physical strength necessary to commit any of the four murders. And he couldn't imagine her participating in Robyn's torture. But she knew something. She had to know something.

"Shhh, relax," Kestrel Firehawk whispered above the gurgle of water. She pulled him under her words and laid him down.

A flash of memory jolted through him. Only a split second but he saw enough. Somewhere with hills of green and mud. Ireland? Some place old. Maybe 1500's. At least, that's the way it *felt*. He knew little or nothing of Irish history.

He stood at the rear of a small mob of villagers. He sensed he knew them. Neighbors, friends, a wife at his side. All angry and jubilant at the same instant. He sensed a terrible sadness and impotence. His wife, a small woman with stringy, brown hair, clutched at his hand. She was smiling, happy. He'd never seen her so happy, not even on their wedding day.

Gloria?

The center of everyone's attention was a huge, newly built scaffold. The local priest stood, waiting, anxious, at the foot of the raw plank steps. A bigger man in dark robes and a large crucifix dangling from his waist emerged from the crowd, dragging a woman by the arm. Dirty red hair spilled down her shoulders and into her eyes. Bruises marred her wrists where coarse ropes bound her hands. The man reached the scaffold and gave her a rough shove up the steps. She stumbled and fell, striking her head against the scaffold and dazing her for a moment.

The old priest bent to help her, but one scalding glare from the other man—the witch-hunter—and the priest quickly withdrew. Damn him for that! The woman had twice saved the life of the priest, once with bread mold that healed an infection on his foot and again with an herb that rinsed poison from his flesh. Yet now the priest, like others in the crowd, watched helplessly as the only healer for miles was dragged up the steps and then a noose of coarse rope looped around her neck.

Head held high, the woman stared into the crowd through dirty strands of red hair, once beautiful and flowing in the night winds. She couldn't have bowed her head if she'd wanted to. The witch-hunter had fixed a spiked choker around her neck to keep her jaw closed or else pierce her throat. It kept the witch from cursing the village, the witch-hunter had explained. And from begging for that wonderful Christian trait known as mercy.

Her face was dirty, bruised. Like many women accused and convicted at trials where they were not allowed to speak in their own defense, the woman had pleaded her belly, but unlike many women who claimed pregnancy to buy an extra thirty days of life, this woman had indeed been with child at her trial. They'd thrown her into a dark, dank prison where she'd taken a chill, despite the blankets the old priest had slipped her, and the baby—Finn's baby—had died inside her, and with it, any chance of a reprieve.

A boy near the front of the mob threw a rock, hitting her hard in the chest. Already her forehead bled where she'd struck the scaffold. Her bright eyes searched the crowd while the seemingly soul-less eyes of the witch-hunter condemned her.

"Witch, witch, witch," the crowd cried in unison. Each one who bore witness against her stood to inherit her lands and properties after the execution.

"Witch, witch, witch," chanted children barely old enough to talk but present for the spectacle.

"Witch, witch, witch," shrieked his wife gleefully. She'd been one of the woman's accusers. She and other women of the village who feared their husbands fancied the red-haired beauty over them. And in his wife's case, though no other, the rumor was true.

He'd loved Fiona. That was her name, he realized. Fiona the Healer. Fiona the Wise. And later, Fiona the Witch. He'd begged her to go away with him, start a new life as his wife in a distant village. But she'd refused to leave the village without a healer. A plague had wiped out the old wise women of the village, and she, their young apprentice, was the only woman left who knew the healing arts. So he'd stayed, not for his scold of a wife, but for the daily hope of catching a glimpse of *her*.

She should have left with him.

In that glimpse through time, Finn knew the future. The witch-hunter would march triumphantly from their village on his way to the next where he would find many more witches to hang. The priest's body would later be found on the rocks below a cliff, allegedly pushed to his death by a demon Fiona the Witch had conjured at her execution to bring misery to her tormentors. Young women of the village would suffer and die in childbirth and old men would waste away in the foodless, bitter winter. Within another year, a plague would visit the town and without a healer, few of them would survive. His own wife would loll feverish in bed, shrieking for Fiona to come to give her some healing herb and forgetting she'd killed her only salvation. The few survivors would flee elsewhere, but he...he would simply go mad and roam the Irish countryside.

But in that moment when the witch-hunter kicked the block from under Fiona's feet, in that moment before she dangled—jerking, dancing, choking, eyes rolling, rope slowly...slowly...slowly strangling her to death—in that moment before the crowd cheered, in that moment Fiona's searching eyes found him at the back of the mob. Their gazes locked, and she started to smile, her only way to let him know she knew he was there.

That they would be together again.

And he knew—*knew*—Fiona was Kestral Firehawk.

Cool water hit him hard in the face.

Chapter Five

~Kestrel~

I'd never seen anything like it. I'd traced his lifeline and he'd jerked away, toppling his chair and falling face-first into the stream and knocking his boots in after him as he tried to grab the rock. He flailed and splashed, finally finding his way to his feet, knee-deep in water. He blinked rapidly, his eyelashes wet and clumping together. With one sleeve, he wiped the water from his face and stared wild-eyed at me.

I stood, too, careful not to step on the sharp, slippery stones beneath the water's surface. "Are you okay?"

"Yeah. Yeah," he sputtered, still blinking away rivulets of water that seeped from his blond and gray hair hair. Cheeks burning, he fished his boots out of the water.

I didn't get many men in this neck of the woods. Men, even pagan men, don't seek out hypno-therapists easily. The frightening thing was that he'd come all the way from Savannah, and if people in Savannah had heard about me, how long before word spread to Greenburg? At least they knew me as Saadia and not as Kestrel the Murderess or Kestrel the Missing Murder Victim. I never sought out customers but never turned them away, figuring any who came to me came with the blessing of the Goddess. They all came to me for a reason. Who was I to question the need? I was merely a tool of the Divine.

On the other hand, I would have been just as happy alone and unheard of. That was something I felt on a soul level, something that had pervaded my life. Stay quiet, stay out of the way, stay alive. I'd learned that from my mother. Yet I'd been reclusive with Grant and Cedric and the outcome hadn't been kind.

"Come on back to the house," I urged my latest visitor. "We'll get you out of those wet clothes and toss them in my dryer before you freeze to death. If you don't mind a sandwich for lunch, I have something you can wear while we wait on the laundry." I wouldn't tell him yet that the "something" was a couple of one-size-fits-all ritual robes that would be a little short on him.

He hesitated, then collected his boots and slid them over his wet feet. Without a word, he trudged after me through a wooded path. His damp boots squeaked, but we both ignored them. I didn't normally invite my clients back to my home, but they didn't usually take a dip in the drink, either. When clients had appointments and paid in advance by credit card over the telephone, I directed them to the privacy of my office on the secluded other side of the stream, but when they showed up out of the blue, I usually conducted their sessions in the middle of the stream where I so often went to meditate. If there were problems—and I'd never had a problem—I could scramble to the bank and hammer a warning on the gong. The twins were safe at home and would hear the gong and call 911. There, too, was Tracey and her daughter just down the mountainside and readily a source of help if help were needed. And, of course, there were weapons of air—swords and bows—hanging on the walls of my office.

He was a good-looking man, this newest visitor squishing and squeaking in his boots beside me. Late thirties, I'd guess. Maybe early forties, but fit and firm and eyes that were ageless, timeless, had seen enough pain of their own. Blond-gray hair to his shoulders. Small rings in each earlobe. Black jeans and a black T-shirt emblazoned with a Celtic dragon of teal, yellow, and ruby. The only thing that gave away his age was the deep smile lines that cut into his cheeks, even though I sensed that he seldom laughed. No, another thing polished his presence. The confidence that comes with age and wisdom.

"Don't you worry," I assured him, suddenly unsure of my talent for small talk. "It's not far."

A rabbit leapt from the path in front of us. The small animal spooked me, which rarely happened. Still barefoot, I chose my footing carefully, using the tree trunks to climb and pull myself up the mountain. My companion, unfamiliar with the terrain, struggled to keep up. His boots were slippery and afforded him little traction.

"Wait up," he said from behind me as he ducked under the trunk of a half-fallen, wild magnolia. He skirted a pile of moss and fern shrouded rocks.

I heard but didn't slow down. I was too busy smiling to myself at the thought of him in a flowing black robe. Years had passed since I'd seen a man in a ritual robe, especially one I'd made. And that made me both smile and sniff back tears.

"Wait up, Kestrel."

Kestrel. Oh, Goddess, he'd called me Kestrel. He knew who I was. *He knew!*

I whirled on him. "What did you call me?" He started to answer but I cut him off. "Who are you?"

He stared blankly at me. Gradually, realization dawned in his eyes, and his expression hardened. Self-defense. "A seeker of the truth," he said at last.

"Then here's the truth: you're not welcome on my land. Leave. Now!"

Oh, Goddess, what was I going to do? I'd disappeared the night Grant and Cedric had died and disappeared for good the night the girls had been born. I'd taken Saadia's name and identity just as Saadia had wanted. No one had uttered the name of Kestrel Firehawk in my presence in years, and that had been Saadia herself and the members of the Coven of the Jeweled Dragon before they'd all decided it would be safest to refrain from further contact with their sisters in North Carolina. If this man knew my true identity, he knew my past, and while I didn't see murder in his aura, I did see danger.

"I'm not leaving without answers." He wasn't angry or threatening. Just...adamant.

I backed up, looking downhill at him as he looked up at me with earnest eyes. He wouldn't hurt me. Not intentionally. I knew it. "I don't have any answers," I said. "I've learned to live with my questions."

"*I* haven't."

"What do you want from me?"

"I told you, answers."

He was strong. His aura pulsated. I could feel the emotions in the finer hues. Frustration. Longing. Confusion. Hatred. Were the feelings current or from a distant past?

My throat tightened. "And I told you, I don't have answers."

His eyes narrowed at me. He took a single step uphill, bringing his face inches from mine. "At least try."

I sighed. If I talked to him, maybe he'd go away and leave me alone, forget he'd found me. I sensed a goodness in him, a willingness to fight, to protect. A warrior at heart, though impotent until I gave him the weapons he needed. How bad could it be? Questions about why I used Saadia's identity? Easy. To stay alive. That much should be obvious to him.

There was one more thing I sensed but I refused to think about it. A flash of past or future, I didn't know. His hands, touching me.

"What do you want to know?"

He took his time, or at least, it seemed that way. "Where's the real Saadia Payne?"

Without thinking, I glanced uphill toward a clearing where more than one grave lay, then back at the man. My throat closed with the memory of the old woman's loving hands. "She's...gone."

"Dead?"

"To this world." I noted the brief flicker of worry in his eyes and added, "Congestive heart failure. She spent a week in the hospital getting well enough to come home and die a month later." Tears stung my eyes. I blinked them away. For everything I knew about the Great Circle of Life and about Death and Rebirth, sometimes I really missed Saadia.

"Oh. Sorry. What was she to you?"

"She wasn't—" No, that wasn't true. Saadia hadn't been nothing to me. "She was my mother."

The man shook his head. "I don't buy it. Not at her age. Not at your age. Besides," he said, lowering his voice gently, "I know for a fact that your mother committed suicide shortly after killing your father."

His words sliced through me. How *dare* he? I lost my balance and fell backward, catching the trunk of a scrawny oak between my shoulder blades. "How did you know that?" I hissed.

"You didn't answer my question. Who was Saadia to you?"

"She was my adopted mother. Maybe not in any court of law, but to me, she was my mother."

He nodded, seeming to accept her explanation. "What about Gloria Stokes? Did you know her?"

Gloria Stokes. That goddamned little bitch. I hadn't thought of her in years. I'd tried so hard to cull the negatives from my life, the awful memories. But Gloria Stokes had interrupted our protection and harmony magick and had brought disaster to my family. It didn't matter that the papers said she'd died the next night—on *our* altar of all places! That stupid little flirt had been the catalyst.

"I can tell by the look on your face that you recognize the name." The man backed off a few inches, giving me precious breathing space.

"Yeah, I knew who she was. She made work a living hell for my husband. Stalked him. She harassed him. Harassed *us.*"

The man took a deep breath and paused as if to decide whether to say something. He nodded to himself. "She told me you killed your husband. Both of them."

"She what? She's a liar. Was a liar. To the core." But if Gloria Stokes had said that, she could only have lied about it within twenty-four hours of....

"I know."

"What?"

"I know she lied. What I want to know is why she fingered you as the murderer."

I shrugged. I had no idea. "Maybe she was mad because my husband chose me over her."

"Or because you had two husbands and she was bored with her one?"

"I don't know. I met her only twice. Once at a cocktail party where she wouldn't keep her hands off my husband. And once at my house—while she was trespassing."

"Do you know of anyone who'd want to kill her?"

"Yeah. Grant and Cedric, my husbands. And me."

He raised one eyebrow and leaned against a nearby pine. "And? Did you kill her?"

I shook her head. "Violence is in my past, but it's not in my nature."

"Do you have any alibis?"

What was he? A detective? "Yeah. About twelve, not including Saadia's husband. Several of them are dead now. Saadia, Edgar, Robyn."

He blanched. "Robyn?"

"Yeah. Robyn Porter. Though we usually called her by her Craft name."

"Robyn was in Saadia's coven? That would make sense." He stared off into the distance, clearly working through the information. His eyes watered. "You...you knew Robyn well?"

Obviously he did. "Not well enough. I was pretty much a basket case back then. She took me out one Thursday night for Moroccan food and somebody tailgated us back to her place. Took me years to figure that out. That was the only time I left Saadia's. With Robyn. She figured I was safe with her because she was a cop."

Silent tears trickled down his cheeks. He tried to speak but couldn't. I wanted to reach out and touch him, heal him, but I held back. This was a kind of healing that only he could do and, like all open wounds, it could heal only from the inside out.

"Robyn died saving my life," I said when a long time had passed. "She bought me time while Saadia and I took off with the babies."

"Wh-what babies?"

"The night Robyn died, I delivered twin girls. Nine years and seven months ago."

"Nine years, seven months, and four days."

Whew. Robyn hadn't mentioned anyone special in her life, but this man must have been. Then again, Robyn hadn't talked much about herself.

"Kestrel, I have to know. Do you know who killed Robyn?"

"No." I couldn't bear the look of disappointment on his face. "But that night, just before Saadia and the girls and I left town, Robyn told Saadia who it was. When we talked about it later, Saadia couldn't remember the name. She was old, you know."

"She couldn't remember anything? At all?" He didn't believe me.

"Once she said she thought Robyn had said 'Reverend.' She wasn't sure. She was hard of hearing and her hearing aids didn't work very well in her last years. And sometimes, when she wanted to disconnect from the world, she simply turned them off."

"Reverend Jones?" His voice rose. "Did she say it was Reverend Jones?"

"I can't be sure." Reverend Jones? Wasn't that the pastor I'd told to call the police that Beltane night? The one with the umbrella in the rainstorm?

He sank his hands into his pockets. "Reverend Jones couldn't have killed Robyn."

"What makes you so sure?"

"Jones was sitting at my desk when Robyn was assaulted. Are you sure you can't give me some clues here?"

I shrugged. "I don't know."

"One more question and then I'll leave."

"Um, okay." I wrapped a strand my hair behind my ear and tentatively looked up. This man hurt the same way I hurt— with all the heart.

"I need to know what really happened the night your husbands were killed. How is it you're alive and they're not?"

So much for peeling away the scars from my wounds carefully. How many times had I asked myself the same question? How could someone as wonderful and full of fire as Grant die such a terrible and early death? How could someone as dear and soothing as Cedric die so violently, so young? Why them and not me? I was the one who hung to myself, sharing my heart with no one but the two men I loved. I wasn't some terrific, outgoing person who made a difference in the life of everyone I met.

"Who *are* you?" I demanded through clenched teeth.

"You can call me Finn."

Robyn's warnings echoed in my head. *If my partner, Finn, ever comes looking for you, you get the hell away from him as fast as you can.*

"No," I murmured. I backed up, feeling my way along the tree trunk for support. I had to get the girls and get away from him before it was too late. Finn had been Robyn's partner, the detective she'd described as half lost puppy and half pitbull. If he was onto me, he wouldn't stop until he'd dragged me out into the open, back to his precinct in Greenburg, back to within a killer's sites.

I twisted to flee, but he seized my wrist. Confusion glazed his eyes. "Where are you going?"

"Get away from me!" I shoved back and shoved hard. He grabbed my shoulders and held on. Desperate, I brought my leg up between his body and mine, and with my barefoot, I shoved him in the chest with all my energy. He let go and tumbled downhill, yelping in pain. I turned and ran for the house.

"Branwen! Deirdre!" I yelled before I reached the front door of the house. I fumbled with the doorknob. It slipped in my sweaty palms. I pushed into the house, snatched up the Jeep's keys, and shouted again for the girls. No time to waste. We had to get out of there before Finn made his way another fifty feet up the mountain and hauled the three of us away.

"Girls!" I shrieked. I streaked through the house, but no sign of them. Had Finn found them already? *Oh, Goddess, if anything happens to my precious daughters....*

I heard giggles through the open window and raced back outside. My feet slid on the porch. I skidded over the edge and to the leaf-ridden ground, keys flying into the underbrush. To my far right, Finn came huffing and puffing up the mountain, dragging his left leg behind him. To my far left, I spotted the girls, dancing and playing, wearing just their pink cotton panties. I scurried after the keys, finding them half-buried in a mound of black-eyed susans. I grabbed the keys and then stumbled toward the girls. I could hear Finn panting behind me.

The girls looked up from the their play, their laughter dying as they saw me fleeing from a stranger. Their eyes widened. They froze. Both of them had stripped down to their underwear. They still had the bodies of children, though the breast buds were starting to bloom. They were flawless and beautiful, the best things I'd ever made. One with unruly blonde hair like Grant's and the other a silky brunette like Cedric had been. They'd scattered an odd assortment of pans on the picnic table. Paint or ink or berry juices, I couldn't tell. And paint brushes.

They'd painted each other with anklets of Celtic knots and Druid spirals. Branwen's upper arm sported an ink bracelet of blue loops and links. But on their chests, just above their hearts, they'd painted an all-too-familiar tattoo: a triskele like the one above my own heart, like the ones Grant and Cedric had worn.

The world went gray around me, and I was vaguely aware I'd fallen to my knees.

Chapter Six

~ Finn ~

Finn sat on the edge of the porch and rubbed his knee. He could hear Kestrel inside the house, crying. He hadn't meant to bring her such misery. He'd done that a lifetime ago, and once he'd seen into a distant past with her, he'd known he could never hurt her again.

The screen door opened and the little girl with dark hair—Branwen, he thought—crept out onto the porch with him. She was cautious, alert, ready to run if necessary. Or to finish the job her mother had done on him.

"Hi," she said, tentative, nervous.

He smiled at her. "Hi. Is your mom all right?"

"I dunno. She doesn't cry much. And she never ever faints."

Great. He'd brought her tears and fainting spells. He could've kicked himself.

Branwen perched on the porch beside him. She was a pretty child with enough of her mother in her that he knew without a doubt that she was Kestrel's daughter. Her sleek brown hair had been pulled back in braids that kept her hair out of her eyes and off her ears. Her coloring, however, was nothing like Kestrel's. She must have been Cedric Firehawk's daughter. She settled down beside him in her freshly laundered denim shorts and a white T-shirt that read "Magick Happens." Most of the paint on her arms had been scrubbed off, but some skin-reddened smudges remained.

"Where's your sister?" he asked. The other child, the little blonde, Deirdre, was also obviously Kestrel's daughter, though the wild blonde fountain of hair scrunched up on top of her head must have been a hand-me-down from her father, Grant Firehawk. They were twins, all right, but twins with different fathers.

"Deirdre's rubbing Mommy's back. She's trying to make Mom feel better."

"Ah. I see." He hesitated. "Is it helping?"

"I don't think so. Why did Mom start crying? You know, don't you?"

"I know it had something to do with the tattoos you and your sister drew on yourselves."

Branwen flinched, for the first time realizing she herself might be a reason for her mother's pain. "They washed off."

He smiled down at her and continued to rub his knee. "I don't think she cares about that. Though it is a good thing that berry juice came off. You're too young to have tattoos."

"Kids had tattoos in the old times," she protested. "In some places, they were like works of art." Then a darkness slipped over her. "And in some places, they were brands meant for criminals and slaves. A way to hurt people and make them feel bad." Her darkness faded and she added, "But in worlds where they were art, they were signs of specialness."

"You must read a lot."

"Some. Why?"

"To know so much about tattoos." She reminded him of Robyn, knowing so much unusual knowledge.

"Oh, I didn't read that anywhere. I dreamed it."

"And the tattoo you drew over your heart—the symbol with three spirals—did you dream that, too?"

She studied him, unsure of whether to trust. Finally, she nodded. "Deirdre and I had the same dream."

The same dream? Not the sort of thing that happened to the typical pair of sisters.

"Does that happen often?"

"No. Just today."

"What do you think caused it?" he pressed.

Branwen shrugged. "Deirdre and me listened to Mom hypnotize this woman and we fell asleep."

Good God. "Are you sure you fell asleep?"

"Yeah. And we had the same dream. Cool, huh?"

"Yeah. Cool." They'd been hypnotized and didn't even realize it. "What all happened in your dream?"

"Lots of stuff. I was this man with blonde hair and Deirdre was this other man—his brother, I think—with brown hair and Mom was this woman we called Kes and she looked sorta like Mom but she was happy."

Finn flattened his hand over his mouth and groaned. The kids had taken a dip into their past lives—as their fathers!

"Are you okay?" Branwen asked. She pointed at his leg. "I can help."

He'd groaned out of wretchedness and surprise, not out of pain. But if the little one wanted to interpret it as pain, so be it. "Thanks, sweetheart," he said, "but you can't help. I took a spill and twisted my knee."

"That's okay. I can still fix it."

Before he could protest, she jumped off the porch and stood at eye-level with his throbbing knee. She laid one hand close to his knee but not quite touching. A warm hand. He could feel it through the black denim. Warm and then hot. Hotter. He started to jerk his leg away but the heat felt *wonderful.* His knee no longer throbbed with pain. The girl lifted her hand and began making odd gestures over his injury, rubbing her thumb against its four opposing fingers. Though her skin never connected with his, he could feel the movements in his flesh.

"H-how did you learn to do that?"

The little girl shrugged and kept working. "In my dream, I knew how to do this but I never told anyone but my brother and Kes."

"Why not?"

217

"It wasn't who I was. Or at least who I let people see."
She kneaded her hand over his injury, still not making physical
contact.

"What else have you seen in your dreams?" Finn asked.
Had she seen her father's murderer?

"Things."

"Like what?"

"Dancing around bonfires. Singing. Laughing. Good
stuff mostly." She stopped what she was doing and glanced
shyly up at him. "Sometimes I see you, too."

"Me? Are you sure?" In Grant and Cedric's lives?

"Yeah. We were brothers. You had red hair then. And
you wore a skirt. I mean, a kilt. We were warriors together in
the same tribe. And there was another time when we were best
friends and we lived in this place where the temple floors were
stone and they were cold to our feet. We were all girls. We
were studying to be priestesses in the Temple of Diana. We
wore long robes, you and me and Deirdre."

Finn stretched his leg. His knee didn't hurt any more.
"That explains why you're not scared of me." He'd had dreams
of his own ever since he'd opened his mind to them.

"Why would I be scared of you?" She blinked at him in
such perfect innocence.

"A strange man comes to your house and you're not
afraid?"

"I knew you were coming, Finn."

"How?" Had she and her sister watched him on the trail
below or at the stream? Had Tracey called and warned Kestrel
of a possible customer?

Branwen leaned closer as if she had a secret. "Deirdre
saw you," she whispered.

"From the trail?"

"No." She tapped her forehead. "Deirdre sees things
sometimes. Just before they happen. And she saw a guy in a
dragon T-shirt and black pants and boots that squeak. And
white and yellow hair. That's you."

"What did she see me doing?" Getting pushed down the
mountainside by their mother?

"You were protecting us."

"From what?"

"From the man who's coming to kill us."

Chapter Seven

~*Kestrel*~

I ignored the man standing behind me and scrubbed down the kitchen counter even harder. No use in running now. My past had caught up with me. It always does, doesn't it? Deep down I knew what was happening, but if I just scrubbed harder, I wouldn't have to think about it.

"You're going to wear a hole in your counter," Finn said. Thunder still rumbled though the unexpected downpour had lightened. We'd had a light shower earlier in the day but this was a full-fledged rainstorm.

"Please leave," I told him.

"All right. I'll wait outside a while if you'd like."

I didn't look up. "I'm not asking you to leave the room. I'm not even asking you to leave temporarily. Please leave...leave this mountain...forever."

"I can't do that. And I think you know why."

The Dark Goddess had foretold the coming of my fourth. And of great joy, which I knew always preceded great pain. The kids, Finn, and I made four, even if he wasn't the fourth I'd hoped for. He wasn't here by accident. Of that, I was certain.

I'd seen quick flashes of him in past lives. He'd been Ainle in my memories of Deirdre and Naiose. He'd been Bran in my memories of Branwen the daughter of Lyr. Other times, too. Once in a monk's robe and enjoying the seclusion of ancient nature with me. I didn't often get flashes like that. Somehow, his presence was responsible for what was happening. And the kids' strange behavior. Somehow his presence had brought that on, too. Just as Gloria Stokes had been a catalyst to that Beltane night ten years ago, Finn was a catalyst to...something.

But the kids...oh, Goddess, how had they known about the triskele tattoos? I'd been so careful to keep my own covered.

"Kestrel, we need to talk."

I whirled on him, fists clenched. "I don't want to talk!" I squeezed the wet cloth in my hand so hard that I sprayed water across the linoleum. Outside thunder boomed, even though the rain had stopped.

"Your daughters are very talented."

"Of course, they are. Deirdre's a fine swimmer. She regularly wins trophies at school swim meets. And Branwen, she's a great artist. Lots of unusual combinations of yellows and reds. Wins all kinds of awards for innovation. So yes, they are very talented."

"I meant less mundane talents."

"What are you talking about?"

"Which of your late husbands was a Reiki master?"

I swallowed. I latched onto the refrigerator handle to steady myself. Grant had studied Reiki healing techniques before setting it aside for his law career. He had thought he could make time for it in the evenings or on weekends and the two of us could combine Reiki and hypnotherapy for people in need of alternative medicine. It had never worked out though. For as much as Grant wanted to explore his talent for healing, all the time he'd hoped could he spare was spent behind a desk, shoveling paperwork and researching thousands of pages of small print. Healing had been a dream unrealized.

"Why would you ask that?" I whispered.

"Because one of your daughters has the talent."

I crossed the kitchen to the doorway, careful to avoid Finn. I peered into the living room where both girls flopped on their stomachs on the floor, legs curling up and down. They were watching that stupid kids' movie again, the one with three so-called witches who were bumbling idiots in search of children to eat. What hogwash! No wonder people think witches are evil. They were taught such drivel from the cradle.

"Girls!"

Both kids scrambled fast to turn the channel. They knew better than to watch TV shows and movies that I raged about.

I closed the door to the living room so little ears wouldn't overhear our conversation and turned back to Finn. "Grant was a Reiki master. Hardly anyone knew. Are you saying Deirdre's inherited his talent?"

"No. Branwen has."

"But that's impossible." I felt the blood drain from my cheeks. "Branwen is Cedric's daughter. I'm sure of it. What makes you so sure she has the gift?"

He extended his injured leg and pointed at his knee. "Good as new."

"But that—" It didn't make sense. Deirdre was Grant's daughter and Branwen was Cedric's daughter. I had been inclined at first to reverse the names but Saadia had insisted.

"Which one of your husbands had a gift for seeing slightly into the future?"

How could Finn know these things? "Cedric."

"Deirdre has his gift."

I laughed but it rang hollow. "No, she doesn't. If she did, I'd know. I'm her mother."

"Would it upset you to find out? Just look at you. All tense at the mention of it."

The chalkboard. It had been years ago. Years. A fluke, I'd told myself at the time. Deirdre had frantically warned her teacher that the chalkboard was going to fall on the teacher's head. The teacher had dismissed her concerns as foolishness. Then the board had fallen and Deirdre had been sent to the principal's office as a prankster. Deirdre had insisted she'd had a premonition but it was easier to believe she was a troublemaking child than to accept the ramifications.

Another time she'd gotten into trouble for reporting a bully even before he punched another kid. There had been other times, too, that Deirdre had been in trouble with teachers but nothing directly related to the clairvoyance—as far as she knew. If Deirdre had had any inklings of the future after her first couple of bouts of trouble, she'd kept them to herself. Poor thing. She'd learned the hard way that visions of things to come were not something everyone experienced.

"But Deirdre is Grant's daughter. How could she inherit Cedric's abilities? She inherited her father's looks—blonde hair, blue eyes, the shape of his hands. How could she inherit something from a man who wasn't her father?"

"A different kind of inheritance, Kestrel."

I pulled a straight chair from the table and plopped down. "I don't get it."

Finn sat down next to me and rested one calming hand on my shoulder, and it *was* calming. "Kestrel, the girls remember their previous incarnation."

How did he think he knew so much about my family? Who the hell was he to make such assumptions? Even if I had known him...before...he'd been on my property for less than six hours. "That's silly. They probably heard me talking about the old days." Except that I never spoke much of my life before I'd flown by night.

"They know about Cedric and Grant. That your name was Kestrel. They know about ritual dancing and fires." He paused to lean close and make certain he had my full attention. "Kestrel, the girls remembered under hypnosis."

"That's ridiculous. The girls have never been hypnotized. They don't even know what it is. They think it's some kook spinning a watch or necklace."

"They may not understand what it is, but they've been regressed. Did you know they were eavesdropping on your counseling sessions?"

"Eaves—" I choked. If they'd overheard, overheard and relaxed, then—oh, Goddess, no! It was possible they'd been hypnotized along with my client. I'd taken my client into her previous incarnation, shown her happy times. If the girls had gone back in time to their previous lives, then....

I slid down to the floor and covered my face. Grant and Cedric hadn't left me the day I'd gone into labor. They'd promised we'd be together again soon, that they'd see me soon. I'd thought they meant I'd die in childbed or at the hands of the beast who'd slain my lovers. But no. They'd come back to me. My guys had come back. As different people but with the same souls. As my beautiful daughters. Cedric as Deirdre, daughter of Grant. Grant as Branwen, daughter of Cedric. And both the dearest loves of my heart.

"Kestrel?"

I felt Finn's hand warm on my shoulder. I knew all about him, courtesy of Robyn, but that had been before he'd found life after birth. He was different now. No longer a stressed-out homicide detective. Wiser. Wiccan.

He sat down on the floor beside me and put his arms loosely around my shoulders. "Kestrel, we have a bigger problem."

"P-Problem?" I lifted my face to his. He brushed away the wetness on my cheeks in a gesture so gentle it caught me by surprise.

"Someone's coming." He didn't have to elaborate. His tone said it all. The beast had found us. "I need to know who killed your husbands."

"I don't know who did it." I backhanded the tears and leaned my head against his shoulder. It had been so long since I'd leaned on anyone. "They were dead when I got there. There was someone hiding in the woods, but he—I thought it was a *he*—ran away when the sirens got closer. And then I ran. I never saw who it was."

Finn jerked his head in the direction of the kitchen door. "They did."

I stared back at him, lost in his unwavering eyes. Sincerity and protectiveness shone through, but he didn't understand. "My daughters didn't see anything."

"Sure, they did. They went back ten years to the time when they were Grant and Cedric. They remember."

"Only good stuff. My client was nervous so I took her only to pleasant moments. You saw the girls a few minutes ago. If they'd remembered their last deaths, they'd be traumatized. They're not." Thank the Goddess.

"Okay," he conceded, lifting me to my feet. "Maybe they don't remember that part. But if they could, then we could find out who killed Cedric and Grant. And Gloria." He hesitated. "And Robyn."

I shook my head furiously. "You want me to hypnotize my little girls? No! They're *little* girls. Do you know what you're asking?"

He held my shoulders, forcing me to look him in the eyes. "I'm asking you to do something that will save your daughters' lives. Maybe all our lives."

"No. I won't do it."

"Kestrel, please. The man who killed the two most important people in your life is on his way here to kill you and your children. Deirdre's seen him."

I shut my eyes, trying to close out the future as it rushed toward me. What a wicked paradox. If I'd not lost my guys to a murderer's fisted stabs, I wouldn't have had my beautiful little girls. Oh, my children might have looked the same, but their tiny bodies would have housed different souls with different purposes in life. I'd always known that we choose our parents before we are born, for what experiences they can give us and that we may give them, but the souls of the two beautiful men I had taken for my husbands had chosen to come back to me and live and grow again in the light of my love. Out of my greatest sorrow had come my greatest joy—my daughters. The Dark Mother had been right. As always.

And now, someone was coming to take it all away from me. Again. Someone who should have been stopped a decade ago. I hadn't know how then. I still didn't. I hadn't been strong enough. And now?

"I won't hypnotize my children."

"You don't hypnotize kids ever?"

Maybe a few dozen times. Always to get over nightmares or to remember, in a few tough scenes, what happened in a car wreck or with suspicious-acting Uncle Gary. "I don't hypnotize children so they can view their previous deaths. Especially violent deaths. They just can't handle it that young. Hell, Finn, most adults have problems accepting violent passings. You expect me to expose my children to something that horrible? They'll be in therapy for the rest of their lives."

"At least they'd *have* the rest of their lives. Kestrel, they could give us their killer's name or at least a description. Right now, we have nothing to go on." He held up his cell phone.

"One of the cops in Greenburg's still a friend of mine. He's working on a few new leads. He was supposed to call me today and let me know what he'd found out."

I sighed long and loud. Didn't he know? "Cell phones don't work around here. The mountains interfere with the signal."

"Shit. Harrison may have found something already and I didn't know."

"Finn?"

"Yes?"

"Why now?"

"Want do you mean?"

"It's been ten years that I've been in hiding. He almost found me the night the girls were born. But I've been careful. I gave up everything in my old life and started over as someone else just to keep my babies safe. I always worried we'd be found but why now?"

Finn shrugged.

The Goddess had said our fourth would bring danger with him. Finally I said what I'd hesitated to voice. "How is it that the killer found us a few hours after you did?"

Chapter Eight

~ Finn ~

God. She was right. She'd stayed out of sight all these years and the second he showed up on her doorstep, a murderer stepped out of ten years of shadows. That had to be more than a coincidence.

Finn stood at the window and scanned the woods below the house. The dirt road Tracey had brought him up on wound like a serpent down the mountain. He couldn't see the road in its entirety, just a curve here or there through the shield of trees, but the road was empty. No murderers stalked openly toward Kestrel and her children.

Far below, at the mountain's base, was the perimeter of the small town of Lingering Shade. Nothing moved in the glare of sunshine, except for a couple of black and white cows meandering toward the creek that descended the mountain and rolled across the meadow. He squinted hard and traced the highway to the snaking mountain road to the cul-de-sac below Kestrel's home where one path forked toward the stream where he'd fallen and the other led to the front yard.

About two hundred feet below Kestrel's stood Tracey's cabin where he'd left his vehicle. Kestrel's nearest neighbor was a five-minute walk through the woods, though the ribbon of dirt road looped back and forth for half a mile to make the incline drive-able. Tracey had left hours ago, so he and Kestrel and the children were all alone on the mountain. All alone with a killer on the way to Lingering Shade. No. No, Tracey's truck was back, though it was in nearly hidden in the shade.

He rubbed the cell phone hooked to his belt and wished with all his heart that the phone were a Glock Model 23. He'd talked to Harrison two days ago, and no word back, thanks to interference from the high mountains and whatever else might have held up Harrison. Finn had told the young detective about Lingering Shade and Saadia Soap. They'd rehashed Robyn's murder and those of the Firehawks and Gloria Stokes. Harrison had volunteered, thankfully, to do a little research on the string of four murder cases that had been deemed "cult activity" but never really closed. Of course, it would help tremendously if Finn had a name to give Harrison to research.

If Finn had led a killer here....

But who? He'd called Harrison, yes, and perhaps Harrison had passed something along to someone in his precinct. It was possible, he supposed. Maybe other murder victims had died the same way as the ritualistic four Finn had investigated. Harrison would know, but maybe Harrison had tipped someone off by accident. He certainly wouldn't do it on purpose. Harrison was a good Christian man who followed the teachings of the Essenes and the early Christians. He embodied the best of that religion.

What if Finn had been the one to tip off a murderer? He had also called Floyd Stokes, Gloria's husband, and asked him if *Saadia* meant anything to him or if Gloria might have mentioned the town of Lingering Shade, North Carolina. The man had broken into tears over the phone, and Finn had felt awful for dredging up old pains. The poor guy had been a broken man ever since his flirty young wife's death. Boring husband or not, he'd loved his wife. He hadn't remarried since, and hadn't seemed able to hold a job more than a few months.

Finn had called Stuart, too, hoping Robyn's gay friend might recall anything he'd left out during his statement nine years ago. Stuart no longer lived in his old neighborhood and according to his elderly mother, Stuart was believed to be in a long-term care facility, near the end of a lengthy illness. She wasn't really sure where, as she hadn't had anything to do with her son in years and didn't really appreciate someone stirring up her old misery.

Finn hadn't fared much better in the calls he'd made to Cedric Wiley and Grant Sullivan's parents. Bitterness had settled in for both families. Grant's mother had spent the decade in and out of psychiatric wards and was barely coherent on the mind-numbing drugs that moved her from day to day. Grant's father had been livid at the interruption into his miserable life. He'd spouted obscenities for a solid five minutes before curtly telling Finn they didn't know anything about this Saadia person who might have destroyed their lives. Finn had to wonder, now that he'd met Kestrel's children, whether the Sullivans might find some small healing in the knowledge that they had a granddaughter or if they, like many Christian grandparents, would launch a campaign to take away their pagan children's children.

Cedric's father had listened intently for a few minutes, then cursed Finn for not catching Kestrel and bringing her to justice and told him to go to hell. Neither of them able to cope with their grief, the man and his wife had divorced years ago. Rumor had it, Cedric's mother and her new husband lived in Asheville, North Carolina, ironically a good two hours' drive from where Cedric's daughter lived. Harrison would know more later.

And then there was Reverend Jones. Finn had kept a copy of his phone number, too, but the woman who had answered said she'd had the phone number for at least two years and had been vaguely aware that a preacher had had the phone number before her.

All the people Finn had talked to were still either reeling from their losses or actively trying to numb their grief. The death of a child was the hardest for a person to get through, harder than the death or a spouse or a parent, and if the effect of Robyn's loss on him was any indication, how could Finn blame the Sullivans or the Wileys for their anger? None of the people he'd talked to had made the connection for him between the violence that had touched their families and Saadia Soap in Lingering Shade, North Carolina.

If only he had some inkling, some small suspicion, of Robyn's murderer!

Oh, wait a minute. Kestrel wouldn't have to hypnotize the kids after all and risk traumatizing them.

"Deirdre!" He sprang for the living room door and yanked it open. Kestrel snapped out of her silent prayer and followed him. "Deirdre!" he called.

Both girls rolled over and looked up expectantly from the floor. Branwen punched the remote control button and the television picture flickered and fizzled out. The twins blinked in unison.

"Is Deirdre in trouble?" Branwen asked, inching protectively in front of her sister.

Finn expelled his breath slowly, careful to check himself. He must've been an intimidating sight, he realized, towering over them with sparks in his eyes.

"No, sweetheart," he said to Branwen. "Your sister is not trouble." He knelt before Deirdre. He hoped she'd be more receptive to a big guy on his knees. "Deirdre, I need to know about the man you've seen in your visions."

Deirdre shot an eat-shit look at her twin, the kind of look that screamed "You told!" Then her gaze riveted to her mother's frown. She squeezed her shoulders back like a soldier at attention. Finn saw the girl swallow a lump in her throat.

"It's okay, Deirdre," Kestrel said. She joined Finn on the floor in front of the little girl. Kestrel understood. Why hypnotize and take the children back to their hideous deaths before their births when the little visionary could describe the killer painlessly? "Deirdre," Kestrel continued, "we know about your dreams. And it's okay to have dreams like that. They have a purpose, and that purpose is to warn us. All right?"

Deirdre's eyes watered. Slowly, she nodded.

"Deirdre?" Finn took her tiny hands into his large ones and smiled at her. "Branwen tells me you've seen me protecting you."

Her head bobbed once. "Your shoes were red."

Hmmm, maybe her vision wasn't that good. Finn didn't own any red shoes, but still he pressed for answers. "Good. Good, Deirdre. And this person I'm protecting you from, do you know him?"

"I've dreamed about him before." Her words came out in a barely audible whimper. "But he was different then."

"Different how? What kinds of dreams?"

She exchanged a glance with her twin. Ah. So the two girls had discussed it. "He wore black in my dreams, with this big, gold cross hanging way down in front. But sometimes in my dreams, he wears old-timey clothes like in the Robin Hood movies and he rides a horse and goes to different villages and he's really mean but he thinks he's right about everything, even when he's wrongest."

The witch-hunter.

"And sometimes he wears funny costumes," she added.

"Like what?"

"Rain stuff. Raincoat and boots and a hat. Yellow. In my dreams, he's hiding in the woods." She shuddered. "He was scary, but I wasn't surprised to see him."

"I was!" Branwen yelled back. "It wasn't fair! You knew he was coming. You should've warned me."

"There was nothing you could do," Deirdre argued.

"You still could've warned me. All you did was hint that something was wrong." Branwen's words simmered with anger too old for a child.

"Whoa, wait." Finn beckoned to Branwen. She stepped forward tentatively. "You've seen him in your dreams, too?"

"Uh-huh. He's mean. He hates us, but I don't know why. He wants to hurt me. He has a knife with purple rocks on the handle. When I was little, I couldn't sleep with my closet door shut because I thought he was hiding inside. I thought he was the bogey-man."

Kestrel sucked in a tearful breath. She scooped both girls into a hug. They went willingly. "You never told me what your nightmares were about. Either of you. You just said the bogey-man and I thought it was a monster out of your imagination. I didn't know. I'm so sorry."

Finn waited for the hugs to subside. "So you kids have both had the same dreams." Memories of past lives, though they clearly didn't remember their deaths. Or, if they did, they didn't understand the sudden release from the body and the rushing forward of consciousness. "But you've also dreamed of my coming here to help you."

"Just me," Deirdre said. "We both dream about things from a long time ago, but I'm the only one who sees things that haven't happened yet."

"Deirdre, I want you to listen very carefully. Have you seen the man in the raincoat in person?"

"No. But he's coming. Without the raincoat this time."

"Can you tell us his name?"

"I never knew his name. He always came out of no-where."

"Can you tell us what he looks like?"

Deirdre hesitated, but her mother rubbed the girl's back and kissed her cheek. "It okay, honey. You can tell us."

"He's old."

"Old?" Reverend Jones? Grant's father? Cedric's? All three were in their fifties or sixties now. Gloria's husband was probably bearing down hard on fifty. No one else connected in any way with the four murders fit the description.

"Yeah, real old," Deirdre continued. "Like you."

Finn blinked at her. Old like him? Sure, he had a few crow's feet at the corner of his eyes and mouth on the few occasions when he smiled, but old? He'd felt older—looked older— ten years ago when he'd been a cop who talked to the dead.

"Deirdre," Finn tried through clenched jaws. *Old, was he?* "Is the man old like a grandfather?"

She shrugged. "I don't know. I don't have a grandfa-ther."

"Okay, okay. Tell me exactly what he looks like."

"He's...." She stared at some imaginary movie screen he couldn't see. "He's wearing hunting clothes."

"Camouflage?"

She nodded. "He had one of those truck-cars that go up mountains but he's not driving it up the mountain. He's push-ing it into the woods down close to the mailboxes. It has a cross hanging from the mirror inside. The kind of cross with a man glued to it. He's covering up the truck-car with broken limbs and bushes. He doesn't have a lot of hair."

Not a lot of hair. Cedric's father was almost bald and in his early fifties. He'd lost his son and his wife. He'd been the rudest of the people who knew Finn was looking for informa-tion on Saadia Soap and Lingering Shade, North Carolina.

"Okay. Okay, thank you, Deirdre. You and Branwen can go back to watching your TV show."

The girls flicked the TV back on and turned away. Kestrel couldn't stop staring at them, longing for them, loving them. Finn could see it, feel it, himself. His spine tingled with warning. He turned quickly to look over his shoulder as Kestrel finally broke away and walked back into the kitchen.

"Deirdre? Just one more question," Finn said. "How soon will this man be here?"

"He already is."

Chapter Nine

~*Kestrel*~

I froze in the kitchen doorway. Only once in my life have I ever been so scared, and it was long before that Beltane night when my guys were murdered.

Daddy had gotten nose-puking, knee-crawling drunk and beat up Mama again and he tried to rape me. I was eight years old, just a year younger than my girls. Mama got Daddy's pistol out of the nightstand drawer. I remember her loading it, not being able to load it fast enough and her hands shaking and her dropping bullets on the carpet and the way they bounced and skittered everywhere. I don't remember screaming, but I know I was. Mama yelled at him that he'd better never hurt me the way he'd hurt her. He had such contempt for her that he didn't even look at her. He just pinned me to the floor and tore my blouse open. I wasn't even old enough to wear a training bra.

Mama shot him once through the head. I remember a splatter, like warm, red rain. I remember blood in my eyes. Then she kept shooting him.

But I wasn't as scared, not even then, as when I saw the look on my mother's face when she realized what she'd done.

She kicked at him, rolled him off me with one foot. Then she gathered me into her arms and told me her place was with my father. She locked herself in the bathroom. I was eight years old, covered with my father's blood, and banging on the door, begging my mother not to leave me. That was the other time I'd been this scared—when I heard a single gunshot and then the sound of my mother's body hitting the linoleum floor.

"Girls!" I rushed back into the living room as I called their names. "Branwen! Deirdre! Grab your shoes—now!"

The two of them jumped up, leaving the TV blaring their forbidden movie behind them. I swore that if we ever got out of this, I'd give that television to charity. Branwen already had her shoes on, but, as usual, Deirdre was barefoot. I picked up a pair of strewn sandals from the floor and thrust them into her small hands.

"What's wrong?" Branwen asked, her bangs in such need of a cut that I could barely see her curious eyes.

Deirdre answered before I could. "He's coming."

"Who—" Branwen's eyes widened under her dark fringe. "Ohhhhh."

"Get your shoes on," I reminded Deirdre, shoving the both of them toward the back door. She squashed her feet into the sandals and let the heel straps fall into place as she walked.

"Where are we going?" Branwen asked, but she asked her sister, not me.

"Hurry," I urged, giving the girls a push toward the door. "You're to run to the deer path and wait there for Miss Tracey. I'll call her as soon as you leave. She'll take you for...for a long walk."

"But Mom, what about you?" Branwen rubbed her nervous palms over the hips of her shorts. She paused long enough to look into my eyes for a truthful answer, a trick she'd learned from me.

"She's not coming," Deirdre answered. My somber, little clairvoyant stared off toward Tracey's cabin as I dragged her down the steps. No, I wasn't going anywhere. I wondered what she saw when she looked at me. My impending murder? Upside-down pentagrams carved into my flesh?

"Listen to me and listen closely." In the shade of the house, I drew them to me in a tight hug and kissed the tops of their heads again and again. "No matter what happens here to-day, I love you. I've always loved you, even before you were born." I blinked back the tears. "And we will be together again. I promise."

I shoved them off toward the hidden path a good twenty-five feet from our back door. I visualized a violet bubble surrounding them, protecting them. *In Your hands, Goddess.* I sniffed back all sign of tears and fears until they were out of sight. I couldn't help but wonder if I'd ever see my babies again. If all went well, they'd make it to the Lingering Shade Inn well before dark and the rising full moon.

Finn stood in the doorway behind me. "Will they be okay? They're so little."

I nodded, more for myself than for him. "They know these mountain paths like the backs of their hands. They could find the way on their own, but I worry about some of the wild-life around here."

"Yeah. Me, too." He touched my shoulder, and I jumped. "Kestrel? Come inside. Now."

Yes. Yes, I had to hurry. I had to call Tracey and tell her to watch for the girls and get them off the mountain, over the top and down the far side. And I had to perform a protec-tive spell for the house and for the coming battle with the witch-hunter. I began composing the ritual in my head. *Water, air, smoke and earth; Keep this day my home and hearth.* I preferred black candles to ward off evil and rosemary to protect. It was the day of the full moon, still waxing in this hour, though it would not rise until very late in the afternoon. Magick under a full moon tended to be more potent. *Keep all bane outside my door—*

"Kestrel." Finn drew me out of my mental preparations and led me back inside. He double-locked the door. "Kes, we have a problem."

Kes. Grant and Cedric had called me that, long ago on a Beltane night.

"The phone," he continued. "I tried to call my detective friend back in Greenburg to see what he'd found out."

"And?"

"Kes, the phone's dead."

Chapter Ten

~*Deirdre*~

Deirdre climbed up on a mossy boulder and sat down, her jaws in her palms. She stared at her toes and then, in an angry flourish, flipped the sandals off her feet. One landed on the far side of the deer path. The other dropped into a pile of thorny ferns.

"What'd you do that for?" Branwen demanded, stopping her pacing. "Miss Tracey's gonna be here any minute and you're not going to be ready."

"Miss Tracey's not coming."

"Yes, she is. Mom said—"

"Mom doesn't know everything." Deirdre chanced a peek at Branwen to see if her sister had a clue. She didn't. Deirdre let out a huge sigh. It was no use. Nothing mattered. She'd seen everything and she was tired of seeing things. She didn't want to see anything else. She didn't want to know. Knowing *hurt*.

"Get your shoes on." Branwen sounded just like Mom. "Mom's gonna be mad if Miss Tracey gets here and you're not ready."

"Shut up." Deirdre shifted her weight and stepped down the rock. She was face to face with Branwen and so angry. It wasn't fair that Branwen got to heal people and Deirdre got stuck with seeing things. "Just shut up!" she yelled at Branwen, pushing her hard.

Branwen's foot caught on a root and she fell, sprawling across the wet leaves and dirt and skinning one elbow. "No, *you* shut up!" she whispered back as loudly as she could. She struggled to her feet and clamped one hand over Deirdre's mouth. "You want the bad guy to hear you? We're supposed to be sneaking away, stupid, not yelling for him to come get us."

Deirdre shrugged out of her twin's grip and shoved her again. This time Branwen was prepared and swung back, landing a fist squarely in Deirdre's nose. Blood seeped from one nostril. The anger in Branwen's eyes mixed with unspoken regret. The two of them rarely fought, but unforced apologies were even rarer.

Deirdre glared back. She wiped the blood with the back of her hand and looked at it. Blood dripped onto the wet leaves. "We're right here!" she shouted, throat hoarse. "Right here! Come slash us into little pieces!"

The rant dissolved into silence. Not even the songs of birds bridged the noise-less gap between the girls. Nothing moved around them. They stared at each other.

Finally, Branwen spoke. "What is wrong with you? Do you want to die?"

Deirdre felt the hot tears seep into her eyes, felt their stinging trails down her cheeks. "I just want to be like everybody else," she sobbed.

"We can't," Branwen reminded her. "We can't be like everybody else 'cause we're witches."

"I mean the dreams. I don't mean to make bad things happen to people."

"You don't make bad things happen to people. They just happen. All for the greater good, whatever that means. That's what Mom says, anyway."

"Then why can't I stop it? And if I can't stop it, why do I have to see it? I don't understand!" She sank against the rock and stared up hopelessly at the sky. "They're like previews of next week's TV show. All I can do is wait, and not in a fun way, either."

"Well, maybe...." Branwen kicked at yellow daisy-like flowers with black centers. "What if Mom's right? Maybe instead of being like next week's episode on TV, they're warnings instead. You can do something about them."

"I tried that already and it didn't do any good. Remember? I saw the chalk board fall on Miss Williams' head and I tried to warn her, but it fell on her anyway."

"Yeah, but she didn't believe. Mom believed you when you said you saw that bad guy coming."

"But believing didn't stop him. He's still coming. He's not far from Miss Tracey's house." Deirdre could see him even now behind her eyes, trudging up the steep, narrow path somewhere beneath them on the mountain on a trail they called the "deer path." She blinked away the vision and stared at the blood on her pink T-shirt with something Gaelic scrawled across it and circled with Celtic knots.

"You could have warned me that the bad guy was coming. I would've believed you."

Through hot tears, Deirdre blinked at her sister. "I did tell you the bad man was coming. And I told you that Finn was coming to protect us. But I don't know if Finn's able to help or not. I haven't seen that. But he does get hurt. Bad."

"No, I don't mean now. I mean then." A hard look settled on Branwen's face. She clenched her fists. "You know what I'm talking about. That night in the woods. In the dream. You knew, didn't you? That's why you sent that woman away. Kes. She was Mom, wasn't she? That's why you sent her to the store."

Deirdre swallowed hard. "You remember. You remember it, too."

"Not a lot. But enough. You sent her away so she wouldn't be hurt. But you didn't warn *me*. You should have warned *me*."

Deirdre saw herself as she had in the dream, staring longingly into the eyes of a woman who was more of a girl than Mom. Kestrel looked so much like Mom. And then seeing an image of two bodies Deirdre barely recognized as a man's—her

body then—and Grant's. Symbols carved into them. Lying naked, sided by side, in the posture of Jesus on the cross. Deirdre
shook the memory from her head.

"It didn't matter," she wailed. "I'd already seen it. It
was going to happen no matter what we did. I thought...." She
paused, trying to remember what the exact emotion was. "I
thought I could save you some...dread? Worry? Pain?" What
was it she'd felt? "I thought it would be better if you didn't
know before it happened. I think it would have been better for
me."

"You should have told me," Branwen grated out. Her
voice seemed deeper, older. "If I was going to die, I had a right
to know."

Laughter gurgled over in Deirdre's throat. "Then
wouldn't we all have a right to know?" They'd studied in school
about ancient Greek myths and how three blind women cut life
threads at random. This didn't feel so random.

"Miss Tracey has a right to know, too. He could hurt
her, too, you know." Branwen stomped away and down the
path. "If you won't warn her, I will."

But it was already too late.

Deirdre grabbed Branwen's shoulder and yanked her
back. For a split second, she flashed on an image of Branwen.
Scared. Running. Dark braids bouncing against her shoulders
and back. The dream-like Branwen reached the edge of the
stream, near the picnic rock. Paused. Looked over her shoulder.
Someone was behind, close behind. The waters were higher.
The rainstorms had filled the stream. Deirdre could see a man's
hand reaching out. Almost grabbing one of the dark braids.
But Branwen ducked. She ventured onto the first stone that
crossed the water. Late afternoon sunlight trickled down,
glinted off the water. Branwen took another step. Onto another rock. And then another. She looked over her shoulder at
a man's feet. Soldier boots. Following her from rock to rock to
rock. Then she stepped toward the one that was slippery.
Deirdre wanted to scream out, "Don't step there!" Not the obvious step that looked safe. Not the one that was as slippery as
a tadpole. Branwen and water didn't mix. Her shoe slipped.
Her leg went up in the air, the shoe came off, splashed down in

the water nearby. A man's hand grabbed her by the throat and pulled her up.

"B-Branwen?"

"What?" Branwen screeched at her. "You don't want to come with me to save Miss Tracey? Fine! Just stay here!"

Deirdre didn't flinch. "You said you wanted to be warned about your own dying. Is that still true?"

Before Branwen could answer, they heard the crunch of footfalls and leaves on the path.

Chapter Eleven

~ Finn ~

Finn shook Kestrel's shoulders a second time. "Did you hear what I said? The phone's dead."

She stared back, then finally blinked. Snapping out of her paralysis. Finn's hands felt like hot coals on her skin. He knew what she was thinking. The phone was dead, and that meant she couldn't call Tracey and tell her to meet the girls on the path and take them to safety. Her babies were out there alone in the woods.

"What kind of weapons do you have here?" Finn asked.

"Weapons?"

"Guns." Most witches held a marked preference for blades over bullets. Damned unlikely that a fellow pagan would have a gun, but it was worth a try. "Do you have any guns? Hunting rifles? Would Tracey have guns?"

She sneered. "We don't hunt."

He'd kill the man himself. Make up some plausible story of self-defense. Or a hunting accident if he had to. He'd spare Kestrel the karmic burden of taking another's life. Anyway, if this was the man who'd killed Robyn, he owed his former partner that much. Vengeance. Justice. All the same where Robyn was concerned.

"Think! Guns, knives, hand grenades—I don't care. Anything we can use to defend ourselves."

"I haven't used an athame in years." She frowned, deep in thought, and studied the floor. "The forefinger makes a decent magickal tool when necessary." Then she jerked her head up. "Kitchen knives," she offered. "I had an athame once, but the witch-hunter has it now."

"Okay. Okay, we'll gather up a few of your sharpest knives. Though I prefer not to use those if we can help it. Unless you've got a real good aim from a distance—and I don't—you'd have to get real close. He's probably stronger than you are. Maybe stronger than I am." Finn still didn't know who "he" was, but killers who fueled themselves with rage tended to have an advantage in physical combat.

Kestrel bolted into the kitchen. She picked up a few small but sharp paring knives out of the sink. Finn plucked a dry washcloth from the countertop and folded it into a makeshift sheath for the blades. He slipped the knives between his hip and his belt.

She mimicked his actions, taking a second cloth from a drawer and wrapping the blade of a butcher knife in the cloth. Then, like him, she slipped the knife between her hip and the belt through her cut-offs.

"I can't believe you're up here in the mountains with nothing else to defend yourself," he grumbled. She seemed more responsible. "What if a bear were to attack one of the girls? What then?"

"We're under the Goddess' protection. We don't bother Mother Nature and Mother Nature doesn't bother us." Then she frowned and added, "But I do have a couple of swords hanging on the wall of my office."

"Office?"

"Yeah. The cabin across the creek. Where I do hypnosis for people with appointments, keep records, things like that. I wanted my business separate from my home, so I built a cabin that was more secluded than here. I found a couple of old swords at a thrift shop. An old cross-bow, too. I use them as decoration."

"Cross-bow? That's better." At least he could get some distance and aim. He had no idea what kind of weapons the witch-hunter would be carrying, but he doubted an athame and a crucifix would be the most of it.

Kestrel patted the cloth-covered blade on her hip. Her bare legs looked fragile. "I'll meet the girls on the deer path and go get Tracey." Becca wouldn't be there tonight, but Tracey might be in danger. "You go back to the cabin and get the weapons off the wall. The cabin's right across the creek from the gong. Can you find your way?"

He nodded. "Across the water from where I found you. I think I can find it." He knew he could find it just by listening for the distant rush of the waterfall, as long as he didn't fall down the steep landscape.

"Good." She plucked a key ring from a hook on the wall near the back door and thrust the keys into his palm. "Small gold key. That'll get you in the door. I have to keep it locked to keep the girls out."

He nodded again. Understandable. The twins were at the right age where they were into everything. They probably knew this neck of the woods better than any rabbit or squirrel.

"The four of us will meet you at the gong. From there, Tracey can take the girls over the mountain, and you and I...we'll stay behind to take care of what must be done. I wasn't strong enough to face him ten years ago. I had to flee to protect my children. But now I'm back at the same crossroads. This time, I have to stand and fight to protect my own." Her face hardened at the thought, and she looked less like a high priestess and more like a warrior preparing for battle. Before Finn could say anything, she headed out the back door.

"Kestrel?" he called after her. His gut yearned for her. He'd been with her so many times before, yet he knew so little about her. Now there might never be time to explore their past...or future.

"Yes?" She didn't even look over her shoulder. She stared off in the distance toward the deer path, toward where she'd shooed her children a few minutes earlier.

"May the Goddess be with you."

"She always has been, Finn. Even in the darkest times."

Kestrel headed one way and he another. He crunched through the leaves toward the direction he'd come. His boots, still wet, squeaked with every footstep. If the crunch of leaves didn't give him away, certainly the squeaking would. He tugged off the boots and carried them instead. After he had weapons more forceful than a paring knife, he'd put the boots back on. For now, he needed to be quiet. Very quiet. As long as he stayed away from red shoes, he mused, he'd be just fine.

He paused in the shade of a wild magnolia and listened. The scent of white flowers around his head made his eyes water. A waterfall roared softly in the distance. As long as he kept on a reasonably straight course—didn't go up or down the mountain—he'd run smack-dab into the stream. Eventually.

It took only twenty minutes to reach the creek banks, but it seemed like forever. He found the waterfall easily, descended the mountain until he saw the gong and then the rope bridge crossing to a cabin on the other side. Two lawn chairs stood in the middle of the shallow stream below where he'd sat with Kestrel in the morning hours which had been considerably warmer before the rains. Finn tied his bootlaces together in a loose knot and hung them around his neck. He pulled himself across the rope bridge. For only a moment did he notice that the waters had risen.

Finn bounded up steps of the cabin, careful not to catch any splinters on his sock feet. He fished the key ring out of his pocket and fumbled with the small, gold-colored key. The doorknob turned and he pushed his way inside, flipping on the light switch in the process and dropping his boots to the floor. He spied a nice selection of rusty broadswords and sabers hanging on one wall and a cross-bow and armored breastplate hanging on the other. The swords weren't particularly sharp, though they could deliver an ugly blow if necessary. And the crossbow? Definitely an antique.

It must have seemed odd to Kestrel's clients that she had swords and weapons of air hanging on her walls, but it made perfect sense to him. If she was, as Robyn had alleged all those years ago, aligned with the Powers of Air, then swords, cross-bows, bows and arrows would all appeal to her. Still, there was little here that they could actually use to defend themselves.

The room was small and dim, even with the lights on. Another hallway led to a tiny bathroom and a larger storage area. The cabin, however small it was, was still homey, with fresh flowers, a straight chair, an oversized recliner, small stereo system in the corner, and an antique desk bearing a computer on top and...and *a telephone!*

Yawning to make his ears pop, Finn bent closer for a better look. The computer was an older model with an external modem, a phone cord snaking its way from a log jam of cords behind the computer, into the telephone, and out the back to a jack near the baseboard. Absolutely archaic! He quickly re-routed the phone cord and tried for a dial tone. He held the receiver to his ear. The phone buzzed to life. The phone line to Kestrel's house had been cut, but this line didn't go to Kestrel's house. It was a separate phone line for the computer, the one she used to maintain her *Saadia Soap* web site and keep up with the world via the Internet. He punched out Harrison's number as fast as he could and waited for the phone to ring in Green-burg. Harrison Weaver was the one person he trusted back home, and the only person who'd been half-civil to Robyn when everyone else had insisted the witch be fired on the spot. Him, included.

"Harrison," he yelled into the phone as soon as he heard the familiar voice. "Harrison, it's me. Finn—I mean, Dylan MacCool."

"MacCool, where the hell have you been? I've been try-ing to reach you all day."

"Just shut up and listen, okay? I don't have much time. I'm in a hole-in-the-road place called Lingering Shade. North Carolina. I'm with Kestrel Firehawk and —"

"Kestrel Firehawk! She's alive? Oh, shit. Man, listen, you've got to—"

"No, you listen to me, Harrison. I don't have much time here." Finn had to get his point across, just in case he and Kestrel weren't successful. "The man who killed Robyn—and Grant and Cedric Firehawk—he's after us. After her and her two kids. I need to know what you found out about Reverend Jones. Doesn't make sense that he's the killer but somebody told Kestrel that Robyn thought he was. We need to—"

"I can guarantee it's not Reverend Jones. The man's been in a nursing home for years. Completely lost touch when his grandson was killed in that liquor store robbery."

"What liquor store robbery?" Even as Finn said it, he remembered. Reverend Jones had been on the other side of Finn's desk the night Robyn had died. Finn had received that desperate call from Robyn and had sprinted away from the old preacher to run, too late, to Robyn's aid. The old man had been upset over the death of the liquor store clerk, the same clerk who'd confiscated Kestrel's driver's license the night her husbands were killed. "When Kestrel left the store that night, that's why the preacher had been there. Not to stalk Kestrel or preach to drunks but to play guardian angel to his grandson."

"MacCool?" Harrison's voice came through quietly over the crackling phone line. "We know who killed Robyn. And the Firehawks. And Gloria Stokes. You interviewed him twice. Once after the Firehawks. Once after Gloria Stokes' death."

Finn gripped the phone. He'd interviewed a murderer. Not once, but twice. And he'd missed it? If he'd been better, if he'd caught on quicker, he could have stopped Robyn's murder. She'd still be alive.

"MacCool? It's Floyd Stokes."

The news sank in. "What? Floyd Stokes would be what? Fifty now? He was a geek, a weakling. I've never seen a many so distraught over his wife's death. This man was hurting over the loss, not hiding."

"He'd be forty-eight now, according to his military records," Harrison continued.

"Military records?" Finn gripped the phone so hard his hand hurt.

"Yeah. Ex-special forces."

"Are you sure? He wasn't military. He was a businessman. Greenburg Self-Defense School or something like that. Taught women how to protect themselves from rapists."

Harrison grunted. "Not exactly. Try gun shop and firing range. He'd been Special Ops about five years before the murders. Then he found God or some version of God and went rabid. Special Ops kicked him out. They want soldiers, not avengers. His team was sent into an Arabic country to rescue a diplomat. Stokes turned the mission into a bloodbath.

247

His own private Holy War. Killed every Arab in the place, including one still in diapers. And by the way, MacCool, this is sensitive information. Trust me: I didn't get this through official channels. You wouldn't believe the kind of digging I've been doing."

The muscles in Finn's hands ached from clenching the receiver. Phone still in hand, he maneuvered toward the crossbow on the wall and gently took down the weapon. He began to load it as he talked. "What tipped you off?" Finn asked.

"Actually, you did. When you called the other day and asked me to see what I could find out about Saadia Soap and Lingering Shade, I started looking back at the Firehawk case. Been a while since I'd studied it with fresh eyes. Amazing what you can see from a distance. Anyway, I looked over your notes and Robyn's. Based on detailed descriptions you'd both written down, I assumed the same person who killed the Firehawks also killed Gloria. And Robyn." Harrison's voice shook. He'd liked Robyn. A lot. He'd been too shy and too young at the time to pursue any romantic interest, but the feelings were still there in his voice.

"I ruled out Kestrel Firehawk right away. She didn't have the physical stamina to stab either man through the heart like that. That kind of wound takes quite a punch. She didn't have what it took, physically, to kill two men in their prime. The only one she might have brought down would have been Gloria Stokes. But not the men. Not unless they willingly went to the blade. And Robyn? I can't imagine that Robyn ever submitted to anybody."

"Yeah," Finn agreed. "Not to mention that Kestrel was a little bit busy giving birth to twins while Robyn was being murdered."

"It didn't make sense," Harrison continued, "for Grant or Cedric's parents to kill their children. Based on your notes, that is. If they'd killed anybody—based on Robyn's notes—it would have been Kestrel. Not their own children. And there was no connection with Gloria or Robyn. Reverend Jones was in the police station the night Robyn died. So I ruled him out, too." Harrison grunted again, deep in thought. "What really bothered me was Gloria Stokes' insistence to you, off the record I might add, that Kestrel was the killer. You noted in your report that Gloria couldn't have gotten a good look at Kestrel's face because of the logistics of the crime scene. The killer's back was to the fire and her—or his—face was in shadow. Seems to me she was trying to accomplish two things. One: she was protecting someone, either because she felt obligated to or she was scared to death of him. And two: she was doing her best to damn Kestrel Firehawk, whom she saw as some kind of romantic rival. According to interviews with Gloria's coworkers, she had some sort of fixation on Grant Firehawk. Now that made me wonder: how would Floyd Stokes, her husband, feel about her interest in another man? Would he feel strongly enough to kill off the object of her affections? Was that why she kept quiet? Did he threaten her, too?"

Damn. Young Harrison Weaver had turned into a really good detective. Maybe if Finn hadn't been so blinded by his emotions and his discovery of Robyn's religion, maybe he could have seen the facts, too. But he'd lost his objectivity, and after that, all had been lost.

"We got a search warrant for Floyd Stokes' home. Didn't find anything there. He wasn't home. Left rather quickly, it seems. Then we hit paydirt."

Finn pulled a cord on the crossbow almost into place. The cord unraveled and snapped. Too old. Too rotten. The crossbow had once been deadly. Now it was nothing more than an ornament.

"We found the makings for a couple of pipe bombs," Harrison continued. "Matched up with a couple of local bombings that took place in the past year here in Greenburg. We've had three interracial couples' homes and businesses bombed this year alone. We thought maybe it was a white supremacist group and that's what we were going for. We didn't realize we were dealing with a Phineas priest. Now it all makes sense."

"Yeah, to you, maybe," Finn said, picking at the blinds of the window and seeing nothing outside. "I don't know much about Catholicism, but what the hell is a Phineas priest?"

"Doesn't have anything to do with Catholicism. There's a group of religious fanatics in our country. All over our country, MacCool. They're very sincere."

Sincere? Sincerity in a religion was a welcome relief after all the hypocrisy he'd seen in his life. Or was it?

"This group of people," Harrison continued, "doesn't believe they're subject to the laws of the land. They don't believe they're subject to any law other than the laws of God. The laws of God as they interpret them. They take their authority from the Bible, from a story about a man named Phineas who killed a couple for cavorting outside their race. This Biblical Phineas was rewarded by God for his actions. These people—these Phineas priests—believe that interracial marriages are so wrong that they are punishable by death, the sentence to be carried out by them as representatives of God Almighty."

"Jesus," Finn whispered.

"No. Doesn't have anything to do with Jesus. Most of their actions seem to go back to the Old Testament. At least, they do where Floyd Stokes' group is concerned. They don't believe in banks or that banks have any Biblical reason to exist; therefore, they don't see bank robbery as breaking the law. They don't believe that abortion is allowable either. Remember the abortion clinic doctor who was shot to death in Florida several years back? The shooter was a Phineas priest."

A shiver wound its way down Finn's back. He dropped the blinds and turned to stare at the room for more weapons. "So we've got a dangerous situation. We've got a bunch of people who believe they're authorized by God to kill those who don't keep the laws of God as they see them. Have I got it right?"

"Right on target. And you know what the Bible says about witches...."

Thou shalt not suffer a witch to live. He knew. And no need explaining to anyone how King James had bastardized the original scripture to suit his own political needs. The original language had nothing to do with witches but instead with murderers. Poisoners. Honorable men fought openly, often in bladed combat. Cowards slipped potions into your drink and slipped away unnoticed while the poison sometimes took days to work its evil. By then, there was simply no knowing whose hand had delivered the fatal cocktail.

"So Floyd Stokes is somewhere out there making sure he doesn't suffer any witches. You're sure of that."

"Absolutely," Harrison answered. "He had a lot of computer gear in his home. Turns out that he had an Internet hate site dedicated to the murder of people he didn't like."

"Let me guess—witches."

"Witches, Druids, Wiccans, gays, lesbians, interracial couples, pregnant teens. Even working moms. He hired models to pose in ghoulish makeup—you know, pointy noses and warts—and pretend to be real witches stirring cauldrons full of aborted babies to show how disgusting pagans are. There are photos of children and young teens holding church rallies with bonfires where they're burning mannequins that are supposed to be witches. The kids are holding placards and chanting, 'Burn the witch, burn the witch!'"

Finn swallowed the bile that rose in his throat. "He's trying to make people believe...." Ugh. He couldn't even finish the sentence.

"He's not just trying. He's succeeding. He's making hate crimes acceptable. Stokes may be burning store mannequins in public, but he's doing his damnedest to desensitize people into thinking murder is okay as long as the victim isn't like them. He's going to make sure people think of pagans as dirty, diseased, evil creatures who need to be killed."

Finn nodded to himself, his fingers pressed against his lips to hold back the nausea. Finn knew well that hate web sites were out there. He'd seen them himself and had thanked the God and Goddess that the web site owners lived a thousand miles away. What did surprise him was how much Harrison knew, how matter-of-fact he was about paganism. He even knew there was a difference between witches and Wiccans. Then again, Harrison had been madly in love with Robyn. He'd probably done what Finn hadn't all those years ago when Robyn's religion had gotten her fired—he'd bothered to find out what she believed and why.

"Fortunately—or unfortunately, depending on your point of view—our country has this freedom of speech and freedom of religion thing," Finn said. "He can say anything he wants and believe anything he wants, and the real witches out there can't stop him. Those same freedoms protect pagans, too. Ironic, isn't it? A few staged rallies and photo shoots aren't illegal so—"

"Those youth rallies weren't staged. They were real. He's even got audio and video on his web site. Some of them were filmed at a church building—we're investigating those now—but most were filmed at his safety range." Harrison's voice rose in excitement. "Get this, MacCool: for the past four summers, he's been holding church youth camp at his safety range. Teens, twelve and up, attend for two weeks at a time to learn how to identify witches, gays, and other undesirables. They have a rally every night, complete with a sermon on their responsibility to God. During the day, they learn to shoot and to work with explosives and poisons." Harrison paused for effect. "MacCool, he's training an army. An army of God."

"And what can we do about it? So he gets a couple of fines for violating safety laws. Harrison, I want to get that son of a bitch for what he did to Robyn." And what he did to Kestrel.

"Agreed. And I think we will. We took Stokes' safety range apart, and in the attic we above one of the meeting rooms, we found a plastic garbage bag. You'll never guess what was in it."

Finn's heart pounded furiously. He peered out the window for signs of life. He could see the gong by the stream, but no one waited there. "Hurry it up, Harrison. I can't stay here much longer."

"A yellow slicker. Boots. A hat. Still stained with blood. Stokes had been so completely covered up when he killed the Firehawks and his wife—and Robyn—that we wouldn't have found a speck of blood on him. The gear didn't leave any fibers. Nothing to trace back to Stokes. It's damned damning evidence, I'd say."

They had him. They had the killer. They had Stokes. Finn had waited so long.

"MacCool? My advice to you would be to get out of wherever you are. Now."

"I've interviewed him before. I'll recognize him."

"That's not the point. He may recognize *you*. I've heard enough rumors about you over the years. I can discern rumor from truth, but we all know you're not the cop you used to be. Stokes will take one look at you and know you're the enemy."

Chapter Twelve

~Kestrel~

"Branwen! Deirdre!" I called in a stage whisper as I reached the edge of the deer path.

The girls weren't where they were supposed to be. Not that that was anything new. The girls were forever wandering off to catch tadpoles or dragonflies. Sometimes it drove me crazy, but I suppose I would have been the same way at that age if the distant aunt that raised me hadn't been so stern. The girls were always outside, lost in their love of nature. Every time I ever considered forcing them to stay indoors more, it was almost as if the Goddess Herself were saying, "Kestrel? Did you not know your children would be in My house? My daughters are doing My work." As a mother, my one consolation was that where one girl went, so went the other. There was indeed some safety in numbers. Even the number two.

All the times I had yelled at the girls for fighting and wrestling and being generally obnoxious—none of those times mattered now. Right now, I needed to see them both, *badly*, waiting where they had been told.

I scanned the twisting trail, toward the mountain peak and back down toward Tracey's cabin. Maybe I'd missed the girls. Maybe Tracey had run instead of walked. Maybe they'd already gone up, over the mountains.

I studied the leafy ground to the left, up the mountain. It seemed quiet, cold. I tried to get a sense of the energies. A vortex swirled to the right, just down the mountain. Yes. My girls had headed toward Tracey's. Maybe they'd grown tired of waiting. It was like them to be impatient. Especially Branwen. She tended to be the leader—or rather, instigator—of the two. I had to find the girls and get them away from here. Quickly. Before the witch-hunter made it up the mountain.

And I had to warn Tracey.

I took several punishing steps through the underbrush and stopped. I missed...noise. The birds around me had stopped singing. All the wildlife around me had gone quiet. Aware. Waiting. Expecting danger. Deafening in their silence.

Then I spotted it. Blood. Just a few drops, but blood, there, on the path. And against a large white boulder, where the girls like to sit sometimes, was smeared a few fingerprints' worth of blood. *My babies!*

I toed off my shoes and left them at the edge of the path. I would pick them up when we came back up this way, but for now, the path was soft and leafy. No briars. No thistles. Too many twigs. I had to be fast, but I had to be quiet.

I padded softly, quickly, down the hill, running at times in the steep descent. I splashed through a trickle that flowed over the path on its way to larger waters. I rounded the corner and Tracey's cabin came into view. I could see Tracey's old truck and a vehicle that must have belonged to Finn. The cabin windows were open. Sheer curtains fluttered in the windows. Wind chimes jangled on the same breeze. All seemed still, yet I heard the sound of children's voices coming from inside. Singing. Soft singing. Goddess chants and prayers.

I ran. I bounded up onto the craggy porch behind the house and knocked briskly on the back door. "Tracey! Tracey," I called, not too loudly so as not to alert the witch-hunter. I hoped they could hear me. "Girls! Girls!"

No answer. Still, the sound of singing from deep inside the cabin.

Why were they singing? And who was hurt? Had the witch-hunter found them already? They needed to be running, not singing. Why were they singing?

I pulled on the screen door. It was open, but that wasn't unusual. Tracey routinely left the back door open, particularly when she was going in and out, potting flowers, and from the looks of the potting soil and vermiculite bags on the back porch, that's exactly how Tracey had spent her afternoon.

"Tracey?" I stepped inside. I followed the sound of song into the kitchen and realized with a sinking feeling in the pit of my stomach that the music came from a small tape player on the counter. I clicked it off and let the silence envelope me.

Nothing moved. The breeze stopped. The curtains ceased their flutter. The wind chimes outside no longer jangled. Birds stopped their song. Nothing but silence, as if time itself had stopped.

"Tr-tracey?"

I pressed my fingers against my jet and amber necklace as if I could somehow choke my fears. I tiptoed forward through the house. Had Tracey left the house so quickly that she'd left the tape player blaring and the back door unlocked? Normally I could sense the presence of other things around me. People. Spirits.

There was no sense of Tracey. Or the girls.

"Tracey?" My voice grew louder, almost hoarse, then broke. "Girls?"

My bare foot came down on something slippery and I almost fell. I stared down at my feet at the place where my path crossed bloody boot prints that led from the living room out the front door.

"Girls!"

I ran, slipping, sliding in the blood on the linoleum. Scrambling to stay upright. I made it to the living room door, grabbing the door jamb and holding on hard to keep from falling forward.

Tracey sprawled face down on the floor in front of me. Lifeless. If there had been any life there, I would have felt it.

I sucked in my breath to fight down the nausea. The sight of Tracey and all that blood brought back too many memories. Grant. Cedric. Daddy. Mama.

Where are the girls?

I glanced around the room, reaching out with my mental antennae. I didn't feel the kids there. The room felt cold, devoid of any life.

And Tracey, her long blonde hair fanned out over her shoulders and veiling her face, looked hauntingly familiar. Tracey was slim, a size 6—as I had been ten years ago before my babies. She was only in her mid-twenties—as I had been ten years ago. On the few times we had gone into town together, we'd been confused for sisters. If the witch-hunter had slipped in the Tracey's cabin and seen her there in the living room, her back to him, then he would have seen that long blonde hair and thought....

But why? Why Tracey's house?

And then I remembered. The two mailboxes at the foot of the mountain, representing two houses. The two mailboxes out of order. He would have come here expecting to find Saadia Payne, aka Kestrel Firehawk the Witch, not my young friend and neighbor.

I took a couple of deep breaths and padded forward. I crouched and very, very gently pulled the veil of hair back from Tracey's face. Blood gushed from a slash across her throat. Her eyes stared into nothingness. I tugged softly at Tracey's shoulder. Tracey—no, not Tracey—her limp *body* flopped over onto her back. Its back. Eyes staring straight up, past me. Tracey was gone. Her presence had already floated away, into the Summerlands.

The thought caught in my throat. Tracey had been a good friend to me. The only friend I'd had since I lost Saadia. Now Tracey had left a child motherless but with the permission of Becca and her father, they'd bury Tracey here on Saadia's Mountain, near the two unmarked graves where the earthly bodies of the real Saadia Payne and Robyn Porter lay.

I stroked Tracey's cheek. Still warm. Tracey's pentacle had been cut from her neck. The little silver star glittered in a pool of bright red blood near her hand. An upside-down pentagram had been carved into her forehead and another into the palm of her right hand. The mark of the beast.

Beast, indeed.

257

Her dress had been torn in front, far enough down to expose the upper cup of her once-white bra, now crimson. Something glittered back at me. An athame driven into Tracey's heart and twisted. Amethyst eyes of ornate Celtic birds embraced in a hilt of silver.

I gasped. My athame had come home to me!

With a shaking hand, I pulled the blade from Tracey's body. Like most athames, it was never meant to taste blood. The blade screamed with misuse, with the blood of too many witches crying out for vengeance.

I rose and held my athame high above my head, pointed it at the sky. Blood dripped down and onto my fingers. "Goddess, Hecate, avenge Your daughters!" I whispered in a shaking voice as I thought of both Tracey and Robyn and wondered about my little girls. Then I saw in my mind's eye that Beltane night, my guys, my wonderful Grant and Cedric. "And avenge Your sons!"

I lowered my athame, but I didn't wipe the blood from it. In some cultures, it is said that the most powerful talisman you can own is something of a murder victim's body. Sometimes a head. Sometimes a hand. My athame had come back to me for a reason. It had never been cleaned. It bore on it the dried blood of both Grant and Cedric. Of Robyn. Even of that whore, Gloria. And now the still-wet life blood of Tracey. All victims in this lifetime of the witch-hunter. And, in my gut, I knew that four of the victims had met the witch-hunter in some past life, too. Perhaps even Gloria had been one of us before and just hadn't found us yet. Perhaps that had been her fascination with us.

Athame in hand, I stalked out the back door, letting the screen slam behind me. I didn't care who heard now. The athame in my hand tingled and stung as if I'd grabbed onto a live wire. My bare feet touched the earth. Air rushed quickly into my lungs. My eyes teared and water ran down my face. Fire burned in my blood. My sense heightened and I could feel the energies around me. No, Branwen and Deirdre hadn't come this far. Not today. They were still in the waking world...somewhere.

But where would they have gone? Finn was at the office, looking for antique weapons. The girls would not have known to go there for help. And if they hadn't come as far as Tracey's, they might have gone back to the house, especially if they had suspected something. Maybe they'd gone to the front door while I'd gone out the back and we'd missed each other.

The dark energy converged on the path ahead of me and lingered as if someone had come around from the front of the house and followed the deer path toward the place where I'd left the girls. I hadn't felt it earlier. I hadn't been looking for it. I'd always had a propensity for feeling presences, but it was Saadia who had taught me to discern energies. Energies were like smells, like perfumes. Sometimes light and sweet like a bouquet of flowers that had been moved from the room. Sometimes rank and overpowering like a kitchen where fish had been fried three days ago.

I followed the dark energy until I neared the place where I'd left my daughters. Their lighter energies mingled with the dark, but they didn't head back up the way they had come. Instead, they struck out across the woods, the two lighter energies ahead of the darker one. Slow. Lingering. Purposeful. Leading the dark energy away! Away from the house? Away from me?

Oh, Goddess! My babies were protecting me!

But where had they gone? The path they had taken led toward the waterfall, a place forbidden to both girls. The rocks were slippery and deadly and dangerous. Then, too, was the man who followed them.

I attuned myself to the earth beneath my bare feet and the sky above my head. I threw my head back, exposing my throat, raising my arms and athame high in the air, becoming one with the universe around me. Exactly as I sometimes did in deep meditations when I became one with the animals, an old druid talent. Not that I became the animal—I was just along for the ride, feeling what it felt on an instinctive level, gathering information through it, purging emotions. Sometimes, accompanying a bobcat or a wolf to a kill left my mouth tasting a little gamy afterwards.

I found myself stepping away from my body and shooting straight up in the air toward where a monstrous red-tailed hawk circled, its wingspan spreading like palmetto branches. I felt myself merging with the hawk, surveying the woods below. I swerved and swirled and swayed as I had so many times before.

259

The air lifted me up, and I soared and glided. I found the stream at its shallowest, followed it uphill, over the waterfall to where nothing moved but the water, and then up to where the entrance to the caves loomed. I whirled on the wind and turned back. I scanned the mountainside with the keenest vision I have ever known, seeing the tiniest wood mouse scuttle under a pile of leaves and then a small rabbit huddle near a clump of bright yellow rudbeckia, waiting, listening, quietly, hoping I couldn't see him.

Then I spotted the girls walking unhurriedly through the trees, single file, Deirdre leading the way for a change and a little bloody at the upper lip but well enough. Someone walked behind them. He wore camouflage, but I could still detect his movements with my hawk's eyes. Some type of sophisticated rifle in his hands. Aimed at my precious little ones.

I had to get closer.

I joined with the rabbit, close to the ground, barely breathing, only my nose wiggling as I sensed danger nearby. I heard the girls tramping toward me. Splashing through a trickle of stream. Climbing over a fallen log. Whispering. Something about waterfalls and caves. The two most forbidden places in their repertoire of play.

"Shut up, up there!" growled a man's voice behind them, and I knew that they were plotting, as they always were.

The girls fell back into single file silence, managing to walk a good ten or fifteen feet in front of the witch-hunter. They didn't have to duck for the branches, but he did, and it slowed him down a little. The brush was thickest here. Tree roots stabbing upward. Slippery edges and ledges. Very little wear in the path. The girls would have known that. They played here often enough.

I waited, quiet and still, sniffing the air as the girls walked past my rabbit self. I had to distract him. I had to give my babies a chance. As long as they were with him, they were in danger. I heard the crunching of his feet on twigs. Saw the boots with Tracey's blood across the toe. Smelled his sweat. I waited...waited...waited until the boots were only half a stride away.

Run, I told the rabbit. *Danger. Run. Run, run, run!*

I felt the rabbit leap up right under his feet. The witch-hunter startled and fell backward, firing off one shot by accident. I heard him cursing. Branwen scurried up the mountain, through the brush, hidden, safe. But Deirdre didn't run. It was almost as if she were waiting for something.

Then I felt the blinding heat of a bullet crashing through my hindquarter and splintering bone. I felt my little rabbit heart fluttering in my chest as the poor animal fell. I heard the witch-hunter reload, heard him fire again, felt my little rabbit body shudder under the impact.

Then I snapped back into my body. Hands still raised to the sky. Athame still in my hand. Too far away to be of any use to Deirdre.

Chapter Thirteen

~Deirdre~

"What are you stopping for?" the man yelled at her.

Deirdre knew him. She'd seen him in both dreams and visions, but she didn't know his name. He'd come out of darkness, filled with hate she couldn't understand, either now or before. He was a stranger to her, but bent on her destruction.

"Where'd the other one go?" He squinted into the underbrush. Thick ferns waved back at him. "Your sister. Where'd she go?"

"I'm sure we'll see her again soon." Deirdre did her best to sound confident. "You just scared her, that's all. She'll show up at the waterfall."

"What's your sister's name? It's not Robyn, is it?"

"No." Deirdre drew out the word. She knew the story of brave Aunt Robyn who'd died the night she and Branwen were born. Mom and Grandma had had her grave moved to their mountain because some mean people back in Robyn's hometown were walking on her grave and stuff. Disrespecting her body. Did the man with the gun know about Mom's friend? "Nope, my sister is Branwen, not Robyn."

"Branwen Firehawk."

"No. Branwen Payne. And I'm Deirdre. Deirdre Payne."

He glared down at her. He was big. Her knees trembled, but she wouldn't let him see them shake. Hunters could smell fear just as good as little animals could.

"Where's Kestrel Firehawk?"

Deirdre shrugged. "I don't know any Kestrel Firehawk." She knew the name though. She'd heard the name, heard herself calling the name in some distant dream. Kestrel. The woman who looked like Mom. Maybe was Mom.

"What's your mama's name, girl?"

"Saadia. Saadia Payne."

"Don't lie to me, you little brat." He shook the gun at her and nearly tripped over a root that snaked across the path. "I've done my homework. The woman named Saadia would be damned near one hundred years old. Now what's your mother's name?"

"S-Saadia."

He reddened. A vein on his forehead threatened to burst. "What do people call her?"

Deirdre swallowed. "They call her Saadia, but Branwen and me, we call her Mom."

"You've never heard the word Kestrel before?"

"Well, sure. All the time. That's what itty bitty hawks are, right? Kestrels." Mom would have called her a smart-aleck right now, but Mom wasn't around.

The man grunted. "She lied to her kids, huh? Just like a witch."

Deirdre didn't say anything. There were things Mom hadn't told her, things she and Branwen knew. They'd talked about it, late at night after the lights were out.

"Where's your mom now?"

"She's usually at the waterfall this time of day." It wasn't exactly a lie. She knew Mom wouldn't be there now, but Mom *was* usually at the waterfall this time of day. Really. Usually.

"You'd better not be lying to me."

Deirdre didn't look at him. Instead, her gaze stuck on the barrel of his gun. Mom had given her and Branwen a couple of stern lectures on never ever touching a gun and on what a gun could do to a person's body, so Deirdre knew better than to do anything that would cause him to use it. Especially after he'd killed the bunny. She'd never seen a bullet wound on a person, but she'd seen it once when somebody had shot a great big deer—dead—and she knew wouldn't like it if somebody shot her.

Better her than Branwen though. If Branwen had done what Deirdre had told her. For a change. It would be just like her sister to ignore and not do what she'd said, just for spite. Deirdre herself was tempted plenty enough times to do something to spite Branwen, but those times never included when a man in hunting clothes held a gun on either one of them.

"Come on," Deirdre said to the man. She wiped her sweaty hands on her T-shirt. It was easy to pretend she was Branwen now—the daredevil—like she was someone outside her own body. As long as she could pretend, she wasn't terribly nervous. If he knew how nervous she was when she didn't pretend, he would probably kill her.

She trudged in the opposite direction. Reaching high, she caught a small oak branch in her palms and pushed it sideways. She let it go just in time for it to hit the man across the nose. She heard the "oof!" behind her and knew she'd been successful.

"Slow down," he growled. "You run away from me like your sister did, and I swear I'll start shooting every clump of grass I see."

Just like he had that poor little rabbit. She remembered the force of the bullet lifting its furry carcass into the air and dropping it several feet away. She shuddered.

"I'm not running anywhere," she said with as much false bravado as she could muster. "You just have to keep up. This path is real hard. Maybe too hard for an old man like you are."

No, she wasn't running anywhere. She had to get him to the waterfall. Even if she had to taunt him, and according to Branwen, she was good at that. If Deirdre ran, he might lose his way. Go after Branwen. Or Mom. Or Finn. He had to come after her. Had to.

Her knees ached as she shuffled through the leaves, kicking them this way and that, scuffing a trail in case anyone should follow. The sound of water falling hard on rocks grew louder. Deirdre knew the stakes. Mom would be mad if she knew what Deirdre planned to do, but Deirdre couldn't let this man find Mom and hurt her. Not again.

Mom would be mad, but Mom would forgive her. The Goddess? She was another story. The Goddess was full of nurturing and love, but just as there was a light side, the Goddess had a dark side, too. Like all the good and bad but neither one existing without the other. The last thing Deirdre wanted was to have the Goddess mad at her.

"Slow down, girl!"

Deirdre kept going, no faster and no slower.

"Slow down, girl, or I'll shoot you." He picked up his pace and burst through the brush behind her.

Deirdre kept walking but glanced once over her shoulder. Several of the limbs above her head had snapped back and hit him in the face. A thin line of blood trickled from a welt on his right cheek. She knew better than to smirk.

"If you kill me, I can't take you to my mother."

"Who said anything about killing you? I just said I'd shoot. You can still take me to your mother if you're missing a couple of fingers."

Deirdre's heart skipped a beat. He meant it. She could tell. She clenched her fingers into fists and drew her hands into her chest. She slowed down. Not much, but enough to prove she could mind.

"What do I need you for, anyway? I can hear the waterfall from here."

He'd stopped somewhere behind her. He was pointing his gun at her back. She knew it as surely as if she'd turned to face him. Deirdre stopped, too.

"You need me," she said in an even voice, "because you don't know where my mom will be at the waterfall. Besides, if you shoot me, she'll hear the shot and run. If she hasn't already when you killed the bunny."

He didn't move.

Neither did Deirdre.

She held her breath, waiting, wondering where he'd aim the fatal shot. Would she feel the bullet crack her skull and bury itself deep inside her brain? She fought the reflex to close her eyes. If she was about to die, she wanted the last thing she saw to be the mountain stream she loved so much.

"All right," he said at last. "Show me where your mother is."

His bootfalls snuffled behind her. Deirdre exhaled and headed toward the water.

"We have to cross here." She nodded toward the stones she and Branwen had crossed so many times, where she'd seen Branwen fall to her death in a vision. The afternoon rain had seeped into the stream and raised the waters.

"Why here? There's a rope bridge downstream."

Deirdre sniffed the misty air that rose from the waterfall between her and the rope bridge over the quieter, shallow waters. "I'm not sure it's safe. It might not hold us." She chose her words carefully to avoid lying. "Mom doesn't like for us to cross it." That much was certainly true. Mom didn't like for Branwen and her to snoop around the office or visit the graves alone. "We usually walk across on the those rocks." She pointed at the stones that led to the picnic rock, the exact spot where she'd seen Branwen slip and fall in a vision. Only to be carried over the waterfall and thrown to the rocks below. She hoped Branwen wasn't anywhere nearby.

The man cursed behind her. "No. We'll take the rope bridge."

Deirdre splashed barefoot into the water. She'd left her shoes behind on the trail, lost in patches of yellow flowers. "What?" she shouted over her shoulder. "I can't hear you too good. The water's loud." Not as loud as she pretended, but the thunder of it gave her a few steps' leeway. She made it to the third stone.

"Come back here, girl!"

"What?" She nearly leapt to the slippery rock, her bare toes gripping the outer rougher edges of the rock like little suction cups. "I can't hear you."

Heart racing, she crawled onto the picnic rock and rolled to the far side before looking back. She flung her arms out for balance as she scurried across the rock. Late afternoon sunlight caught the shimmer of mica in the stone.

"See, it's easy," she yelled back. "As long as you're co-ordinated."

She heard him curse again, and by the time she looked back at him, he'd reached the third stone. Uh-oh. His balance was better than Mom's and Miss Tracey's and any other grown-ups. Better than Becca's. Maybe better than Branwen's. Maybe even better than hers.

"Come on," she coaxed. "You're nearly half-way across."

His face was purple with rage. One more step and he'd cool off for sure.

Just stay calm, she told herself. *Don't let him see how scared you are. Keep your voice steady. Don't let your knees knock. He thinks you're a stupid kid. He doesn't know who you are. Who you were. He probably doesn't even know who he was or how many times he's done this before. Witch-hunter.*

She crouched on the picnic rock and waited. Like a rabbit ready to jump. She watched the bend of his knee, the rise of his leg, as he aimed for the slippery stone. She didn't dare look him in the face for fear that something in her eyes might betray her.

Center of the stone, center of the stone, she willed the booted foot. *Take that nice, safe indention in the center of the stone. Then put your other foot on the side and fall, fall, fall!*

His right foot, his boot with the little grippy things on the bottom of it, touched the slippery-ness. His left foot came up on the higher, rougher side of the stone. Deirdre felt her heart sink. The plan hadn't worked. If he'd been barefoot, maybe. Or regular boots, maybe. But not soldier shoes. They were made for crossing slippery stones over deep streams. She didn't understand. Not ten minute ago, she'd seen a flash of him falling, right after he shot the rabbit and Branwen took off into the underbrush.

He angled toward the fifth stone. She watched open-mouthed as his shift in balance moved just to the boot, just to the side, just enough, just enough! Down he went! The gun flew up in the air, twirled once, and splashed into the water. The gun bobbed twice before it went over the waterfall.

The man splashed and cursed in front of her. She saw the glint of a hunting knife as he pulled himself back up onto the rock, glaring at her, still cursing her. "Spawn of a witch!" was all she heard.

He drew back the knife and aimed it in her direction, but like a new frog in summer, Deirdre sprang from the rock. She splashed down next to the boulder, down to the water she loved so much.

Chapter Fourteen

~Finn~

Finn stood beside the pounding waterfall and squinted upward thirty feet. He couldn't believe what he was seeing. The little girl with her fountain of blonde curls had picked her way across the deep stream. If she fell, she could easily be swept right over the edge. The stream bed was carved of rock, with plenty of jagged rocks protruding from the water like standing stones. Others were buried under the surface. At the very least, she'd slash her foot and risk infection. At worst, the rushing was would carry her over the cascade and onto the jumble of sharp rocks below where the stream spread out wide and shallow and only gurgled past Kestrel's cabin office.

He'd heard the cursing and rushed out of the building. He hadn't had enough time to grab his squeaking boots but enough time to seize a dingy, rusted, antique sword from the wall. Not that it would slice a tomato, but it could wield a few nasty bruises and it was better than anything else he had. He gripped the hilt in one hand and dragged it along the ground as he started up the steep incline, pulling off his socks as he went.

The little girl, Deirdre, made it to the big rock as if she'd gone that way many times before. She crawled over a small pine limb freshly littered by the surging stream. She chattered back at the man in camouflage as if having a gun held on her were the most natural thing in the world. Finn could barely hear her above the waterfall. She had a bad case of smart-mouth, a dangerous move for a small kid.

She crouched on the big rock and waited for the man. He bore little resemblance to the Floyd Stokes Finn had interviewed ten years ago. This man was older, harder even in the face. He was leaner and harder in the body, too, than Finn remembered. Again, the man Finn had interviewed had been a businessman in three-piece suits and a fancy watch fob hanging from his vest. In more ways than one, the expensive suits had done a good job of hiding what was underneath his meek exterior.

Cursing his way across the rocks, Stokes pursued the child. With the agility of a cat moving in for the kill, Stokes stepped from the third rock to the fourth and then toward the fifth. Just as quickly, his foot flew out from under him. His semi-automatic rifle twirled up into the air and came down into the water. The current carried it over the rocks. It bounced along the rocks below, then disappeared beneath the swirling depths.

Stokes caught the fourth rock with one arm and pulled himself back up, cursing and shrieking at the girl. He jerked a hunter's knife from its sheath. He drew back and aimed it at the child.

"Spawn of a witch! Just like your mother, aren't you? Invoking the devil to make me fall! That's what you did, isn't it?"

The little girl turned away, back arching to dive for the water.

Good God! Stokes meant to kill her! She was just a baby. *Just a baby!*

The water was swift and deep. She splashed into the stream and a second later emerged. She clung for dear life to a crevice in the rock. If she slipped, she was less than ten feet away from the gushing water at the cliff's edge of ragged stones and to a watery grave below on the rocks.

"Come out from there, you god-damned little bitch! I'll put an end to your devilry. Cut your throat from ear to ear like I did your father's!"

Stokes picked a path across the stones to the large boulder and dropped atop it as if claiming the territory for his own. A few more steps and he'd be able to see Deirdre, pressing her tiny body hard against the rock. Still and quiet, trying to blend in as if she were a tiny fish, she stayed in the shadows.

Stokes peered over the boulder's edge to where the recessed stone met the water. In a wild movement, Deirdre cupped her hands and swooshed water into his eyes. It caught him off-guard for a split second. She bolted forward, heading as fast as she could out of the water, toward the last few stones and the other bank.

Stokes grabbed her fountain of ponytail and pulled her back. He raised his hunter's blade to the sun. The child clutched at a broken pine limb bobbing downstream but missed it.

"God of Wild Things," Finn whispered. "Let it be me and not an innocent."

Not quite touching, a beam of sunlight slashed in front of the girl's throat. Finn pulled a paring knife from his belt and aimed at Floyd Stokes. It didn't really matter if Finn hit Deirdre instead. It was a chance he had to take. The worst case, if he flung the knife, was that he'd hit the child. The worst case, if he didn't fling the knife, was that Floyd Stokes would cut her throat. That was always the worst case, wasn't it? There had to be a happy medium in there somewhere.

Finn flung the little knife—hard. The blade spun in sunlit circles. The hilt struck Stokes in the ear—a wonderful aim had the blade turned another 180 degrees.

Stokes jerked back in surprise. He relaxed his grip on the girl's ponytail. She wriggled free and scampered back across the rocks toward the bank. Already, Finn had the second paring knife out of his belt. He aimed it and let it fly. The aim wasn't quite as good as the first but the blade struck the man in the side of the knee. Stokes howled and fell to the rock. He dropped his hunting knife. Before he could pull the paring knife's blade from his knee, Finn was half-way up the incline, a heavy sword swinging in one hand.

Panting for breath, Finn reached the top of the difficult incline before Stokes could drag himself up from the rock. Fresh blood dripped across the white stone, like the remnants of a sacrifice not quite made.

Sword over his head, Finn waded in the water and toward the rock. The stones in the water jabbed into his bare feet but he ignored the pain. He slipped and slid but caught his balance. He didn't wait for Stokes to produce a second weapon. No sense in fairness now. It was a matter of kill or be killed. No matter of who struck the first blow.

Finn brought the sword down hard. The blade came powerfully close to Stokes' shoulder before he dipped and rolled away. The antique blade struck the stone and cracked, the blade breaking into three brittle shards. Finn stared at the hilt in his hands. Only a few rough edges of steel protruded. Still, enough that he could defend himself.

Something cruel and wooden struck the side of his head. Finn felt cool water splash against his face. He blinked up at Stokes who stood over him, over the water where Finn had fallen. Stokes still held a pine limb in his grasp. Before Finn could surge upward through the water, Stokes planted the ragged end of the limb squarely in Finn's chest and pushed him down against the jagged rocks on the streambed. Finn choked and sputtered. Bubbles of air gurgled up from his throat. Finn clawed at the limb but it wouldn't budge. Stokes pressed down on the limb with all his strength, holding Finn under water, doing his best to drown Finn.

Not exactly Stokes' style, Finn found himself thinking as the seconds dragged out in to an eternity. The man preferred to slash and mangle. No doubt, there'd be enough of that later.

Finn's fist closed around a rock. He was only a foot or so under the water. Maybe a scant six inches from air. He brought his arm up to the water and sailed the rock through the air. It hit Stokes in the jaw, then splashed into the water at Finn's feet. Stokes didn't let go of the pole, but his grip relaxed just long enough that Finn rolled out from under the limb, then lunged out of the water, gasping for breath, deep and bloody scratches in his chest. Finn heaved in a good breath and backhanded the wet hair from his face so he could see.

Finn stood, precariously balanced on the rocks above the waterfall. He blinked the water out of his eyes. Before his sight could clear, he saw the limb swing fast for his head again. He ducked, just in time. His feet slipped on the slimy rocks. Down he went. The water pushed him, pushed him, closer, over the edge of the falls. Slipping, slipping!

He grabbed for the last piece of Mother Earth he saw.

Chapter Fifteen

~Deirdre~

What was she supposed to do now? This wasn't fair.
Her plan should have worked. But at least this time she was
doing something, not just standing there, waiting to have him
cut her neck and stab her in the heart. Not like last time.
Sometimes, it was better to do something, even if it was wrong,
than to do nothing at all. That's what Mom said, anyway.

But what was she supposed to do now? Was she supposed to go back and help Finn? Should she keep running for
the caves where she and Branwen were to meet? What was she
to do now? Over the water, she had the advantage, but.... Oh,
this was so unfair!

Maybe she should have prayed about it. Or paused to
cast a spell or something. Maybe that would have helped. The
kids at school sometimes said they prayed and got things, but in
her family, they did spells and rituals and got things. She knew
not to say spells for things like who would win a game at recess
or for her to make a good grade. Better for her to do a ritual
that she'd be healthy and feel well rested so she might win that
game or that she would study well so she might get a good
grade. Ethics, Mom called it.

Was it ethical to do a spell to get rid of the man who wanted to kill her family? To kill him back? She'd never killed anything. Never hurt anything. Well, except for punching her sister occasionally. She'd never asked the Goddess to hurt anything either, but she had to find a way to stop the man who would certainly kill Finn and Mom and Branwen. And her. The man who'd already killed Miss Tracey. The man who'd killed two men on a spring night before Deirdre was born.

She stopped running long enough to catch her breath. Her legs ached from running uphill so long. Branwen was waiting for her in the caves and they could hide safely there until the man left the mountain. Or.... Deirdre felt the Goddess' caress on her shoulder. The caves were deep and dark. A person could get lost in there.

The first time she and Branwen had explored the cave, they'd taken a huge roll of string and tied it to a tulip tree outside. That and a couple of candles and they'd found their way back. If Mom ever knew, she'd have a conniption fit. There were legends of an Indian princess who went into the caves and never came out, but the girls thought Mom had made that up. They'd been warned never to go near the caves. Of course, they'd gone.

"Help me lead him into the caves," she whispered to the Goddess, "and I'll leave him up to You."

Deirdre took a deep breath. She trudged back down the mountain a good ten feet until she reached a clearing and could see the waterfall below. No sign of Finn. Darn son-of-a-something she wasn't allowed to say! They'd lost Finn. She was too late. The witch-hunter had won.

"Hey, you big bully!" she screamed down at the man emerging on the dry bank. "What are you waiting for? The Second Coming of Jesus?"

Chapter Sixteen

~Kestrel~

"Deirdre! Oh, my baby, no!"

I heard her run before I saw her. I gripped my athame and bolted for the light at the end of the dark tunnel of shady trees. I stared at my baby in the distance, far up the mountain and beside the stream. The witch-hunter was only twenty or thirty feet behind her. And closing in great strides. I was amazed at his agility on the steep path. I myself sometimes had trouble with the landscape, and running up and down the mountain paths was my favorite form of exercise. Physically, the witch-hunter would be a formidable foe.

Deirdre scurried a few feet at a time, her wet ponytail bobbing up and down on top of her head and slinging water as she bounded forward. Then she would slow down, pause, waiting for him! Oh, Goddess, what was she doing? Deirdre was going to get herself killed.

"Kessssssss!" the waterfall seemed to say.

I squinted into the rising mist. I could barely believe what I saw. Finn dangled over the edge of the waterfall. The current splashed against his face, leaving him gasping for air.

He'd somehow managed to wrap both arms around an oblong-shaped boulder that protruded from the edge of the falls. He wouldn't be able to hold out much longer.

I glanced up the mountain at Deirdre, the witch-hunter close behind her and Branwen nowhere in sight. Then I squinted at Finn. I had to save my baby! On the other hand, the Goddess had brought him to me for a reason. Maybe the reason was to save my baby.

Another crossroads. Damn! Another crossroads! One path would save Finn and the other might save my little girl. If I were quick enough...if I were quick enough, I might have both paths. *Oh, but everything is about the choices we make, and there is no going back.* Just as I made a choice to fly by night rather than risk the fight. Still, Hecate had warned me of Finn's coming. My fourth. *Our* fourth.

Then I knew what I had to do.

I ran across the stepping stones, almost as if I were walking on water. I'd been careful never to let the girls see me do that, but sometimes it really was the fastest way to cross the stream and I was quite good at it. My knees felt weak. A spot in the pit of my stomach ached as if I'd been punched. I made it to the largest rock in the stream, a big flat one the size of my bed and crawled on top.

Blood stained the white rock. I glanced again at the witch-hunter and realized he was limping. A dark splash of blood bloomed at his camouflaged knee. I placed my athame criss-cross the red on the stone, a visual symbol that I would defeat him.

In what seemed to take forever, I maneuvered around to the side of the rock, between the rock and the falls, closest to Finn. I eased down into the swirling waters of the stream, careful not to lose the paring knives belted to my hips. The rocks under the water were sharp and bruised my feet, but I knew how to step to avoid the worst of it.

Finn had grabbed a rock that wasn't going anywhere, though his fingers might slip. The rock was an appendage of an underground boulder that would take an earthquake to move. I squatted all the way down in the water, its coldness chilling the base of my spine, washing over my thighs like ice. I wrapped my legs around the cold stone that had—at least temporarily—saved Finn's life. I pressed my knees into the rock for balance and leaned forward across the rock.

He was near surrender. I could tell. The water, constant and furious against his face, must have been torturous. I grabbed his left biceps and hung on hard, digging in with my fingernails. He was a bigger man than I'd realized. Most of his athletic bulk had been well-hidden beneath his clothes. With my right hand, I grabbed him behind the shoulder, underneath the arm and pulled him toward me. His newly laundered T-shirt was ripped in a dozen places, and skin shone through.

My grip on his biceps failed. I simply couldn't get my hand around his arm to get a good grasp. I plunged my free hand down into the water and grabbed his belt buckle. My fingers reached embarrassingly deep inside his jeans and pulled him forward with all my strength. He pulled himself up just enough so that the water clipped his chin. Grunting, he pulled himself up a few more inches. I saw blood on his fingertips. He struggled to bring one bare foot up onto even ground but couldn't quite make it.

One hand still gripping his belt buckle, I reached down with the other and seized his thigh behind his knee. His foot landed this time on solid ground, and he shoved himself up onto the rock and into my arms. He faltered atop the rock, me still there, my legs wrapped around the rock. He panted, gulped, gasped as if air had never before touched him.

I cradled his head against my neck like a lover on the first night—or the last. It seemed so right to have him there. As if he'd come home.

The right place, but not the right time.

"Come," I urged into his hair. His long wet tangles streaked across my damp shirt. "Come. My baby's in trouble."

He nodded. I helped him up onto the flat rock.

"Are you going to be okay?" I couldn't hide the urgency in my voice. I had to get to Deirdre. I'd risked my daughter's life to save his, but I felt the Goddess' touch on my willingness to sacrifice and I knew I'd made the right choice. On to the next crossroads....

Finn coughed and sputtered. "Need...a minute to...catch...my breath...."

"I have to go after the girls." I reclaimed my athame and holstered it with the paring knife at my right hip.

I turned to go but he caught my hand, clung to it. He coughed again. Water spurted from the corner of his mouth. His hands were bleeding. One fingernail was gone. The skin on his feet looked as if it had been shredded. I'd saved his life, yes, but there was little he could do to help me now. The wounds on his feet and the pain in his eyes told me wouldn't be able to follow. Even at a limp.

"You know where they've gone?" he asked.

I had one of those awful feelings I couldn't explain to anyone else except a fellow pagan. "Yeah, I'm afraid I do know."

And because I did know, I truly was afraid.

Chapter Seventeen

~ *Branwen* ~

The third match went out before she could light the candle. Branwen wasn't very good at matches. Not yet, even though she loved fire. Mom knew how much Branwen liked flame and always fussed at her about playing with fire. Then again, Branwen wasn't supposed to be in the cave either.

She and Deirdre didn't keep flashlights in the cave because Mom would miss one and they'd have too much explaining to do. Plus, Branwen hadn't had time to run back home and find a flashlight before running away from the mean man and off to the caves as she and Deirdre had planned in whispers. Even if she could find a flashlight at home that quickly, the battery would most likely be dead because the two girls played with flashlights late at night when they were supposed to be asleep in their beds and not hiding in the closet and reading. As a result, Mom always fretted about never having a working flashlight when she needed one.

Instead of flashlights in the cave, the girls kept a box behind a rock at the cave's entrance. Candles. Lots of white altar candles. Mom had so many candles and burned so many of them every week that she'd never miss the few dozen the girls had, well, *borrowed*. They had several boxes of matches, too. Mostly little boxes that they kept inside a plastic bag that sealed to keep water out. The only other things in the box were some small branches off a willow tree. Deirdre insisted willow was best for magick wands. Not like the kind in the Harry-Potter-the-Wizard books, but real wands for real magick. They'd watched Mom and Miss Tracey often enough to know how it was done and they liked to experiment alone. Usually things like making it snow so much they couldn't go to school on test day. Funny, but that spell always failed. Or sometimes they asked the Goddess to help make Mom forgive them for something stupid they'd gotten into trouble about. Those spells usually worked.

Branwen paused. Deirdre was near. As twins, they recognized each other's presence, finished each other's sentences, and couldn't sleep without the other nearby, even if they did fight like cats and dogs half the time. Typical sibling stuff, Miss Tracey had said.

Branwen stood as still as a frightened fawn in sunshine and strained to hear her sister's footfalls. An eerie whistle of wind moved through the cave, bringing with it the stench of damp, cool stone and causing the flame of her lone candle to flicker. The distant, steady drip of water from the jagged stalactites into an underground lake that fed the falls outside echoed through the emptiness of the rocky rooms. Then she heard the rustle of leaves outside as Deirdre swerved between the tree trunks that helped hide the cave's entrance. Then Deirdre rushed through the door, blinking in the blackness and silhouetted against the oval of blinding light behind her.

"Branwen?" she whispered. Her voice trembled.

"Here." Branwen touched her sister on the arm and held up the candle to light her face. Deirdre jumped at the touch. "It's okay," Branwen told her. "It's just me. Did he fall into the water?"

"Yes," Deirdre answered breathlessly, at the same time shaking her head. "But he's right behind me."

Branwen's heart skipped a beat. Their plan hadn't worked. The bad guy was supposed to slip and fall over the waterfall. He'd lose his weapons and be hurt, maybe even killed, if it was the Goddess' will. Deirdre would collect Branwen from her hiding place in the caves and they'd both go back to let Mom and Finn know everyone was saved. But it hadn't worked. Now what?

"I'll put out the candle. We can hide in here, and he'll never find us."

"No." Deirdre squinted into the dimness and felt her way along the wall. She bumped into the box that held the candles. She fumbled through it and scooped the other candles into her arms. She stuck one of the willow limbs into the waistband of her shorts. "We have to light them all."

"All the candles? But he'll see—"

"All. We have to have help."

"But—"

"The Goddess' help." Deirdre grabbed her by the arm and led her into the dark rooms deeper underground. "To the Altar Room. Come on!"

With the light of a single candle, they stumbled from the outer chamber through a narrow doorway. The shadow of a huge boulder over the entrance made Branwen cringe. The rock hung there precariously and threatened to fall. Was that Deirdre's plan? Trap the mean man inside the cave where he'd starve before he found his way out into the light? Branwen always worried about that rock falling—not just to the hard ground, but on *her*.

"Come on," Deirdre urged. "We have to hurry."

They tiptoed down through a deep chamber they called the Cathedral Room, named so because the ceiling went straight skyward like something medieval. Sometimes the ceiling seemed to move. Bats or shadows, she wasn't certain.

The room opened up into another, the Altar Room. Indian drawings of ancient council meetings had been scratched into the walls. It was by far the largest room the girls had explored. The wind whistled louder here. The rushing sound of an underground stream and the dripping of stalactites made Branwen want to pee as they descended further underground.

"We have to hurry." Deirdre thrust several of the candles toward Branwen. "Light these. Light them all."

Without the candles, they wouldn't be able to see their hands in front of their faces. The darkness was total and damp and earthy. The girls held cold wicks to the flame, setting each candle afire. Deirdre took each one and planted them one at a time in a crevice between the cones of rock. Together they planted the bright-burning candles until the candles formed a giant circle around the altar stone, a large circle-shaped flat rock covered with a thin sheen of dry dirt. Out of a reverence she remembered but didn't understand, Branwen hooked her index finger under the strap of her shoe and flipped it off. In another second, she was as barefoot as Deirdre. Branwen's toes spread against the slick, cool Mother Earth beneath her feet.

"Should we—I don't know—get naked or something?" Branwen distinctly remembered stripping off a long dark robe sometime long ago.

"Don't need to." Deirdre straightened a wayward candle. "If magick can work across miles and time, it can for sure work through our clothes. That's what Mom says, anyway."

Deirdre stopped dead still. So did Branwen. All they heard was the dripping was water and whisper of wind. What they felt was ancient and full of hate. A presence. They'd been here before, sensing his coming and waiting for Death on a night meant for Life. Neither had to look up. They both knew a darkness stood at the opening of the cave, obliterating the light.

Deirdre took a deep breath and reached for her wand.

Chapter Eighteen

~ Finn ~

The blood wasn't so bad now.

Finn curled up on the flat expanse of rock, his cheek against the cool, dry stone. Like a subdued sacrifice, he felt the closeness of Death all around him. It lapped against the boulder and raced beyond to the rush of the waterfall where Kestrel had hauled him to safety. It glinted down in the sunshine to the silver freckles of mica speckling the rock. It flew by on wings of late summer air when the passage above the creek should have been breezeless. With every movement Finn made, the gashes in his feet reopened and blood gushed out, trickled down the white of the rock and then mingled with the clear water.

He tried to lift his head but failed. Tired, so tired. He'd made an effort for over two decades to stay in the best physical shape possible, more out of concern for stamina than vanity. The workouts had paid off and his muscles had served him well, but there was only so much a man could do in the face of his own death. He'd hung on to the rocky waterfall until the sheer effort of supporting his weight sapped all his strength. He'd braced and climbed and flung his feet against the razor-edged rocks in a futile effort to scale the wall of water. Without Kestrel, he would have fallen to the rocks below.

Again Finn tried to raise his head. Failed. He turned his eyes toward the steep incline of the mountain, to the path where Kestrel had gone and Stokes before her and Deirdre before him. He caught a red flash of a woman's shirt as she disappeared between stone and wood high above him on the path. Kestrel. Off to defend her children. Her soulmates from ten years ago. Off to deflect Stokes' blows where she had not on that fatal Beltane night. And now that she was stronger, off to confront the evil she had fled by night.

He needed to do something. Anything. He couldn't let her face Stokes alone. Not like that time when she'd faced the witch-hunter at the gallows and Finn had stood by silently in the crowd and watched her die. He'd been physically stronger then and had done nothing. What use could Finn be now? He couldn't even walk.

"You have to get up."

Finn wasn't sure if he'd heard a voice on the wind or in his conscience. Maybe he was losing consciousness. Or his mind. Either that or he was dying.

You have to get up.

The thought echoed in his mind, more felt than heard.

He had to get up. He had to go after Kestrel. Nothing to lose. Either he fought by Kestrel's side, or waited for her to fail and for Stokes to come back to finish him off, this time with pentagrams carved into his dead flesh.

"God and Goddess, help me." Panting, he forced his shaking elbows to raise his chest from the cool rock. Tears of pain stung his eyes. He heaved in summer air and then swung his legs up and over the boulder's edge. His black shirt hung in tatters, flopping against his chest. Finn stared down at his bare, bloody feet. Red with blood. Red like the shoes Deirdre had thought he wore. His feet no longer dripped but throbbed instead. In a few days—if he lived a few more days—his feet would be sore, unbearable to the touch. But for now, they hurt less than they would later. Weakness from loss of blood was his biggest worry.

With half a push and mostly a fall, he splashed down into the rippling water beside the rock. The cool water felt good to his wounds, freezing cold, though he had no feeling left in the soles of his feet. Numbly, he stumbled forward, knowing only from the pressure in his bones that his feet touched the dozens of small, sharp stones on the bottom of the creek.

Shivering, Finn waded ashore. Leaves and grass stuck to his feet. He lurched forward, enough effort to reach a small oak and hang on. Finn looked back at the bloody footprints he'd left behind. No, no more looking back. Only forward now. The past was too filled with grief, and the landscape of the future was only slightly less bleak. Such was the crossroads of a man at thirty-nine and alone.

The trip up the mountainside seemed to take forever. The steep terrain would have left a healthy man breathless, but for a lame ex-cop-turned-witch, the incline was nearly impossible. He fell, again and again, finally pushing himself with his knees up the slanted wall of leaves and ferns. His feet hurt, but soreness would set in with time and only pain him more.

"Lord and Lady, hear my prayer," he whispered, stretching out on the ground. "Help me, God and Goddess. Don't let it end here."

He'd given up. Not that he wanted to. He had no choice. No strength. And his feet were bleeding like sieves.

Somewhere near the top of the mountain, Kestrel and at least one of her little daughters were facing a self-righteous madman, spurred on by his own version of God and Right. A much different version from the spiritual path Finn had chosen. And the stronger disciple of his own God would live to see darkness fall over Kestrel's forests. And there was nothing Finn could do about it.

You need to get up.

He lifted his head, then damned himself. No one was there.

The scent of peppermint drifted along the leafy ground. Robyn?

No. No one. Certainly not his beloved Robyn. Yet...she felt close.

A tendril of late sunlight curled through the shade and landed on something yellow. He thought at first he'd spotted a bed of wildflowers, but these yellow blossoms were scattered on the ground in wilted spirals. The girls. They'd been there, probably, playing yesterday. He squinted at the tall standing stone above the flowers.

A grave?

Using elbows and knees, he prodded himself toward the stones. Rosemary grew in a long rectangle, the wildflowers alongside in intricate designs. The petals had wilted, maybe a day ago. He studied the surface of the standing stone, but no name or inscription marred it. Nothing but a spiral carved thinly into rock.

Saadia. He knew it innately. Kestrel had buried the old woman near the stream, in the forest, amid the breezes and sunlight.

There was no longer a newness about the grave. Most of the rosemary had filled in, but the herbs were still at a height that needed water and encouragement. The old woman had died not so long ago, and Kestrel had buried her there and taken her identity to be safe. Kestrel had been alone since then with just her girls and the neighbors down the mountain.

And what of the lovely Tracey? He had a bad feeling about that, too. Only one of the girls had returned, and even then with a mad man at her back. He'd seen no sign of Branwen or Tracey.

You must get up. Again the voice in the back of his head.

The scent of peppermint wafted over him again. He closed his eyes, inhaled, remembering Robyn and those damned peppermint candies she always carried with her on stake-outs. Then it struck him—the peppermint wasn't his imagination and wasn't memory. It was real.

He opened his eyes, searching frantically for the little green herbs. There it was, six feet or less away from Saadia's grave. Why hadn't he seen it before? Then again, he knew well enough that the Lord and Lady revealed everything in its own time. The herb-covered rectangle was at least eight feet long and three feet wide. An ordinary trespasser on the mountains or a magickal traveler in the woods would have thought it to be an herb garden, growing finely for the making of Saadia Soaps.

He felt Robyn close again, closer than he'd felt in years. And even if it weren't for her spirit hovering around him, he would have known it was her grave by the standing stone at the head of the plot of peppermint. Someone, probably Kestrel, had carved an equi-armed cross into the stone and wrapped it in a Celtic knot to symbolize an eternal life—no beginning, no end—in union with Spirit.

Finn had always thought Robyn had been his soul mate and he'd learned too late. Yet now he realized that it was possible to love someone who wasn't a soul mate. Really love them. With all your heart. But soul mates were different. Maybe not life mates as Robyn might have been. It went deeper than that. It cut through time and physics. He'd wanted that with Robyn, but it wasn't mean to be.

All these years, Robyn's body had rested here. He'd wondered about her resting place, after that last desecration of her tombstone when some anonymous relative had had her grave removed and taken far from Greenburg where no one could harm it. Kestrel and the old woman had done far more for his partner in death than he had done for her in life. For that, he owed them.

He might as well die in service to the Goddess as to sprawl on the leafy mountainside and forfeit all.

Chapter Nineteen

~*Kestrel*~

For the first time in my life, I wished for a gun.

I knew all too well what bullets could do to a man's head and a woman's heart. But I wanted—*needed*—a weapon that could close the distance between the witch-hunter and me.

Deirdre had long since disappeared up the steep trail with the witch-hunter not far behind her and now out of my sight. I scrambled forward, upward, my bare toes digging into the damp dirt and leaves. My pulse thundered in my ears, drowning out the trickle of the stream and distant roar of the waterfall far below.

I caught sight of the witch-hunter, far above me. I didn't have the traction of his boots as I fell, again and again, scraping knees and knuckles until they were bloody. I swallowed the bile of frustration that rose in my throat and prayed for strength.

"This time, Goddess," I whispered between heaving breaths, "make me strong enough to stand against him." I hadn't been strong enough so long ago. I hadn't been able to stand against him. I could stand against him only when I was complete.

I fell again as I topped the ridge in time to see the witch-hunter disappear into a hole in the rock. The caves! He'd followed Deirdre to the caves! Branwen waited there, too, somewhere deep inside. She'd run in this direction when I'd taken the rabbit's form, and I could feel her there, now. Sense her. Almost as if I could hear her unsteady breathing.

The caves were filled with night and danger. I wasn't sure which was worse: the chasm or the witch-hunter. I had often told the girls stories of Arthur and Merlin and the battle of the red and white dragons beneath the earth, of the fall of Vortigern's tower, of the way the shaking earth was blamed on dragons in those darkest of ages. My brave little girls were probably wanting their mommy as much as I wanted them.

"Great Hecate," I prayed, bowing my head and pressing my forehead into the ground. "Great Goddess of the Crossroads, take me and mine into Your dark embrace. Send dragons to hide and protect us until we emerge again into light."

Chapter Twenty

~*Branwen*~

"Back!" Branwen grabbed a candle and thrust it at the man. Hot wax splattered across the ground in front of her and onto the witch-hunter's boots. "Get back, I said!"

The eerie light of the flame licked at his face. The farther parts of his face seemed to disappear into the darkness but the protruding chin and cheekbones and the ridges over his eyes stuck out as the soft glow made him look even scarier.

A twisting grin spread across his face. "Keep your candle, little girl. You'll need it in the dark abyss of hell."

Branwen gulped and almost took a step backward. Then she remembered who she was. She was a child of the Goddess, and it was the Dark Goddess she'd called upon to protect her. The Dark One, yes, on the night of the full moon when the power of the witch and Goddess was at its peak.

But it was already too late. Deirdre grabbed Branwen's shoulder and yanked her back. Deirdre stood a few feet behind her, just within the edge of the circle of candles. Deirdre didn't back Branwen up with a rousing "Yeah, go to hell, you fiend!" or even so much as a whimper. Deirdre had gone silent. Goddess help them all if Deirdre had gone deep within herself and saw things she wouldn't say.

The witch-hunter paused and sniffed the air, then looked around the cave. He let down his guard. A bad sign, Branwen decided. He didn't think he had anything to be afraid of. He thought he had enough strength to kill them both, and Mom and Finn, too. That was bad, really bad. Because he probably did. Branwen bit her lip and desperately wanted to step backward.

"Pretty stupid of you," the man said. "Coming up here into the caves. Kind of like painting yourself into a corner. Where do you go now? Huh?" He laughed, his eyes glinting in the flickering light.

Silence shrouded the cave. Only the whistle of wind and drip of water broke its bonds.

Branwen ground her teeth. *If only Mommy were here, she'd know what to do.*

"Branwen?" Deirdre whispered behind her. "Branwen?"

Branwen swallowed. She was the braver of the two. Always had been. She had to do something. She was the first line of protection for her family. Wait. No. That had been a long time ago. She'd been someone else then. Someone else who should have protected Kestrel and Dei—*Cedric.*

"He won't hurt us," Branwen whispered over her shoulder to her sister. Not that she really believed it. "We're just kids. We haven't done anything wrong."

"Kids!" he snorted. "Demons in the guise of innocents is more like it. You're the devil's spawn. Both of you. You're still children of the devil. You even look the same."

The girls exchanged glances as if they were a lifetime away, to a time in a dark and sacred grove of oak trees. Deirdre had had brown hair then. Long hair. Really long for a man. She'd been older. Not so old as Finn or Mommy but closer to Miss Tracey's age. And she'd looked like one of those sword-wielding warriors with a chest of bulging muscles that Branwen thought were really gross. Deirdre—*Cedric*—had had almost no hair on his chest but on the side of his heart and above one of the flat nipples was a tattoo with three spirals coming out of it like long tongues. The symbol of the three phases of the Goddess, but it meant more than that. It meant three people—one named Cedric and one named Kestrel and yet another name Branwen heard in her dreams. *Grant.*

"You!" the ugly man spat, pointing his finger at Deirdre. "I remember you. Blond, jackass lawyer who took my wife away from me. I'll be damned if I have a wife who's nothing more than a roommate."

Deirdre shook her head furiously. He was looking at her blond hair and thinking of the DNA she had shared with Grant's body. But Deirdre wasn't Grant. *Branwen* was Grant.

The man pointed one long finger at Branwen's nose. He thought Branwen had been Cedric, the man with long hair. "I knew you were a demon by the way you just stood there. You didn't fight. Didn't run away. You didn't even flinch."

Branwen flinched. She had those memories, too, but from a different perspective. Her soul had already left her body and drifted up into the canopy of trees before racing to find Kestrel. Branwen had seen it all from above. The man in the yellow raincoat and hat using Kestrel—*Mommy's*—dagger already thick with her own... no, his own...no, *Grant's* blood.

"You're not children. You're the spawn of devils."

Branwen shook her head. "I don't understand." Her knees hurt from holding her legs so still. "I don't understand," she repeated.

She hadn't understood before. Why would a man come out of darkness, out of nowhere, and rip her and her family to shreds? Why wouldn't it matter to him that she was only nine-and-a half? She'd never done anything to this man. Either in this life or...before. She couldn't remember ever seeing him any time before now except in her dreams. But none of it mattered to him, she realized with a terrifying feeling rising in the pit of her stomach. None of that mattered at all. All that mattered was his hate.

"Goddess, help us," she whispered.

"Goddess?" He rolled his eyes. "Goddess? You little fool! God is a man. Don't you know that?"

She nodded once. "Uh-huh. God is a man's spirit but Goddess is a woman."

"There is no Goddess. She's a usurper. There's only God. And even if you were to fall on your knees and beg for His mercy, it's still too late for you. You or your sister. You're whore children, conceived in sin." His face turned uglier than any monster in Branwen's nightmares.

"What's a whore?" Deirdre asked. "Is that what your wife was?"

Branwen stared at her sister for a second, but she remembered, too. Yes, the man had had a wife. Something had happened in an office with computers and a desk. She could see flashes of it, but nothing stuck. Like a dream she couldn't quite remember. Something about...the woman asking for Grant's help. Begging for help in leaving her husband. Escape. And a lie. And Grant had said no and walked away.

Before more memories could come, the man outside the circle raised his hand to backhand Deirdre. Then he laughed. "You're playing with me, aren't you, little one? That just proves my point. Only a demon would remember those things. A real child would not remember my Gloria, but you do. Don't you?" He leaned in toward the circle but didn't cross it. "Don't you?"

Deirdre took a half step backward. She held the willow wand in her hand like a sword.

"I'll carve you up, too, you little brat. When I'm done with the others, I'll carve you up. Show you on the outside for what you are on the inside."

Branwen glanced down at the booted feet and sprinkles of cooling wax she spattered on him. He hadn't stepped over the circle. Somehow, the circle they'd cast was working, protecting them. All he had to do was reach out and grab either one of them by the neck but he didn't seem to realize—at least not consciously—the wall of pure energy surrounding them. The circle hung like a thick mist in the air, and either he couldn't see it or he thought it was dampness in the cave. She couldn't imagine how he could miss it. The electricity of a Greater Presence loomed all around her. She felt it like ants crawling on her flesh.

Deirdre lowered her chin and raised her eyes to the man. "You'd better leave," she said in a voice that sounded much older. "Our Mother is coming."

Branwen squinted at the distant oval of light at the high end of the cave. Mommy wasn't there. But Deirdre's sight was always right.

Chapter Twenty-One

~Finn~

Finn grabbed a half-rotted limb and pulled himself to his feet. Like a crutch, the branch fit perfectly under his arm, but the mountain's incline was too steep. After only a couple of shuffles, he pitched forward. He dropped the limb and fell to the ground.

Panting for breath, he studied the trail of blood behind him. The sprinkling of scarlet on the brown leaves had turned into a trench where he'd dragged one foot. Leaves and dirt coated his wounds, soaked up blood. Stung. He felt his heart in his feet with a dull, aching pain that threatened to move up his leg and consume him. If ever he needed little Branwen's healing touch, now was the time.

He lifted his hands to his face and stared at his palms. There were cuts, but not nearly so bad as his feet. Those were hands that had sought out murderers and brought them to the door of justice. But there was no strength in them now. Hands that had led covens in great feats of magick. But there was no power in them now. Hands that held Robyn as she had died in his arms. But there was no tenderness in them now. Hands

296

that had clenched, swearing retribution. But the promise of justice was gone now. Here on the mountain was where it would end.

One way or another.

A frown inched into his brow. He closed his eyes and saw Robyn's face. The bruise-broken skin. The tufts of shorn red hair. Her bleeding lips. The five-pointed star carved upside on her forehead, an aberration he had not even begun to understand at that time.

Never thirst! Her dying blessing still rang in his ears. *Never thirst.* Hot tears seeped under his lashes and down his cheeks. His love for Robyn had been the opportunity of a lifetime, and he'd cast it off, thrown it away, dismissed it. Because he hadn't understood until too late.

It's never too late, he heard in his mind. *There's no such thing as futility.*

He opened his eyes and, on one elbow, pushed up from the ground. No way in hell would he let Floyd Stokes carve up Kestrel and her two little girls. He would get to them first, even if he had to crawl.

Finn looked down at his feet. Yes, and he would have to crawl.

I ducked under the boulder, precariously balanced over the doorway. Legend had it that Indians and explorers alike had vanished in these depths. What went in never came out.

If I could get to the girls, get between them and the witch-hunter, then I could free them long enough for them to scurry to safety and I could dislodge the boulder. Then it would be just the witch-hunter and me. Trapped in here. For eternity. Hell, as some might call it.

Finn would care for the girls. He'd know what to do. For some reason only the Goddess knew, I was sure Finn would devote the rest of his life to raising my children and honoring my memory. Sacrifices are easier to make when you know vital matters are taken care of.

The witch-hunter circled around again, quoting scripture, praying and damning at the same time. Jesus surely would have been pissed off to see how He'd been misquoted, how His words had been twisted by hate.

My blood turned hot in my veins. I could barely breathe. This monster had taken my guys away from me, and no matter how they may have come back to me, the self-righteous bastard had ended the lives of too many people I had loved. I wanted to cut his throat, to stab him a thousand times, to hurt him as much as he'd hurt me. And to hurt him slowly. How could I give back ten years of agony without making it too quick?

I waited in the shadows until his back was turned and then I pounced, slashing and screaming all my hatred and hurt and loneliness. The sounds echoed back harshly like a banshee's screams and shook the house of stone and darkness. I didn't recognize my own voice. I swung at his throat, but at the last second, he pivoted and ducked.

Then he stood there between my girls and me, laughing at me. A second later, his hand flashed toward me. I saw the glimmer of candlelight on the blade. His knife was small but deadly.

I parried with my athame. Sparks spewed from metal on metal. Somehow I managed to clip both his hands in one thrust. I slashed at his groin. My magickal blade seemed longer, fiercer. It glowed and buzzed in my hand like a live wire. He leapt back, and I caught his ankles in a shallow cut. I didn't stop. I felt my face contorting, determined. I had to end this. I had to. Me or him. My kids or him. Finn, all of us, or the witch-hunter. There could be no truce.

"Run, girls!" I shouted over my shoulder. "Get out of here! Now!"

But they weren't moving. They froze, watching. They were little girls, just little girls.

The witch-hunter jabbed back. I reeled and spun below the aim of his knife and rebounded from the cave floor, slashing hard across his middle. I saw the fabric slice, the quick seep of blood, and his startled face. Enough to anger him but not enough to stop him. Before he could move, I brought my athame down hard against his blade, grinding, shooting sparks, sending it skittering into the black stoniness beyond the candles.

"You bless me, witch, to try to give me the five wounds of Christ!" His eyes gleamed in the candle glow.

"And you blaspheme. Jesus was a master teacher and great leader. How dare you compare yourself to your Christ!"

"I'm not the sinner here. You are. When I'm done with you, your blood will seep into the ground and call out to God, but He won't hear you."

"I thought we were all sinners. Isn't that what your book says?"

His faced turned a deep purple. His eyes bulged. Obviously he didn't expect me to know anything about the Bible. "No," he growled. "I mean, yes, but—but I have redemption and you don't."

"Is that what you think? Is that what you honestly believe? Deity somehow favors you over others?" He took a sideways step but I held him at bay with my athame. "What is it you've done that God so owes you?"

"I keep God's laws. That's what I do. All of them. I don't commit adultery or gamble or dabble in sorcery or marry filth from another race or kill unborn babies."

"But you'd kill *my* children? Fully born?"

"They're not children. They're the spawn of a witch— and the Devil. They're *not* children."

What was the use? He'd already gone so far, so deep into his own righteousness that he could not even see humanity

Chapter Twenty-Two

~Kestrel~

I reached the rocks near the cave and realized that the witch-hunter had probably heard me. How could he not? All my huffing and puffing and scrambling. In my mind's eye, I saw myself as a mama tigress, stealthily sneaking up the mountain. In reality, I was anything but quiet.

I stopped outside the rocks, grasping a boulder to keep from falling forward. I was in excellent shape for a thirty-five-year-old woman with two children. Still, the steep incline and the thin air took their toll. Thank Goddess, I wasn't injured like Finn. The burden of the crossroads was too great. If I'd had one more thing to contend with, I couldn't have made it.

Bracing myself with one hand on my knee and the other against the rock, I bent forward. Gradually, the oxygen filled my lungs. My breathing calmed. My girls were in a dangerous cave with a monster and here I was barely able to catch my breath. So much for Super Mom.

I wished I'd taken more than the two paring knives from my kitchen drawer. I still had my athame, but the two paring knives I'd tucked carefully into my belt were gone. Lost somewhere on the mountainside. Such mundane blades had forsaken me as if they were too weak and insignificant for the task of facing the witch-hunter. The ritual dagger, however, vibrated with an aura of its own. It had been given to me years ago by the stern aunt who'd introduced me to the Craft and had been intended for ritual use only. Instead, it had tasted the blood of too many witches. Regardless, the athame was the only weapon I had left.

"Hecate, Cerridwen, Goddess of the Dark," I whispered.

I squinted into the open mouth of the dark abyss of caverns. No wonder the people of old times had once thought dragons rumbled inside the earth. The blackness, the hard stoniness of the walls, the damp.

"Dark Mother, I call on you to send dragons to move inside this underworld I am about to descend as Inanna did when she embraced the shadow. Finish this ancient curse on me and mine. End it today. End it now. Rid us of this plague upon witches. Dark Mother, I pray Thee."

Athame in my fist, I took a deep breath and stepped inside. I held my breath, waiting, half-expecting to be slashed to death on the spot as my eyes adjusted to the blackness beyond the realm of light at the entrance. Nothing happened. Slowly, oh-so-slowly, my vision changed to meet the test of darkness. I could hear shouting and echoes of shouting. Branwen. I'd recognize her little voice anywhere. It shimmered with terror and defiance all at once.

I took an unsteady step forward, my eyes by each second growing more accustomed to the lack of light in the caverns. A gray dimness glowed along the walls and dots of candle flame sparkled deep within the belly of the Earth Mother, beckoning me. I could see two figures—the girls—standing inside a faint blue bubble of energy and the witch-hunter on the outside, stalking around the circle like a cat toying with its prey.

Prey indeed.

I dared not run. My bare feet tingled with the power of Earth and Mother until it felt more like pins than slippery stone beneath my heels. I couldn't afford to slide and fall in the darkness. No, one step at a time. Athame in my grip.

any more. He could no longer distinguish between two innocent children—who'd never done anything to harm anyone or
even each other, except to pull each other's hair—that he was
blind to everything that made a man human.

He'd hardened his heart against my little girls. He was
like a machine now. No longer feeling any emotion. Not capa-
ble of feeling sympathy or pity. And never ever stopping. A
living, breathing, human terminator of those who broke God's
laws. Laws as he saw them.

He thought it was okay to kill in the name of God. To
kill those who loved as he would not have wished. To kill those
who saw God in a different way. What next? Kill those who
don't honor a father and mother? Kill those who covet? Kill
anyone with any opinion different from his?

"Great Goddess," I began, my voice rising, calling the
prickly energy around me.

"Goddess," he sneered.

"Great Goddess—" The walls trembled around me. I
felt another presence enter the caves. Finn. He was too near.
He needed to leave, take the girls. But it was too late. I felt the
cave floor rock under my bare feet. I heard the boulder over
the door shudder and move, sliding down hard to the ground,
blocking the doorway. But Finn was inside, limping toward me,
dragging one foot behind. I knew it without looking. I dared
not look, dared not take my eyes off the witch-hunter.

We were trapped inside—my little girls, a crippled witch,
and me—trapped with the witch-hunter in the bowels of the
earth.

I raised my arms to pull in energy. Dangerous, I know,
leaving my body open to the witch-hunter to grab his knife or
some other weapon I hadn't seen and stab me in the heart, but I
cloaked myself in ritual.

"Great Goddess," I implored, "send your warriors here.
Protect me from this ancient fear."

I inched around a quarter of a circle, facing East and the
witch-hunter. Out of the corner of my eye, I saw Deirdre cut a
door in the protective shield she and her sister had cast.
Deirdre planted her feet firmly on the other side of the witch-
hunter and faced me. Her sister edged to one side, facing

South. Then Finn, his feet wrapped in bloody rags, closed the circle. Together the four of us moved in a complete circle around the witch-hunter. He glanced uneasily at each of us and turned back to me. His hands clenched into fists.

The circle was cast.

My voice rose and rocked the walls with each syllable. "Hail ye Dragons of the East, on wings of air and wind you come. Join me. Bear witness. Protect and blessed be."

Before I could continue, Branwen took over. She thrust her arms upward. Her tiny voice rose to a pitch I knew from years ago. I recognized Grant's soul in its timbre. "Hail ye Dragons of the South. Burn your eye and breath with fire. Join me. Bear witness. Protect and blessed be."

"Hail ye Dragons of the West," Deirdre chimed in, lifting her arms. She opened her mouth but the words belonged to someone older, someone long ago. Cedric's soul. Cedric's memories. "Swim and sink on loch-land waves. Join me. Bear witness. Protect and blessed be."

Finn grimaced as he raised both arms. His hands were bloody and ragged, but full of power. "Hail ye Dragons of the North, with feet of soil and skin of earth. Join me. Bear witness. Protect and blessed be."

In a heartfelt moment, I invited Hecate into our circle, though the Dark Mother, the Goddess of the Crossroads, had been with me for years. She wrapped her dark cape around me, around me and mine, with the witch-hunter at the center of our circle. I let the words of ritual flow through me, my voice as loud as it has ever been.

> "Dragons red and dragons white,
> Circle now within the light.
> Dragons white and dragons red,
> Balance light and darkness wed.
> Struggle, fierceness, conflict, strength,
> Ancient battle, eternal length.
> Take my struggle from my heart.
> I give the fierceness from my arms.
> Take the conflict from my mind.
> I give the strength to fend off harm.

Struggle, fierceness, conflict, strength,
Ancient battle, eternal length.
Dragons ageless, dragons bright,
End the battle with this night,
Crush the troubles that follow me,
As I will it, so mote it be!"

The girls and Finn joined in as we circled the witch-hunter, each chanting again and again, "Crush the troubles that follow me; As I will it, so mote it be!"

Somewhere in the walls of stone, the dragons rumbled. Somewhere under our feet, they moved. Somewhere above, they writhed. With every decibel, they shuddered inside the earth.

The witch-hunter glanced at each of us. I saw the fear in his eyes. Yet he didn't call out to his God, and I knew he thought he himself was too powerful to need even his own twisted version of God.

Then everything crumpled and closed in around me. A rock struck me hard on the shoulder and I fell sideways into the shadows. Then all was darkness.

When I woke, I saw a single candle flame on the other side of a pile of rocks. The witch-hunter, what was left of him, was somewhere underneath. My athame was gone, buried with him. The shimmer of our circle was gone, dispersed into rock, but the air still buzzed.

"Gotta find her," I heard Deirdre sobbing. "Mommy's here. Gotta find her."

"It's okay, baby," I called. With Deirdre's sight, she could look just into the future and see me. In the present, I was still lost. "I'm here." But my voice was hoarse. I tried again. "I'm here."

"Mommy, over here!" the girls echoed at once. Branwen sat crossed-legged on the cave floor a good ten feet away. She held both hands a half inch above Finn's ravaged feet, busily healing him as he moaned. She had a cut on her arm and more dirt on her face than I'd ever seen, but both my babies and Finn looked absolutely wonderful.

Except that we were trapped inside a black underworld with a candle that wouldn't burn for much longer.

I crawled over the rocks, over the final resting place of the witch-hunter. Bruised, knees scraped, aching tired, I reached my daughters at last and hugged them hard.

Finn grunted nearby, pushing himself up on his elbows. It was hard to tell how much blood he'd lost. I pulled him to me and held him for a long time in my arms, kissing his damp forehead as he melted against me. His mouth found mine and I knew by the warmth and passion in his touch that we were meant to be together, even if we weren't meant to survive. The witch-hunter was dead, and it had taken the four of us, the complete circle, to defeat him.

This was to be our tomb as well. The candle would fail in a few hours. Then we would sit in darkness and wait to starve to death. Finn, the worst wounded of us, would likely die the easiest.

"We need to go home," Deirdre said with a sniffle. "Finn needs to see a doctor before it gets dark."

"Honey...." I choked. The caves were pitch black. Soon, it wouldn't get any darker.

"Mom," Deirdre wailed. She backhanded a tear from her scraped cheek. "We need to go. Now. Finn won't live if we don't go."

"There's nowhere to go, sweetie." How could I tell my babies the brutal truth?

"Yes, there is," she insisted, tugging at my arm. "Come on. Everything will be okay if you'll come with me. You'll see." She picked up the candle and scampered deeper into the caverns.

I had trusted Cedric and his vision all those years ago. Deirdre's gift came from the same place. I had to trust it.

Branwen and I helped Finn to his feet and half-carried him between columns of stone. He limped and grimaced. I didn't want to think whether the slipperiness on the cave floor was ground water or life blood. The feeble candle glow flickered and sputtered.

"There," Branwen said, pointing at a knot of dark yarn tied around a stalagmite. The colored string held tautly between two columns of white onyx and disappeared through one of five openings ahead.

The candle sizzled. The light vanished.

"Follow the cord," Deirdre called from somewhere ahead. Her voice echoed in the chambers.

The trickle of an underground stream grew louder. I could hear the vague whistle of wind. Beneath my feet, the cave floor rose slightly, then more remarkably. The girls had mapped the cave, obviously, with candlelight and balls of yarn. Against my express instructions never to enter these dark caverns.

Then finally I saw it: a glimmer of light up ahead where I had not looked before, dimmed and shaded but there. It always had been.

Both girls and Finn paused and let me through. I grabbed the yarn and followed it to where it turned red in the dim light. My heart pounded. Freedom. Freedom from the past, freedom from darkness.

I pushed through the curtain of dark green magnolia leaves and squirmed out onto solid rock. I stood shakily, overwhelmed by the view in front of me. An early evening haze had settled over the lush valley below with blue-purple mountain peaks rising toward a full golden moon.

I cupped my left hand to Her in reverence. I felt the joy spread across my face. Like Inanna, Goddess of the ancient Sumerians, I had emerged from the Underworld, resurrected, whole again. I had faced the shadow, embraced it, been stripped and dishonored and sacrificed, and yet made whole again. Though not undisturbed by the darkness.

I stepped out into the light and raised my open hands to Her. Behind me, the girls and Finn ascended from the darkness. Branwen kicked at a rock above the hole and the stones rumbled down to seal the tomb. No one would enter there again. No one would leave there again. I paused to offer my thanks.

"Hail to Thee, Goddess of Earth, Goddess of Sea.
Hail to Thee, Goddess of Flame, Goddess of Air.
And in the stillness of this hour
I give thanks to that Ancient Power
That courses through our veins, every one.
That shines within our souls, ever more.
Bless us now as this day is done,

That our four souls are reunited this day and ever more. So mote it be!"

"So mote it be," echoed the three most important people in my life.

And then I saw it clearly—how the Goddess had brought us all here together, more powerful together than alone, enough to defeat the one who had tortured all of us so for so many centuries.

I smiled at the moon, the covenant of my Goddess, and knew. The four of us would spend the rest of this lifetime together. Finn and I were destined for each other, with Branwen and Deirdre to grow up in love and light as our children. I was thirty-five years old, and I had come home.

The frightened girl who had flown by night all those years ago could settle down at last.

The End

More Spilled Candy Books
By Lorna Tedder

Waiting on the Thunder
A woman who has lost her faith in Gods, a man who has lost his faith in everything but revenge, and a murderer who doesn't believe in anything but the kill.

Thunderstorms & Convertibles
A small town woman on a quest for answers about her family history picks up a stranded motorist with a baby girl—and soon discovers he's on the run.

Flying by Night
A polyamorous woman is accused of murdering her two husbands and must flee an ancient enemy as well as a burned out detective who will lose everything in the process of finding her—and himself.

Access: An End Times Thriller
An End Times thriller filled with time travel, reincarnation, biological warfare, a spiritual journey, and a love story between the savior of the world and her protector.

Witch Moon Rising by Maggie Shayne & Witch Moon Waning by Lorna Tedder
Wiccan women face questions of love and ethics in 2 short novels. Includes 40+ spells, rituals, charms from the authors' personal Books of Shadows.

Metaphysical Fiction

Field of Jonquils
By Selene Silverwind
Two people on similar spiritual quests find themselves crossing over into each other's dreams and realities.

Dream of the Circle of Women
By Dahti Blanchard
Can the daughter of a witch find answers to long-hidden mysteries--including her mother's death—before she loses her own life?

Hidden Passages by Vila SpiderHawk
An anthology about girls and women of different cultures and epochs, each of whom seeks and finds wisdom with the help of one or more Crones.

The Prophet's Lady By Vicki Hinze
A spiritual romance of reincarnation and getting it right.

Pelzmantel by K.A. Laity
The Grimm Brother's "Allerleirau" is retold from the viewpoint of the princess' caretaker, a crone who infuses the story with tales from medieval Ireland and Scandinavia, herbal cures, and magick.

A Reverence for Trees by Lorna Tedder
A love story about healing and forgiveness.
Read it FREE at www.spilledcandy.com!

The Priestess Diaries

The Archangel's Return: Angels, Protection Rituals, Entities, Spirit Guides
Read it FREE at www.spilledcandy.com!

Salt and Fire: Cleansing/House Purification Rituals

Bound for All Time: Handfasting/Spiritual Blending Ritual

Celebrating the Tower Card: Third Degree Status, Shielding, Witch Wars, & Cult Detection

Drink of Me: Science / Magick Theory, Visions, Rituals for Clarity and Prosperity

An Interference of Angels: Astrology, Visions, Fighting Manipulative Magick

Flying with Scissors: Forming a Circle or Coven, Soulmates and Twin Flames

Heat Beneath My Winter: Crystal Healings, Energy Healings, Coven Dynamics

This Sadness Shall Pass: Medical Empathy, Chakras, Energy Healings, & Crystals

News from the Ether: Spirit Guides, Channelings, Possessions, & Ouija Sessions

Trusting the Voices: Spirit Guides, Pendulums, Trusting Your Intuition

A Wicked Twist of Fate: Astral Projection, Visions, & Fate vs Free Will

By Lauren Hartford

Lauren's Hartford's ongoing series, *The Priestess Diaries,* features combined novelized diaries of several High Priestesses, each book emphasizing certain spiritual techniques and lessons in story format, with an overarching romantic subplot, intrigue, mystery, suspense, humor, and heartache.

Look for extended excerpts presented as free ebooks at our website.

A Banishment of Devils: Ouija Sessions, Past Lives, Atlantis, & Banishings

Giving It To the Gods: Coven Dynamics, Higher Selves, & Letting Go

The Indigo Promise: Indigo Children, Earth Changes, & Time Shifts

Return of the Archangel: Angels, Entities, Spirit Guides, Protection Rituals

The Key to Hell's Gate: Pleiadeans & The Nolalalns, Astral Healing, Discerning Good Mediums from Bad

A Wedding of Souls: Spiritual Unions, Hand-fastings, Initiations

Guardian of the Portals: Interdimensional Portals, Interpretation of Dark and Light

She Who Feeds on Grief:: Ethics of Magick, Psychic Vampires, Altering Outcomes

Printed in the United States
57845LVS00005B/1-15